MW01485948

# WEIGHTLESS

*a novel*

# KANDI STEINER

Published by Kandi Steiner
Edited by Betsy Kash
Cover Design by Kandi Steiner
Formatting by Elaine York/Allusion Graphics, LLC/
Publishing & Book Formatting
www.allusiongraphics.com

# DEDICATION

*To Staci and Becca, for*
*believing in me even when I didn't.*
*This one's for the Tribecycle.*

# PROLOGUE

I remember the lights.

I remember I wanted to photograph them, the way the red and blue splashed across his cold, emotionless face. But I knew even if my feet could move from the place where they had cemented themselves to the ground and I could run for my camera, I wouldn't be able to capture that moment. There was no shutter speed, no lens, no lighting technique that could properly encapsulate everything I felt as I stared into his eyes.

I had trusted him, I had loved him, and even though my body had changed that summer, he'd made sure to help me hold on to who I was inside, regardless of how the exterior altered.

But then everything changed.

He stole my innocence. He scarred my heart. He took everything I thought I knew about my life and fast-pitched it out the window, shattering the glass that held my world together in the process.

I remember the lights.

The passionate, desperate, hot strikes of red. The harsh, cruel, icy bolts of blue.

They symbolized everything I endured that summer.

And everything I would never face again.

# CHAPTER

# 1

My mom and step-dad thought I couldn't hear them mumbling in the kitchen about my well-being over the volume of the fifth consecutive episode of *Lost* I was watching, but I could hear every word. So I sighed heavily and turned the volume up when they approached the couch.

I was still in my pajamas, and I knew I should have at least changed into shorts and a t-shirt so they thought I got up and lived a little that day. The truth was I hadn't done a damn thing, other than watch that utterly confusing show, anyway. But I lost the ability to care after my second Little Debbie snack.

"Love this show," Dale said, sitting casually on the arm of our dark brown leather sectional. I pulled my legs up to my chest so Mom could sit down next to him. "Hated the ending, but still."

"No spoilers, Dale!"

He threw up his hands in mock surrender. "I'm just saying. You're going to wish you didn't waste the hours."

Mom appraised my sweatpants, her eyes lingering a little longer when she spied the frayed edges where I'd dragged them on the ground. Jillian Poxton didn't do sweatpants and she didn't think any other woman, or girl, should either. Her choice was always a dress or neatly pressed skirt paired with the perfectly complementary top. Even then, on a Sunday afternoon hours after church had ended, she sat with her hands in her lap and her ankles crossed in a bright, summery-blue dress that cinched her tiny waist and flowed down to her knees.

"Sweetheart," she sighed the word, her hand reaching to gently squeeze my leg.

"Mom, please." I leaned up and away from her touch, keeping my eyes fixed on the television. "Don't."

"Honey, don't you think it's time to get out of this house? I let you stay home all week, but today was the second time you missed church… and you know how people talk."

I chewed my lip because as much as I wanted to argue, she was right. People *did* talk in Poxton Beach, SC. The fact that my step-dad, Dale Poxton, owned pretty much everything in the small tourist map-blip didn't help my case much, either. His ancestors founded the cozy beach town and, surprisingly, the family never did pull up roots and venture out. Dale had lived there his entire life and he knew he would die there, his grave filing in right next to his parents'.

Still, I hated how stern Mom was being with me. Given the circumstances, I didn't think it was that big of a deal to wallow in self-pity and Zebra cakes for a while longer. But apparently Mom had reached her limit. She may have been my mom, but she was also Dale Poxton's wife, which meant she had eyes on her, too. Questions. Still, I wasn't ready to face the music of my new reality.

I had graduated high school just a week prior, and on that same night, my boyfriend of two years had broken my heart.

"Exactly. I do know how this town talks. Which is why I'm not keen on leaving the couch at the moment," I challenged, trying again to end the conversation by raising the volume on the TV.

"Now listen, Natalie," Dale chimed in, grabbing the remote from where I'd just dropped it next to me. He pressed the pause button and I sighed heavily. "Your mom and I understand what you're going through, we do. Believe it or not, we were young and in love once, too. But you can't waste your summer lying around and…" He trailed off, but his eyes fell to the mess of processed food wrappers gathering on the mahogany coffee table.

"Eating my feelings?"

He exchanged a worried glance with Mom and I wanted to crawl under the couch cushions and die. I hated being looked at, I hated being judged, and I felt both happening from the two people I trusted and loved most.

I was thicker than most girls my age —hell, than most girls, period. I had love handles that hung over my jeans and arms twice the size of my best friend Willow's. My cheeks were chubby, there wasn't a single space my thighs didn't touch when I stood ankles together, and I couldn't remember a time I'd bought anything smaller than a large when I went shopping with my friends.

I had always been the "big girl", and up until that point, I had never really thought to feel ashamed about it. It was only the Friday before, at my graduation party, that I realized how insecure I had always felt but had never admitted. I didn't come to that realization softly. No, I was hurled into it like a high-speed train. Because Mason didn't just break up with me that night, not for the reason he gave me. He said we were growing apart, that he had plans and I didn't, that he needed to start thinking about his future. But when he started dating a petite little brunette not even a full two days later, I knew the real reason he let me go. I didn't even know who she was, but I saw a photo of them on social media and that was enough for me. She was skinny. She was gorgeous.

She was everything I wasn't.

"Can I have a minute with her, Dale?" Mom asked, like I wasn't still in the room with them. Or like I was twelve and not eighteen. He nodded, smiling and ruffling my hair before excusing himself. Again, I felt the need to shove my diploma in their face and remind them of my age. Once he was gone, Mom turned back to me.

"Do you want him back?"

I blanched. "What?"

"You heard me. Do you want him back?"

"I don't really think that's an option, Mom," I mumbled, picking at the already chipping gold nail polish on my thumbnail. I wanted to peel every last inch of that high school off of me forever, including the forest green and gold colors I had sported so spiritually every year of my life. "He's…" I paused, crossing my arms tight over my chest. "He's not available anymore."

Her face softened and she moved closer to me, reaching out to place a hand on my leg again. I didn't pull away this time. "Oh sweetie, you give up too easily. If you want him, fight for him."

I shook my head. "It's not that easy, Mom. This isn't a Rom Com."

"I'm serious," she said, lowering her head and forcing me to meet her bright blue eyes. They were so different from my own chocolate ones. I assumed I had my father's eyes, though I couldn't be sure. He was around for a total of ten months of my life and I'd never seen so much as a picture of him. Not that I ever asked to see one — Dale was the only father I needed as far as I was concerned. "You know what the best revenge is after a break-up, right?"

I lifted a brow, clearly not versed in the subject. At all. Mason was the only boyfriend I had ever had. I was going through my first break-up, my first heartache, and all I knew was that it hurt like hell and eating on the couch seemed like a perfectly fine way to spend my summer — especially the summer after I graduated high school. I just had two and a half months to make it through and then I'd be gone, anyway.

Maybe.

If I could decide what I wanted to do with my life, that is.

Or maybe I'd still be right here, on this couch, eating Oatmeal Cream Pies.

Mom stood, pulling me up with her to give me the answer to her question. "Looking drop-dead gorgeous the next time he sees you. And if you can score some man-candy to tote you around, that helps, too."

She winked and I scoffed. "Yeah well, I don't think that plan is going to work in my case," I pointed out, gesturing to my body with an open hand. Sure, I had long, thick, dark blonde hair and skin that easily tanned in the southern sun, but I was a size fourteen. And everyone in my circle of friends, including Mason's new... *thing*, was a size four or smaller. It wasn't that I was ever really confident, but before graduation, I hadn't really thought that much about my size — at least, not enough to care. Whether because of Dale's money or stature, I had always been a part of the "in" crowd, and I never had to try to be anyone I didn't want to be. I was shy, quiet, but fun once I opened up. At least, that's what I liked to think.

"Well, I have an idea that might change your mind. But you have to promise you'll hear me out before you say yes or no."

I crossed my arms again. "This doesn't sound good."

"Just listen," she insisted, holding out her hands. I was already skeptical, given that my mom's ideas usually involved retail therapy or traveling. I wasn't in the mood to deal with either at the moment. "There's this personal trainer at the country club. He's completely transformed at least a dozen of the women members. I swear, the guy has a gift. And I know if you would give him a chance, he would be able to help you look and feel amazing."

"A trainer? Really, Mom?" I shook my head, turning toward my bedroom. I was doing my best to seem annoyed, but in reality, it stung a little hearing my mom essentially say that I needed to hit the gym. "Not happening."

"Just try it," she pleaded behind me. "Just for a week or two. If you hate it, you can quit."

"Maybe I like being fat," I threw behind me, still stomping toward my room. "Ever think of that?" I knew I was being dramatic, but I was still clinging to my adolescence and using it as an excuse to act as desperate as I felt.

"At least promise me you'll think about it, Natalie." She sighed, pleading again. "You're not fat and you know I don't think that. I'm just trying to help you look and feel your best."

I paused at the bottom of the staircase, looking back at my beautiful mother. Shiny blonde hair, thin frame, high cheekbones. She had always been gorgeous, it had always been easy for her, and maybe part of me resented her for it. Maybe I was jealous. Maybe I was in denial, thinking my weight didn't matter. Maybe I was just deathly afraid I'd fail. Regardless, I nodded, promising to think about it, but I knew I would never set foot in the gym at the Poxton Beach Country Club.

Mom seemed satisfied with my promise. She smiled and clasped her hands in front of her again. "Mason is a great kid. He's from a good family, and he's going places. Don't give him up so easily."

I didn't get the chance to respond because Willow bounded through the front door, pulling a glittery purple suitcase behind her. "Alright, where is she?"

I groaned, my right hand hitting my forehead with a slap before I dragged it down over my face. Mom chuckled.

Willow and I had been best friends since kindergarten, and she was the kind of friend who took charge. This was the first break-up I'd experienced in our thirteen years of friendship and she'd jumped into action as soon as it happened. If I couldn't get my parents off my back about binge-eating my summer away, there was no way I could escape Willow.

Her deep brown eyes found me on the foot of the staircase and she smiled, white teeth bright against her dark skin. "There you are. Okay, here's the deal." She yanked her suitcase up the first stair when she reached me and kept heaving it up, talking through labored breaths. "We're going to get you all dressed up." Another stair. "I'm doing your hair and makeup," she exhaled, still tugging. "We're going to go out to Hay Stacks tonight, and you're going to show Mason what he's missing."

"That sounds like a really terrible idea," I assessed, leaning back on the stair railing and watching her struggle. It was comical really, her slim frame lugging a glittery piece of luggage at least twice her size. "What do you have in there, anyway?"

"Just the essentials. Now come on, you need to find your cutest pair of boots."

I scrunched my nose but Mom placed a dainty hand on my shoulder, reassuring. "She's right, honey. Just get all prettied up and go have some fun."

"Being around Mason sounds far from fun." Willow and Mom both sighed together, which made me chuckle and throw up my hands. "Ugh! Fine. But if tonight sucks, I get to spend my entire Sunday on that couch with Josh Holloway." I pointed my finger up at Willow first before turning back to my mom. "Deal?"

"Deal," Willow answered quickly from the top of the stairs, bending down to grip her knees and catch her breath. I cocked a brow at mom, who was chewing her lip, but finally she nodded.

"Okay. Tonight will be great, so I don't have to worry about it."

"Mm hmm."

I drug myself up the stairs unwillingly and followed Willow back to my bedroom. She already had the suitcase open on my bed with everything inside it sprawled out on the white and gray comforter. I fell face-first onto the puffy goose down comforter and sighed, letting my hot breath warm the cool fabric.

"You have ten minutes to mope before I start curling your hair," Willow said, popping into my bathroom to plug in her iron. She brought a small makeup mirror, too, which was smart because she knew I didn't have any in my room or bathroom.

I never was a fan of mirrors. I didn't particularly like to stare at myself, especially since I could look down at my body and see quite enough.

Willow sat down next to me, braiding her hair over her shoulder before placing a hand on mine. "Talk to me."

I sighed again. "Mom is disappointed I lost Mason."

As much as it stung, it made sense. After all, his family was one of the most well off in Poxton Beach other than ours. He was heading to college in a couple of months to take the same path to being a lawyer as his father did. And after graduation, he'd be right back here in Poxton Beach until the day he died. To my mom, that sounded like the ideal situation for my future marriage.

But I didn't care about any of that.

What I did care about was that Mason would no longer be kissing me. He wouldn't be holding my hand as we walked the beach with our friends. He wouldn't brush my hair behind my ear or wrestle me for the remote on a Friday movie night at my place. I may not have agreed with my mom about *why* I should be with Mason, but we did both feel the same. I wasn't the same without him — that much I could tell in just the week it had been since he broke up with me. For the first time, I was trying to figure out who I was as a solo entity, as Natalie Poxton without Mason Carter as my boyfriend. And I was failing.

"She's not disappointed, Natalie, she's sad for you. We all are. Which is why I'm going to get you super dressed up and take you out to show him what he's giving up."

"I think he knows."

She sighed. "Do you really not want to go?"

Chewing my lip, I thought hard about her question. Did I want to see Mason? Of course. Still, my stomach felt like it was being squeezed by Hulk fists anytime I thought about it. Because if I saw him, I would want him, and for the first time in two years he wasn't mine.

But I couldn't spend my whole summer mourning him, even if that was the easy thing to do. I'd have to face him sometime, and maybe he would see me and realize he'd made a mistake.

"You have any magic makeup in there to make me look better than his new girlfriend?"

Willow grinned, waving her hand at me. "Oh please. Like anyone can out-makeup me." She winked and grabbed my hands, pulling me up off the bed and into the bathroom. I stared at the photographs I'd taken on our family vacation to Hawaii a few years ago as she prepped everything on the counter. The images of the straw huts and fires on the dark beach always soothed me.

Photography was my passion. It had been for longer than I could remember. I was the lead photographer for the yearbook all through high school and I had more digital files of my friends and hometown on my computer than I had hard drive space to store it. It was the one and only thing that made me feel comfortable and safe.

Other than Mason.

Who I didn't have anymore.

"Can I take my camera tonight?"

Willow dabbed foundation below my eyes. "If you want to. You have about a million photos of all of us out at Hay Stacks, though."

"I know. It just makes me feel better to have it with me."

She chuckled. "You're kind of weird, Nat. But I love you anyway."

"I love you, too. Thanks for this," I said, gesturing to her spread. "I know you guys are right. I'm scared, but I know I can't hide forever."

Willow smiled, outlining my eyebrows with a light pencil. "Don't worry. Everything is going to be fine."

I tried to return her smile, but it fell flat and I settled my vision on a photo of Mauna Loa, instead.

That was the first moment where I felt the shift.

There was something about that summer that would change me, it was already beginning, and a part of me knew it. It was like I was walking in the dark toward a distant light, but I couldn't drag my feet fast enough to figure out what it was. I could only think about one thing at a time, and that night, it was about being in the same place with the boy who had broken my heart just one week prior. I wanted to be prepared, I wanted to be confident, I wanted to be okay, but the truth of the matter was that I just wasn't.

I was far from okay.

Two hours later, I wiped my sweaty palms on the harsh fabric of my jeans as Willow and I weaved through the weekend crowd to Hay Stacks. Crowds were never my thing, but I felt particularly uneasy that night and Willow sensed it. She held out her arm and I looped mine through hers, clinging to her like a lifeline the closer we got to the bars.

The Crawl was a small strip of clubs, bars, and restaurants near the Poxton Beach boardwalk and pretty much the only place to go out within a thirty mile radius. It was always crawling with tourists, but locals were there in heavy crowds, too. Poxton Beach was the second best tourist spot in South Carolina, right behind Myrtle Beach, and The Crawl was just about the only adult entertainment in the town. Everything else was very family-focused, just the way Dale's ancestors wanted it.

Even though I had just turned eighteen in November, I had been to The Crawl more times than I could count. Hay Stacks and a few other bars were eighteen and up, which made them favorite spots for my group of friends on the weekends. When we weren't at The Crawl, we were throwing house parties or bonfires on the beach.

Still, on that night, my stomach lurched when the neon sign for Hay Stacks came into view. It was the only country bar at The Crawl and though I loved country music, I was the exact opposite of excited to be there. I knew Mason would be inside, probably at the same bar he had kissed me at the night after homecoming, and I had a pretty good hunch he wouldn't be alone. Willow tried to soothe me with her never-ending flow of wise words and clichés, but nothing she could say could make me want my couch any less.

"If you don't loosen your grip, I'm not going to have an arm left for them to slap a wristband on," Willow said as we reached the doors. The twangy music was spilling out onto the strip and I swore I heard Mason laugh through the noise.

"Sorry," I murmured, removing my hand from her arm and stretching out my fingers as she rubbed the spot I'd been holding fast to. My nervous hands reached for my camera next, and once they found their comfortable placement on either side of the sleek, black object, I immediately felt a subtle calm wash over me. I idly ran my thumbs up and down the cool metal. "I don't think I can do this, Lo. Everyone is going to judge me."

"Try being one of only three black girls in the town, Nat. Trust me, you'll get used to it." She winked and I shook my head, smiling a little. She was exaggerating, of course, but not by much. Poxton Beach definitely wasn't known for its diversity and Willow stood out both with her skin color and her personality. She was confident, smart as hell, and usually the life of the party.

So basically, she was my polar opposite.

Still, I trusted her more than anyone. I questioned a lot of my friendships in Poxton Beach, but never hers.

She liked me before we were old enough to realize money meant something in the world. It wasn't that I thought my friendships were fake, but after graduation and the lack of phone calls from friends to see if I was okay, I wondered if all the people who claimed my friendship actually wanted it. Maybe they just wanted the privilege that went along with it.

If only they knew *everything* that went along with it. The Poxton name was splattered all over that town, on everything from the local pharmacy to the bank and everything in-between. I couldn't even walk into a convenience store to get a pack of gum without everyone knowing who I was. There were eyes on me at all times, and that was more pressure than I knew how to handle most of the time. I wasn't born a Poxton, I was married into it — and sometimes I felt like I let Dale down.

Like right now — when I couldn't even handle a stupid break-up.

When I started chewing my lip and clicking the shutter buttons on my camera, Willow realized how shaken I was. She inhaled a deep breath and pulled me to the side of the building, away from the crowd waiting to get in.

"Listen to me, Natalie," she said, her hands finding my shoulders as she leveled her eyes with mine. "Mason made a huge mistake letting you go, and I know he'll recognize that some day. I'm not going to lie to you and say it'll be tonight because it probably won't be. If I had to bet money, I'd say he's going to have that new brunette Barbie hanging around his arm and he'll likely pretend like you don't exist or like nothing happened between you two at all and everything is normal. Either way, don't let him get to you. Hold your chin high and walk in that bar like you haven't been fazed at all. Take illegal shots out of this flask with your best friend and dance until those cute red boots of yours shred to pieces." Willow smiled, holding up her favorite, sleek black flask, her bright white teeth glowing against her dark skin in the neon light of the bars. Her long hair was still braided to one side, elongating her face even more than usual and reminding me how flawless my best friend was. I put her in the same category as my mother — effortlessly beautiful.

"I'm just scared, Willow. He was my best friend. He was my everything." Saying the words out loud made my chest sting.

Willow threw her arm around my shoulder, steering me back toward Hay Stacks. "I know, babe. And maybe that's part of the issue, you know? If you give your all to someone else, realize you may one day have to change all you know about yourself."

I nudged her playfully. "You and your words of wisdom."

She shrugged. "What can I say? It's a gift. Now put on your happy face and let's do this. And please don't hide behind that lens all night," she added, eying my camera.

I sighed, looking around at the crowd gathered like someone out there would have the mental strength

I needed and I'd be able to steal it from them with one glance. We walked straight up to the bouncer, ignoring the small line that had formed. He smiled at us and tipped his hat to Willow as he moved to the side to let us in, my hands still holding fast to the camera around my neck. I heard a few groans from the out-of-towners, but the locals didn't even bat an eye. I was Natalie Poxton. And that meant I didn't have to wait.

If only I were as powerful on the inside as the name I'd been given.

I let out a long breath as my hands tightened their grip around my camera. I felt safer with it hanging around my neck, and my fingers played with the flash, clicking it up and back down again as we made our way to the back bar where our friends would no doubt be gathered.

I spotted Mason immediately.

I half hoped he wouldn't show, but he did. And as soon as my eyes found him and witnessed his signature, full-faced smile break across his face, I almost fell to my knees. He looked more handsome than usual, if that was even possible, and it absolutely killed me. I pulled my bottom lip between my teeth out of habit and followed Willow a little closer.

"Lo!" Stephanie shouted over the music, throwing her arms around Willow's neck when we reached the group. "Okay, it's official. The party can start now."

"I have arrived!" Willow yelled in response and the group laughed. I felt hot eyes burning holes through me as I gripped my camera even tighter and waited for the first person to speak to me. I tried to hold my head high like Willow said, but I was pretty sure I was failing miserably.

"Nice to see you, Natalie," Dustin said first, offering a kind smile. Dustin was Mason's best friend and, from what he had said to me after the break-up the week before, he didn't exactly agree with Mason's choice. I smiled back at him and dropped my hands from my camera, trying to relax.

"You too, Dustin." I'd chewed off all the lip balm I'd put on in the car ride over, so I retrieved a small tube from my purse and reapplied, using the old habit to calm my nerves as Dustin continued smiling at me.

Dustin and Mason were practically twins, though Mason's features were perfectly symmetrical, giving him just a small edge up on Dustin. They both had shaggy brown hair and matching chocolate eyes. While Mason was always tan from working on his parents' land, Dustin's skin was light and dotted with tiny freckles. And though Mason was tall with broad shoulders, Dustin was at least six inches taller, his frame lanky in comparison.

I tucked my lip balm back into my purse just as my eyes moved to Mason, who was officially staring at me along with everyone else. "Hey Mase."

He paused for a moment, like he wasn't sure what to say to me, and it made my stomach twist into an awful knot. I swallowed, but kept my posture as calm as I could, hearing Willow's words in my mind. All I wanted was for him to wrap me in his arms and tell me it was all a joke, but I knew that wasn't going to happen. So I needed to at least pretend to be okay. That town loved to gossip and I didn't want poor, dumped Natalie Poxton to be their next subject of focus.

"Hey, Nat." He paused again and lowered his voice a bit, moving a little closer. "You okay?"

His words made my stomach twist more, but Willow's eyes narrowing behind him reminded me that I needed to seem in control. Even if I was far from it.

I shrugged. "Why wouldn't I be?"

There were a few raised brows and whispers after that remark and Willow gave me a subtle *thumbs up* sign, but I felt awful. I never lied to Mason, and I knew he could see I was bluffing. But he didn't call me on it. He just smiled, nodded, and turned back to Dustin. It was like his attention was tied to everyone else's because as soon as he and Dustin started talking about baseball, everyone else went back to their conversations, too.

Stephanie grabbed my hand and hauled me to the bathroom with her and Willow. "Let's drink!" She bounced a little, her smile bright as she tugged us through the crowd.

Stephanie was by far the prettiest girl in our class, though Willow closely rivaled her. Both of them were tall and lean, but Stephanie had perfect, long, auburn hair that twisted into beautiful curls effortlessly. Her smile revealed dimples that drove every boy insane. She was always nice to me, but we never hung out unless Willow was involved. In fact, Willow and Mason were the only two people I ever hung out with outside of our group outings.

After Mason dumped me, I was down to one.

Stephanie and Willow took shots out of their flasks in the handicap stall we all crammed into but I waved my hand when they offered them to me. I probably could have used the alcohol to calm my nerves, but I was more afraid of breaking down under the haze, so I opted for water when we got back to the bar, instead.

Sipping on my water allowed me to relax a little and the more everyone else drank, the better I felt. For some reason, buzzed eyes were easier for me to stand than sober ones.

We were leaned up against the back edge of the bar, still in the same group as Mason and Dustin but with enough space between us to hold separate conversations. Willow and Stephanie were chatting about their dorm room assignments at Appalachian State while I pretended to listen. As far as I was concerned, that college was essentially high school number two. Besides, Mason's girlfriend had just walked in, and I was far more interested in torturing myself by watching them together. She had just strutted in and thrown herself into his arms as everyone around them smiled. He wrapped his arms all the way around her and pulled her tight into him, kissing her lips like he'd kissed mine a week before, and I couldn't help but realize that he could never wrap his arms that far around me.

"What about you, Nat?" Stephanie asked, stealing another sip from her flask before pouring half of it in the soda she'd just ordered. "Where are you rooming? I'm surprised you and Willow aren't together."

I shrugged, tilting my plastic cup until an ice cube slid between my teeth. I crunched on it loudly with my eyes still on Mason. "I haven't decided if I'm going to Appalachian State, yet."

Stephanie blanched and Willow's mouth pulled to the side. She already knew I was still debating my options, but to Stephanie and everyone else in this town, it was practically a sin not to go to Appalachian State. It was where everyone in Poxton Beach went. We "stuck together," as Dale liked to put it, and most of us would end up right back in that town.

Again — high school number two.

But me? I hadn't made a single move toward college, other than take the standardized testing.

"What do you mean? Like, not this semester?" Stephanie was twirling the small black straw in her drink furiously as she waited for my response.

Embarrassment shaded my cheeks, though I wasn't sure if it was from her judgmental questions or from Mason's eyes catching mine briefly before I flicked them back to Stephanie. I hated having to explain my decisions, especially when I wasn't quite sure why I made them, either. The only thing I knew for sure was that I didn't want to go to a college just because everyone else was doing it. "As in maybe not at all. I don't know, I haven't decided yet."

"But don't you have to get a room? And enroll in classes?"

I shrugged again. "I'm not worried about it right now." That wasn't exactly true, but it wasn't exactly a lie. I did worry about it — about the decision I had to make, about being behind the rest of my classmates when it came to knowing my future. But, it was also true that, at the moment, my only *real* worry was that Mason had his tongue halfway down another girl's throat.

Willow followed my gaze and shook her head, stealing a shot from her flask before grabbing my arm. "Nuh-uh. Not happening, Nat. You are not going to sit here and torture yourself all night. Let's go dance."

But before she had the chance to pull me away, Mason's girlfriend made her way toward us. She smiled at Stephanie first, eying her outfit.

"I *love* those boots! Where did you get them?"

Stephanie returned her smile, flattered and clearly unaware of my discomfort. "The boot boutique in town. They have the best colors and styles! I'll have to take you sometime."

"I'd love that," she answered genuinely before turning her gaze to me. It soured immediately. "You're Natalie, right?"

My throat was too dry to swallow, which meant I definitely couldn't answer, so I just nodded.

Her smile was pinched at the corners. "It's nice to meet you. I've heard a lot about you from Mason."

My heart backflipped at her words before sinking to the floor. She heard about me from Mason? Was that a good or bad thing?

"I'm Shay," she finally said, but she didn't extend a hand for a shake. "Listen, I hope things won't be weird between us. I mean, being that Mason dumped you to date me and everything. We're young, right? These things happen." She smiled wider now, happy with herself.

This time I swallowed, feeling sick. Her eyes were on me along with Stephanie's, both of them waiting for a response. What was I supposed to say?

Willow narrowed her eyes, tugging my arm again. "Come on, you don't have to play this game with her." She turned to Shay next. "Maybe you should go back to your boyfriend."

Shay shrugged, linking her arm through Stephanie's to mirror Willow's through mine. "You're probably right. Come on, Stephanie is it? I want to hear more about this boot boutique."

Stephanie lit up, chatting animatedly as Shay pulled her back toward where Mason and Dustin were standing, oblivious to what had transpired at our end of the bar.

Willow pulled me out to the large wooden dance floor before I had the chance to completely process and we joined in on the line dance, finding a spot just in time to stomp twice and turn before it started from the top again.

"Don't let her get to you," Willow shouted over the song as we fell in line with the other dancers. I wouldn't say I was shy, but I was far from the attention-seeking type of girl, which was part of the reason I loved line dancing. There was something about moving to the music without having to stand out that pulled me in.

"Kind of hard not to, Lo. Did you see her?"

"Yeah. And? She's nothing special, Nat." Willow flipped her braid over her shoulder as we hit another turn.

I inwardly frowned, noting the brunette's petite frame and large... lady parts. She wore jean shorts that looked like they had been purchased in the kids' section and her smile was almost too perfect. If she was "nothing special," then what the hell was I?

"Who is she, anyway?" I asked as the song changed and we fell into the next dance.

"New girl. She's a junior — or well, I guess a senior now. She's from Lee County but just transferred here for her senior year. I guess her dad got a new job here."

"What?" I stopped abruptly, careful to avoid another dancer crashing into me when I halted. "Where?"

Willow cringed. "He's the new VP at the bank."

I smacked my palm against my forehead. Of course. It only makes sense that my ex's new girlfriend moved to town because *my* dad hired hers. Awesome.

I turned to leave the dance floor, clearly done dancing, but before I had a chance to register what had happened, I slammed into Colleen Masterson, knocking her straight down to the floor.

"Oh my God, are you okay?" I leaned down quickly, Willow taking her other side as we helped lift her up. Colleen was a couple of years older than us and was the smallest girl I knew. At just five-foot-one and maybe one-hundred and ten pounds, she was the perfect size to be the best flier on the cheerleader squad that she had been all through school.

Colleen nodded, leaning up as Willow and I helped steady her. She seemed shaken and I felt like a complete oaf. Suddenly, a loud ring of laughter came from behind Willow. I looked up through the paused dancers that had gathered around us and saw Shay pointing our direction. Everyone around her was laughing, save for Mason, who was making his way toward us with a concerned pinch between his brows. Dustin joined him, but not before throwing a disapproving look over his shoulder toward Shay.

"Hey, are you all right?" Mason asked, not pointing the question toward Colleen but at me, instead. I didn't answer, because my focus was still completely drawn to where Shay was making jokes. I couldn't hear what she was saying, but she was definitely staring at me, and Stephanie was laughing with her. I swallowed, heat rushing to my face as Willow turned to look behind her, too — just in time to see Shay call me a "fat klutz".

And that time, I heard her.

"I'm sorry, Colleen," I mumbled, standing as quickly as I could and bolting for the door. Willow chased after me, calling out my name and asking me to wait but I didn't stop. Tears stung at the back of my eyes as I shoved through the crowd, using more force than necessary. I hated that I couldn't hold myself together. I didn't even cry when Mason broke up with me, why the hell was I about to cry over something someone I didn't even care about said?

Because *he* cares about her, that's why.

How could Mason go from dating someone like me to dating someone like her? She was awful. He deserved better, he should want better.

He should want me.

Moses had Dale's Range Rover pulled up almost as soon as I sent him the text and I slid into the backseat quickly, locking the door behind me, like that would shield me from the cruel reality I had just faced.

"Take me home, Moses," I said through the tears still building. I tried to catch a deep breath, but came up short each time. My chest was too tight. My lungs weren't big enough.

Moses didn't hesitate or ask a single question, just pushed the Rover into drive and tore out of The Crawl like he felt the urgency, too.

Moses used to be Dale's family's butler, but he transitioned into more of a family friend by the time mom and I made our way into the Poxton tribe. He was in his sixties, though his bald head and tan skin made him look more like a biker in his late forties. He had barely any wrinkles to speak of, which I swore I would find the secret behind. He eyed me curiously in the rearview mirror for just a moment before looking straight ahead again. I was waiting for the questions to come, but thankfully they didn't.

My phone rang as soon as the light from The Crawl faded behind us. Willow's name and striking smile lit up the screen and I hit the red *ignore* button hastily before turning off my phone completely. I knew she wanted to help, but I was past the point of being pulled back by *Willow's Words of Wisdom*. Each mile we drove brought us closer to home and farther from the club, yet still I felt my heart ripping. I closed my eyes tight and saw their faces, heard their laughter, felt the embarrassment. I'd never been the butt of any of my friends' jokes — at least, not that I knew of. Why was it that Mason's new girlfriend could make fun of me and get away with it so easily? Why didn't anyone stand up for me?

Then again, could I really blame Shay for my embarrassment? It wasn't her who ate the way I did. It wasn't her who watched me put on more and more weight over the years. It wasn't her who knocked Colleen to the floor in the middle of a crowded bar. All of those things were my fault, and the saddest truth was that I wasn't even doing anything to change the way I looked. Or felt.

Maybe it was time to start.

Like a strobe light of assault, little moments that I hadn't thought twice about struck me violently in the backseat of the Range Rover. I remembered covering myself at the beach while all my friends laid out in two pieces. I remembered having to shop at a completely different store for my prom dress after the attendant told me and Willow that they didn't have anything above a size nine. I remembered having to order a large gown for graduation, even though they were already so flowy and loose. I remembered it all, all of a sudden, all at once — all in striking detail.

It was the first time in my life that I realized I wasn't comfortable in my own skin.

When we pulled up the long drive to Dale's house, my mind was still replaying the laughter I'd heard. Mason hadn't joined in on it, but he hadn't stopped it. Still, he asked me if I was okay, and that was all the hope I needed to think that maybe I did stand a chance of winning him back.

But before I could think of going after him, I had to go after a better life for myself.

"Thanks, Mo," I whispered quietly, my voice strained. He offered a soft smile and only nodded in return. Again, I was thankful that somehow in this town, he'd lost the interest in finding out every detail of a bad situation.

It wasn't even midnight yet when I stepped through the door into our massive foyer. I heard mom and Dale talking in the kitchen and I let my feet carry me there without even thinking about what I would say. Dale was mid-bite and Mom was laughing as they stood around the kitchen island, large bowls of ice cream in front of them, when I walked in.

Dale dropped his spoon when he saw me and Mom whipped around, cutting her laugh short. She immediately rushed to me when she saw my face and I let her pull me into her. For a small woman, she had a fierce hug.

"Oh baby, what happened?" Dale asked, moving toward us. I pulled back from Mom's grip and shook my head, my eyes falling to the wood floor.

"I think I change my mind," I said softly, not sure if I was really on board with what I was about to say or if I was just acting in the moment. Either way, the words were there. "About the trainer."

Mom looked back to Dale who crossed his arms over his chest, a worried look on his face. "Are you sure?" I nodded, though my eyes stayed down. He sighed. "Don't do this for some boy, Natalie."

"It's not for him." *Not entirely, anyway.* I cleared my throat, lifting my eyes to meet his. "I need this. For me."

Mom pulled me in for another hug. "Oh sweetheart, it'll be okay. You're so strong. I know you can do this. And Mason will kick himself for ever letting you go."

I shrugged out from under her and pulled my arms over my chest to mimic Dale. It felt safer to stand like that. "Can I start tomorrow?"

Mom smiled softly and nodded. "I'll call the club first thing in the morning."

I felt the tears pricking my eyes again, but I somehow managed to hold them in check. "Thanks, Mom. Dale. Really." I shook my head, my eyes finding the floor again. "I'm sorry."

Dale frowned. "What on earth are you sorry for, baby?"

I shrugged. "I knocked a girl down tonight. I'm so big I—" a sob finally choked its way through my throat and my hand flew to my mouth. I shook my head as they both moved to comfort me, the tears I'd been holding back breaking free. "I don't want to feel like this anymore."

Saying the words out loud finally made me realize how far I'd let myself go. No matter how I had played it off in the past, my size had always bothered me — just not enough for me to care to make a change. But that night was the breaking point. I knew the road ahead of me wouldn't be an easy one, but I didn't have a choice anymore.

Mason had weakened me. And that night, his girlfriend had finished the job he started, successfully breaking me into pieces. They were scattered on the floor around me and I knew it was time to pick them up and start rebuilding.

I hoped I'd build a better me.

A *stronger* me.

And definitely — a smaller me.

# CHAPTER

# 2

I walked into the Poxton Beach Country Club just after two in the afternoon the next day. The club sat on the west edge of town, a large, grand building right at the front of our one and only golf course. I'd only been to the club for Dale's parties and Sunday brunch before, and never once had I been curious enough to ask if there even *was* a gym, let alone ask to see it. As I followed a club associate through the large hallway toward the back of the building, I was regretting my word vomit to my parents. Yes, I had been upset. Yes, I wanted to start making changes — but was a trainer really the best way to do that? When we walked through the large glass doors and I found myself standing in a room full of slim, ripped, beautiful people, I was sure I'd made a crazy decision in my haste.

I definitely did not belong in that room.

"Your trainer is just finishing up with his last client," the older woman informed me. She tilted her head toward a small fitness room behind the row of treadmills. "Go ahead and walk back there. He should be done soon." She paused, her smile still radiant. I guessed she was maybe in her late thirties and her PBCC polo shirt was perked up by a set of what I was sure were very fake assets.

When I only smiled and nodded awkwardly, she turned to excuse herself, but not before adding, "And have fun. He's the best trainer in this place." She winked and I felt myself blush, though I wasn't exactly sure why.

I made my way toward the small room the woman had referred to, crossing my arms over my body as I walked past the various members in their tight workout gear. I was dressed in yoga pants and a Poxton Beach High School t-shirt from homecoming two years ago with my thick hair pulled into a high, messy bun. I looked frumpy and I knew it, but with my body, I didn't really know how to look otherwise.

When I reached the glass windows that separated the private fitness room from the rest of the gym, I paused, watching the two people inside. There was a man knelt down on the ground, his muscular back showing through the ripped up, wide-sleeved black tank top he wore. From that angle, I could see there was a woman on a spongy black mat in front of him.

She was on all fours, but all I could see was her back right leg extending up toward the ceiling with a flexed foot as the man gently guided her knee. I watched the muscles in his arms flex as he moved, the ripples and ridges changing with each lift and fall. I had never seen muscles like that — not that close, anyway. Just the partial view of his backside had me crossing my arms tighter and wishing I would have at least tried not to look like a bum.

After another minute, the woman dropped her leg and sat back on her heels, giving the man a high five and a smile so big it made *my* cheeks hurt. Though when he stood and turned around, I completely understood why.

Suddenly, it was hard to breathe.

He threw a small white towel over his dark, damp hair, dragging it down his face slowly to wipe away the sweat he'd worked up. His arm muscles were even more defined from the front, his biceps tightening with every movement of his hand. As he pulled the towel down and around his neck, I noted his strong, tense jaw, covered with just the smallest bit of scruff. His bright green eyes were lasered in on the woman and he continued his slow assault with that damn white towel while she asked him questions. He was scowling, almost as if the towel had greatly offended him or he was contemplating a world issue and for some reason that scowl had my body feeling a heat it had never felt before.

My trainer was none other than Rhodes — Poxton Beach's closest thing to a bad boy. Other than the fact that he was a senior when I was a freshman and he was absolutely terrifying, I really didn't know much about him. I only had one year of roaming the same halls as him at PBHS, but that was all I needed to know it was best to keep my distance. Rhodes was a mystery to most of the town, and the fact that he would be getting up close and personal with my body in a matter of minutes set me on edge. It was like a red *DANGER* sign lighting up over and over again as I watched him closely, that same fear I'd felt toward him in school creeping up. Still, my feet wouldn't move.

When the woman gave one last wave and walked out the door to my right, I was still standing and staring like an idiot on the other side of the glass. Rhodes dragged the towel over his face once more before lifting his shirt, revealing a sliver of tan skin as he tucked one corner of the offending white fabric beneath the band of his shorts. It was then that his eyes found mine, and for the second time in twenty-four hours, I felt a small shift in my universe.

Rhodes frowned, assessing me through the glass that was my only safety from the unfamiliar sensation I was currently experiencing. Slowly, he walked through the door and leaned against the frame, crossing his arms. "Natalie?"

I was still standing a safe distance from him, my body angled toward the glass. I nodded before finally finding my voice. "Yes. Yeah, um, yeah I'm Natalie. Natalie Poxton." I extended my hand for his, but he just quirked a brow as he appraised it before looking back at me again, jaw set. Suddenly I felt like an idiot and I let my hand fall.

"I see. I'm Rhodes; I'll be your trainer. Come on," he said, moving from his leaning pose on the frame to stand straight. "Let's get your numbers."

I tried not to analyze what that *I see* meant as I followed him back to a small office behind the section filled with weights. It was tiny, but elegant, like only a Poxton Beach office would be. There was one desk and a matching bookshelf that held mostly files. The desk was vacant except for a white, sleek computer and a green notepad, which Rhodes picked up as soon as we entered. He gestured to a large glass scale in the back corner near the bookshelf. "Step up."

I snapped my head toward him but he was already scribbling away in the notepad, leaving my pleading eyes to fall on the scale in front of me. But that scale wasn't sympathetic. I swallowed, shifting. I knew it was part of the process. I *knew* that. Then again, what I *hadn't* known was that Rhodes would be my trainer.

Cool, life. Cool.

When I didn't move, Rhodes glanced up from his notepad and used the pen in his hand to point to the glass monster again. I sighed, shaking out my nerves the best that I could, and stepped up. I was far from excited about the number that popped up on the digital display in front of my face and even more horrified when Rhodes proceeded to calculate my body fat percentage. When he wrapped a long, blue measuring tape around my waist, hips, thighs, arms, legs, and neck, I was pretty sure my face could fry an egg I was blushing so hard. When all the poking and prodding was done, he sat behind the desk and asked me to sit on the small, dark blue cushioned chair across from him.

"So, what's your goal?" He asked, pulling out a new file to store my information. His arms were still slightly glazed with a sheen of sweat that I couldn't help but fixate on while I tried to think of the answer to his question.

*To get my boyfriend back.*

Yeah, suddenly that didn't sound so smooth.

I fidgeted, unsure of what else to say. "I don't know, I suppose I'm here for the same reason everyone else is," I offered, hoping he would nod and continue on. But he didn't. He lifted his eyes to mine, the piercing green capturing my gaze as he studied me. After a moment, he sighed and leaned back, balancing the pad on his knee.

"Okay, who is he? Who's the guy?"

I blanched.

"What?"

"The guy. The one you're trying to get or *for*get or whatever." His voice was booming, but with an edgy rasp that somehow smoothed it out.

I crossed my arms, defensive. "There's not a guy." *Not that you need to know about, anyway.* "I'm here because *I* want to be."

He shrugged, not fazed in the slightest by what I felt was a huge act of standing my ground. "Fine. Then what's your goal?"

I chewed my bottom lip, working from the left side to the right and back again. It was a nervous habit I'd had my entire life, and I had to carry copious amounts of lip balm to make up for it. Rhodes' eyes fell to my lips and I snapped my mouth shut. They stayed there for a moment longer before he found my gaze again. I had forgotten he asked me a question until he lifted a brow, waiting.

*What was my goal?*

"I just want to be pretty," I finally answered, my voice just above a whisper. I had let my eyes fall to the floor, just like I did with my parents the night before, and when I lifted them to meet his again I slightly regretted it. His brows were pinched together over the bridge of his nose and he shook his head before quietly scribbling in that damn notepad of his.

I imagined he was writing something along the lines of, *"No chance. Never happening. Poor girl."*

"All right." He stood and I followed, though I wasn't sure what we were doing just yet. "Let's go do your first workout. It'll only be a twenty minute toning session today and then I'll have you do twenty minutes of cardio. This will be your easiest day. You're set up to train with me for two hours every day of the week except for Wednesdays and Saturdays. I'm working on your meal plan and I should have that ready by tomorrow's session. Until then, I'll give you the name of a fitness app to download to your phone so you can start logging your meals. Log everything, even if it's bad. You have to be honest for this to work." I was nodding feverishly, hanging on his every word. "You'll weigh in once a week and we'll take your measurements once every three weeks. Here," he handed me a business card from a small stack behind the computer. "My cell number is on here. You can call me anytime, day or night, if you have questions about what you're eating or anything else related to your training."

I took the card, startling a little when our hands touched, then he was on the move. "We'll start with legs. Do you know the proper way to do a squat?"

And I didn't. I didn't have the slightest clue how to properly execute a squat, a lunge, a calf-raise or anything else he showed me in that insane twenty minute session he put me through that day. But the way he looked at me, the strange way he appraised me when he thought I wouldn't notice, had me wondering if my attention should even be on my form at all.

There had always been mystery in Rhodes' eyes, I remembered that from when we went to school together. There was danger. There was ice. But that day, there was another element that I never expected to see.

Curiosity.

I just couldn't figure out why.

I thought I knew what sore was, but I had no idea. Muscles I didn't even know existed were aching, making me groan every time I had to stand up. Or sit down. Or really move in any way at all. I'd only trained with Rhodes three days but already I felt like I was dying a slow, muscle-torturing death. Even after having all of Wednesday off, I still couldn't walk, and worst of all — I had to leave for the gym in an hour.

Might as well start drafting up my obituary.

Waddling into the kitchen, I pulled the snack-sized pack of celery out of the fridge and grabbed the jar of fat-free peanut butter I'd bought to pair with it. It wasn't anything I really craved, but I was determined to stick to the meal plan Rhodes had designed for me. I even went shopping and meal prepped myself instead of letting our in-house chef, Christina, take care of it. Meal prepping was a new adventure for me, but Rhodes tried to make it easy and Christina helped when I asked. She had been cooking for me since I was in diapers and I think she almost took offense to the fact that I wanted to do this on my own. Still, she supported me. I was going to be leaving for college at some point in the next year — well, maybe at least — and I wanted to be able to eat without her when the time came. I knew it wasn't going to be easy, but I had an entire summer off from school to focus on the habits I needed to make a lifestyle.

That's how Rhodes had explained it — a lifestyle. He kept telling me that I wasn't on a diet and I wasn't on some get-skinny-quick fix, either. His goal was to help me change my lifestyle, to teach me how to live my life in a healthier way. And even though I knew my main goal was to see the look on Mason and Shay's faces when I looked amazing in a bathing suit at the senior send-off party, I was kind of intrigued by his bigger plan. After all, it wasn't all about Mason. It was about me. It was about my life and my future.

As I bit into my fourth stick of celery, Dale walked into the kitchen. He lifted a brow when he noted my plate and I frowned. "Don't even go there, Dale."

He threw his hands up and laughed a little. "I'm

not saying a word. Who am I to judge if you want to eat plants?"

I stuck my tongue out and took another bite, the celery and peanut butter crunching between my teeth as he reached in the fridge for a beer. He popped it open and leaned back against the counter. Dale was tall, his hair jet black and his eyes almost the same color. When he stood next to my fair-skinned, blonde-headed mother, their differences were on full display. "In all seriousness, I'm really proud of you, Nat."

"Thanks," I murmured, looking down at my plate. "I don't feel like I'm doing anything special yet. Nothing is changing."

He chuckled. "It hasn't even been a week. Give it time." Taking a drag from his bottle, his smile faded and he assessed me more seriously. "You know you're beautiful, don't you, Natalie?" I rolled my eyes and thought about throwing a celery stick at him, but refrained. Before I could say anything, he set his bottle down on the counter and crossed his arms. "I mean it. You're a gorgeous girl. Mason is an idiot and he should have realized that by now, regardless of the trainer."

Dale was great at being a dad, even though he didn't have to be. Still, I could tell he wasn't any more comfortable handling my first break-up than I was. Dale and I were close, but we never really talked about girl stuff like that. I knew I was insecure, I knew I was dramatic, but Mom was always the one to help me through the high school insanity — not Dale. He watched me closely as I finished my last celery stick, not sure what to say back to him.

"Well I don't see it, I guess."

He smiled again, making the tension melt a little. "Not yet. But you will." He grabbed his bottle and tilted it toward me in a cheers. "Have fun at the gym."

I groaned, my muscles protesting at just the sound of the word. Dale chuckled and made his way back into the living room as I grabbed my water bottle and shoved it in my gym bag before heading out the door.

It was a beautiful May afternoon, the sun blazing high in the sky with a gentle breeze rolling in from the east coast. I knew the beach must have been absolutely packed. Rolling down the windows in Dale's Range Rover, I tried to enjoy the weather and relax my mind as I drove the short fifteen minutes to the club. When I pulled up, Rhodes was waiting for me outside, his arms and ankles crossed as he leaned against one of the front pillars.

He was wearing a dark pair of sunglasses, but still his brows were furrowed over in a squint as he watched me exit the SUV. When I reached where he was leaning, he stood straight and uncrossed his arms, giving me full access to gaze at his chest muscles stretching out the tight fabric of his navy blue shirt. Thank God I was wearing sunglasses, too.

"We're working outside today. Did you bring a towel?"

I reached into the front pocket of my gym bag and pulled out the towel I'd packed, waving it around slightly like a white flag of surrender.

"Good," he assessed, walking toward the back of

the building without checking to see if I was following. "You'll need it. Lose the shades."

I swallowed, but followed quickly behind him, removing my sunglasses and tucking them in my bag as he did the same. It was my fourth day with Rhodes, yet he still hadn't said more than a few words to me. I'd tried conversation a few times, but to no avail. He was cold, reserved, and not the least bit interested in becoming my friend.

Not that I could really blame him.

He was beautiful. Crazy? Maybe. Intimidating? Definitely. But, beautiful nonetheless. And beautiful guys like him didn't befriend girls who looked like me.

Still, he was my trainer. My parents were paying him for his service. The least he could do was provide it with a smile, right?

We started the session with a three mile jog around the club property. We ran up and over the hills of the golf course, through the garden, around the tennis courts, and finished with a sprint up the stairs leading to the top balcony of the space used for weddings and events. I had to stop at least ten times along the way, but each time I did Rhodes would scream at me to keep going and threaten me with added distance. The beautiful day I had been admiring in the drive over felt more like my own personal hell halfway through the workout. By the time we reached the top of the stairs, I was completely spent.

"Nice job," he said simply, wiping the sweat from his face as I chugged from my water bottle. He leaned over the railing for a moment, his gaze caught somewhere across the course. I was panting so hard I had to take short breaths between sips. I felt like I couldn't drink fast enough and he was just standing there all calm and collected, like we had just watched a movie rather than ran for almost an hour in the Carolina heat.

"Don't drink too much too quickly," he said smoothly, lifting himself from his leaning position on the rail. "Take a few minutes and meet me downstairs when you're ready." Without another word, he turned and jogged back down the stairs we had just run up. I watched the ridges of his back muscles move in sync as he disappeared from view.

I wasn't one for cursing, but I could think of at least seven swear words I felt like yelling out to the entire club in that moment. Instead, I focused on my breathing and sipping water until I felt a little calmer before walking down the stairs to join Rhodes. He was setting up some sort of obstacle course with tires, ropes, boxes, and bars.

Good Lord.

It wasn't that I hadn't worked out before training with Rhodes, but I'd never experienced anything close to his methods before. I realized at that point that my high school gym classes were a complete joke. Even the Zumba classes that had kicked my butt when Mom and I took them paled in comparison to the sessions I had with Rhodes. He was fierce. He surely had a goal in mind for me, whether I did or not.

"How do you do that without dying?" I asked, nodding toward the path we'd just run.

He shrugged, dropping another, slightly taller box down beside the one he'd just placed. "I just do."

I fidgeted with the bottom of my t-shirt, waiting for more of an explanation that never came. Sighing, I tried again. "How many days a week do you train?"

"Seven."

"So you don't have a single day off?"

"Nope."

"That's crazy." He didn't respond. "What got you into fitness?"

He paused after placing a weighted plate on the taller of the two boxes, his arms bracing himself on either side. Turning toward me slowly, he locked his eyes on mine as his mouth flattened into a thin line. Small beads of sweat dripped down the ridges of his nose and jaw and I watched them with fascination, wishing I had my camera with me to capture that shot in a stunning black and white monochrome.

"You ask a lot of questions."

"I asked four."

"That's a lot."

I scoffed, but he didn't give me a chance to argue further.

"Let's start here. Grab these ropes." He gestured down to two, thickly woven ropes that were anchored to the thick pillar below the stairs we'd just climbed. I slowly bent to pick them up and held one in each hand facing the tied end. They were heavier than I expected and I immediately worried about where the workout was heading.

Rhodes stepped up beside me with his arms outstretched, mimicking the position I was holding the ropes in. "These are battle ropes. They're going to work a lot of different muscles simultaneously and give you an all-over workout. We're only going to do ten minutes, but it's going to feel like hours." I swallowed, gripping the ropes a little tighter. "Start like this," he instructed, standing with his feet shoulder-width apart and bending his knees slightly before lifting both of his hands up and bringing them down with force. "It's a simple double wave. Just lift the ropes with both hands and bring them back down as hard as you can, making a wave."

I lifted the ropes as high as I could and brought them back down with as much force as I could muster, turning to Rhodes for approval. He nodded, his brows bent in that beautiful way that I'd begun to realize was a signature look of his, and I continued. Immediately I noticed my arms burning, but the more we worked, the more the burn spread throughout my entire body. He had me change positions every minute to everything from an alternating wave where each arm worked opposite the motion of the other to shoulder circles, which were exactly what they were called except with heavy ropes that made my upper back and shoulders burn like they were on fire.

"Let's finish with snakes," Rhodes said after what must have been about nine minutes but what felt more like nine days. "You're going to get into a squat," he said, illustrating the move. "And move your arms out and then together, but not all the way crossed, making snake-like waves across the ground." He lifted his brows to ask if I understood and I nodded, turning back toward the anchor. I did my first attempt and laughed out loud at the failed result. When I looked over at Rhodes, his eyes were brighter, the wrinkles in his forehead leveled out. If I didn't know it was impossible, I'd say he was almost smiling.

"Here," he said, moving behind me. I stopped breathing as his strong hands found my middle, somehow making me feel small as he lowered me into a squat. Slowly, he snaked his arms up under mine and gripped the ropes just above where my hands held tight to them. His hard chest was pressed against my back, our bodies sticking together slightly, and his breath was hot on the skin of my neck. "Like this." He moved our arms out and then back toward each other and I watched how the ropes mimicked the movements of a snake, trying to focus on anything other than the buzz I was feeling from being so close to Rhodes. I felt him swallow, the muscles in his arms tensing as he waited for me to do the move with him.

When he was sure I had it, he stepped back, straightening himself as I finished. He eventually called time and I dropped the ropes and stood, shaking out my legs. I was breathing hard, though I wasn't exactly sure if it was from the ropes. I peered up at Rhodes, hands hooked on my hips as I tried to steady my breathing. He was watching me closely, that same curiosity buzzing in his eyes. I felt like he had a question for me, and I begged him to ask it — to say anything at all. The air between us was charged with an unexplainable energy, and I wondered if he felt it, too.

But he just cleared his throat and motioned to the boxes he'd set up earlier. "Grab water if you need it. We're doing box jumps next."

My eyes fell to the ground and I retied the messy bun high on my head as my cheeks heated. Foregoing the water, I followed him to the box jumps, which I wasn't able to successfully complete. I was terrified of falling on my face and it felt like my feet were glued to the ground each time he demanded I jump. We moved on to the next part of his make-shift obstacle course and continued through it until I was so drenched my light orange shirt was stuck to every curve of my body. Rhodes clapped me on the back like a football player and told me to take an ice bath, then he turned and disappeared inside the club and into the small gym office.

I did take my first ice bath that night, right after drinking the disgusting powder-based post-workout shake Rhodes told me to buy. As I sank down into the freezing water, ice cubes shaking and shifting as I lowered myself in, I hoped it would cool much more than just my aching muscles.

# CHAPTER

# 3

Thursday's workout was tough, but Friday's was absolutely brutal. Rhodes seemed pissed off, for whatever reason, and apparently taking out his frustration on his clients was his favorite pastime. So when Saturday finally rolled around, I was beyond thankful for my day off from training. Spending Saturday night with Willow was just what I needed, though I wasn't sure I'd be able to lift myself out of the booth when the night was over.

Hookah wasn't really my thing, but I loved going to Rook with Willow. It was a small, dark hole in the wall with plush maroon couches and acoustic music — sometimes played by a live artist. There was something about the vibe that helped me relax, even with the smoke clouds around me. When Willow called me wanting to go out, I was far from excited, but she promised just the two of us. Girl's night. And that was pretty much the only kind of outing I was okay with at the moment. Plus, I owed her an explanation for shutting her out after the Hay Stacks incident. So, I caved, and after the hard part was over and I'd apologized for ditching her, I finally relaxed and started to enjoy myself.

Willow was going on and on about the program she applied for at Appalachian State when the waitress brought us our second hookah. She had already been accepted in the fall, but the program she was waiting to hear back from was an early acceptance program that would kick-start her academic career and set her up with some of the best professors and smaller, more intimate classes. Plus, she'd get a full ride if she was accepted. She said *if*, I said *when*. Willow was too intelligent not to get accepted. In fact, she could have landed a full ride pretty much anywhere in the country, but — just like every other normal kid in Poxton Beach — she wanted Appalachian State. Part of me wanted to go, too, if only to have at least four more years with my best friend.

"I'm just so nervous," she said for the fiftieth time, taking the first drag from the new hookah set up on the small wooden table in front of us. "I want this more than anything I've ever wanted in my entire life, Nat. What if I don't get it?"

I shook my head, wishing I had a bank of intellectually deep phrases to pull from like she always did. I wanted to calm her, but I could only laugh. "You're going to get in. I know it, you know it — everyone knows it. You got your acceptance letter to Appalachian State months before anyone else and you were Valedictorian. This kick-start program committee would be absolutely freaking insane not to accept you.

And when you do get in, I'm going to cry for days wondering how the hell I'm going to make it through the rest of the summer without you."

She smiled softly, reaching over to pat my leg before inhaling through the long hookah hose again. She was smoking a peach and vanilla combination of sheesh that made my mouth water a little. It wasn't that I didn't enjoy the taste of it or that I hadn't tried it before, I just didn't really have an addictive personality. I could drink if I wanted to, but I rarely did. I could smoke if I wanted to, but I almost never felt that need. Overall, I didn't need much to have a good time — just my friends. And Mason.

My stomach lurched and I shifted on the couch, pulling my legs up closer to my chest. Willow noticed my shield and narrowed her eyes, letting a cloud of smoke escape her plump lips. Her hair was long and curled tonight while my dark blonde locks were pin-straight. Even dressed in distressed jeans and a Fall Out Boy t-shirt, she looked flawless. I, on the other hand, still felt less than average — even with the make-up I'd taken almost twenty minutes to apply.

"You better not be thinking about Mason," she warned, handing me the hose so she could drink her water. She had a weird stigma about not letting the hose touch the table until the hookah was tapped.

"I just still can't believe what happened last weekend," I confessed, sighing a little. "Mason used to be my best friend. I mean, he can't have changed that much in the two weeks we've been broken up. How could he be with someone like that?" I shook my head. "He might as well have laughed with her."

She scoffed and rolled her eyes, taking a small sip of water. "An insecure man would rather laugh with the hyenas than chance failing a run with the lions."

I cocked a brow. "What the heck does that mean?"

Willow laughed. "It means he's a follower, Nat. His new girlfriend has him pining for her attention and he'll do anything to be what she wants. It takes a real man to stand up for what he knows is right and not be afraid to go against the crowd. Mason is just a boy."

I sighed, picking at the plastic mouthpiece on the hookah hose. "Yeah, but he used to be *my* boy."

Willow snatched the hose from my hand and took a drag, kicking back further on the couch. "You want to know what *I* still can't believe?" she asked, changing the subject. "That you're training with fucking *Rhodes*."

My cheeks flushed. I had debated telling Willow about my personal training, but she was my best friend and would have found out anyway. I did swear her to secrecy, though. The last thing I wanted was Mason or Shay finding out I had signed up at the club the day after they publicly humiliated me. "Scary, huh?"

"That's putting it lightly. Remember when he was a senior when we started high school? Dude was terrifying. He was in juvie more that year than I was in gym class."

I chuckled. "I don't remember what he was always in trouble for."

"What *wasn't* he in trouble for? Him and that group of kids he hung out with were always up to something.

Stealing, partying, drunk driving, public nudity — you name it, they were doing it."

"That's the thing, though. I don't really remember him having many friends. He was always kind of a loner, wasn't he?"

Willow exhaled a long puff of white smoke. "I guess. But anyone he *did* hang out with was just as rough around the edges as he was."

Clearing my throat, I pulled my feet up to tuck them under my thighs. "He's different now."

"Oh yeah? Different how, Natalie Poxton?" Willow's brows shot up.

I blushed harder. "I don't know, he just is." I wasn't exactly sure what it was that made me think he was different. He still didn't talk to me, he was still terrifyingly strong, and he still had a glare that could make a full grown man run and hide. I had no way of knowing if he did drugs or partied with thugs or stole old ladies' purses. He could very well have been doing all of that and more. But there was something about him that made me think he wasn't as scary as he seemed.

"You crushin' on your PT, Nat?" Willow teased, waggling her brows as she handed me the hose again and reached for her water. I narrowed my eyes to glare at her and she laughed out loud before lifting the bottle to her lips. Suddenly, her eyes grew wide and she almost choked on the water. "Holy shit. Isn't that him?"

I rolled my eyes. "Ha-ha, Willow. You're hilarious."

"No." She swallowed, twisting the cap back on her bottle. "Seriously, look."

I turned to face the same direction as her and fought to keep my composure when I realized she was right. Rhodes was there, walking straight toward our table. His arm was draped around the shoulders of an older woman. A very, *very* pretty older woman.

"And is that Mrs. Landers?" Willow asked, her voice raising an octave. Rhodes' eyes found mine just as the words left her mouth. They were dark in the dim light of Rook, but I could still feel their intensity. He was dressed in dark jeans and a light gray quarter sleeve button-up that accentuated the tan muscles of his forearms. He frowned when he saw me and, like an idiot, I lifted my hand in a small, non-committal wave.

His face hardened further and he strolled right past our table without a word, pulling Mrs. Landers closer into him and moving the hair from her neck so he could whisper into it. She giggled and placed a hand on his stomach as he opened the door and ushered her out into the night.

I was still staring at him open-mouthed when Willow snapped her fingers in front of my face and grabbed the hose from my hand.

"Hello? You there, Nat?" She laughed, shaking her head. "What the hell was that? He acted like he didn't even know you. And why is he with our anatomy teacher? Maybe she's teaching him a thing or two. Or vice versa." She giggled at her own joke and I finally closed my mouth, crossing my arms over my chest.

"We should probably get going. Church in the morning."

"Ugh, don't remind me," she groaned, dropping the hose on the table after one last pull. "I love Jesus, but this town on a Sunday is something else."

I laughed a little, but my stomach was still in knots as we walked out to the Rover and drove across town to my place. Rhodes had straight up ignored me, which I guess wasn't really any different than what he did when we trained together, but it still bothered me. Did he always have to have a stick up his ass? And why *was* he all cuddled up with Mrs. Landers?

My brain ran wild with possibilities as I tossed and turned in bed that night. When I finally did fall asleep, I dreamed of shoplifting with Rhodes and getting arrested. But for some reason I didn't cry or scream when they put the handcuffs on us and threw us into the back of the cop car. Instead I laughed, and for the first time, Rhodes laughed, too.

I woke up angry on Sunday morning. I thought praying and singing in church would calm me down, but it didn't. Instead, I found myself not listening to Pastor Mike and thinking about Rhodes and Mrs. Landers. I convinced myself that it wasn't him with her that upset me, but rather that he didn't even acknowledge my existence. Up until that point, I thought he just didn't like to talk much, but acting like he didn't know me in a public place gave me a new idea. It hit me then that maybe he was ashamed of me. He was my trainer —

not my friend — and I knew that, but I wasn't okay with him treating me like I didn't matter. I may not have been as beautiful and fit as the other women he trained, but I still deserved to be treated like a paying client.

He didn't owe me anything. He didn't have to be my friend. But I couldn't for the life of me figure out why he insisted on always being such a jerk. He dodged my questions when we trained, opting for silence, instead, and he ignored me the one and only time we bumped into each other outside of the gym. He didn't want to be my friend? Fine. But I was his client, and he at least needed to be nice to me.

After church, I changed quickly and ran out of the house to head to my training session. I was fuming in the car, going over all the things I would say when I finally got face-to-face with Rhodes. *What's your problem? Am I really that hideous that you can't say hi to me? What the hell were you doing there with Mrs. Landers?*

Of course, as soon as I actually made it inside the training room and was met with those sharp green eyes, everything I'd planned to say flew out into space, leaving me with my arms crossed and foot tapping on the spongy gym floor like a moron.

Rhodes cocked a brow, though his mouth remained a thin line. "You're late. Get on the treadmill. Bump the incline up to four and the speed to five."

I glared at him, willing my mouth to open, wishing the words I'd recited would flow from my mouth like I imagined they would if we were in a movie. But I came

WEIGHTLESS

up empty, and I couldn't take the heat from his glare any longer so I huffed and climbed onto the treadmill, doing as he said.

Rhodes didn't take it easy on me that day. After forty-five minutes on the treadmill changing the incline and speed every three minutes, I was drenched and on the verge of passing out. I couldn't drink water fast enough. Then he had me on the machines. It was leg day, which was news to me, and I found out quickly that leg day sucked. But, I had anger on my side, and I pushed through everything he threw at me.

I tried to take every question I had and use it for fuel to go faster. I focused on the embarrassment and anger I felt when Rhodes ignored me the night before and geared my frustration toward lifting more and lasting longer. I was doing everything I could to ignore what I was feeling and think only of what my body was doing.

Almost as if he knew I was fighting something, Rhodes pushed me harder than he had the entire week before. He made me do more reps when I thought I was done, yelled for me to run faster when I slowed down even the slightest, and got in my face when I murmured that I couldn't do another set. He knew I was perturbed, but he didn't ask me about it. He made me work through it. And that just pissed me off more.

When two hours had passed and he told me to get on the Stairmaster, I'd had enough. I tried to push through it, but two minutes in I felt my breakfast threatening to make a second appearance.

"I'm done," I said, gasping for air as I hit the stop button on the machine. The stairs halted and I rested on the top one, laying my head on my slick forearm as I stared down at my sneakers. Suddenly, Rhodes' hands gripped the bar and he lowered his eyes to mine.

His jaw was so square, so set — just having his face inches from mine made me uncomfortable. When he spoke, his voice low but firm, a chill ran down my neck. "No you're not."

"Yes." I lifted my head, wiping the sweat dripping from my forehead with my towel. "I am."

"Stop quitting. Tell your mind to get out of the way so your body can work."

"I have been working!" I yelled. I was surprised at the level the words left me, but I wasn't sorry. I was exhausted. I was pissed. And I was officially at my limit.

"And you're *still* working. You're not done. Let's go." He pressed the green button and bumped the speed up to six, forcing me to walk. I smacked his hand away and stopped it again.

"I'm going to throw up."

He sighed. "No you're not. You're just psyching yourself out."

"I CAN'T DO THIS!" I screamed at the top of my lungs, my chest heaving as I dropped down to the ground from the steps. There were people staring at us then, but I didn't care. I stepped right up to Rhodes, putting me chest-to-chest with him. I felt intimidated, but I didn't dare let it show. "All you do is scream at me and push me and I feel like nothing is happening other than me feeling like I want to die every night when I leave here. You never let me breathe, you never smile, you never talk to me, and last night you pretended like you didn't even know who I was. I don't know if you're ashamed to be seen around me or what but I'm not putting up with it. You may be my trainer, Rhodes, but that doesn't give you the right to be an asshole."

Rhodes' eyes were on fire as he stood back, arms crossed, taking every lashing I handed out with my verbal beating. At first he seemed amused, but with every word, his face fell a bit further.

Satisfied with his dumbfounded expression, I tossed my towel over my shoulder and snagged my gym bag from the floor, swinging it over my shoulder, heading for the Rover.

I was shaking as I strapped on my seatbelt, physical proof that though my words were confident and sure, I was far from both. Starting the car quickly, I pulled out of the club without looking back to see if Rhodes was trying to stop me. My breaths were still hard in my chest and my heart hammering against my ribs when I made it home.

The house was quiet as I dropped my bag at the door. I heard Mom on the phone down the hall, but I headed for the kitchen first, grabbing a Gatorade out of the fridge. I chugged half of it before heading toward where I heard Mom's voice. I wasn't sure the whole training thing was for me anymore, but before I made any decisions, I wanted her advice. My hand lifted to knock on the door frame when I heard my name.

Pausing, I tucked my hand back to my side and leaned back against the wall, straining to hear what she was saying.

"I'm proud of her, I just hope she can stick to it. You and I both know the kids in college won't be as kind as the kids here in Poxton Beach. No one knows who she is or who her father is there. They'll judge her based on her looks. I think she sees that, too. I'm just glad she's finally doing something about it."

My chest tightened and my throat grew thick with something I couldn't quite swallow down. I silenced my breath as much as I could, trying to hear her soft voice more clearly, but my heart was beating like a helicopter in my ears.

"Yeah, exactly. Natalie has always been pretty, but I can't wait to see what she looks like once this trainer is done with her. And she'll feel so much better when she's not carrying around so much weight."

An ache ripped through my chest as she paused on the phone, the other person talking now.

"Oh, no, I, um… I think he's getting better. We haven't had any instances recently. He's just a man, I don't hold any of it against him."

She had moved on to something else, something that I didn't have a clue about. But I clearly understood the conversation before that. A familiar sting hit my nose and I sniffed, wiping at it quickly before walking as quickly and quietly as I could back to the living room. I snagged my camera off the coffee table and slipped back out the front door, pulling it shut almost silently behind me.

I was shaking even worse now and I dropped the keys to the Range Rover twice before finally climbing inside, carefully setting my camera in the passenger seat beside me. My hands found the wheel and I gripped it tight, heart beating in my ears, breaths coming erratically. When I pushed the START button and the engine purred to life, it was like a sort of numbness settled over me. My muscles were becoming more aware of the hell I'd put them through that afternoon while my mind tried to process everything I'd just heard.

Mom was right. I did know that college would be different, should I decide to go. I knew that no one would know who I was, that maybe who I was had something to do with the friends I had here in Poxton Beach. But hearing those things from her killed me. Had she always thought I was overweight? Had she always wished that I would do something about it? Was she ashamed of me, too?

My mind was spinning as I drove to the beach. I felt tears stinging the corners of my eyes but they didn't fall. I pulled into Dale's reserved parking spot near the pier and threw my camera strap around my neck before peeling off my sneakers and socks and walking slowly onto the beach.

When my toes hit the sand, I powered on my camera and lifted the viewfinder to my left eye, snapping the first photo.

*Click.*

Just hearing the soft, familiar sound let my breaths come easier than before.

I shot everything and nothing. The water, the sand, a seashell stuck in seaweed, a man and his daughter down the beach building a castle, the old and decaying building on the other side of the pier. I snapped and clicked until my arms were numb from holding the camera and my face was numb from the tears I hadn't realized had started falling.

It was the first time in my life I fully admitted to myself that I wasn't happy.

I wasn't happy with who I was. Or how I looked. Or how I felt. Ever since I could remember, I depended on food for everything — comfort, celebration, mourning. And now that I had finally started to take control and do something about it, I didn't feel support from anyone around me — save for Willow, who would likely be gone in just a few weeks.

Even my trainer didn't believe in me.

It was like they all looked at me with pity in their eyes. *Poor Natalie Poxton.* But I didn't want to be that girl anymore. If my life was to be a story, I wanted to take control of the pen. I wanted to change the paper, crumple up what had been written so far and start over.

I just hoped I could actually do it.

I wasn't sure if I was still crying when the sun started to set, only that I didn't care anymore. I let myself break as I shot the pink and purple streaks across the Carolina sky. I knew right then and there, on a warm Sunday evening with my feet sinking into the sand at the edge of the ocean, that this summer would be the hardest of my life. It would either change me for the better or shatter me completely.

## WEIGHTLESS

But maybe I *needed* to break, to fully fall to pieces,
before I could ever truly be whole.

# CHAPTER

# 4

I debated not even showing up for my training session the next day, but I dragged my butt to the gym against my own will. I knew I'd have to face Rhodes after going off on him the day before but I hoped he would just let it go. That's what I was prepared to do. The night before had set a new resolve for me and I was ready to get to work. Even if I was the only one in my corner, I was going to fight for a new me. The summer after high school was supposed to be about change, movement, progress. I was determined to turn my life around and I wasn't going to waste a single second because of some jerk who'd always been a jerk, anyway. He didn't think I could do it? Fine.

I would prove him wrong.

Just like I'd prove Mason wrong, and he'd realize giving me up was a mistake. Then, I'd be back under his arm, under his sheets on rainy Sundays — back where I belonged.

Even with my new determination, I couldn't meet Rhodes' eyes when I walked through the gym door.

Walking straight up to the treadmill, I hit the QUICK START button and began walking, staring straight ahead out the window that overlooked the golf course. After a minute had passed, Rhodes walked over to stand in front of the machine. He leaned over and paused it, bracing his hands on either side of the display and blocking my view of the course, forcing me to look at him. When I finally did pull my eyes to his, his features were softer. I tried not to notice the way his hair flitted over his brows as they pulled together and he exhaled.

"I'm sorry, Natalie."

I shivered a bit when he said my name, but I wasn't sure why. Maybe because he was just saying it like a normal person yet for some reason the three syllables rolling off his tongue shot straight down between my thighs.

"I'm not sorry for pushing you, but I'm sorry for upsetting you." His lips pressed together for a moment before he continued. "And I'm not ashamed of you." Rhodes held my gaze. Even when I tried to look at the ground, he moved his head down into my view until I looked at him again. "Exactly the opposite, actually. You work hard. You want this, for whatever reason, and I can see it. *That's* why I push you. I know you can work harder, go faster, lift more. I'm proud to have you as my client."

I scoffed, the anger I felt from Saturday night resurfacing. "Oh yeah? Is that why you completely ignored me at Rook when I saw you with your..." I paused, not sure what to call Mrs. Landers. "Girlfriend?"

His mouth flattened into a thin line. "She's a client, Natalie."

"Is that right? Well damn, do you kiss on the necks of all your clients? I've been getting jipped." I couldn't believe those words just left my mouth and my cheeks flushed immediately, but I stood straight and kept my eyes on his.

He glared at me for a moment, his steady eyes threatening to weaken my resolve, but I remained poignant.

"You shouldn't be smoking."

I rolled my eyes at his attempt to change the subject. "I wasn't smoking. If you hadn't treated me like the plague and actually talked to me instead, you would know that."

Again, I was surprised at the words leaving my mouth. They were a hell of a lot more confident than the girl saying them.

"I was just holding the hose for my friend. She doesn't like to let it touch the table until it's tapped." I waved my hands in the air flittingly. "Some weird superstition or something."

Rhodes kept his eyes on me, looking for a lie that wasn't there. Finally, he nodded. "Fair enough," he assessed, then he held out his hand.

I stared at it for a moment before grabbing it and letting him help me down off the machine.

"We need to get your weight. It's been a week. Come on," he said, nodding toward the office. "Let's do it before you drink a bunch of water."

I followed him back, my hand still tingling from where it had touched his. I couldn't figure out if I was still angry at him or not, so I kept a frown in place just in case. He was always scowling, maybe I should do the same.

When we reached the office, he pointed to the tall, glass scale as he scoured his desk for my file. I eyed him silently, wondering if I had more questions for him or if I wanted to yell at him again. He had apologized for upsetting me, and he said he believed in me — which was exactly what I needed in that moment, wasn't it? He was "proud to have me as a client," which was why he pushed me. Maybe I didn't need him as a friend, if I could have him as a pillar of support, instead.

It was too much to figure out in that moment, so I sighed and stepped up, closing my eyes as I waited for him to write down what was probably the same number as last week.

"Down eleven pounds," he said and my eyes shot open. "Nice job."

I stared at the number on the digital screen, my mouth hanging open. *No. Way.*

Rhodes let me stare for a moment and, thankfully, he didn't make fun of me. When it had finally sank in that I was eleven pounds lighter than the week before, I slowly stepped off the scale, wincing at the pain I still felt in my legs after yesterday. Walking in the sand all night probably wasn't the best way to recover from leg day.

Rhodes must have picked up on my expression. "How do your muscles feel?"

"Tight," I answered, bracing myself with one hand on the wall as I lifted my foot and pulled it up toward my lower back to stretch out my quad. It killed me just to lift my leg at all. When I pulled it in toward my body, I cried out and let it drop back down to the floor.

Rhodes furrowed his brows. "Follow me."

We headed back into the gym and I expected him to tell me to jump back on the treadmill, but he grabbed a yoga mat and a tennis ball, instead, before leading me out back to where we had our first outdoor session. I watched his back move as we walked, the muscles flexing beneath the thin fabric of his tattered blue tank top. His skin seemed darker today and I wondered if he had enjoyed the beach yesterday, too.

He found a shady spot in the grass beneath a Spanish oak tree and laid out the black mat. It was hot in the sun, but there was a slight breeze that, combined with the shade, made me glad we had moved outside.

"Lay down," he commanded and I shivered again. His eyes were on me as he moved down to sit beside me, holding the tennis ball in his hand. "I'm going to roll out your muscles. You can do this at home, too — with a foam roller, a tennis ball, or just your hands."

I nodded and he slowly moved his right hand to my right quad. The moment his hands touched my leg through the thin fabric of my workout pants, I sucked in a breath that I forgot how to let go of. He applied pressure, softly rolling his fingers over the muscles. I winced, and then groaned in a mixture of pain and pleasure when he hit a spot that sent an electric current through my entire leg and up to my hip.

His eyes snapped to mine when I groaned, but he didn't say anything. Instead, he moved the ball to replace his hand and began rolling it up and down my quad. I tried not to make any noise, but every time he hit that spot, I involuntarily moaned again, closing my eyes and letting the unfamiliar mixture of feelings overtake me as I gripped the edge of the mat. It hurt like hell but then again it felt amazing. I was so confused.

"It's a trigger point," Rhodes finally said. "It's like a knot that forms in your muscle. Rolling it out will release it and allow you to move properly again without the pain you're feeling now."

I nodded, but words were lost for me at the moment. He moved to the opposite leg and the process started all over again. It started off incredibly painful, but at the same time I enjoyed it, and when I stopped moaning, he would move to a different area of my body. He worked meticulously, and I peeked an eye open to glance at him from time to time, watching as his eyes skated over my body while he worked.

When he moved to my abdomen, I cringed, my hands flying down to cover my fat. It was then that I realized how vulnerable I was in that position.

Rhodes paused, the ball just above my navel. "It's fine, Natalie," he said softly, grabbing my hands and placing them back at my sides. "You need to do abdominal work today and it's not going to be effective if you're hurting this badly."

I chewed the inside of my cheek, but timidly laid my head back down and stared up at the moss flowing in the breeze. It moved fluidly, casting the sun's light in a wave over Rhodes' face as he tenderly rolled the ball around my upper abs. When his thumb grazed the bottom of my sports bra, I had to suck both of my lips between my teeth and bite down to keep from moaning for a completely different reason. *What was wrong with me?* Rhodes eyed me cautiously, but didn't acknowledge it.

"You went to Poxton High," he said after a moment. I waited for him to say something else, but he left it at that.

"Yeah, I was a freshman when you were a senior." I groaned a little louder as he moved to my upper chest. I was incredibly sore there from the push-ups and burpees we'd been doing.

"Poxton High," he mused. "That title have anything to do with your last name, by chance?"

I laughed a little. "My step-dad. He kind of owns, well, almost everything in this town. Including the high school."

He nodded, but didn't comment. "And you were a freshman when I was a senior?"

This time I nodded, but he had moved the ball to my biceps and I was focusing on not making noises that would cause my cheeks to heat.

"Roll over," he demanded. As I did, I noticed his brows knitted together in concentration, even when he wasn't rolling the ball. I wasn't sure why he was suddenly talking to me. Maybe because of the fit I threw the day before. Whatever the cause, I wasn't going to question it. I was thankful to not work in silence. And as strange as it sounds, getting that ball rolled over my muscles felt a lot like work.

"I just don't understand," he said as he began rolling the ball up my calf. I moaned out loud, realizing that area was packed with trigger points, as he had called them.

"Don't understand what?" I asked, still holding my breath as he rolled over my other calf. I leaned up on my elbows and turned my head back to meet his eyes.

He paused, holding the ball in place as he gazed back at me. "How could I never have noticed you before?"

I swallowed, almost more afraid of the brief tenderness I caught in his eyes in that moment than the usual hardness that existed there.

Shrugging, I answered his question just above a whisper. "I'm easy to miss."

I held his eyes for a moment more before laying my chest back to the ground, resting my head on my arms. He started rolling the ball up my hamstrings and I closed my eyes tight. I thought I might explode from the mixture of pain and pleasure that rocked through my body. After a few moments, he spoke again.

"Maybe I just wasn't looking."

My eyes shot open, but I didn't respond.

Rhodes finished rolling out my muscles and then we headed back into the gym without another word. He didn't work me any less than the days before, but he was more patient, taking the time to explain the drills to me and making sure I took the rest I needed between sets. Still, he pushed me hard, and sweat was dripping furiously down my face and into my eyes as I drove home that evening with the windows down. The salty water was irritating my contacts, but I didn't swipe it away. In fact, I didn't even care. My mind was too busy running over the words I'd heard Rhodes say to give attention to anything else. They played over and over again in my head until I was sure I'd dream of them that night.

*Maybe I just wasn't looking.*

No matter how many times I replayed the words, I couldn't for the life of me figure out what he meant. And I was right. I thought about it so much that when the night came, I dreamed of Rhodes for the second time.

And for what I knew wouldn't be the last.

I told Mom and Dale about my weigh-in the next morning and they both flipped out. Mom jumped up from her barstool excitedly and wrapped me in a bone-crushing hug while Dale clapped me on the back. His hand lingered there as I told them about how my sessions had been going. Dale joked about taking us out for ice cream to celebrate and I shrugged out from under his hand and glared at him. He laughed, then, and I joined him. I was happy. It was a good start to what I hoped would be a life-changing summer.

My session with Rhodes was pushed back to six that night and by the time we finished at eight, I was starving. We'd had another great session, and I felt us falling into a comfortable rhythm. He talked to me a little more, which made me happy, and I learned not to push him when he stopped talking and focused on working, instead. Maybe we were figuring each other out, after all.

My stomach growled loud enough for him to hear as we did a cool-down walk around the golf course and he chuckled, which was sort of a foreign sound when it came to Rhodes.

"Hungry?" he asked, the sky fading from a gold to a light blue behind him. It was an intriguing contrast, such hard features against such a soft background. No one was left on the course but us, and other than the buzz of the trail lights and insects, it was silent. I welcomed the quietness.

"You have no idea," I murmured, rubbing my stomach. "All this rabbit food is killing me."

"Rabbit food?" Rhodes quirked a brow. "Are you hungry like this all the time?" I nodded and he shook his head. "You shouldn't be, if you're eating enough protein. Do you have plans tonight?"

I stopped mid-stride, staring at Rhodes like he'd just asked me to take my pants off, but he just waited for my response with a calm demeanor.

"Um, no?"

"Good. Come over to my place and I'll cook us dinner, show you that eating *rabbit food* isn't as bad as it seems if you know how to do it right." He continued walking but it took me a minute before my legs would move again. Did Rhodes just ask me to come over to his house? And did he just say he was going to cook for me?

The same guy who would barely say more than two words to me before was asking me to come over to his place for dinner. He'd gone from ignoring me to asking me to hang out with him, like we were friends.

I smiled at that possibility.

"I just need to lock up the office real quick."

I nodded and he jogged off while I pulled out my favorite strawberry lemonade lip balm, gliding the tube over my lips repeatedly as I waited for Rhodes. I was counting my breaths and trying not to overthink.

It was just my trainer making me a healthy meal. That's all.

Rhodes led me around to the front of the club after he locked up. I traded my lip balm for my keys as he climbed onto a sleek black sports bike. The way he straddled it highlighted the defined muscles in both his arms and his legs and I couldn't help but stare as he pulled on the matching all black helmet.

"I'm not too far from here," he said, nodding up the street. "Just follow me and flash your lights if I'm going too fast. Cool?"

"Cool," I replied, but it barely croaked out. I smiled to try to cover the weakness in my voice. For a moment, I thought Rhodes crooked the tiniest smile, but he pulled the helmet the rest of the way down and I couldn't be sure.

I threw my bag in my trunk and slipped in behind the steering wheel, my knuckles turning white from the ferocious grip I had on it. I was going to Rhodes' house. His *house*. I tried to breathe steadily, but I was pretty sure I sounded more like a horse than anything.

*Deep breaths, Natalie. Deep breaths.*

Yeah. Easier said than done.

# CHAPTER

# 5

We pulled into a small apartment complex less than ten minutes later. His place was in the exact opposite direction of my house from the club and even though I was only a half hour from home, it seemed like I was in a different country.

When I stepped out of the Rover, I locked the doors and stared up at the chipping blue paint on the wood-paneled building. The upper apartments had small balconies that I could see some residents sitting on. They were staring at me like I didn't belong, their eyes hard and cold. I crossed my arms over my chest and walked to Rhodes just as he hopped off his bike. Surprisingly, he started pushing it up on the sidewalk toward the building.

"Don't you need to park that?"

"I am," he responded simply. I didn't understand until he unlocked the bottom floor apartment door on the back right side of the building, pushed the bike inside, and leaned it up on the kickstand just inside the small foyer at the entrance. He was parking it — just not outside.

It was dark inside the apartment and when Rhodes flicked on the light, I blinked my eyes until they adjusted. It was small, that was for sure, but I was surprised by how it looked on the inside. It was clean, nice. Simple — but nice. We were standing in the small foyer with basic, white-tiled floor. It led right into a living room with beige Berber carpet and one dark brown leather couch facing a flat screen mounted on the far wall. There was an entertainment center filled with cookbooks and movies and a simple coffee table — wood with a glass center. There were no photos, no paintings, no quote embellishments — just a clean white wall, furniture, and the TV.

I followed Rhodes further into the space as he stashed his helmet in the hall closet and caught a view of the kitchen. It was pretty large, considering the size of the apartment as a whole, and it looked like Rhodes had renovated it from the original setting. The countertops looked like new granite and he had installed a hanging rack above the stove to hang pots, pans, and utensils. The sink had a fancy faucet that looked like something Christina would want installed in our kitchen. All the appliances were a dark gray and seemed brand new and there was one cabinet above the fridge that had the cabinet doors removed. The shelves housed at least a dozen more cookbooks. And one lone apron hung on a small hook just beside the pantry.

Rhodes ran a hand through his still-damp hair as

he watched me look around. "You want something to drink?"

My eyes found his but dropped a little to note the way his shirt was still sticking to his abdomen. "Just water is fine."

He nodded, stepping into the kitchen long enough to grab a glass and fill it with ice and water from the fridge. Setting it down on the counter in front of me, he lifted a thumb and pointed to the room down the hall behind him. "I just need to shower real quick. You can too, if you want."

I swallowed hard, my eyes practically bulging from my head. And for the first time — Rhodes laughed.

Well, he chuckled.

"I meant when I'm done, Natalie."

"I know," I said quickly. *I totally didn't know.* "I will. When you're done. I have extra clothes." *Why did I say that?*

He quirked a brow. "Guess I won't be seeing you naked tonight, then." I thought he was joking, but couldn't be sure because he left it at that without so much as another smile before turning and disappearing down the hall.

I quickly guzzled down the glass of water he'd given me and refilled it. I needed to cool down. *Way* down. It was the first time I'd seen Rhodes smile, the first time I'd heard him laugh. I thought it would be weird to see him like that, but it was the exact opposite. He seemed more comfortable with a grin on his face, no matter how fleeting it was.

Rhodes emerged from the back room ten minutes later fully dressed in large gray sweatpants and a plain black t-shirt with the sleeves cut off. His hair was wet and unruly and his skin still shone a little from the water. He walked straight into the kitchen and started pulling dishes out. "Towels are above the toilet and you don't have long with the hot water so be quick. You can use my soap and whatever else you need." He didn't turn around when he said the words and I swallowed, the thought of standing in the place where he'd just been naked rattling me more than I cared to admit.

But my legs eventually started moving and I walked down the hall with my gym bag. When I pushed through the door, I was surprised to find myself in Rhodes' bedroom. The bathroom was straight ahead, but his room filled out the right side of the room. It was just as clean and simple as the living room. Queen bed, dark blue comforter, no headboard, white walls and an old box TV sitting on top of a dark brown dresser. There was one framed photo on a small bedside table that matched the dresser. Curiosity getting the best of me, I walked over and picked up the silver frame to examine the photo inside.

It was of a young girl standing against a row of dark green lockers. If I'd had to guess, I'd have said she was sixteen or so when the photo was taken. She had long brown hair and dark olive skin. At first I thought she might have been Rhodes' girlfriend, but when I studied her closer and noticed familiar green eyes, I realized it was his twin sister, Lana.

I didn't really know much about Lana, other than she was Rhodes' twin. She was sort of quiet when they were seniors and we were freshmen. Honestly, in a kind of sad way, she was overshadowed by Rhodes — all the girls wanted him and all the boys were terrified of him. Lana was an afterthought… that is, until she was front page news.

A loud clamor in the kitchen startled me and I quickly placed the photo back and hurried into the bathroom with my bag, shutting the door behind me and leaning against it to view the space. It was small, but again — clean. The shower was just that, there was no bath tub. I undressed quickly, pulled a towel out and hung it beside the one Rhodes had just used, and stepped inside.

The hot water felt incredible on my freshly rolled muscles. Although it hurt when Rhodes was rolling the ball across my legs and back, that pain had almost completely vanished and the soreness melted away. Though, I was sure it would be back the next day. Rhodes would be sure of it.

I lathered up my body and hair with Rhodes' body wash and couldn't stop smelling myself even after I had tied my hair up into a messy bun, dressed, and rejoined Rhodes in the kitchen, tossing my bag on the floor by his bike. I had caught so many teasing whiffs of the earthy, evergreen scent when he'd been near me at the gym, but now it was amplified, with nothing else to drown it out. I hoped it wouldn't wash off.

"Would you prefer chicken or salmon?" Rhodes asked, sautéing some sort of concoction in a skillet. His arms flexed with each stir and I couldn't help but be mesmerized. The kitchen already smelled tantalizing and my stomach growled.

"Chicken. I hate fish."

He paused, turned to face me, and deadpanned. "You live in a beach town and you don't like fish?"

I shrugged. He shook his head and went back to whatever he was doing as I pulled out one of two barstools and took a seat. For a few moments he cooked in silence, pulling out chicken and vegetables and chopping them on a cutting board before adding them to the pan. His fingers worked quickly, methodically, like cooking was to him what breathing is to me — effortless. The silence was comfortable as I watched him, but I couldn't let my curiosity about what I'd seen in his bedroom go.

"Is that your sister in the photo by your bed?"

Rhodes stiffened at my question, stopping mid-stir for a beat. When he started again, he didn't turn to face me. "Yes."

"She's beautiful."

"She was."

He didn't falter with those words, but I noted the past tense. I remembered when Lana was reported as a missing person close to the end of their senior year, the sorrow that washed over the school as the days stretched on without anyone finding her. But after a while, the story about her disappearance faded. I realized as I sat at Rhodes' kitchen island that I never did hear if they ever found her, though his past tense reference made me think maybe I didn't want to know.

I sensed Rhodes' discomfort, so I changed the subject.

"I like your place."

He shrugged, spinning in place to wash his hands in the sink in front of the counter I was sitting at before turning back toward the cabinets and reaching up for some spices. "It's not much."

"How long have you lived here?"

He paused, his arms still stretched out above him as he dug through the spices, revealing just a small sliver of skin between the top of his boxers and the hem of his black t-shirt. Facing me once more, his eyes sparkled in the soft kitchen light. "There you go with your questions again."

I blushed and murmured, "Sorry."

His eyes were still on me but he nodded toward my bag. "Why do you always have that camera with you?"

I followed his gaze to my camera tucked in the side pocket, the neck strap hanging out just a bit. It was my smaller camera, not the nicest one I owned, but I always carried one with me just in case.

"You know how you geek out about everything fitness-related?"

He glowered. "I don't geek out."

I stifled a laugh. "Okay, well, I was trying to say that that's how I am with photography. It's my thing, I guess. I've been into it my whole life and I want to go to college and do it professionally." I paused at that admission. "Well, maybe anyway. I don't know, I kind of always have a camera with me."

He nodded, his arm muscles flexing with each movement of the wooden spoon in his hand. My nose was in a frenzy and my mouth had been watering since I got out of the shower. "You going to Appalachian State in the fall?"

I sighed. "I don't know. I probably should but I don't really want to."

"Wow," he assessed, covering the skillet with a glass lid. He leaned back against the stove and crossed his arms over his chest. "The Poxton Princess doesn't want to follow in her family's footsteps and do what all the PBH kids do? What a travesty."

I wanted to narrow my eyes at him and tell him not to call me that, but all I could do was shift uncomfortably under his gaze. It was hard to confront the scariest person I knew. Luckily, I was saved by my phone ringing before I had the chance to answer. It was Willow.

"Sorry, one sec."

Rhodes didn't show any shift in emotion. He just turned to face the stove again and went back to work.

"Hey, Lo."

"Hey! What are you doing Wednesday?"

"Um." Wednesday wasn't a training day, but I wasn't sure I was going to be down for whatever she was about to propose. Still, I couldn't think of any excuse, so I sighed. "Nothing. What's up?"

"Perfect. We're going to the town fair with the group. Now before you tell me no because Mason will be there, let me remind you that you're looking super hot lately and you should prance around in front of him and Shay and show them you're not afraid of them. And we can go shopping for something super cute for you to wear." I tried to cut her off but she just spoke louder over me. "AND this is our last summer together before college and we have way too many memories to make to let that douche hose ruin it."

I laughed at her expression, but couldn't help but note Rhodes' glare when she mentioned Mason. Could he hear her?

"I don't think this is a good idea, Willow."

"Oh whatever, Nat. He's a pansy and so is his new Barbie doll. Please come with me? I'll protect you and fuck up anyone who tries to mess with my best friend."

I sighed, but couldn't help but smile. I knew she was serious. "I don't know…"

"Think about it. You need to stay relevant and in the picture if the end game is to get him back, right?"

I chewed my lip. She did have a point. I wasn't sure I was exactly ready to see Mason just yet, I'd only been training for a week and a half, but as the saying went — out of sight, out of mind. I didn't want him to forget about me while he got all caught up in Shay.

"I'll buy you a funnel cake," she sang into the phone and I laughed again.

"Well, when you put it like that."

"Yay!" she squealed. "I'll pick you up after your training on Tuesday. Love you, Nat!"

I shook my head when the line went dead and tucked my phone back in my bag before sitting at the bar again. Rhodes assessed me as he plated our food. There was chicken, seasoned to perfection, along with vegetables and brown rice — none of which would have sounded good to me a week before but all of which was making me drool at the current moment. "Gnat, huh? Like the bug?"

I scrunched my nose, pulling my attention from the saliva-inducing food porn. "What?"

"Your nickname?"

"Oh, no." I shook my head. "It's Nat. Like, short for Natalie."

"Ah," he said, handing me my plate. He nodded to the couch and I followed him over. "I think I like Bug better."

I frowned, wondering what he meant, but didn't comment further. Rhodes flipped on the television and kicked back on the couch, propping his feet on the coffee table. I hugged the arm opposite him and crossed my legs, balancing my plate in one hand and taking the first bite with the other. When I did, I couldn't help but moan.

"Oh my God, this is amazing."

Rhodes smiled, which still made me falter even though I'd seen it already before that night. It was such a rare thing, such an amazing thing. "This is nothing. Simple. Just chicken."

"Well it's better than any chicken I've ever made. Or had. Ever." I was scarfing down bites between my words but I wasn't even sorry. "Do you cook like this all the time?"

He shrugged. "You said I geek out over fitness, but I think the better comparison would have been cooking. I watch a lot of cooking shows, read cookbooks, upgrade my kitchen when finances allow it. There's just something about creating healthy food that also tastes great. It's hard to do. A challenge, you know?"

I nodded, though I didn't have the slightest clue, but it was the first time Rhodes talked about something he had a passion for and it was kind of amazing to witness.

He chuckled. "I'll have to really wow you next time."

Wait.

Did he just say *next time*?

I swallowed the bite I'd been chewing and chased it with a long pull of water. He eyed me over his plate, the sports channel he had on the television filling in the silence. "Why did you agree to go to the fair if you didn't want to go?"

I frowned, wondering how much of my conversation with Willow he'd heard. "I don't know. Willow wants me there. She's my best friend. It's whatever." I stacked another piece of chicken on my fork. "Besides, we go every year. It'd be weird if I didn't show up."

He watched me for a beat before taking another bite and turning toward the TV again. "You're so nice you make other nice people look like assholes."

I giggled, flushed, and took another drink of water to cool my cheeks. He peered at me from the corner of his eye, brow cocked and a slight smile on his face.

We ate the rest of our dinner in silence and I helped him with the dishes, even though he tried to fight me on it. The one appliance missing from his kitchen was a dishwasher, so I washed and he dried. And he coached me on other foods to eat to keep my hunger at bay while I pretended to listen but paid more attention to the way the muscles in his forearms shifted as he dried each plate.

And we talked.

He listened when I spoke and he didn't punish me by not saying anything at all. He talked, too. About the club, about the plans he still had for his kitchen. And by the time we finished and he walked me out to my car, I had seen Rhodes smile more than I had in all the years I'd known him before that night.

I drove home in silence, not even turning on the radio. I played through every word, every laugh, and every detail in my head. And my shirt still smelled like his body wash mixed with the chicken he'd cooked. I didn't change before I crawled into bed and let the exhaustion from the day melt with the fullness in my belly, lulling me into a stupor. Mom peeked in to check on me at one point but I pretended to be asleep and she left again. Just as I was about to really drift off, my phone pinged. The bright light blinded me as I checked the screen, but then my eyes snapped open when the words came into focus.

**— Hey. You awake? —**

Mason.

# CHAPTER

# 6

The next day was miserably gray and humid with thunderstorms rolling through off and on all day. It matched my mood perfectly and I found myself wishing the sun wouldn't show at all. Dale had to go into town for some banquet, so he offered to drive me to my training session. I stared out the window and thought about my phone call with Mason the night before.

He just called to check on me, but it was the first time we'd really talked since the break-up. I think I'd almost forgotten how badly he'd broken me until I heard his voice saying my name the way he used to. And then saying Shay's in the exact same way. It killed me to hear him talk about her, even though I knew in his head he was doing what he thought was right. He was showing me sympathy and mercy, but I didn't want it. Training with Rhodes was thickening my skin and numbing my mind. I liked numb. Numb didn't hurt.

I sighed, resting my forehead against the passenger side window of Dale's Corvette. It was raining, so I had no idea why he chose that car in the first place. It's not like he could put the top down. But then again, that was Dale — he liked to show off his toys.

"I heard you on the phone last night," he said, stirring me from my thoughts. I glanced at him and he was staring at me carefully. I just sighed again and put my head back on the window. "Was it Mason?"

"Yep."

He paused, gripping the steering wheel a little harder. "And?"

"And he talked to me about his new girlfriend." I swung back to look at him, hoping my eyes would convey that I didn't want to talk about it. The truth was that it stung, and I realized on the phone with him that I wanted him back even more than I realized. I didn't want to hear him talk about Shay because I wanted to be the only girl in his world.

Dale frowned, but nodded. "How's training going?" he asked, changing the subject.

My stomach did a small flip when I thought about Rhodes and the night before. The dinner paired with Mason calling made for an interesting night. "It's good," I said, smiling.

He appraised me carefully. "I can see a difference already, you know," he said. "I know it's just been a little over a week, but you can tell. In the way you carry yourself."

"What do you mean?"

Dale grinned, shaking his head. "I don't know, I can't really explain it." He glanced over at me again. "You've always been beautiful, Natalie, but the confidence you're gaining with this training takes you to another level."

I smiled, trying to take the compliment but not really feeling up to the challenge. My self-esteem was low, and though Dale always seemed to see the best in me, I just couldn't see it myself. Adjusting the messy bun on my head, I smirked. "Let's just hope taking it to another level doesn't mean another level up on the treadmill because I don't think I can handle that."

He laughed as we pulled into the parking lot of the club. Rhodes was standing outside beneath the overhang, sheltering himself from the rain. His arms were crossed and he was leaning against the brick. His signature pose. I swallowed at the sight of him and unclicked my seatbelt, my eyes still on his.

"Come here," Dale said as he threw the car in park. He pulled me in for a long hug, squeezing me tight, and when he pulled back he leveled his eyes with mine. "You're an amazing girl, Natalie. Don't ever forget that. You can do anything you want to do. Talking to Mason hurts right now but one day you're going to wake up and not even care about what he's saying or doing because you'll have moved on from him."

"Isn't it Mom's idea to get me back together with him?"

He waved his hand at me. "Your Mom and I don't agree on everything."

Grinning, I leaned over the console and grabbed my gym bag from the tiny backseat. "Thanks for the Dadvice, Dale."

"Always."

"Don't forget I'm staying the night with Willow tonight. She's picking me up after my session," I added.

"Got it. Have fun tonight. You deserve it." He threw me another wide smile as I stepped out of the car, opening my large bubble umbrella as I did. I returned his smile, feeling a little more like I could conquer my training session, and waved him off before turning to Rhodes. When I did, my feet wouldn't move.

Rhodes was staring hard at the Corvette as it pulled out of the lot, his green eyes piercing through the rain like laser beams. I glanced back and saw Dale glaring at Rhodes with the same disapproval. When I turned back toward Rhodes, he shifted his gaze to me in an instant and kept the same dark expression as I moved toward him.

"Who was that?" he snapped.

"My step-dad?" I answered hesitantly. "Why?"

He blanched. "That's Dale Poxton?"

I nodded. Most people in this town knew who Dale was, but hardly any of them knew what he looked like — not unless they were in his circle. Dale liked to keep to a certain type of crowd.

Rhodes still hadn't moved. His eyes were hard for a moment more before he shook his head, kicking off the wall and making his way toward the gym. "Let's head back."

"Wait," I said, jogging a little to catch up with him. "Why? Why did you ask who that was?"

"It's nothing. He just looked at you funny, I wasn't sure..." His voice faded to a low murmur and he shook his head again. "Nothing. I was mistaken. How are your muscles today? Are you still sore?"

I eyed him cautiously, but let him change the subject. I was ready to work, too. "I feel a lot better. A little sore, but I can move."

"Good," he said, patting the treadmill as we entered the gym. "Hop up and turn the incline to six, speed to four."

I groaned, but tossed my bag down in the corner and did as he said.

We worked in mostly silence for just over an hour as he moved me around the gym. He had set up an obstacle course similar to the one the week before, complete with the ropes and all. When I bent low in my squat to do the snake in the grass move, I shivered at the memory of his arms around my waist when he showed me how to do it before.

"So what are you doing tomorrow night?" I asked as I lunged across the gym with two plated weights in my hands. My leg muscles felt stronger, steadier, far from the shaky mess they were the first time I did a lunge.

"We don't train tomorrow, it's your day off," he replied simply, head down, eyes on his clipboard.

I huffed, straining against the pain in my quads. "I know that. So what are you doing? Want to come to the fair with me and my friends?"

"No."

I dropped the plates and put my hands on my hips, turning to face him. "Why not?"

"Pick up the weights, you're not finished," he answered, standing straighter before dropping the clipboard and crossing his arms over his chest. I mimicked him in the stance and instantly felt tougher.

"Not until you tell me why you won't come tomorrow night." Since when did I have the courage to ask Rhodes to hang out?

He sighed, running a hand through his dampening hair. "Natalie, last night was just me showing you how to cook a decent meal, okay? It was about your training. You're my client. We have a relationship in the gym, but not outside of it."

I swallowed what felt like a wine cork wrapped in sandpaper and uncrossed my arms, picking up the weights again. He was right, of course, and I knew that. Still, he was friendly last night — we had fun. I was kind of hoping it wouldn't just be a one time thing.

Which was stupid of me.

Because Rhodes was Rhodes and I was me. He could hang out with anyone he wanted to, including the beautiful women he trained that he seemed to find company with often. Why in the world *would* he want to spend time with me?

"Okay. Sorry."

He nodded, his eyes watching me carefully. "Three more sets. Watch your back, you're leaning forward too much."

I muttered under my breath but kept my eyes forward and made my way back across the room, lunging each step. My teeth still worried my bottom lip as I thought over the night before, wondering if I looked too much into it. Was he acting like a friend or was he really just showing me that eating healthy could work? I didn't recall us really talking much about food, other than when we were doing dishes, but even still we talked about other things, too.

Sighing, I shook my head. Whatever. It was fine because he was still my trainer, which was what I needed him to be. He knew how to help me reach my goals, and that was enough for me.

Each lunge burned more than the last and I knew I was about to hit my limit. When I reached the other side and turned around, I hit something with the weight in my left hand.

"Oh!" I turned to check on whatever I'd hit, thinking I'd be apologizing to some tiny club member in booty shorts and a sports bra, but when I came face-to-face with Mason, I dropped both weights and stumbled back a bit. One of them fell on my foot and I howled out in pain as I fell to the ground.

Rhodes cursed and rushed toward me while Mason bent down to my level. "Oh my God, Natalie. Are you okay?" He moved to touch my leg but Rhodes beat him to it, pulling my foot up and tugging my sneaker off to inspect it as he squatted down next to me. His thumb moved across the delicate skin of my ankle and I hissed at the pain as chills raced up my legs and straight between my thighs. Rhodes followed the chills and lifted his eyes to mine. I blushed and looked away.

Which left me staring at Mason.

He watched Rhodes and made a face before turning to me and asking the same question again. "Are you okay? What are you doing here?"

Rhodes dropped my foot gently, leaving the sneaker off as he helped me to my feet. Mason stood with us. His eyes never left mine and I leaned on Rhodes for support, putting weight on my foot as slowly as I could. I was fine, but it smarted. "I... train here." I swallowed. I wasn't exactly ready for him to know that, but I guess I didn't have a choice.

"Oh," he said simply. This time his eyes shifted to Rhodes and then back to me before he spoke again. "I didn't realize you were into fitness."

I shrugged. "It's, uh, a new hobby."

He nodded. "Cool. Well I don't want to interrupt your session or anything. I was just dropping off a donation bag from my mom for the fundraiser this weekend and saw you through the window. I wanted to say hi."

I smiled, though it was strained. "Hi."

He chuckled, and for a moment his chocolate eyes shined the way they used to when he looked at me. When I was his. It warmed my stomach and made me want to throw up at the same time, shooting an all-too-familiar pain straight to my chest. "It was nice talking to you last night. I've missed that, our late night phone calls." He shifted. "Is that weird?"

Every muscle in my body was wound too tight, but I shook my head. "No. I get it."

He smiled, just a tiny little curl on his lips. "Are you going to the fair tomorrow?"

I glanced at Rhodes then. He was still gripping onto my forearm and steadying me, though I had practically put all my weight on my foot again. "Yeah, Willow is dragging me," I said, still watching Rhodes. When I faced Mason again, his smile was warm.

"Cool. Well I'll see you tomorrow, then." His eyes landed on Rhodes again and he looked him up and down slowly with a slight snarl in his lip. I waited for him to extend a hand to shake his or at least introduce himself, but he did neither.

I wasn't sure how Mason was surviving Rhode's glare.

After a moment, he nodded to me once more, his smile returning, before he stepped out of the gym and I was alone with Rhodes again.

"Thanks," I said, pulling free from his grasp and rolling my ankle around before bending down to tug on my sneaker and retrieve the weights again. "I'm good. You want me to do another round?"

Rhodes was staring at me, his face completely void of emotion. "Not about a guy, huh?"

I swallowed, and suddenly the weights felt too heavy for me to hold. I placed them back on the rack and turned to face Rhodes. He hadn't moved. "He's my ex."

"Yeah, I caught on to that after you dropped a weight on your foot at the sight of him."

I blushed. "I haven't really seen him much since it all happened. I was caught off guard."

He crossed his arms. "You told me this wasn't about a guy."

"It's not," I tried and he scoffed, heading toward the back of the room. I followed. "It's not, I swear. This is about me. Yes, at first, it was about him." *And still kind of is.* "But I want this for me, too."

He stopped mid-stride and spun to face me. My eyes leveled with his chest and I had to strain my neck to look up at him. "Do you want him back?"

I chewed my bottom lip, unsure of how to answer. Rhodes' eyes fell to where my teeth worked the tender skin and I watched the muscles in his jaw tense before he found my eyes again. "That's what I thought. This is about him."

"It's not *just* about him."

He swallowed, but didn't argue. Instead, he sighed, his chest deflating, and stepped back to put distance between us. "It's okay. It actually makes sense now."

"What does?"

He shook his head. "Nothing. I'll help you get your boyfriend back, Natalie." He pointed to the elliptical. "Finish with the cardio drill we did the other day. The intervals. Do thirty minutes." He pulled the white towel from his pocket and wiped his forehead before turning away from me.

"Wait," I tried, but he kept walking. "Where are you going?"

"I have another client to tend to. We're finished

with weights today so just finish with the cardio and you can go. I'll see you Thursday."

He didn't face me again as he said the words. He just threw them over his shoulder and let the door close behind him as he exited the gym. I stood there for a moment staring at the door he'd walked through like it would open again, but it didn't. Sighing, I climbed onto the elliptical and took a long drag from my water bottle before starting the session.

Rhodes told me to do thirty minutes but I did an hour. I texted Willow when I was finished and told her I was going to hit the hot tub but she could start heading that way. She was just finishing up at her weekly coffee house poetry slam, which was just about a half hour from the club, so it worked out perfectly.

I changed into my one-piece quickly and grabbed a towel from the locker room before heading out to the pool. The rain had cleared, but the pavement was still wet as my feet padded across the small garden area to where the pool and hot tub were tucked away. It was a full moon and the light from it reflected off the soft blue of the pool water, casting a cool glow over the white folding chairs lined up on either side. I tossed my bag and towel on one near the shallow end of the pool just as I heard light laughter.

Following the sound, I glanced toward the hot tub on the other end of the pool and sighed when I noticed it wasn't vacant. Probably two old, drunk, Poxton Beach Country Club members doing God knows what. *So much for steaming out the soreness in my muscles.* I grabbed my towel and wrapped it around me again, though my muscles cried out in disagreement. There was no way I was going to join whatever party was happening over there, though. I lifted my gym bag strap onto my shoulder but as I turned to head back inside, I glanced at the hot tub again.

And I was met with fierce green eyes.

Rhodes was staring at me, brows low, his mouth narrowed out into a straight line. An older woman who I didn't recognize was kissing up his neck. She caught his earlobe in her mouth and wrapped her long, manicured nails around his jaw, pulling him into her touch.

I swallowed, but I couldn't look away. Rhodes watched me carefully, but his gaze was just as unwavering as mine. When the woman's hand dipped below the water line, my stomach sank and I felt a wave of something roll over me. Nausea? Jealousy? I wasn't sure, but I'd had enough. Averting my eyes, I tucked my towel around me tighter and skipped going back inside, heading straight for the entrance, instead.

I thought maybe he would come find me. I thought maybe he would tell me not to worry, she's just a client, blah blah blah. But he never came. Then I realized, why would I think he would? Rhodes didn't owe me anything — least of all an explanation for having a woman's hands in his swim trunks. I was trying to figure out why it bothered me so much but fifteen minutes went by with my head spinning and no answers coming. Willow pulled up in her cherry red Jeep and snapped me out of the spell.

"Ow owww," she whistled when she came to a stop. "I can't believe I get to spend all night with this sexy beast. *And* I stole some wine from my parents' stash? Oh yeah, tonight will be trouble." She winked and I tossed my bag in the back before plopping down beside her and fastening my seatbelt. When I didn't smile or joke in return, she frowned, but didn't ask me what was wrong. She just threw the car in drive and turned up the volume on the radio.

She would ask me for details when we got to her house. I knew that. This was only a temporary relief. And I knew I'd have to tell her what I was feeling. I'd have to tell her what was going on with Mason, with Rhodes.

The problem was, I wasn't sure I really knew, myself.

# CHAPTER

# 7

The fair that came to Poxton Beach in late May was nothing like the state fair that rolled through South Carolina each October, but it was an event that drew all the locals out in addition to the tourists passing through. It was themed around corn, being that it was held right in the middle of harvesting season, and there were food competitions, Future Farmers of America showcases, and rides for a promising night of entertainment. I always got excited for it before, but Willow had to practically drag me from her house this time.

"I promise we'll have fun, Natalie," she said for the seventh time as we made our way through the dirt lot to the entrance. I was struggling, trying to balance and walk somewhat gracefully in the nude, strappy wedges she'd forced me to wear. "Just ignore Mason and Shay. They'll probably be off doing their own thing, anyway."

"Wishful thinking."

She glared at me, applying another coat of lip gloss.

"Fine," I sighed. "I'll try. For you and only for you, Lo," I trailed off, watching my feet as we walked. "You're right, we don't have much longer together. I want to have a fun summer with you, regardless of them. Especially since you're probably leaving me early, too. Because we all know you're going to get into the advanced program."

Willow wrapped her petite arms around me and gave me a squeeze. "I love you! Don't get sad on me now, though. Tonight's about fun." She pulled out a purple sparkly flask. "And that fun starts now." She winked, took a swig, and passed it to me.

Smiling, I accepted her offer and threw back a shot. Last time we were out I made the mistake of turning down alcohol. This time, I wouldn't be so stupid. I was down for anything to numb all the feelings bubbling up inside me.

"I wish you would have let me wear sneakers," I complained. "It's a fair. It's mostly dirt and grimy concrete covered in fair food. Why did we have to get so dressed up?"

"Because Mason is going to be here and if you want to get him back, you need to look drop dead gorgeous every time he sees you. The more he sees that you're doing fine, the faster he'll realize how badly he messed up."

"I haven't changed," I pointed out as a driver waved us to pass in front of his car in the gravel parking lot. "Not yet. I'm still the same girl he dumped less than three weeks ago. Plus, he saw me yesterday when I'm pretty sure I looked like a sweaty walrus."

She laughed but stopped me just before the entrance. "You *have* changed, Natalie. You're already walking with your chin held higher, and believe it or not, I can tell you've lost weight. Especially in your face."

"It hasn't even been two weeks, Willow."

"Well, then Rhodes must work magic." I eyed her and though I tried not to, I blushed. Rhodes *definitely* had some kind of voodoo juice happening. "Besides, from what you told me about yesterday, Mason said he missed you."

"He said he missed our calls."

"Exactly. Which reminds me that he called you in the middle of the night the night before. I don't think getting him back is going to be as hard as you think. *Especially* after he sees you in this dress." She smiled.

I fidgeted, shifting on my feet that were already sore. Every time I heard Mason's name, my stomach fell to my feet. But I couldn't tell if it was for the same reasons as before. "I love Mason, Lo. You know that. I know that. But this is about me, too. It's about getting me back. Or rather, getting a new me. A me that's never existed before. A better me."

She smiled at that, linking her arm through mine and leading us through the entrance. "Every life-altering change stems from a series of small, seemingly meaningless amendments." She winked as they scanned our tickets and I shook my head. My best friend was a wacko.

We passed by Dale and my mom on our way to the spot the group had agreed to meet at. They were judging the cornbread competition, against my mother's will, I'm sure. She hated eating any kind of carb — she preferred to drink them. Willow and I wished them luck and then continued on through the fair, sneaking swigs of the flask she'd packed as we walked.

I really did love the vibe of the fair, and with each passing step, I started to relax a little. It might have been the alcohol, or it might have been the bright lights, loud, tacky music, and array of aromas wafting in around us. Aside from the few children crying, everyone was in good spirits at the fair — it was hard not to be. And though my stomach was still in knots over all the confusing thoughts whirling around in my head, I did my best to push them all down and focus on having fun.

When we met up with the group by the Himalaya, Mason and Shay were already with them. Shay rolled her eyes when she saw me, tossing her long brown hair over her shoulder before whispering something in the ear of a girl I didn't recognize. She had platinum blonde hair and long tan legs like Shay's. They really did look like walking Barbie dolls.

Dustin gave me a hug when he saw me and I squeezed him back, thankful to still have him in my life regardless of what was going on with me and Mason. "Heard you were training at the club," he said as he pulled back. "That's awesome."

Shay scoffed. "Waste of money, if you ask me. No amount of workouts can make up for eating your weight in fried food and Twinkies."

My cheeks flushed and I felt a pain stab at the back of my stomach as Shay and her friend giggled. I looked to Mason, waiting for him to put her in her place, but it was Dustin who shook his head.

"Stop it, Shay. It's not funny."

She shrugged, eyes on her nails like she was filing them with straight laser beams. She was still smiling. "Maybe not to you."

I silently thanked Dustin with a soft smile and he just nodded, frowning in Shay's direction.

Willow missed the interaction, she had run off to the restroom nearby, but when she returned, she could sense the tension. Mason seemed a little uncomfortable, but still held his arm tight around Shay as Willow eyed them both before turning to me. "What happened?"

I sighed, not wanting to ruin our night within the first five minutes. "Nothing. Let's go ride something."

"Something or some*one*?" She waggled her brows and I smacked her arm playfully before we made our way with the rest of the group to a spinning, flipping, high-speed ride that I was absolutely positive couldn't be safe. Willow handed me the flask to finish off when we took our place in line, the purple glitter sticking to my hands a bit as I stole the last drag. I tucked it in my purse just as Mason sidled up beside me.

"Hey," he said softly, his brown eyes warm in the fair lighting. He looked like he'd been drinking, and without Shay on his arm, he almost looked like the old Mason. Brown hair mussed and wispy in the wind from the ride, same familiar grin on his face.

It made my stomach ache.

"Hi." I returned his smile, but I wasn't sure what to feel. He was nice at the club yesterday, but then he just let Shay say what she did without so much as a disapproving glance. I couldn't figure him out.

"You look really pretty tonight. Is that a new dress?"

I tried to fight it but my cheeks burned and I nodded. It was a new dress — a knee-length, cream dress with a pink rose pattern splashed across it. Willow and I had gone shopping at the mall earlier that day and she had practically flipped when she saw the way it accented my cleavage and made my waist appear smaller than it really was. My heart hurt when I realized Mason was the only one in my life who would notice something like a new dress. No one else paid that much attention to me.

"Well, I like it." He grinned wider, tucking his hands in his front pockets. "So, you're training with Rhodes?"

I chewed my lip, debating an answer. I didn't want him finding out about my training and now that he knew, I still wasn't sure what I wanted to tell him about it. *Did he already think I was doing this for him?*

I didn't have the opportunity to reply. Shay slid up beside Mason and wrapped her arms around his middle, nudging her way in until his arm was around her shoulder, her sharp hazel eyes on me like I was a bug that needed to be killed.

"What are you talking to her about, baby?" She

asked the question to him, but her gaze was still fixed on me.

Mason smiled down at her and kissed her forehead. A little piece inside me broke in that moment. "Just chatting. You ready?" he asked just as the line moved and we had to file into the death contraption. She giggled and grabbed his hand, leading him forward and casting another frown in my direction. When she looked away, Mason looked back at me, an apology in his eyes.

I just sighed.

Regardless of Shay's attempts to throttle the night with her glares and snide remarks, Willow's promise held true. We did have a good time. We rode ride after ride and took ridiculous pictures with my camera. I even took a few photos of Shay and Mason, though it almost killed me to do so. Maybe Rhodes was right. Maybe I really was too nice.

Willow wasn't the only one who brought flasks. Everyone in the group was passing them around all night and when they ran out, we found a local carny who knew me. He hooked us up with Coca-Cola cups filled with booze and we were pretty much set after that. No one questioned the red cup and by eleven, most of us were sloshed.

I had avoided eating all night, trying to stick to the meal plan Rhodes had prescribed, but the drunchies were catching up to me. When the gang started to head toward the Ferris wheel, I told Willow I had to pee and snuck away into the bathroom to eat the protein bar I'd packed in my purse. It felt a little weird eating in the bathroom stall, but it was better than doing it in front of Shay. I could only imagine the remarks she'd have for me eating a protein bar.

When I finished, I let myself break the seal, which always made me feel even more intoxicated when I stood back up again. Thoughts of Rhodes and the hot tub were creeping in as I washed my hands but I didn't have time to dwell on them, because as I dried my hands on a harsh brown paper towel, the bathroom door opened and Shay stepped in with her friend.

My heartbeat accelerated.

"Oh heyyy, Natalie," she cooed sweetly, but she blocked the exit and I knew that sweetness was laced with venom. "Fancy meeting you in here."

"I don't want any trouble with you, Shay," I said, tossing the paper towel I'd used into the trash can. "Let's just get back to everyone else and finish out the night. We're both mature enough to do that, right?" Even as the words left my lips, I shook. I wasn't confident in my ability to be mature any more than I was hers.

She barked out a harsh laugh that seemed too big for her body. "Oh, Natalie. Sweet, naive Natalie. Don't you get it?" She paused, her lips pressed together as if I were a poor child on the side of the road and she was offering me a grilled cheese. "You don't belong here anymore."

Her words slammed into me hard, but I lifted my chin. I was determined to stand tall. She seemed to notice, so she stepped closer to me, her eyes leveling out to mine. They were so menacing for such a tiny thing.

"No one cares about you, Natalie. Can't you see that?" She pointed to the door. "Everyone in that group uses you because you can get them things. Your step-dad owns the town and you have privilege. You're useful. But no one *cares* about you. Maybe Willow, for reasons I'll never understand, but no one else. Stephanie doesn't care about you, Dustin doesn't care about you, and Mason doesn't nor has he ever. They all feel *sorry* for you, Natalie. You're the fat girl with a lot of money who's good to keep around for resources. That's *all* you are. And that's all you'll ever be to them."

My resolve cracked and my shoulders slumped, tears biting at the back of my eyes. I tried blinking them away, but the liquid only pooled between my lids, blurring my vision.

"Aw, look Tawnya. She's crying." They both snickered and I shoved through them, wiping my face as I did. When I made it outside and the warm, thick air hit my skin, Mason was just a few steps from the bathroom door. Everyone else stood several yards away, laughing and looking at something on Willow's phone, but Mason was too close to pretend he didn't know what just happened. He'd heard everything, I knew he had, so I waited. I waited for him to stand up for me, to take my side, to put Shay in her place, but when Shay walked out behind me, still laughing, she slid her hand into his and he took it.

I crumpled as I lifted my eyes from where their hands were clasped to stare at Mason, open-mouthed.

He still wore apologies in his eyes but no words came to support them. It was then that it hit me.

He wasn't my Mason, anymore.

"Who *are* you?" I asked, voice cracking. I shook my head, tears still streaming down my hot cheeks. Then, before I embarrassed myself further, I broke through my group of friends — or, what I had always thought were my friends — and bee-lined for the parking lot. Willow chased after me.

"Natalie! Natalie, where are you going?"

"I'm leaving, Willow. I can't do this," I called out behind me, eyes forward.

"What? What are you talking about? What happened? I thought we were having fun," she pleaded as she caught up to me. She wore a confused expression and it tore me up to think that maybe I'd held her back all these years. She was friends with the loser fat girl.

"*You're* having fun," I corrected her, spinning to face her and halting in my tracks. "I'm miserable. I have been since we got here. Shay just ripped into me in the bathroom and I was mad at her at first but now I almost want to thank her," I admitted, a short laugh escaping my lips. "Because she's right, Willow. I don't belong here. Not in this group, not at this fair." I motioned to the rides around us, my arm falling to my side with a slap. Pulling my bottom lip between my teeth, I shook my head. "Not in this town."

"Natalie," she reached out to touch me but I shrugged away from her.

"I'll call you tomorrow. Please, don't follow me."

With that, I spun on my heels and walked as fast as I could in the stupid shoes I was wearing away from the group. I wasn't sure if they'd heard what I'd said to Willow. Part of me hoped not, part of me didn't care. I tried to hold myself together as I made my way through the crowd, but the further away I got, the more it seemed like the string tethering me to the ground was shredding into nothing. My breath was labored, tears flooded my eyes and ran down my face, and I felt a pain like nothing I'd ever experienced racking my chest.

I was nothing. I didn't belong.

I was almost to the exit when I stopped in line at a fried food booth. I knew I shouldn't, but I couldn't stop myself. Food was always my answer. When I hurt, I turned to food. And at that moment, I didn't have the fight to stop myself.

"What would you like, miss?" the man asked me when I reached the front of the line. He had dark, leather-like skin and lines on his face that told me he had worked his entire life. He eyed me cautiously and I realized I probably had makeup smeared everywhere. I chewed my lip, something inside me still trying to fight against what I was about to do.

"Miss?" he asked again.

I choked on a sob, feeling myself breaking again, when warm arms wrapped around me. I didn't even know who they belonged to yet at the same time I somehow sensed him. I caved, leaning my weight back into his hard body, letting him hold me steady.

"She changed her mind." I turned to meet Rhodes' intense eyes and he pulled me into him, his arm tight around my shoulder. Something shifted in that moment — something small, almost too small to acknowledge. It was like the world tilted off its path just a millimeter, but I felt it shake everything inside me.

"Miss?" the man asked again. He seemed alarmed by the way Rhodes was staring at me. I can't say he was alone in that sentiment.

I shook my head, pulling my gaze from Rhodes to him. "Sorry, I'm fine. Not as hungry as I thought."

The man appraised us carefully, then shook his head. "Have a good night, folks."

"Thank you," I said softly as Rhodes tugged me away from the stand and in the opposite direction of the one I'd been walking in. He didn't say anything else, but it was then that I realized he was holding my hand.

"Are you hungry?" he asked behind him as we walked. "Be honest."

"Yes."

He frowned as he looked back at me again. "You've been crying."

I swallowed, eyes on my feet as I forced a weak smile and shrugged. He tightened the grip on my hand.

"Let's go. I'll make you food."

"It's almost midnight."

"So I'll make breakfast."

I almost giggled, but I couldn't find the strength. He was pulling me toward the south exit, the opposite side of where I'd been trying to leave. I prayed we wouldn't run into the group and thankfully, we didn't. I was far from ready to face them. I wasn't sure I'd ever be able to again.

"Why are you even here?" I asked as we walked. "I thought you were busy."

He swallowed. "One of my clients wanted to meet here. I was on my way to find her when I saw you."

A strange sickness rolled through me. "Why were you meeting a client here?"

He didn't answer, and visions of him in the hot tub the night before hit me once again. I wanted to ask him more about it, but I didn't have the energy, so I let it go. It wasn't my business anyway, which he'd made clear the day before.

Just as we reached the gate, a huge confetti canon let loose announcing the final fireworks show. Small pieces of colorful paper started raining down over us and I pulled my hand free from Rhodes before retrieving my camera from my purse.

He turned and watched me carefully as I adjusted the lens and focus, snapping different shots of the kaleidoscope paper rain.

"What are you doing?" he asked after a moment.

I smiled. "Finding something beautiful in the chaos."

Rhodes didn't share my smile, but he didn't pull me away, either. He stood and let me take photos until nearly every scrap of paper had fallen and the last firework exploded in the sky. When I reviewed the pictures on the screen, I shook my head.

There are some sights in life, some little moments, that never look as pretty in a picture as they do in real life. I couldn't capture depth with my camera — not true depth, anyway — like the depth of the dark night sky that surrounded each rainbow-colored morsel as it fell in the bright firework light. I couldn't record the way it felt when that soft tissue paper hit the skin on my tear-stained cheeks. Or the way my chest felt heavy as I snapped each photo knowing he was watching me. It was a breathtaking moment frozen in time by an unremarkable photograph.

But it would live brazen in my memory forever.

# CHAPTER

# 8

I rode on the back of Rhodes' bike to his house, since Willow drove us to the fair and I didn't have the Rover. It was terrifying and exhilarating and I was already a complete mess, so everything felt intensified as the wind whipped through the hair that hung lower than my helmet. He didn't have an extra one, since he wasn't exactly counting on running into me, so I wore his and he went without one, even though I tried to fight him on it. Rhodes seemed completely at ease with my arms wrapped around his middle, but I could feel the chiseled abs I'd yet to see beneath his shirt and it made it hard to catch a breath.

When we reached his apartment and he wheeled the bike inside his foyer, Rhodes flicked on a few lights before dipping into his bedroom. I stood by the kitchen island for a moment, looking around, wondering how I'd found myself back at his place. After a moment, my feet reminded me how much they hated me with a shooting pang and I slowly eased my way out of my wedges. Wiggling my toes, I groaned with relief as I stripped each shoe off and let them hit the floor. Rhodes appeared again and watched me with a shake of his head as he moved straight into the kitchen and pre-heated the oven.

"Why the hell did you wear those things to the fair, anyway?" He scowled, leaning up against the counter and crossing his arms over his chest. He was dressed more casually now than when he picked me up, sporting a heather-gray t-shirt with PBHS Weightlifting written on the front in dark green and simple black basketball shorts. He was also wearing a flat-billed hat, which I'd never seen him wear before. It framed his face in a way that somehow made his defined jaw look even stronger — square, symmetrically perfect.

When I didn't answer his question, recognition hit his eyes and he nodded. "Ah. I get it. You wore them for your ex, didn't you?"

I cringed. "Willow's idea."

"Mm hmm," he murmured under his breath. He was watching me more carefully than usual that night, questions that he wouldn't say out loud hidden behind his gaze. The silence of his apartment wrapped around us as his eyes drifted down to the hem of my dress and back up to my mouth. I wanted to break the quiet, ask him why he was staring at me like that, but he turned too quickly and began grabbing ingredients from the fridge. "What's your favorite fair food, Bug?"

I scrunched my nose. "I don't know, probably corn dogs. And don't call me Bug."

"Why?" he asked, turning to drop an armful of

food and seasonings on the counter in front of me. "Your friends call you gnat. It's the same thing."

I giggled. "It's far from the same thing."

"It's similar," he argued, pointing the fork he'd just pulled from the drawer at me. "And it made you smile, so you can guarantee I'll be saying it again." His eyes glistened and for the life of me I couldn't figure him out. Last night, he was pissed at me and wrapped around an older woman in the hot tub. Not that he couldn't be friendly with me and do the same thing, but still. He was different then — angry, distant. Now, he was grinning and making jokes. And cooking for me. Again.

He said we were just trainer and client, but this was the second time he'd invited me to his place. And, he brought me here because I'd been crying and he wanted to help take my mind off it. That seemed like something a friend would do.

I was going to need a chiropractor for the whiplash.

Rhodes went to work on whatever he was making and the minute the herbs hit the air, my mouth started watering. I was still kind of buzzed, which just made me that much hungrier. After he whipped up what looked like little muffins and popped them in the oven, he set the timer for ten minutes and we moved to the couch. He sat on one end and I hugged the arm at the other, like I was scared to touch him even though I'd just had myself wrapped around him on the way over.

"How are your feet?" He nodded toward where I was still stretching out my toes. There were red marks from the straps indented along the bridges of both of my feet, the edges of them outlined by dirt.

I shrugged. "They've been better, that's for sure."

"Here," he said, leaning forward and lifting my right leg into his lap. I instinctively yanked it back.

"Ew, absolutely not. You are not touching my feet, especially after I walked around in wedges in the dirt all night."

He chuckled, and it revealed a smile I hadn't seen on his face before. It was mischievous, curious, and sexy as hell.

"Relax, Bug. I've dealt with way dirtier things than your feet."

His electric eyes glimmered at that remark and he held his smirk. Hesitantly, I let him take my leg again. The minute his strong hands started working the balls of my feet, I melted back against the couch.

"Oh," I groaned, squirming under his touch. He stopped, but just for the tiniest second, before continuing his slow assault. I watched his hands carefully, but I felt his eyes on me, not the work he was doing.

"You were drinking tonight." It wasn't a question, but I felt like I was being reprimanded.

"I needed to drink, Rhodes."

He paused, switching to my left foot. "I get that, but alcohol isn't going to help you reach your goal," he said sternly. "I'm not saying you can't ever drink, but it shouldn't be often. And when you do, try drinking the low-calorie vodka and water. It doesn't taste as good, but it still works the same and it won't crush your nutrition for the day."

I nodded. "You got it, boss."

He smirked, but the crooked smile fell just as quickly as it had come. "Why did you need to drink tonight? What happened?"

A pain shot through my stomach and I pulled my legs into me instinctively. Rhodes didn't try to pull me back. He let me retreat, pulling his right ankle up to rest on his left knee as he waited for me to explain.

"Well, my ex's new girlfriend basically told me that I don't belong anymore and that none of my friends even care about me, nor have they ever cared about me before. I'm the 'rich fat girl,'" I word-vomited. "Her words, not mine. Though I can't really argue her point."

Rhodes balled up his fists, but he didn't say anything. He just kept his eyes on mine, waiting.

"Willow, my best friend, didn't hear her say it. But Mason did. And he didn't do anything about it." My stomach tightened at the admission and I felt tears sting my eyes again, but I shook them off. "So I bailed. And I just wanted to feel okay, I wanted something to make me happy, so I went to get food. Like always. Even though I knew I'd regret it. And..." I trailed off. "Well, you know the rest."

He seemed to chew on what I'd just told him, his jaw flexing beneath his flawless skin. It was peppered with just the slightest hint of stubble, which worked with the shadow from his hat to frame his jaw in the low light. "You shouldn't hang out with people who treat you like that, Natalie."

I shrugged, untucking my legs from my arms

124

and pulling them up under me to sit crisscross style, instead. "My friends aren't the ones doing it. It's Shay."

"But like you said, Mason didn't stop her. And did anyone else?"

I didn't respond.

"Exactly. Don't let these people make you feel like this, Bug. Not them, not anyone else. I know it seems like what they think about you matters right now, but it doesn't." He bent down a little lower, trying to get me to look at him. "Remember what I said in the gym after you reamed me out?"

"Hey! I didn't *ream you out*. I yelled at you. And you deserved it."

He chuckled, the noise low and throaty. "The point is, I push you because I believe in you. So when they get in your head, just think about that. Maybe it's time to start believing in yourself, too."

I could smell the faint scent of mint on his breath as it hit my skin, sparking a wave of chills. I didn't know what else to say about me, so I turned it around to focus on him. "Was that your girlfriend last night?"

He sighed, leaning back and scrubbing his hands down his face just as the oven timer sounded. "Don't, Natalie."

I frowned as he moved from the couch back into the kitchen. "What? I'm not allowed to ask?"

"Not when you know the answer."

I chewed my cheek, standing and moving to the other side of the kitchen island so I could watch him finish dinner. Or breakfast. Whatever you consider food after midnight to be. "But that's just it," I corrected him. "I don't. Not really."

Rhodes carefully removed the pan from the oven and set it on top of the stove. "She's not my girlfriend, Bug. None of them are. They're my clients."

I shook my head, the word *client* sending a familiar yet uneasy zing through my chest. "What? Did they pay for the platinum package to get that kind of extra time?" I scoffed. "Remind me to change my membership before our next training session. Don't want to be missing out on the perks." I cringed a little at my words, shocked that they came from my mouth.

Rhodes was plating our food but my words halted him, too, his hands dropping down to grip the handle of the oven hard. I watched as his knuckles turned white and he hung his head, shaking it just slightly. I almost spoke again when he silenced my sass with a loud slam of his hand on the counter. The force shook our plates and he rushed toward me, pinning my hips to the counter with his own before I even comprehended what was happening. He was flush against me, and he snaked his hands into my wind-blown hair like he owned me. "Is this what you want, Natalie?" His tongue licked his bottom lip before he drug his teeth across the tender flesh. I watched fascinated, my breath caught in my throat. "You want me to kiss you in the hot tub? Touch you in the sauna?" His voice was low but gruff, each question laced with lust I'd never experienced before. He flexed his hips forward and I inhaled stiffly. "Fuck you on the treadmill?"

I didn't answer. I couldn't *breathe*, let alone form words. Rhodes stayed there a moment, his body now firmly between my legs, his hands still grasping my neck. He swallowed, his fervent eyes falling to my lips briefly before he released his hold and backed away.

I exhaled the moment he did, oxygen finding me in a rush. It felt like my first breath and my last one, too.

"What if I did want those things?" I murmured, surprising myself more than him, I was sure. "It wouldn't matter, would it? I'm not hot enough. I'm not skinny enough…" my voice trailed off. "I'm not like them."

"Why don't you get it?" he growled roughly, reaching into the cabinet above the stove before slamming it closed again. He turned to me then and his eyes were piercing, like the sharpest blade slicing right through my fragile defense. Suddenly, and for the first time in my life, I felt small. "You're right. You're *not* like my other clients. Them?" He gestured in the direction of the door, his voice raised. "They don't have goals. They're selfish, greedy, and entitled. They sign up for sessions with me so they have a solid excuse when they want to dip out on their rich ass husbands to come fuck me." He slammed his hand against his chest when he referenced himself and I flinched at his honesty. Rhodes swallowed. He knew he'd struck a nerve, but he kept going.

"I'm not a good person, okay? I train and screw around with other people who are just as shitty as I am." He moved closer, his palms flattening out on the counter in front of me as his eyes leveled with mine. "That's why when you walked into the gym, I couldn't figure out why."

Breath was a fleeting thing.

"Why? Because I'm the only one who's actually fat?" I whispered. I was certainly more overweight than those other women I'd seen him with. I waited for him to scold me, or roll his eyes, or sigh, but he just watched me. He studied me. And then, his eyes softened.

"You're not, Natalie. You," he paused, lifting his hat to run his hands through his hair before pulling it back on again. "You're weightless. The world hasn't touched you yet. You're not heavy with the weight of pain, and guilt, and selfishness." He shook his head, biting his lower lip in that same way that made my skin heat just moments before. "You're *light*. Don't ever lose that. Don't let the world weigh you down like them." He shifted, looking away. "Like me."

With that, he turned back to the stove and finished plating our dinner, effectively ending our conversation while his words still swirled in my head. We moved back to the couch and again I found myself hugging the arm. I had so many questions. What had weighed him down? Why did he think this was his only path in life? How many women did he sleep with? Did he like it? But he was done talking about it, I knew that, so I changed the subject again.

"You made us muffins?" I asked when he clicked on the TV.

"They're corn dog muffins. Eighty calories each."

I smiled at his thoughtfulness and he shrugged, the flickering light of the television dancing across his face. "You wanted fair food, so I'm giving it to you. Just modified."

I just smiled harder, even though I knew I probably looked like an idiot. When I noticed a change in Rhodes' breathing, my smile melted. His eyes flickered to my lips momentarily, but he looked away so fast I almost questioned if I'd seen it.

"Thank you, Rhodes. For tonight. For… everything, really."

He shifted. "I didn't do much."

"It's a lot, to me."

I noticed his Adam's apple bob in his throat, but he just nodded. We watched the sports channel he'd pulled up and ate our midnight snack in quiet. It was mouthwatering and delicious and I had a hard time not eating five-hundred calories worth of those low-calorie muffins. I made sure to tell him that at least eight times before we walked out to his bike. It was almost two in the morning, but I felt wide awake.

He drove slower on the way to my house than he had earlier on the way to his. The night air was warm, but the wind was cool, and the moon was bright enough to light our way without his headlight. I didn't know what to make of what he'd said earlier or of what he'd done for me, so I tried not to dwell on it, but my mind was racing as fast as the bike. My heart was beating fast, my mouth was dry, and I felt myself leaning closer and closer to an edge I wasn't sure I was prepared to fall over.

When we pulled up to my drive, he cut the engine and propped his bike up on the stand at the end of the road. My parents didn't expect me until late, still, they *certainly* didn't expect me to arrive on the back of a motorcycle, so I had him pull over by our brick mailbox. Rhodes pulled my helmet off and chuckled as I tried to tame my hair. When I sighed and gave up, he held his smirk.

"Can I ask you something before you go?"

He leaned back, half-sitting on his bike seat and crossing his arms over my helmet. His eyes took on an entirely new appearance in the light of the moon. They were darker, yet the green still shone through the night. "You and your questions."

I blushed, but asked anyway. "Your sister..." He stiffened, and I almost didn't ask, but I couldn't hold the words back. "You said she *was* pretty. Is she... did they never... what does that mean?"

His jaw tensed. "She's dead."

Two words. He said them so unflinchingly, like they didn't hold the weight that they did. I knew I probably should have said I was sorry for his loss, but Rhodes didn't strike me as someone who would want to hear that. It wasn't personal, it wasn't sincere — it was laced with bullshit that I didn't want to feed him. So, I asked another question.

"What happened?" I shook my head. "I mean, I know, kind of. I remember when she... when they said she was missing."

Rhodes wouldn't look at me. He would look up toward the sky, to the left down the road, down at his sneakers — but never at me. "She just disappeared. We drove to school together, I saw her at lunch, then again right before weightlifting practice, but she never came home that night."

I gulped.

"What about your parents? Did they try looking for her?"

"I don't have parents, Bug. We were in a home."

My heart broke. It was all starting to make sense. "I know she disappeared, but how do you know she's dead? Did they… did they find her?" I felt sick even asking, and I couldn't bring myself to add *body* to the end of that question.

"They never found her." He breathed slowly. "I don't know for sure that she's dead, but I have to believe she is."

"Why?"

He shrugged, and his eyes finally met mine again. There was a pain there that was indescribable, a pain I knew I could never fully understand. "Because it's better than the alternative."

I bit my lips against the tears threatening the back of my eyes. I didn't have the right to cry. "I'm sorry, Rhodes," I whispered.

"Are you finished with your questions?" he asked, standing. I nodded. Without another word, he packed the helmet I'd worn into his backpack and pulled on his own, mounting the bike and sparking it to life. He peered at me through the lens for a short second before pulling off, leaving a light cloud of smoke as he did.

I stood there motionless, scolding myself for asking questions, for effectively ruining the night. He was the only thing good about mine, and I'd just wrecked his. I sighed, dragging my feet inside and up to my room, head not spinning any less than it had been when I woke up that morning.

Before I let myself go to bed, I stood in a scorching hot shower. I tried to burn the night from my skin — the words Shay spoke to me, the words Mason didn't say to make it right, the words I wished I could take back that I'd said to Rhodes. I imagined the water washing them from me and pulling them down the drain, along with all the hurt they'd caused.

But when I succumbed to my bed and pulled the covers up high over my head, I still felt them on me.

I didn't dream about Rhodes that night.

I didn't sleep at all.

# CHAPTER

# 9

My stomach was in knots as I dressed for my training session the next day. I was nervous about facing Rhodes again after what I'd asked about his sister the night before. Would he be angry? Hurt? Sad? Would he ever want to talk to me again?

It didn't help that I could hear Mom and Dale arguing down the hall. I swallowed as Dale's voice rose louder when I packed the last of my gym bag. Zipping it up, I tossed it over my shoulder and hurried out of my room and down the stairs, trying my best not to eavesdrop on what was being said. All I'd picked up was that Dale had been drunk the night before, which wasn't anything new, and Mom was pissed — again, not anything new. It wasn't that they fought all the time, but Dale did tend to get into trouble when he drank. I wasn't sure what it was — if he embarrassed himself or Mom or both — but there always seemed to be a bit of a tiff after he had a night of drinking.

I padded down the hall to the kitchen where I figured their voices would be mostly drowned out, pulling up the meal plan Rhodes developed for me. Meal prepping was still far from my favorite pastime, but I was getting better at it.

"Want some help with that?" Christina asked, wrapping an apron around her waist as she entered the kitchen. I smiled and nodded, and in her soft, almond-shaped eyes, I could see that she heard them fighting, too.

Christina had been cooking for me ever since I could remember. She was from Venezuela and her family had moved to Poxton Beach when she was a teenager, fleeing the dangerous conditions of her home country. She had two little boys — Junior and Luis — and she treated me like the daughter she never had. I always welcomed her advice, but I loved it even more when she knew I didn't want to talk at all. She and Moses were a lot alike in that respect.

We cut and cooked and prepped for the next thirty minutes, not really talking but not feeling uncomfortable in the silence, either. That was, until it wasn't silence anymore.

"I don't care what you call it, Dale. If you don't get it under control, you're going to have to say goodbye to the woman who has looked past it for so long!" My mom stormed down the stairs and I stood frozen with two packed Tupper-Ware containers in my hand, waiting to go to the fridge. Christina had already excused herself, leaving me to stare alone.

Mom's face was tear-stained with streaks of mascara marring her cheeks like scars. When she saw me, she sniffed, shook her head, and laughed. "Men," she said, wiping her nose with a balled up tissue in her hand. "They are just silly sometimes, aren't they?"

"Mom…" I dropped the containers and moved toward her. I would be late if I didn't leave soon, but I didn't care. They'd fought before, but I'd never seen my mom cry like that — ever. "What's going on?"

"It's nothing sweetheart."

"Come on, Mom. It's okay. Talk to me."

She sighed, shaking her head again and grabbing the containers I'd abandoned. She carefully placed them in the fridge and then turned to face me, propping herself back against the counter. "I'm fine. It'll all be fine."

I just stared at her, trying to decipher if she was lying. She waved me away.

"I promise. We're just having a tiff. He'll realize I'm right and come around. He always does." She smiled. "You heading to see your trainer?"

I nodded, letting her change the subject, and her smile widened. Mom didn't really ever talk to me about her relationship issues, which made sense, being that she was my parent. Still, we were also best friends, and I hated not knowing what was making her cry.

She lifted from the counter and tucked a fallen strand of my hair behind my ear.

"He's really doing a great job already, Natalie. I can tell."

I shrugged, suddenly feeling odd under her watchful eyes. I was concerned for her fight with Dale, but I still hadn't forgotten her conversation on the phone that I'd overheard. She was finally seeing me turn into the daughter she could be proud of. I just wished it wasn't because I was losing weight.

"Oh!" She clapped her hands together. "Let's go shopping after your session! I bet you need new workout clothes. Invite Willow. It'll be fun!"

"Mom..." I groaned. "I don't want to buy fat clothes."

"Oh stop," she scolded, clicking her tongue. "You shouldn't be wearing raggy old high school t-shirts to the club and I could use the girl time. Please?"

I sighed, not excited about the idea of shopping, but I also knew that retail therapy was her favorite. This was Mom's way of telling me she needed me. "Okay. I'll call Willow."

I needed to call her anyway. She'd blown my phone up all night and morning trying to apologize for last night.

"Perfect!" Mom scampered off toward the stairs. "I'll get showered and dressed. By the time you train, get back, shower, and get ready, I should be almost finished."

I laughed at that. "I could probably eat and take a nap beforehand, too."

She giggled, but didn't deny it, before trotting up the stairs. At least she seemed better than when she'd come down them. It took a lot to knock my mom down for longer than a few minutes. After the hell my dad put her through when I was younger, there wasn't much that could faze her. Though, when she told me stories about her before Dale, it was always so hard for me to imagine. To me, she'd always been a wealthy, classy, refined woman. It was hard to imagine the poor, rough around the edges version of her.

In fact, I didn't really know much about that time in her life. My dad left her when I was born, not even leaving so much as a note. She met Dale two years later and only a year after that they were married. He'd been around my entire life. Dale *was* my father, as far as I was concerned. Still, my grandmother often told me how Dale brought out the best in my mom and saved her from a really dark time in her life. I guess in a way, Dale sort of saved me, too.

I shook off the feeling of the house as I made my way to the Rover. I wouldn't say I was necessarily excited about going to the gym, but I wasn't dreading it, either. I was nervous to see Rhodes, but anxious to workout. There were plenty of things I wanted to get my mind off of, and unlike my mother, shopping wouldn't help. But, working out might.

On my way to the club, I dialed Willow. She answered on the first ring.

"Okay, I've decided you can't hate me. Because you're my best friend, Nat, and if you hate me, my life will plummet into a downward spiral the summer before college and I'll never come back from it. I won't get in the early admittance program, I'll probably fail out of college my first year from sheer depression, and then I'll live the rest of my life trying to be a carny at the

Poxton Beach fair and wondering where I went wrong that fateful night years ago."

Willow was breathless by the time she finished spouting off her story and I couldn't help but laugh. "Lo, I'm not mad at you."

"Oh my God," she said, exhaling a long breath. "I've been freaking out all night. I'm so sorry. Whatever happened, I'm so sorry. I shouldn't have forced you to go out with everyone. I don't know what's going on with Mason and his chick but I'm sorry I pushed you. We don't have to hang out with anyone else the rest of the summer. Just me and you. I promise. I'm so sorry."

"Lo," I cut her off. "It's fine. I promise. I'm good."

"What happened?"

Sighing, I gave her the cliff note version in the five minutes I had left before I would pull into the club. She cursed the entire time and vowed to strangle Shay the next time she saw her, which made me laugh more.

"So did you just go home? Did you call Dale? Or your mom?"

I hesitated. "Um…"

Willow waited a moment before speaking again. "What? What is it?"

"Well, don't freak out, but I may or may not have gone home with Rhodes."

"Oh. My God." She said the first word with a punch and the second two altogether. "Shut up."

I cringed. "Well, he kind of found me. And—"

Willow squeaked, drowning out my explanation. "I need details. Now. All of them."

This time I laughed. "You're going to have to wait. I'm pulling up to the club for my training session. But," I started just as she began whining. "My mom wants to go shopping this evening. Come with us?"

"Like that's even a question. Call me when you're on your way. And I better get every single detail with you making me wait like this."

With that, Willow ended the call and I tossed my phone in my gym bag and trudged into the gym. When I entered through the double glass doors and saw Rhodes running on the treadmill, sweat pouring down his face and drenching the top of his shirt, the nerves I was feeling earlier rushed back in full force. His eyes lifted as soon as I entered and he killed the machine, wiping himself with a small white towel as he made his way toward me.

"You're late."

"Sorry," I murmured. "My parents were… well, it doesn't matter. I'm here."

He nodded, and I waited for him to rip into me. About last night, about being late — anything to get him to just get it over with before we started. But, surprisingly, he didn't.

"Do you know how to check your heart rate?"

I scrunched my nose. "I mean, I watch it when I'm on the treadmill or the Stairmaster."

"But do you know how to check it without a machine?"

I shook my head.

"Okay," he started, moving closer to me. "You know how I tell you to get your heart rate up to at least one-hundred-and-sixty beats per minute when we're doing treadmill drills?" I nodded. "That's because at that rate, you're in the hard-core cardio zone. If you're between one-forty and one-sixty, you're in cardio. One-twenty to one-forty, fat burn. Anything over one-eighty is max effort and anything less than one-twenty is warm up."

I was looking at him like he'd just told me I have a thigh gap.

He chuckled. "I'll get you a chart. But, the point I'm trying to make is that you should be able to do this on your own, without a machine. You should always monitor your heart rate to know what zone you're in, regardless of if you're working out outside or on a treadmill."

"Okay, so how do I do that?"

Rhodes took my wrist and my stomach dropped, but I didn't let it show. Turning my arm so that my palm faced upward, he pressed two fingers into my skin on the thumb side of my wrist. "Using two fingers, push hard between the bone and the tendon over your radial artery right here. Then, count how many beats you feel in fifteen seconds and multiply by four to get your heart rate."

"You can feel my heart right now?"

His eyes lifted to mine and the slightest smile curled on his lips. "Yeah. Yeah I can feel your heart." For a moment, he stayed staring at me like that, but then he cleared his throat and dropped my wrist. "You can check it on your neck, too, but I like the wrist way myself. Try it."

I did, and I was embarrassed by how fast my heart was beating while we were just standing there. I knew he had felt it too, which only deepened that embarrassment further.

"Got it?"

I nodded. "Yeah, I think so."

"Good. I don't want you to have to depend on the machine." He paused, then pulled something from his pocket. "That being said, I got you something."

He opened his hand and revealed a small white box with a watch depicted on the packaging. It was kind of bulky, but it was pink and feminine at the same time. "What is it?"

"It's a lot of things. It's a heart rate monitor, a watch, and a GPS system. It can log how far you run when you run outside. It's waterproof, so even if it's raining, you can still wear it. And it has a voice-memo feature so you can record how you're feeling at certain times during your workout. You can track your workouts each day and look at data that compares how many calories you burned over the weeks and months and what your average heart rate was. And you can even toggle a setting for it to coach you while you train." He shrugged. "It's kind of like a mini me on your wrist."

I smiled, but my stomach was caught in a wave, dipping and surging over and over again. Rhodes was giving me a gift, and I had no idea how to react. "Wow."

He shifted on the heels of his feet, shrugging as he ran his free hand back through his damp hair. "Yeah, I mean it's just something I like to give my clients to help out." He tossed it to me quickly. "Go ahead and put it on and I'll show you how it works."

I did as he said, but I couldn't help the disappointment I felt when I realized it wasn't just something he'd done for me. But *why* was I disappointed? He was a trainer, giving a workout-related gift to the person he was training. It made sense that he would do it for everyone.

I was overly annoyed with my emotions.

Once we'd toyed with it and figured out how it worked, we set in on the day's training schedule. We weren't talking much, but that was mostly because I could barely breathe, let alone talk. Rhodes went a little harder on me each day, but the crazy thing was — I was beginning to be able to handle it. In fact, I almost wanted him to push me harder. The adrenaline, the rush of endorphins, the ache in my muscles — I kind of loved all of it.

Who was I?

"Tomorrow's our last workout before your second weigh-in on Sunday," he told me, tossing me my water bottle as we finished up the final round of weights. "I'm going to do one of my more advanced sessions with you, if you're up for it."

I nodded, though in my head I was trying to figure out how it could get more intense than it already was. "Bring it."

He almost smiled, but opened his mouth and tongued the inside of his cheek instead, staring at me amused. "You're *so* going to wish you hadn't said that. Bring your watch. I can't wait to see how many calories we blast." He winked before turning toward the showers and I let out a long, slow, shaky breath.

I was relieved. He didn't bring up the night before, he didn't ignore me or lash out at me, and if anything I'd even go as far as to say he was *nice* to me. I didn't know what to think about the watch, but I decided not to dwell on it. I had two girls waiting on me to unleash their inner shopping beasts and I did not want to keep them waiting.

Packing up my bag quickly, I made my way out to the car. On my way out, I passed by several women, two of which I knew were Rhodes' clients. I swallowed as I passed them, his words from the night before ringing loud in my ear.

*"I'm not a good person, okay? I train and screw around with other people who are just as shitty as I am."*

One of the women, a tall, blue-eyed redhead, eyed me cautiously as I passed, almost as if I didn't belong there. And I guess in a way, I didn't. I didn't really belong anywhere. But I was trying to figure out who I was, exactly, because I needed to know that before I could find out where to place myself. So, I held my chin up and strolled past them without cowering away.

A smile met my lips when I realized neither of the two who I knew Rhodes trained with were wearing watches like mine. Something told me Rhodes had lied.

But for once, I was okay with it.

# CHAPTER

# 10

Willow made me spill all the details when we went shopping that night, and of course she overanalyzed everything — that was her specialty, after all. She was convinced Rhodes was into me, which was the most ludicrous thing I'd ever heard. When she turned the conversation back to Mason, anger rolled through me.

All summer I had been working to get him back, but that night at the fair when he'd neglected to stick up for me, I realized I didn't even know the guy I was fighting for anymore. So, I shifted gears. Did I still want him to see me when I dropped my weight and looked amazing? Yes. But now, it was less about getting him back and more about showing him that I could do whatever I wanted, whether he believed in me or not.

Willow co-signed.

The next day, Rhodes came through on his promise, completely murdering me in the gym. But it was worth it when I weighed in on Sunday. I had lost another eight pounds, which meant I was already down nineteen pounds in just two weeks.

It was hard for me to wrap my mind around that. It had only been two weeks, yet it felt like years. I could already feel my body changing, yet at the same time I found it hard to believe that I could have already lost almost twenty pounds. But the number on the scale didn't lie.

Another week went by and I felt myself start to fall into a routine. Eating right was beginning to be less of a chore and more of an instinct. I still craved sweets and sodium-packed easy meals, of course, but it was easier to fight off those cravings when I knew how hard I had to work to get that same number of calories in that chocolate bar to show up on my watch.

The watch had become an obsession for me. I loved seeing my heart rate sky rocket when I was working hard and the "calories burned" number climb right along with it. Rhodes scolded me when I drained the battery in the first few days. I accidentally left the voice memo function on after I had noted how much easier I was breathing during a run and it killed the battery life. But, I was getting the hang of it, and it was by far the best gift I'd been given in years.

Rhodes and I hadn't hung out since that night of the fair, but training with him was becoming fun. He was different with me than before, showing me a softer side. He wasn't a tiny meowing kitten by any means, but he wasn't the pit bull I'd become used to, either. He talked to me more and listened to my concerns, helping me see the finish line in sight when I couldn't. He wasn't cooking for me anymore or running into me outside of the gym, but we were falling into a comfortable zone. Trainer and client. Jedi and Padawan.

On the flip side, Mason had texted me more than ten times since the night of the fair. The texts ranged from apologies to just asking how I was to reminding me of inside jokes we had. I'd yet to respond, but mostly because I wasn't sure what to say. Or think, really. Where my body was making progress, my mind seemed to be falling deeper and deeper into a confusing pit of feelings. I wanted to decipher them, but I kept my focus on training and eating right. Thoughts and feelings could wait.

The problem was, when Mason texted me, I still felt that same pull to him that I always had. I knew my priorities had shifted and the lifestyle change I was making was for *me*, but I couldn't figure out if Mason was still driving part of my desire to train harder, too. I would be lying if I said I didn't still have moments where I wanted him back, and part of me hoped he was thinking the same about me, too. Still, I longed for the old Mason — the one I wasn't sure still existed. I wanted our comfortable date nights in, our crazy nights out with our friends, the way he smiled sideways at me as he tucked me under his arm. I missed it.

When I wasn't training or hanging out with Willow, I was still watching *Lost*, and I was in the middle of season four on the Saturday evening before my third weigh-in when Willow called me with news I wasn't prepared for.

"I got in."

She said the words with a mixture of excitement and caution, and it took me a moment to realize what those three syllables meant. She meant the kick-start program. When the news settled, I bolted up from where I'd been lounging on the couch and switched the phone to my right ear.

"Oh my gosh, Willow! Congratulations!" I swallowed hard, powering off the television completely. "I'm so happy for you."

And I was. I really was. But at the same time, I was selfish. Willow was the only friend I had in Poxton Beach — the only *true* friend, anyway — and with all the drama going on with Mason and Shay, I didn't want her to leave. I knew that made me a crappy friend but I couldn't help it. I needed her.

Willow let out a breath. "Oh God, I'm so happy you're happy. I was nervous to call."

"Why?"

"Because…" her voice trailed off. "I just know you have a lot going on right now. I don't want you to think I'm abandoning you."

Reaching for my egg-shaped lip balm on the coffee table, I ran it over my lips to buy me a minute before I exhaled a long breath. "Are you kidding me, Lo? You're my best friend. And this is amazing news. Can I come over to celebrate?"

"My parents are taking me out to dinner, actually," she answered.

"Oh. Well that's okay. Can I come by tomorrow?"

"Well…" Something in my gut told me I wouldn't like what Willow said next. "I won't be here tomorrow.

They want me to come up for orientation on Monday and Mom wants to leave tomorrow to make the drive."

My stomach sank along with my shoulders. "Oh. Okay. Well, we'll just get together when you get back. When do you leave for the program?"

I heard Willow swallow. "Three weeks."

"Three weeks?" I repeated back to her in a high shrill I didn't know my voice was capable of making. Clearing my throat, I tried to calm down. "That's so soon."

"I know."

We were silent for a moment, and I knew I was making her accomplishment seem like something she should be sad about. Which was dramatic and immature, and I was trying to be better at both, so I forced a smile. "Well, we have a lot of shopping to do in three weeks if we're going to get you ready for college."

Willow squeaked. "Oh my God, Nat. I got *in*! I'm going to the advanced program at Appalachian State!"

We both screamed together and I felt a surge of pride for my best friend. I didn't want her to go, but I was proud of her. She deserved every bit of success I knew she would achieve.

I just wasn't sure where I fit in her new plans.

Or what *my* plans would be.

"Gotta go, we just got to the restaurant. I love you!"

"Love you too, Lo."

When we hung up, I stared down at the phone in my hand, the heavy silence of the empty house giving me goosebumps. Mom and Dale were out of town for the week traveling for business and to see a few family friends. Other than Christina, all our other help was off for the week, too. I was alone, and the one person I would call to comfort me was the one currently causing the pain.

I had no right to be upset that Willow was leaving — that much I knew. Still, whether that was the case or not, I felt like a part of me was being ripped away. Willow had been my best friend since we were toddlers. We never went more than a week without seeing each other. We were supposed to go to college together — it was always in our plans. But she was going to college and I was staying in Poxton Beach.

I had no idea how to handle that.

Even worse, it was my fault I was staying. I could have joined Willow a couple of months later in the fall, but I hadn't so much as looked at how much the application fee for Appalachian State was, let alone apply. Because at the end of the day, I still didn't know what I wanted to do. I was lost. I was idle. And the world kept spinning on without me.

It wasn't that I hadn't thought about my options, because I had. The truth was that the biggest part of me really wanted to go to an arts school, if I was going to do the college thing at all. But admitting that to myself wasn't nearly as hard as it would be to tell Mom and Dale. They would want me at Appalachian State. With my best friend going there, it shouldn't have seemed like such a big deal to me to *not* go, but it was. I didn't want to be like everyone else in Poxton Beach. In fact, I wanted out of the town altogether.

The shock of that admission hit me in the chest and I exhaled a long breath.

I flipped through my contacts, landing on Mason's number and staring at it. My thumb hovered over the call button, my breath labored as I tried to figure out what to do. I needed to get out of the house, I needed to be with someone, but I knew Mason wasn't that someone. I could call Christina, but she was with her boys, and I didn't want to pull her away when she was finally getting some quality time with them now that Mom and Dale were out of town.

My knee bounced as I thought hard about who to call. Rhodes popped into my mind out of nowhere and I shook my head, but then I paused. Maybe he *could* help. He did kind of save me from my thoughts after that night at the fair, and we were joking around more. He wasn't Willow, by any means, but he cared about me. Right?

Before I could overthink it, I dialed his number.

"Hey, everything okay?" He answered after five rings, and I could tell by his breathy voice that he was busy.

When I didn't answer right away, he muffled the phone with his palm but I could still hear him speaking to someone through it. My throat felt thick with something I couldn't swallow as my mind raced, wondering who was there with him. When the phone cleared, he spoke again.

"What's going on?"

"Can I come over?"

He paused. "Uh, it's not really a good time. Did something happen? Are you hurt?"

"Please, Rhodes." I hated the way my voice sounded when I pleaded with him. "I don't really have anyone else to call right now. My parents are out of town and Willow… well, she's not available. It's kind of a long story but I really need to clear my head right now. Go for a run with me or cook for me or something — anything. I just need to… I need to do something."

Rhodes drew out a long breath laced with curse words and I paced as I waited for him to answer.

"Okay. Give me thirty."

He hung up before I could answer, but I exhaled, feeling some sort of unexplainable hope that he would hold the key to making me feel better. I realized then that Rhodes often gave me a hope that no one else could, and that recognition scared me.

I dressed in workout clothes, tossing my hair into a bun before packing a bag with extra clothes just in case we did something after. I didn't know why I expected Rhodes to want to spend his Saturday night with me, and I guess that's not really what I was asking. I just needed to pass some time, to get out of my thoughts and into my body for a while. Rhodes was actually a pro at ignoring me and not talking, which is more of what I needed in that moment. Maybe that was why I called him — it just made sense.

I left my house earlier than I needed to, mostly because I couldn't stand to be in there alone anymore. I couldn't believe I was taking the news of Willow leaving as hard as I was. It wasn't like I thought she wouldn't get into the program. Still, the hit of her news crashed through my already shaky emotions and I'd found myself spinning. I needed something to ground me.

Pulling up to Rhodes' apartment complex ten minutes earlier than he'd asked, I tried to pass time playing on my phone in the Rover. Pictures of Mason and Shay along with *congratulations* posts to Willow flooded my social media networks and I tossed my phone into the passenger seat, letting out a frustrated sigh.

I tapped my fingers on the steering wheel, applied another coat of lip balm, cleaned my Ray Bans with the end of my t-shirt before placing them back in their case. I popped in a piece of gum and chewed it for a minute before spitting it out my window. Not even sixty seconds had passed.

I knew he was with someone when I called, but surely he had time to get back home by now, right? I didn't see his bike, but then again I *wouldn't* see his bike because he parked it inside. Sighing, I gave up trying to wait.

"Screw it."

I grabbed my bag and jumped out of the SUV, locking it behind me. The closer I got to Rhodes' apartment, the more the familiar nerves my body associated with his proximity consumed me. He always made me anxious and I had no idea why.

When I reached his front door, I lifted my hand to knock, but it swung wide open before my knuckles could tap the light blue exterior. Rhodes stood in the doorway, but he wasn't the only one. A busty woman with razor cut brunette hair and a fake tan was wrapped around him, her lips hard on his. She was giggling, but startled as Rhodes ripped his mouth from hers to stare at me.

"Shit."

I snapped out of my trance and let my eyes fall to the ground. "Uh, sorry."

"It's all good, babe," the woman said, her leathery hand touching my arm as she excused herself from Rhodes' apartment. "We just finished up." She threw a wink back at him and my stomach lurched, my cheeks burning. "See you at the club Monday, stud."

With that, she swayed down the hallway, intoxicated by a high I was sure only Rhodes could provide. She didn't even have her shoes on. She was waltzing away barefoot, her high heels hooked on two dainty fingers over her shoulder.

Rhodes and I both watched her until she was out of sight. I lifted my eyes to meet his again, but he'd already turned his back, leaving the door open behind him.

"Who was that?" I asked, following. I closed the door and tossed my bag on the floor.

"A client."

"Uh huh."

He leveled his eyes at me. "Don't make this about me. I told you thirty minutes. It's been twenty-five."

"Well at least you have your timing down," I scoffed.

"Why are you here?"

His question knocked the cocky smirk from my face. "Willow got into the early admittance program. She's leaving in three weeks."

Rhodes didn't soften his glare or offer an apology. He simply nodded, turning toward his bedroom. "Let me get changed and we can run."

And run we did. We didn't talk the entire time, save for random things I spouted off on my watch, like how the first mile we ran was my fastest mile yet. Rhodes led me through the trail that lined the back of his apartment complex, showing me a side of Poxton Beach I'd never seen before. We ran past a few homeless colonies, their shaded eyes wary of us as we did. I swallowed, running faster to stay close to Rhodes.

I wasn't sure how far we ran, but we were out for at least an hour before we made our way back to his place. Neither of us said a word as we took turns showering, and I knew he really was what I needed most in that moment. I already felt better about Willow, the run helping my thoughts settle, and Rhodes didn't ask me to talk about it if I didn't want to.

Still, after our showers, I sat on one of his kitchen bar stools with my hair in a wet, messy bun and watched as he pre-heated the oven, finally feeling like maybe I did want to talk. Even if just a little bit.

I waited as Rhodes began pulling ingredients and cooking utensils out onto the counter, wondering if maybe he'd ask me to talk about it, but he never did. That was part of his allure, which I knew, so the ball was in my court if I wanted to talk. For a while, I just watched him cook in silence. Every now and then he would glance up at me, but then his focus was drawn right back into the meal. He seemed to be working through something, too. Even while we were running, I could feel some kind of emotion steaming out of him, too.

"She's my best friend," I started as he cut a mango. "It's always been me and her. We had our group of friends and everyone loved Willow, but at the end of the day, it was always us. We were supposed to go to college together. We want to have houses right next to each other. That was always the plan. Get married, have kids…" I trailed off. "I sound so stupid, don't I?"

Rhodes shrugged. "You're going to miss her. There's nothing stupid about that."

"But I wouldn't have to miss her if I were going with her."

"So why don't you?"

I sighed. "I don't want to do what everyone else in this town does. Go to Appalachian State, travel for a while, and then end up right back here. It's like the cycle of life around here."

"Yeah," Rhodes said sarcastically, the knife in his hand clacking against the cutting board. "Sounds awful."

"Oh like you want to be here any more than I do."

"Some of us don't have a choice." He met me with hard eyes. Dumping the mango into a bowl along with diced tomatoes, he continued. "Besides, Appalachian isn't the only college out there. What's stopping you from going somewhere else?"

"My family."

He mixed in a few spices, but didn't look at me when he responded. "It's not your family's life you're living. It's yours."

I chewed on that, falling silent. He had a point. I wasn't sure exactly what it was that was holding me back from making decisions about my future. Part of me did want to go to Appalachian State University. They had a great photography program and Willow would be there. But then again, so would Mason. I could go somewhere else, like an elite art school where I'd *really* learn more about photography, but Dale would fight me on it and that wasn't a battle I wanted to tackle. I was surprised he was even letting me slide with the *I'm taking time off* excuse for not applying to Appalachian State right after SATs. Maybe it wasn't even about college. Maybe it was about the way I felt about myself, the feeling I was trying to change by training with Rhodes.

I was lost. I was frustrated. And though I knew in my head that I had the power to change it, I still felt so helpless.

I sighed, sipping on the water Rhodes had poured me. I had no right to be upset about Willow leaving. I could miss her, but I couldn't feel much else than that. She was following her dreams and I couldn't fault her for that just because I didn't have my own.

Watching Rhodes work, I wondered who the woman was earlier and what they had done. It was stupid to wonder, really, because the implication was pretty clear — but I couldn't figure out why he did what he did. He was young, attractive, smart — he could have any girl he wanted. Why was it the stuck-up house moms who got to live between his sheets? Was it the only way he could keep his job? Why didn't he just work somewhere else, if that was the case?

I traced the lip of my glass with my fingertip, eyes skating with it. "You know you can file sexual harassment against those club members. They can't make you do the extra… training."

Rhodes scoffed. "Don't be naïve."

"Do you choose to do it, then?"

"Yes," he snapped. "I choose to. And stop skirting around the word. I fuck them, Natalie. *Hard*. Long. And until they scream like they used to when they were in their twenties."

I tried to swallow, but found no moisture to aid in the process. Rhodes' scowl was intimidating, but I saw him shaking slightly. And that's when it hit me.

He was embarrassed.

There was a reason he asked me to show up after that woman was gone. He didn't like this part of himself, which prompted my next question.

"Why?"

"Because not all of us have a rich daddy." He slammed the fridge shut with those words, popping the top off a bottle of beer.

"That's not fair."

"Don't talk to me about fair," he said, bringing the bottle to his lips. After a few chugs, he set it on the counter and splayed his palms out, facing me. "My twin sister disappeared when I was a senior in high school and as soon as I graduated, my foster parents kicked me out. The money stopped, right? So why would they want to keep me?" He shook his head. "I was glad to leave though, Natalie. Because being out on the streets without a clue as to what to do with my life was better than being beaten by my alcoholic foster dad every night."

My throat was so tight, so dry. I wanted to say something, but I had no idea what.

"But I made it on my own. It wasn't easy, but I learned real quickly that earning enough to live means not always doing what you want to do. I lived on the streets for months before I figured out the kind of work I could do to make real money. It was drugs at first, and then it evolved into… other things."

"They pay you?" I asked softly.

"Of course they fucking pay me." He shoved back from the counter. "And not shit money, either. I make more off one *session* with them than I do an entire month of working at the club. They toss hundreds around like food scraps." He took another long pull from his beer, his eyes wild. It's like he wanted to stop himself from talking, but he was at the point where he couldn't. "You think I can pay for an apartment on my own with the twenty dollars a training session the clients pays me? You think I'd be able to afford the private investigator I've had searching for my sister for the past three years on the paychecks from the fucking country club?" He wasn't yelling, but I felt anger pouring out of him. "I fuck sad, rich women to pay my bills. I'm a shitty fucking person. Is that what you wanted to hear, Natalie?"

He moved from the kitchen into the living room and plopped down on the couch, draining the rest of his beer before slamming the bottle on the coffee table. I jumped, but he just stared at his clasped hands, his elbows on his knees and his head down.

Cautiously, I moved over to sit next to him. There was something about the torture in his eyes and the tenseness of his jaw that made me want to photograph him. His edges were so hard, but in moments like that I saw his softness. I almost reached for my camera, but thought better of it.

"I'm sorry, Rhodes," I whispered as I sank down in the couch cushion next to him.

He cringed, shaking his head. "Don't."

I bit my lip. I knew saying sorry wouldn't make him feel any better. He wasn't just angry, he was embarrassed — and it was my fault.

"You pay for an investigator?" I asked and he nodded, head still in his hands. I swallowed. "Has he found anything?"

"Not yet," he answered gruffly. "But I have to believe one day he will. Or believe she's dead. I alternate between the two daily."

My eyes skated over his skin as he breathed steadily, trying to calm himself. I watched his chest rise and fall, watched the muscles in his back strain and stretch against the thin fabric of his cut off shirt. I guess I should have been disgusted with his confession about the women from the club, but I only found myself yearning to take away the pain his words were laced with. I knew what it felt like to be embarrassed, to feel not good enough.

Before I knew what I was doing, my fingers reached out, touching the smooth skin of his forearm. He stiffened as I slid them lower, wrapping them around his wrist. He lifted his head to watch me and I tilted his wrist toward the ceiling, my heart thumping loudly in my ears. It was the first time I'd been brave enough to touch him.

"I'm sorry," I whispered again. Rhodes' nose flared, his eyes closed tight. I was shaking, unsure of the movements my body was so confidently making without me, but Rhodes was perfectly still. Carefully, my fingers found the inside of his wrist and I pressed hard. "I can feel your heart too, Rhodes. You're more than what you think you have to be."

His forehead wrinkled as if my words had caused him pain and his eyes connected with mine, staying there for a moment, studying me, asking me for something before they fell even slower than before to rest on my lips. My stomach dropped as his breath came harder and mine did, too — like we were breathing in a fire, filling our lungs with smoke, starving for oxygen. It was the first time I admitted it to myself.

I wanted Rhodes to kiss me.

I waited, my fingertips still pressed into the inside of his wrist. He leaned forward, just a fraction, barely enough for me to notice but enough to make both our heartrates beat faster. I felt his through the vein in his wrist and mine thumping loudly in my ears. When I licked my lips, Rhodes closed his eyes again and let out a frustrated breath through his nose. His rough hand trailed down my arms and hooked around my hand on his wrist, gripping it for just a moment before pulling it away.

"We should eat."

He dropped my arm to the sofa and stood, making his way into the kitchen. I just sat there, my breath still shaky, my lips parted. A wave of embarrassment crashed over me, strong and merciless.

I'd tried to kiss Rhodes, and he'd denied me.

I crossed my arms over my chest and fought against whatever emotion was rising in me, but it was too late. My cheeks hot, I shot up from the couch and hastily grabbed my bag from the floor.

"I'm actually not hungry."

"Natalie," Rhodes started but I didn't even turn to acknowledge him. The door slammed behind me, and I wasn't sure if it was intentional or not but I didn't stop to contemplate it. I didn't stop at all until I was in my car and halfway down the road. The tires on the Rover screeched as I whipped into the parking lot of a Circle K, throwing the car into park and letting my head fall to the steering wheel.

I thought I knew what it was to be embarrassed, to feel like a naïve little girl, but nothing compared to what I felt as I tried to keep myself together in that parking lot. I squeezed my eyes shut, forced them open, tried with everything I had left in me to breathe normally under the wave. But I couldn't fight it anymore. I was surrendering. I was letting it take me under.

And it was in that moment that I realized Rhodes was like lightning. White hot and electric, but fleeting and dangerous. Beautiful to watch, but perilous to touch.

But it was too late for warning signs.

I'd been struck.

# CHAPTER

# 11

Rhodes cancelled our training the next day and I weighed in with a female trainer I'd only seen around the club a few times. Her name was Sophia and she had beautiful tan skin and the tightest body I'd ever seen. I lost another four pounds, and though I should have been happy about it, I couldn't find it in me to feel anything other than disappointed. Because as embarrassed as I was about the night before, I still wanted Rhodes to be there for the weigh-in. Since it had been three weeks, Sophia took my measurements, too — for the first time since I'd started training. I was down inches in every area, and officially, I was a size twelve.

I didn't even celebrate with a smile.

Sophia trained me for an hour after the weigh-in, but her session was a cakewalk compared to Rhodes'. When he cancelled again on Monday, I didn't even go to the club. I ran my neighborhood, instead. Twice. I ran and ran until my legs were numb and my watch hit quadruple digits, then I collapsed in my driveway, staring up at the blue Carolina sky. Clicking the record button on my watch, I decided to talk — even if it wasn't to an actual person.

"My muscles hurt today, but not half as bad as my heart," I started, but then shook my head, realizing how stupid I was being. I didn't need to impress the watch with my words. So, I started speaking freely. "I don't know what is going on in my head." I sighed. "I can't stop thinking about Mason. I know he's with Shay, but not seeing them together has made it easier to pretend that maybe he's not. I want to believe that everything I'm doing to change my life is completely for me but then I think about him and her and I just…" My voice faded off and I watched as a soft white cloud slowly floated in front of the sun, granting me temporary relief from its rays. "He was my best friend. I don't know how to lose him and Willow, both." I swallowed. Saying the words out loud scared me and for the first time I wondered if I truly wanted to be with Mason or if I just didn't want to be alone.

"And then there's Rhodes." Just saying his name sent a familiar pang through my chest. "I don't know what to even say about him." I let the watch record nothing but my breathing for a moment. "He makes me so angry, like I'm forcing him to be my friend. But the truth is that I went into this whole thing knowing that wasn't the case. *He* was the one who made me feel that way, because he invited me over. And he gave me advice. And he made me believe he cared about me." I sighed. "I don't know. He just makes me feel like maybe I have the ability to be someone I only dreamed I could be. He makes me feel powerful, strong, and sometimes… beautiful." I blinked, knowing I was about to admit it out loud for the first time. "And I wanted him to kiss me."

A twinge kicked in my stomach and I sat upright, ending the voice recording on my watch. I had a headache from trying to figure everything out. Talking about it didn't help like I thought it would. Maybe it was because I was talking to myself instead of someone who could offer resolution.

Sighing, I slowly lifted my sore body from the concrete of the driveway and walked to the house, dialing Willow as I did. She didn't answer and I remembered she was still at orientation. And Mom and Dale were still out of town.

I felt as lonely and empty as the house I lived in.

Rhodes finally showed up for our training session on Tuesday afternoon. He was drenched in sweat when I got to the gym and I had a feeling he'd already been there for hours. His fiery eyes caught mine as soon as I walked in and my legs were instantly weak. I wasn't sure if it was from my run the day before or the conflicting emotions running across his face, but I felt like I would fall to my knees at any moment. When I somehow managed to make it to him, I dropped my gym bag to the floor.

Rhodes didn't say anything at first. He wiped the sweat from his face with a small white towel and tucked it into the back of his shorts, frowning as his eyes fell down my body. I swore every part of my skin ignited as his eyes raked over me.

"New clothes?"

I laughed, rolling my eyes and crossing my arms hard over my chest. "Really? That's the first thing you're going to say to me?" Rhodes had a way of bringing out someone inside me who had never existed before. I was bold around him — unabashedly bold. It felt strange and incredible at the same time.

Rhodes swallowed. "We need to train, Natalie. I've been out for two days."

"Oh I'm Natalie now? I'm not *Bug* anymore? And you're right." I pointed at his chest. "*You've* been out for two days. Why was that? Did you not show because of Saturday night?" It was like violent word vomit that I couldn't control. Rhodes confused me, and I couldn't figure out why I allowed him to make me feel embarrassed and sad one moment but then angry as hell the next. Before seeing him in the gym again, I felt like I had myself together. I thought when I eventually did see him, I'd be fine. But the truth was that I wanted to yell at him, to get a reaction out of him — any reaction.

Instead, he just sat there, looking calm and collected and completely unaffected by me standing my ground.

"I had some things to take care of." He nodded toward the treadmill next to him. "Climb on and bump the incline up to four, speed two. Let's get you warmed up."

"So we're going back to you just being my trainer? Is that what this is?"

Rhodes let out a frustrated sigh and jumped off the treadmill, landing hard in front of me. His eyes leveled with mine beneath a scowl. "I *am* just your trainer. Now you can either get on the damn treadmill and warm up or you can walk out. Either way, I'm getting paid. The choice is yours." He snagged my empty water bottle from my hands and walked to the water fountain, filling it up along with his own.

I pursed my lips, but decided not to argue further. Once again, I felt a little embarrassed by my actions. He'd made me feel like a friend… maybe even something more. But now he was insisting he was just my trainer and I his client — nothing more, nothing less. I shook my head, trying to clear it. I needed to train after being away from him for two days and more than that, I *wanted* to train. I wanted to work out every ounce of anger, pain, and sadness I had inside me. And at that moment, I had enough to work for hours.

So we did.

Every time Rhodes tried to end the training session, I begged him for more. I was exhausted, I threw up, my legs and arms were cramping but I didn't stop. Every drop of sweat seemed to take a tiny ounce of my frustration with it as it rolled off the tip of my nose. When I worked my body, my mind was silent — and that's exactly what I wanted.

Finally, after just shy of four hours, Rhodes called it.

"You have to stop, Natalie. You need rest. Go shower and change."

"I'm hitting the pool," I said softly, wiping the sweat from my face and reaching for my bag. Rhodes' hand darted out and caught my wrist.

"I'm serious. You're done for the day."

"I don't want to stop," I said loudly, standing up as tall as I could to look him in the eye. "I have a lot of shit going on right now and the only time I'm not thinking about all of it is when I'm here."

Rhodes' brows pulled down over his eyes and he released his grip. "Fine. But let's at least go to the sauna, instead. You don't have to go home and it'll be good for your muscles. Deal?"

I nodded, grabbed my bag, and stormed toward the locker room. After quickly changing into my one-piece, I joined Rhodes in the sauna. But when I swung the door open and the heat hit me in a rush, I was still somehow frozen in place.

Rhodes was the only one inside and I faltered at the sight of him.

Every inch of his body was covered in a thin sheen of sweat, making his skin glow in the soft, warm light of the sauna. His bright eyes contrasted the darkness and the only clothing he wore was a lone white towel wrapped around his lower half. He was bent over, elbows on his knees, just like he'd been on Saturday night when I'd been bold enough to touch him for the first time. To wish for his lips on mine. When he saw me, his mouth parted slightly and he glanced briefly at my curves before snapping his eyes back to mine. His jaw tensed and I watched him swallow, his Adam's apple straining in his throat.

"You okay?" he asked when I didn't move.

I bit my lip and let the heavy wooden door of the sauna close behind me, leaving us alone and blocked off from the world. In an instant, Saturday night came flooding back to me, along with the embarrassment and anger I'd felt.

"No. No, Rhodes, I am not okay." I tried to say the words with confidence but my voice shook with every syllable. I had no idea what I was about to say but I didn't give myself the chance to think about it. "I am completely and frustratingly confused. You say you're just my trainer but then you look at me like... like that." I thrust my hand out toward him. "Like you have to sit on your hands to keep from touching me." I blanched at my own words and Rhodes' mouth hardened into a thin line, but I kept going. "I never expected us to be anything, okay? I'm not trying to force you to be my friend but you make me feel like I am, when in reality, it's *you* who blurred the line. You invited me over — *twice*. You go from talking to me and giving me advice one minute to making me feel like I annoy you the next." I threw my hands up, exasperated. "You want to be friends? Great. I'd like that. You want to just be professional? That's fine, too. But make up your mind and stop whipping me around like a damn rag doll."

I ripped the door open again and thought about running to the Rover, but decided to walk instead. I knew he wouldn't chase after me, and I held my head high with the dignity I was still managing to hold on to. I did fumble with my keys, though — adrenaline rushing through my veins like never before. The shaking didn't stop until fifteen minutes later when I made it inside my house and closed the front door behind me. Christina was just on her way out, her bags draped over her shoulder, but she paused when she saw me.

"Everything okay, Miss Natalie?"

Closing my eyes, I sighed and nodded. "I'm fine. You heading out?" I forced a smile, but she eyed me questioningly.

"I am. Junior has a baseball tournament in Charlotte. I'll be back on Saturday, though. Will you be okay until then?"

"I'll be fine, Christina," I reassured her. "If all else fails, there's always take out."

She laughed at that and her shoulders released the tension they'd been holding since I walked through the door. "Okay. You have my cell if you need me. And no need for take out," she said as she opened the door. "There are dinners in the fridge with heating instructions." With that, she winked and excused herself.

I took an ice bath instead of a shower, trying to calm both my anger and the raging soreness awakening in my muscles. Working for four hours felt like a solid plan when I was at the gym, but I regretted it now.

When I finished, I dressed in a large t-shirt and boy shorts and fell onto the couch downstairs. Even the thought of reaching for the remote made my body whine in protest, so I audibly sighed when the doorbell rang. With no help to answer the door like usual, I heaved myself up in one motion to get the pain out all at once and waddled into the foyer. Peeking through the peep hole, my stomach fell.

It was Rhodes.

I cracked the door open slowly, trying to hide behind it. My hair was still sopping wet and soaking my t-shirt and my shorts were much shorter than the pants I usually wore to the gym. But when Rhodes saw me, his eyes didn't fall to acknowledge them. They stayed on mine as I noted his still-wet hair and the grocery bags in his hands.

He shrugged. "Hungry?"

"Depends."

"On?"

I shifted. "Am I Natalie or Bug right now?"

Rhodes grinned and the sight of it nearly knocked the air from my chest. "Bug. That is, if I still have the privilege to call you that." He frowned again, waiting for me to respond.

Slowly, I opened the door further. "Come in."

Rhodes' shoulders were still tight as he moved inside. I closed the door behind us but he remained in the foyer. His eyes moved all around the house, taking in the living room and the large vaulted ceiling above it before settling on what little of the kitchen he could see from where we stood. He swallowed.

"Your house is… wow."

I shrugged, grabbing the grocery bags from his hands. "It's not my house. It's Dale's. And you're not cooking tonight."

Rhodes followed me to the kitchen. "I'm starving, though."

"Me too. But you always cook and tonight I want you to talk." I put his groceries in the fridge and cabinets before pulling out one of the meals Christina had prepared. It was baked lemon chicken with zucchini and squash. Pre-heating the oven, I followed her instructions written on the sticky note on top of the container and then turned back to Rhodes. "What does you being here mean?"

Rhodes paused, leaning his elbows on the edge of our kitchen island. "I don't know."

I shook my head. "Nope, not doing that. That's what got us here in the first place. So are we friends or what?"

"Or what." He chuckled, but I pursed my lips and he cleared his throat, running a hand through his hair. "I don't know, Natalie. What if I told you I'm still figuring it out?"

I opened my mouth to argue, but then snapped it shut. I was still figuring out a lot of things, too — so could I really be upset with him for feeling the same way?

"Okay."

"Okay?" he asked, one brow shooting up. "That's it?"

I nodded. "That was honest. That's all I can ask for."

And it was. At the very least, I hoped he'd be honest with me more often, even if it meant hearing something I didn't want to. For now, I didn't want to think about it too much — he was here, which meant he did care about me, and that was enough. I needed him in my corner. After all, I'd already lost Mason and I'd be losing Willow soon. I was just thankful I hadn't completely lost Rhodes, too.

We sat in the kitchen while I made dinner, talking about a little of everything. He asked me more about Willow and her program and I asked him more about his skills in the kitchen. I was careful not to dive into the family territory, not wanting a replay of Saturday night. Rhodes seemed to relax the more we talked and after dinner, I poured us each a glass of wine before moving us to the living room.

"You know you shouldn't be drinking if you want to stay on your meal plan," Rhodes scolded.

I scoffed and reached for the remote to turn on the stereo. Soft music poured from the speakers and Rhodes looked all around us, awe lighting his face. "You know I've had a pretty shitty week and don't exactly care about my meal plan right now, right?"

"Can't argue that, I guess." He cheersed his glass to mine and we both took a sip, but his eyes were appraising me. "You're cursing more now than when I first met you."

"I guess I have more to curse about."

Rhodes laughed, swirling the wine in his glass. "If that's the way it's measured then I should be a sailor by now."

"You practically are."

"Maybe I'm the bad influence, then," he mused. His eyes were playful, his smile easy. Most of the time, Rhodes was shielded under a hard exterior, but in that moment, he was open. I wasn't going to miss the opportunity to find out more about him.

"So," I said, pulling a small couch pillow over my lap. I was more than a little self-conscious about the shorts I was still wearing. "Have you ever thought about going to culinary school?"

"Of course I have."

"And?"

"And I don't have the money for it," he clipped, but he wasn't upset. He was just being honest.

"You can take out a loan."

"It's not that easy, Bug. There are things that still tie me to Poxton Beach... some things that need to be resolved."

I took another sip of my wine, the bitter sweetness tingling on my tongue. "Your sister?"

Rhodes swallowed hard and took a long pull from his own glass. I immediately regretted bringing her up again and cursed under my breath.

"I'm sorry. It's not my business."

"It's fine," he breathed, but I noted the way he gripped the glass tighter. "I don't want to *not* talk about her. She deserves to be talked about." He paused, eyes on his hands. "And yes, she's the biggest reason why I can't leave yet."

I chewed my lip. "Do you think she'd want you to stay?"

"Fuck no." He said the words with absolute certainty. "She'd probably kick my ass if she knew I was still here, especially if she knew what I've done since she disappeared." His eyes caught mine for a moment and he looked back down at his lap. He was thinking about the drugs, the women, and embarrassment shaded his cheeks. "She'd tell me to get the hell out of here and go live my life. But I can't do that yet." He shook his head, lifting his eyes to mine again. "She wasn't just my sister, she was my twin — we're tied together in ways that other siblings just aren't. And something inside me tells me if I look long enough, if I try hard enough, I can figure out what happened to her. And I owe that to her." He paused. "I can't leave without answers, Natalie."

"And if they never come?"

His shoulders lifted slightly and he drained the rest of his glass even though I still had over half of mine left. "Then maybe I never leave." Setting his glass on the coffee table, he stood and looked around the room, effectively ending the conversation. But I let him, because I knew with Rhodes I was lucky to get everything I had already.

"Oh my gosh, I'm so rude," I said, quickly standing to join him. "My mother would murder me if she knew I hadn't given you the tour yet."

"That's a little extreme," Rhodes said, a hint of a smile playing at his lips.

"Well, she's an extreme woman," I said. "Come on."

We toured the bottom floor first, everything from Dale's office to the four car garage. I led him upstairs next and watched him closely as we went from room to room. His eyes were wide, but he didn't say much. He just took in everything I told him about each room and sipped slowly on the second glass of wine I'd poured him before bringing him up. When we reached my room, he walked the walls slowly, his eyes scanning the photographs lining every inch of the soft, mint-colored paint. My room was small for the house, but gigantic in comparison to his. Mom hated that I covered the walls with photos but she knew there was no way to stop me. Photography was the one thing in the world I was unapologetically passionate about.

"So this is why you always have that damn camera with you."

Every wall was filled with memories. Some of my family, some of my friends, and some of just Poxton Beach scenery. One of my walls was dedicated completely to places I'd traveled with Dale and Mom. My favorites were of Mykonos, an island in Greece we traveled to last summer. Rhodes traced his finger over the bright blue water in a shot I'd taken on the beach, the beautiful Grecian architecture lining the horizon in the background.

"Stunning, isn't it? It's even better in person."

"It's beautiful," he said, shaking his head. "I can't even imagine seeing a place like this."

"Maybe you will one day."

A short, soft laugh escaped his lips. When his fingers lightly brushed the newest addition to the wall — one of the photos from the night of the fair — he paused, and I wondered if maybe he realized it was so much better seeing it in real life the same way I did. We were both quiet for a long moment.

"What are you afraid of, Rhodes?" I asked softly, moving a little closer to him. He kept his back turned, his fingers still lightly on the photo, and for a moment I thought he might not answer.

"Starving." He just barely whispered the word, but it was loud enough to knock every other thought from my mind. "I know what it feels like to be hungry. In many aspects." He turned to me then, his eyes slightly glossed over, like he wasn't quite there anymore. "Nothing scares me more than the possibility that I may never cure that hunger."

I swallowed, but didn't comment. His eyes fell over the rest of the photos on the wall and then he turned, scanning the others. "There are no photos of you. There's your family, your friends." He turned back to me. "But none of you."

I laughed lightly. "Yeah, well, I'm not exactly worth taking a photograph of."

Rhodes' brows pulled inward and he went to speak, but then he glanced around again. "Wait. Where is your bathroom?"

"Um, through that door," I replied, pointing.

He moved past me and through the bathroom door, flicking on the light. He peered around for a moment and then turned back to me. "You don't have a single mirror in your room. Not even in here."

I shrugged. "Mirrors aren't exactly my thing either, Rhodes."

"Why?"

I let out a sharp laugh this time, gesturing to my body hidden behind the baggy t-shirt. "Seriously?"

His face hardened and he dropped his glass on my bedside table before taking mine from me, too. Grabbing my hand in his, he pulled me down the hall.

"What are you doing?"

Rhodes didn't answer. He opened door after door until he found our master guest room. It was my mom's favorite, the one she always reserved for the most important guests we housed. When Rhodes pulled me in front of the grand full-length mirror set up beside the bed, I cringed.

"Stop, Rhodes," I said, pushing against his chest to try to move him toward the door again.

"No, Natalie." He grabbed my arms and turned me back toward the mirror. Rhodes was standing behind me, tall and picturesque as always. His hair had dried naturally and had a soft wave to it. His defined jaw matched the cut muscles that ran along the arms he still had holding me firmly in place and his electric eyes were hard on mine. "Tell me what you see."

"I see you."

"Don't look at me," he commanded, his voice firm. "Look at yourself and tell me what you see."

I sighed, but let my eyes fall from his to my own. They were a dull brown, no life sparkling behind them.

My skin was oily, my face bland without any makeup on, and my dark blonde hair was lying almost pin-straight over my shoulders. I swallowed as I let my eyes fall further. It wasn't that I didn't ever look in a mirror — I saw myself in the gym mirrors and when I was anywhere in public — but I never studied myself this way. I could see that I'd lost weight, but I was still far from looking anything like Willow or Shay. I had curves. I had large breasts, thick thighs, and big hips.

"I see everything I still need to work on and everything I don't want to see when I look in the mirror five years from now."

Rhodes breathed heavily behind me, but he didn't say anything. I watched his face in the mirror and saw a mixture of emotions cross it — from pain to confusion and everything in-between. Slowly, he moved to my left, staring intently at me as I still faced the mirror.

"Show me."

The way he said those two words made me shiver. He commanded attention, he always did.

"Show you what?"

Rhodes swallowed, stepping a little closer. "Show me what you hate."

I let out a shaky breath, my eyes roaming all the imperfections of my body. "Well, my stomach—"

"*Show* me," Rhodes interrupted. "Don't tell me."

Swallowing, I lifted my hands from where they rested at my sides and gently touched my stomach. I knew it was smaller than just a few weeks before, but it was still thick — there was still a roll when I sat down and I had muffin tops that fell over my tiny shorts.

"Lift your arms."

I looked at Rhodes questioningly, but the way he stared back — his eyes intense and determined — I didn't question him out loud. I lifted my arms above my head and waited. Rhodes' throat constricted and he seemed to be battling with what he was about to do, but before I had the chance to think more of it he grabbed the hem of my shirt and carefully pulled it up and over my head.

My heart accelerated from a slow trot to a full-throttled gallop. He was stripping me. Rhodes was stripping off my clothes.

Slowly, he bent to his knees and glanced up at me. I could never forget the way he looked kneeling below me — vulnerable, yet still so strong. He pulled his eyes from mine long enough to wrap his large hands around my waist and press his lips gently to my stomach.

And I remember it hurt that first time he touched me. Not because it was painful, but because it was everything but. It hurt from somewhere deep inside my gut that told me I would never get to have him, to keep him, or to feel the way I felt with his hands on me with anyone else for as long as I tried.

"Where else?"

His eyes were lifted to mine, and though my heart was still racing, I somehow managed to move my hand to touch the upper part of my opposite arm. Rhodes stood, grabbed my hand in his to straighten my arm, and then kissed where I had just touched.

I was catching on.

My breaths were ragged, but I moved my hand to the next area without him asking. I didn't know if I was supposed to be looking in the mirror, but I couldn't pull my eyes from the sight of him. He bent and moved with each new place I touched, following it with a sensual kiss.

My breath caught in my throat as I touched my inner thighs. I couldn't believe I was doing this, that I was standing in front of a mirror practically naked with Rhodes touching me in ways I'd never imagined. He licked his lips before falling back to his knees and tucking his fingertips into the top band of my shorts. I gasped at the touch, and he inched the fabric off my hips slowly before letting them drop to the floor.

I was standing in front of Rhodes in nothing but my bra and panties, and though I felt like squirming, hiding, or running away, the weight of his gaze held me locked in place. His eyes flicked to mine and he kept them there as he leaned in to press his lips to my left thigh. I couldn't help it, I moaned low under my breath and he gripped the back of my legs tighter as his lips moved to the other thigh.

When he looked back up at me waiting for the next direction, I swallowed. I knew it was a bold move, but I felt alive in that moment — completely unstoppable. With shaking fingertips, I reached up and just barely touched my lips.

Rhodes lifted himself from the ground, towering over me once again. I could see how I was affecting him through the thin fabric of his gym shorts and my breaths came harder. I was turning him on. It seemed impossible and yet it was true, which only fueled my confidence. "You hate your lips?"

I didn't answer. I *didn't* hate my lips. In fact, they were probably what I loved most about my body. They were plump, a deep pink, and I religiously used lip balm to keep them soft. Rhodes knew we'd moved past touching what I hated about my body. I wanted him to kiss me. I didn't know if I should want that, if I could even allow myself to want it, but I didn't fight it in that moment. I just waited.

Rhodes bit the inside of his bottom lip, his brows pulled down low over his bright emerald eyes. They flicked to my mouth and back to my eyes several times, as if he were debating the same thoughts I had just had.

"Natalie," he warned, but at the same time his hands moved to cradle my face between them. My lips parted and I let my eyes fall to his. I desperately wanted to taste him.

"Rhodes," I breathed back, my hands finding his waist. I let them rest there, still waiting. Rhodes expelled a breath, shook his head just barely enough for me to notice, and then closed the space between us.

Heat is never a sign of something good. It's an indicator that you're burning, a symptom of an infection, a side effect of fever. But the heat I felt when Rhodes touched me — when he kissed me — was the best sensation. It was white hot and electrifying. It seared my skin and blazed through every inch of my body. It burned me. It *scarred* me. But I loved it.

My hands fisted in his t-shirt as he deepened the kiss. His tongue slipped inside to massage mine and I moaned into his mouth, making the erection in his shorts grow even more noticeable. Hastily, he pulled me back onto the guest bed and we fell into the soft goose down comforter, the fabric swallowing us like a cloud.

Rhodes' hands explored my body as he kissed me. He sucked my bottom lip between his teeth before moving to my neck and across my collarbone. I was breathing so hard I was sure I'd hyperventilate. I'd never experienced a kiss so passionate, so laced with desire. His hand was rough, callused from the weight bars as he dragged it down my neck, over my breast, across my stomach and finally rested just above the hem of my panties. I squirmed beneath his touch, anxious to feel his hand just a fraction lower.

Rhodes sighed, stilling his movements and resting his forehead against mine. "There's so much I want to do to you, Bug. I'm fighting against it right now."

"Don't," I breathed.

"You don't understand."

I ran my fingers through his hair and pulled him closer, kissing him with more confidence than I knew I had. "So help me. Help me understand."

He groaned against my lips and I could feel him pressed against my thigh. He was so hard, so ready, and I was physically uncomfortable waiting for him to deliver.

"Not tonight," he finally said, sighing. "Tonight is about you seeing that you're beautiful. Do you hear me?" He waited for me to lift my eyes to his. Suddenly, the confidence I had before was completely gone. "You are, Natalie."

I nodded, but I wasn't sure I really believed his words. I was cute, maybe — and even that was pushing it. But when Rhodes brought his lips back down on mine and kissed me like it pained him not to, I thought maybe there was something he saw that I just didn't.

We stayed tangled in the sheets for hours, but all we did was kiss. His hands explored my body and I explored his. He never stripped down with me, and I never reached to pull my clothes back on. We buried ourselves under the sheets, making us a hot, sweaty mixture of lips, breaths, and moans.

Now I understood what he meant when he said *or what* earlier, because this was far from how you treated someone who was just a friend.

Sometime around midnight, Rhodes paused. "I should go."

I was breathless, cheeks heated, hair a mess as I stared up at him. I didn't want him to go, but I couldn't ask him to stay — not when he'd already given me so much that night.

"Okay. Let me walk you out."

After I dressed and fixed my hair back into a bun the best I could, I walked him to the front door, mind racing. I had so many questions, but none of them would form on my tongue.

"I wish you didn't have to go."

He smiled a lazy smile, his hair still mussed from our activities. "You'll see me Thursday."

My heart sank. In a way, he was telling me that I wouldn't see him on my day off from training tomorrow. When he noticed my face fall, he pulled me into him for a long, soft kiss, sliding his index finger to rest on the inside of my wrist like he had the first time he told me he felt my heart. It was an unspoken promise, but he broke away too quickly for my liking and jogged off to his bike. It took him less than a minute to fasten his helmet and then he was gone.

I closed the door in a daze. I felt numb, yet every nerve in my body had been awakened. I stumbled to the couch and fell against the cool leather cushions, though they did nothing to stunt the heat growing inside me. I could still feel Rhodes pressed against me. I could feel his lips on mine. Something deep in my gut told me I should be scared, that I should worry about what was happening between us. And, though I wanted to ignore it, a small part of me thought of Mason in that moment. I thought of how different it was to kiss him and wondered what he would feel if he knew another man had kissed me the way Rhodes just had.

A smile spread across my face and I covered my eyes with my hands, letting out a short squeal. I refused to overthink it. At the end of the day, no matter what was to come, I had enjoyed it.

It was the best damn kiss of my life.

# CHAPTER

# 12

I was a mess the next day. I felt elated, but mostly sick, and I barely ate — which was a new sensation for me since I usually turned to eating when I was overly emotional. When I was with Rhodes the night before, everything felt right — but the moment he left, the uneasiness set in. I second-guessed everything, wondering what version of Rhodes I would get the next time I saw him. The more I thought about how quickly he had left the night before, the more worried I became. Was he going to be with another woman? A *client*? The thought crippled me, which also terrified me, because I felt so intensely for him in such a short span of time.

And what if he was just trying to get away from me? What if he changed his mind? What if he didn't want me the way I wanted him?

I watched episodes of *Lost* and worried myself with questions I couldn't answer the entire day. Somehow, the euphoria I'd felt after his lips left mine the night before was replaced by this sickening realization that it could have meant nothing. I had a pit in my heart that told me I would walk into the gym the next day and he would be gone. Or worse, there — but not in the way I wanted him to be.

Then, just as those feelings would take over, I would sit up in shock at the fact that I wanted him. I *wanted* Rhodes. I wasn't sure exactly what I wanted from him, but I knew it was more than just a training session at the gym five days a week. Mason was still in my head, too — which only complicated things. I was a mess, and without my mom or Willow to talk to, I was sure I'd go mad.

Dressing in one of the new workout outfits Mom and I had purchased, I tried to hold my chin high as I strode into the country club that Thursday.

I saw him before he saw me.

He was lying on a weightlifting bench, his strong legs braced on either side, the muscles of his arms tightening and releasing as he bench pressed more than I weighed. No one was spotting him, but he made it look so effortless — as if he didn't need help and never would.

I wondered if that were true in many aspects of his life.

After a few more reps, he set the bar back into place and sat up slowly, wiping his brow with the same white towel he always had with him. He tucked it back into the back band of his shorts, and then his emerald eyes were on me.

I couldn't breathe.

I waited for him to frown, or curse, or roll his eyes or shake his head. I waited for him to order me to a treadmill or ask what the hell I was doing wasting training time just staring at him like an idiot. All of those things I expected.

But Rhodes just smiled.

That smile lifted the pressure from my chest and I inhaled like it was my first breath.

It hadn't been a dream. It was real. It was all real.

Rhodes' eyes stayed fixed on mine as he crossed the room to where I was standing. He crossed his arms, legs spread shoulder-wide in a confident stance. "Really?" he asked, shaking his head. His eyes trailed from my own to take in my full appearance. "You choose *today* to wear shorts for the first time?"

I glanced down at the tighter-than-preferred black shorts my mom had convinced me to buy. My legs were getting toned, and I had to admit — the squats were paying off nicely in the glutes area — but I knew I was far from looking like the other girls at the club. Eying Rhodes through my lashes, I tucked a loose strand of hair behind my ear. "I look stupid, don't I?"

His smile fell. "Hardly."

Rhodes looked around the room, as if it weren't safe for us to speak, then he nodded toward the back office. "Come on, let's check your numbers."

I frowned. "But it's only Thursday."

He gave me a pointed look that told me not to ask any more questions before leading me back. Once the door was closed behind us, he motioned to the scale and I stepped up. Rhodes sidled up beside me, looking at the numbers on the scale that I refused to acknowledge. I just looked at him, instead.

"Did you forget everything I said to you the other night?"

I laughed, but Rhodes didn't. "I don't think I'll ever forget anything about that night." I blushed at the admission, but Rhodes just offered a soft smile.

He leaned in closer, but paused, resting his hand on my lower back so lightly I thought I might be imagining it. "You are beautiful, Natalie," he whispered. A chill sparked where his hand touched my skin and traveled in all directions until it covered my entire body. "I can't touch you the way I want to while we're here, the way I did two nights ago, to show you that. So, I need you to just start believing it."

I nodded, though I was far from believing I was beautiful. Rhodes clearly had on goggles I wasn't yet accustomed to. Still, hearing his words, I wanted to believe him — I wanted to feel beautiful.

Rhodes cleared his throat and removed his hand quickly. "Good. Come on, we have work to do. Only two more workouts until weigh-in day."

He didn't tell me what the numbers were on the scale and I was grateful. The rest of my life was such a mess — I needed something scheduled, something reliable and stable. Weigh-in day was Sunday. I needed that to look forward to and dread all at the same time.

Rhodes worked me just as hard that day as he usually did. It almost felt like normal, except his hands touched me more, his eyes almost never left me, and the energy between us caught fire.

When our session ended and I all but limped to my gym bag, I waited for Rhodes' next move. I half expected him to dismiss me like usual, but the other half of me was anxiously awaiting something — anything — that meant I wouldn't have to say goodbye yet.

Rhodes held up his hand for a high five and it took more energy than I cared to admit to meet his hand with my own.

"Nice job today. See you same time tomorrow?"

I was smiling, but I couldn't help the disappointment I felt when I realized the first half of me was correct. "Okay."

He grinned, a sexy, not-safe-for-the-gym grin, and then turned toward the men's locker room. It was when his hand left mine that I realized he'd replaced it with a small, folded piece of notebook paper.

*Dinner. My place. 8 o'clock.*

*Bring your camera.*

Biting my lower lip, I shoved the note into my bag and made my way out of the gym. The workout was over, but the heartrate on my watch display only climbed higher. It took eight words to send my body into overdrive. Just eight words scribbled on an off-white sheet of paper.

Rhodes was better cardio than a marathon.

"Did you bring your camera?" Rhodes asked as he hand-washed our dishes from dinner. I was full and sore and exhausted, but being with Rhodes somehow made me feel like I could run miles.

Nodding, I slid up next to him, grabbing the soft blue towel hanging from the oven and using it to dry each dish as he finished. "I did. Why?"

"Do you have the photos you took at the fair still on it?"

"Yes?" I said the word almost as a question.

He nodded. "Go grab it."

Rhodes took the last dish from my hands and finished drying it before dabbing his own hands on the towel and following me over to the couch. He fell down onto it easily, propping his feet on the table as I rummaged through my bag for my camera. When I had it powered on and pulled up to the photos he referenced, I sat down carefully on the middle cushion of the small couch. Though I wasn't hugging the opposite arm like usual, I was still nervous to sit too close to Rhodes. I felt like he was a caged animal. One wrong move might send him running or cause him to attack. I wasn't sure which was worse.

But as soon as I sat, Rhodes pulled me into him, wrapping his arm around my shoulder. I stiffened before easing into him, focusing on my breaths. He was dressed in relaxed sleep pants and another Poxton High

School weightlifting t-shirt. His hair was still damp from his shower, mussed, and sexy. He was always so sexy.

Am I just now noticing that? Or just now admitting it?

"Show me the photos you took that night."

"I hate all of them, just so you know," I prefaced, scrolling through the photos with him looking over my shoulder. "I couldn't capture what it felt like to be there."

Rhodes studied each photo carefully, stopping me if I scrolled through too quickly. When we reached the end, I watched his face with curiosity. His brows were furrowed, his eyes contemplative.

"You don't feel in control of your life."

He said the words as a statement, not as a question, and so I didn't answer. I kept my eyes fixed on his, though suddenly it was difficult to swallow.

"Looking at the pictures on your wall and at those you just showed me, there's so much control in the shot. It's almost *too* by the book, like photography is the only thing you think you can fully control and follow a manual to figure out."

His words hit me square in the gut and I had to fight the urge to double over from the weight of them.

"It's not that you don't shoot beautiful photos, because you do," he clarified, sitting up straighter. His arm left my shoulder in the process and I reached out to touch his leg, desperate to be connected. "But I see what you don't see, Natalie. I see the beauty in the

192

imperfections of the world. I think you need to look a little closer."

My breaths were loud, my voice hoarse. "You don't see the beauty in you."

Rhodes' face hardened and he pulled away from my grasp, propping his elbows on his knees and clasping his hands together. He stared forward at the television, though it wasn't powered on. "There's nothing beautiful about me."

My heart ached, and I reached for him once more. He flinched when my fingers found his back, and he remained still — almost statuesque — as I trailed them lightly up until I found his neck, his hair, and I pulled him close.

"You told me I had to start believing I was beautiful," I said, louder than before but still just above a whisper. "If I do, then you do, too."

Pressing his forehead to mine, Rhodes shook his head slightly. "I'm not like you, Natalie. Can't you see that?" He exhaled, the air leaving his lungs and reviving my own. "I stayed away from you for so long because I know who I am. I know what I'm capable of." He pulled back, his intense eyes locking on my own. "We both know I'm going to hurt you. It's one of the reasons we avoided this for so long. Admit it," he said, swallowing. "You know I'm not good for you."

I chewed my bottom lip, blindly thumbing at the settings on my camera until I knew they were where I wanted them. His assessment couldn't be farther from the truth, in my mind at least. He was maybe the only thing good in my life that summer. Slowly, I lifted the camera, and snapped one, single photo. It was close — too close to focus without taking more time — but I didn't know if I'd have it. I expected Rhodes to hide or flinch or turn his body away, but he didn't. I aimed the lens at his left eye, the one that always squinted slightly when I knew he was thinking about something he wouldn't speak out loud. Glancing at the photo on the camera screen, I smiled, and then showed it to Rhodes.

"How's this for looking a little closer?"

Rhodes smirked, his eyes hard on the photo as if it were the only one he'd ever been in. For all I knew, it very well could have been. Slowly, I slipped my hand into his and pressed my index finger hard to the inside of his wrist. I felt his heart pulsing through the vein, hard and steady, but nowhere near as fast as mine. He moved his own finger to mirror mine, and we were connected, hand to hand, heart to heart, and I'd never felt closer to anyone in my entire life.

Rhodes wrapped his index finger around my wrist to join the rest of his fingers and he gripped tight, pulling me into him and closing the distance between us. His lips found mine in a mixture of passion and need. I moaned instinctively, which only made Rhodes kiss me harder.

I could sense him holding back. His hands gripped me hard and I winced, though not from pain — from the shocking pleasure of it all. Still, a small wrinkle formed where his brows met and he kissed me softer, taking his time. When my hand slipped under his shirt and fingered the hem of his boxers, he growled, lifting me hastily from the couch. I wrapped my legs around him and it felt natural — like I wasn't as heavy as I knew I was. He held me as if I was just a dainty doll, but he eyed me as if I were a vixen. He wanted me. I could feel it pouring out of every inch of his body, and I'd never experienced a power rush quite so strong.

He threw me onto the bed when we reached his room, quickly pulling off my tight jeans as I maneuvered out of my shirt. My heart kicked against my ribs in an unsteady rhythm as I stripped for the second time in front of Rhodes. The first time I'd felt self-conscience and unsure, but this time, my need to be skin on skin with Rhodes outweighed my embarrassment. For a moment, I let myself believe I was beautiful — just like he'd said.

Rhodes fell down on top of me, bracing himself on his elbows. My fingers found the hard muscles of his biceps and I gripped them tight, holding on for dear life. He lifted me just enough to unsnap my bra and toss it to the side and then his mouth was on my breast, sucking hard, awakening every sleeping cell in my body.

I bit my lip, soft moans escaping through the slight opening of my mouth. Rhodes trailed his rough hand down my skin, leaving an electric fire in its wake, until he found my center. He didn't even bother removing my panties. He swiftly moved them to the side and before my brain could process what was happening, he slid two fingers inside me.

I cried out, the intense pleasure surrounding me.

"Christ," Rhodes muttered, and I wasn't sure if it was a curse or a prayer. He removed his fingers slowly before reentering them once more. His arms were tense and I felt him focusing on his breaths. He was restraining himself, touching me gently as if he was afraid he'd break me.

It was a slow build, and I wriggled beneath his hand, asking without words for him to move faster, harder, deeper. He would give in, give me what I want, and then pull the reigns back once more. Cupping his hand around me, his palm massaged my clit each time his fingers slid inside, the combination stirring an energy deep inside me. I pulled my lips between my teeth and bit down harder, stifling my moans. Each time I released them, Rhodes would catch them with his own lips. They were plumping, swelling from the pressure and the pleasure.

My cheeks were on fire as I squirmed, holding my breath. There was something slowly coming together inside me. It was a cool fire, and I reached for it as much as I cowered away.

"It's okay to let me know you like it, Natalie," he breathed, slowing his movements. I felt every inch of his long fingers as he slid them in and then withdrew them. He was steady, calculated, the perfect equation for impossible satisfaction. "You can moan, or scream…" His words trailed off and he sucked my nipple. Hard. "Or say my name."

I moaned, arching into him. His erection was pressed against my inner thigh and I desperately wanted him inside me, but I knew that wasn't his intention. He wanted me to come apart at the touch of his fingers, and I was only moments away.

"Let it out," he demanded, this time a bit louder. His hand moved faster, his fingers hitting a spot inside me I'd never known existed. I moaned a little louder, but it wasn't good enough. Rhodes flexed his hips, lighting my insides on fire. I groaned, but again, I knew he wanted more.

He removed his fingers long enough to make quick work of my panties, and then I was completely naked in his bed. He still had every stitch of his clothing on, but I was fully exposed — spread out, panting, *needing*. Rhodes' eyes devoured me, breath hitting his chest like a fist. It was a constant battle — he would take me hard one moment and pull back the next. I was the elixir for everlasting life and he wanted to drink me slowly and yet consume me quickly and all at once. I felt his own need radiating like heat from his body, but he subdued it with each breath.

Hooking his hands around my hips, Rhodes yanked me to the end of the bed and then stopped himself, dropping to his knees slowly and finding my eyes with his own before sliding two fingers inside me once more. His teeth raked over the flesh of his bottom lip when I moaned and slowly, with restraint, he lowered his mouth to my clit.

Oh. My. God.

As soon as his hot mouth surrounded my sensitive skin, I moaned uncontrollably. Each flick of his tongue mixed with the pressure of his fingers inside me in a deadly dance. My moans turned to screams, and though I gripped the sheets and tried to hold on, I flew off the edge, losing every ounce of balance left in my already unsteady world.

It was like a wave, slow and steady at first and then crashing down on me all at once. I was drowning, suffocating, fighting for air as the electric current ripped through me. I didn't just scream Rhodes' name, I moaned it, and cried it, and offered it up to the gods as an excuse for the sin I knew I'd never let go.

When the sensation passed, my legs fell lax against the sheets and I closed my eyes tight. I had no idea what I sounded like to Rhodes, but my cheeks blushed from embarrassment the moment the unbridled passion faded. He kissed up my body slowly, taking his time, leaving no inch of skin to feel jealous of another. When his lips found mine again, he kissed me slower, softer, and his eyes were open, fixed on mine.

"That was incredibly sexy."

I shook my head. "That, I, I've never, I don't—" Words were lost. *I* was lost.

Rhodes's eyes widened and he pulled back, propping himself up on one elbow. "Wait," he said the word tentatively, brushing a strand of my fallen hair from my face. "Was that your first orgasm?"

"Is that what that was?!" He laughed a little at my reaction and I blushed harder, covering my face with the sheets. "I thought I'd had one before. I thought I knew what it felt like. But that…"

"That… what? Say what you want to say, Bug."

Dropping the sheets, I leaned up to mirror his position. "That was the hottest thing I've ever experienced."

Rhodes grinned, slowly dragging his teeth over the tender, swollen flesh of his bottom lip. Sliding his hand up my neck until his thumb brushed my jaw, his smile faded. "You're the first girl I've ever wanted to take my time with," he whispered, shaking his head. "But then again, I feel like I'm racing against time. Like I only have so long to touch you."

I covered his hand resting on my cheek with my own, leaning into him. I didn't know what to say, because as much as I wanted to tell him he had all the time in the world, he was somewhat right about what he said earlier. I did feel what he felt — like what we had was fleeting.

A soft smile found his lips again when I didn't answer. "That was nothing, by the way. You have no idea, Natalie."

And maybe I didn't.

But I couldn't wait to find out.

# CHAPTER

# 13

So that's how it was.

Rhodes trained me like normal, and he never touched me inappropriately in the gym. We were client and trainer, behaved and natural. He pushed me harder, and I fought him less. He smiled more, which made me do the same.

Rhodes loved to touch me when we weren't in the gym.

He brought me pleasure in ways I'd never experienced before, yet we still hadn't gone all the way. In fact, I had yet to give *him* a release, which bothered me. When I would try, he would tell me to wait. For what, I didn't know. But, I didn't argue — the truth was, I enjoyed his attention. We were practically inseparable, and I was learning more about him every day. He was even opening up about his sister, though those conversations were few and far between. When he let that part of him be seen—when he opened himself to me — those were the times I loved the most.

With Mason, sex was always rushed. It was sloppy and purposeful — we went until he grunted out a release and collapsed on top of me. I thought that's all sex was, but before Rhodes had even touched me — when he had only heated me with his gaze — I knew there was more.

And *God*, did Rhodes show me more.

I lost the desire to talk to Mason at all. After the way he let me down at the fair, I wasn't even sure who he was anymore. And the more attention I got from Rhodes, the less I cared about the lack of attention I was getting from Mason. Soon, his texts became fewer and fewer, he gave up trying to get me to talk to him, and I fell easily into my new reality with Rhodes.

But every now and then, Rhodes would slip into the same person I met at the beginning of the summer. He would shut down, block me out, or be evasive. Sometimes, he would have to leave my house to "go somewhere" or "do something", but he never told me what. I questioned him a few times, but he would always change the subject or tell me not to worry, which in turn only made me worry more. I didn't want to suspect another woman, not with the way he looked at me, but that's where my mind immediately went. Sometimes I could talk myself out of it, but then my mind would go to even darker places. Because if it wasn't another woman, what exactly was it? Mostly, I just felt this uncertainty deep in my stomach. Something was off, but he wasn't telling me what.

It was just over a week later at our Sunday weigh-in session that I knew I was losing him again.

"Oh no..." I stared at the number on the large glass scale in Rhodes' training office, the same one I'd seen the Sunday before, and I felt my stomach sink. This was it, I'd hit my limit. I was failing.

"It happens, Bug," Rhodes said, but he seemed distracted as he scribbled something on my file. "We'll switch up your diet and cardio, see if that helps and go from there."

"What if it doesn't work?"

Rhodes pursed his lips, shaking his head slightly. "Then we'll figure it out."

"How are you so sure?"

"Because I know what I'm doing. I've trained hundreds of women. This happens to everyone. It's called a plateau."

I flinched when he mentioned how many women he'd *trained*, because we both knew what usually went with that. I shuddered once more when I realized that, technically, I was one of them.

But that was a lie.

Because I knew, deep down, that I was more to him. Or maybe I just *wanted* to know that. I longed for that reassurance. That was what both terrified me and gave me hope at the same time. Rhodes wasn't an easy break. I knew there was more of him to discover. But just like he didn't treat me like any of the other women in his life, I was determined to help him find his own value. He looked at me as if I were an investment — something he believed in — and I saw him in the same light.

"I feel like I'm failing."

Rhodes pinched the bridge of his nose. "Natalie, you've lost twenty-six pounds. In just over a month. Trust me, you're fine."

I could tell I was annoying him, but I couldn't stop myself from talking. "Did I do something to upset you?"

"Other than complain about a problem that isn't a real problem? No." My mouth popped open. He glanced up from where he was scribbling on his notepad and sighed, tossing it on the desk. "I'm sorry. I just have some shit going on."

I chewed my bottom lip and fought against the urge to reach out to him. Rhodes was adamant about keeping our relationship private, if that's even what you would consider it. Whatever we were, we existed outside of the club. Here, we were just a customer and a service provider.

"Talk to me about it. Maybe I can help."

Rhodes scoffed, and the sound was so harsh I tucked my arms tight across my chest.

"Trust me. You can't."

"How do you know if you don't tell me?" I asked defensively.

"Can you just let it go?" He pleaded, his eyes finally meeting mine. They were darker than usual, a green forest with a storm looming. "Please?"

Sighing, I nodded, but I didn't feel good about it. I wanted him to talk to me, and that was the first time I realized that what we had — whatever it was — was on his terms.

"Crap," I muttered under my breath when I checked my watch. "I think I drained the battery again."

"Did you leave the voice recorder on?"

Silence.

He sighed, and I half-hoped I could muster a smirk from him, but it didn't happen. Instead, he just dug through the top drawer of the desk and handed me a new battery. We were done talking for the day.

Rhodes wrote up suggestions for my meal plan and sent me to do cardio. Then, without another word, he left. I watched the muscles in his back flex as he moved farther away from me. Once he disappeared through the men's locker room door, I frowned.

I'd barely cracked him open and already I was losing him. He was pushing me away, and my heart sank at the thought of what it would mean if he succeeded.

Mom and Dale came home from their trip that night. Dale was drunk, or high, or some sort of messed up. It was the first time I'd seen him like that, *really* seen him like that, and Mom tried but failed to hide it.

She ushered him to their room quickly when they got home. I was lying on the couch watching *Lost*, debating on calling Willow. We hadn't seen each other much since she'd returned from orientation and her going away party was in less than a week. Truth be told, I'd kind of fallen off the face of the earth. Mom and

Dale had been gone, Willow was busy getting ready for school, and I had no other distractions to keep me from Rhodes. Even Mason had left me alone.

I heard my parents arguing upstairs, their voices muffled but loud enough that I knew whatever was happening wasn't good. It's not that they hadn't fought before — every couple had their issues, right? But it seemed more intense that summer, more saturated.

When the slam of the door upstairs echoed down through the living room, I paused the television, waiting. Mom snailed down the stairs, her hand lightly brushing the railing, her eyes swollen and puffy and streaked with mascara. Even still, she was beautiful. Mom was always so beautiful.

Rhodes had evaded me at the gym earlier and I knew Mom would try to do the same. Everyone was trying to hide me from something — shield me — but I didn't want to live in a world where everyone knew the truth but me.

Mom slunk down onto the couch beside me and I softly hugged her, resting my chin on her shoulder as we both stared at the paused television. She was done crying, or so it seemed, and I watched the tears dry on her cheeks. After a few moments, I finally spoke.

"Mom, what's going on with you and Dale?"

She shook her head. "It's nothing, sweetheart. It'll be fine." She patted my leg and I ground my teeth.

"Stop that. Talk to me, Mom. What's happening?"

Mom paused, but I could tell she felt my insistence. I wasn't going to let it go. "I don't know, honey. Dale has an… addiction."

The air in the living room grew heavier, and I felt it weigh in around my ears. "What do you mean?"

"Oh honey, I don't want to talk about this. It's fine. He's okay. *We're* okay. I promise." She smiled at me, but I still found it difficult to swallow. Dale had an addiction? How had I never seen any of the signs? Dale had a few drunken nights, sure. He liked to party, he liked to let loose — but an addiction?

I shuddered at the thought.

Then, I studied my mom closer, and wondered what this addiction meant for her. I'd never once questioned that he could lay a hand on her, but seeing her so upset that summer made me think twice. My mom was strong, she always tried to handle her issues on her own, but would she really keep something like that from me?

She sniffed, leaning away from me just an inch.

"Mom, I know you think you need to be strong for me, but if he's hurting you, you can tell me. We can leave. We can figure this out together."

She laughed at that, shaking her head and wiping her nose on a tissue. "Oh stop. You and I both know Dale would never hurt me." She said the words, I almost believed them, but something in her eyes told me she doubted their truth, too. It made my stomach lurch.

"I love you," I whispered. I didn't say it much to my mom, but I did — I loved her fiercely. She gave up more than I would ever know for me as a child, and I wasn't sure I could ever repay her. Thinking of Rhodes and how easy it was for his parents to just abandon him when they were in a similar situation, I realized how truly lucky I was.

"I love you too, sweetie. So," she said with a pop, wiping the remaining tears from her face and replacing them with a smile. "Tell me all about what you've been up to since I've been gone."

Though I wanted to ask more questions about her and Dale, I knew that wasn't what Mom wanted — so I humored her. I told her about Willow's program and about the going away party Saturday. I caught her up on the latest developments in *Lost*, which made her giggle. I filled her in on every stupid, boring detail of my life in the last few weeks.

I left out everything about Rhodes.

Later that night, Rhodes texted me that he was outside. I didn't ask questions, I just carefully snuck out of the house, nearly running to the end of my street where Rhodes had dropped me that night after the fair.

He was leaning against his bike, one foot kicked up on the side, arms crossed, head down, and only the moon revealed that he was there at all. He almost blended with the darkness. I guess in a way, he kind of *was* darkness — and I was just a tea light candle trying to illuminate him.

When I reached him, I slowed my pace, hesitant to get too close. From the way he was acting earlier, I wasn't sure the purpose for his visit — was he breaking things off? Did we even really have anything *to* break off?

His eyes lifted slowly to mine when I stopped in front of him.

"Can I take you somewhere?"

I didn't answer. I simply grabbed the spare helmet from where he'd strewn it across the seat, strapped it on, and straddled the leather. Rhodes climbed on in front of me and sparked the bike to life, and then we were off.

We drove for almost an hour, and I could tell we were a ways from Poxton Beach. When he finally slowed, we pulled into a small park, and Rhodes quickly parked before smoothly climbing off the bike and helping me do the same. He held my hand in his as we made our way to one of the picnic tables beneath a small pavilion.

The park didn't have any lights, and in all honesty, it was more worn down than any of the ones I'd ever played at as a child. The dark red paint was chipping off the tables and benches, two of the swings were missing a chain or a seat, and the jungle gym was in desperate need of a facelift.

I sat on the edge of the picnic table Rhodes led us to, but he remained standing. He stared across the park, his hands tucked into his pockets, his bright eyes wider than I'd ever seen them before. I waited for him to drop the bomb. I could feel it, he was ending it — he was ending *us*. I wasn't even sure what we were, but I knew with more absolution than I'd ever had in my life that I didn't want it to end. Not yet. Not like this.

He blew a breath out of his nose, and that breath lay suspended between us. I held my own, afraid of tainting his, afraid of what that breath meant.

"We used to come here every Sunday when we were little." Rhodes' arms flexed, and he tucked his hands deeper into his pockets. "Our foster parents always had their card games on Sundays, and the house would fill up with strangers, smoke, and booze. So Lana and I would ride our bikes out here. My old house is right up this road," he said with a nod toward the street we were just driving on. I noted how he called it a house, not a home.

"We would play around for a while, but eventually we always ended up on the swings. I tried to swing higher than her, and I always fell on my ass trying." I smiled, but Rhodes' expression hadn't changed. He licked his lower lip and swallowed, shaking his head. "Today is her birthday."

His words hit me softer than they should have because I didn't quite understand their magnitude. I'd lost my grandmother when I was really young, but I had no idea what true loss felt like. Staring at his face as his own loss engulfed him, I was sure I'd never want to.

Rhodes was opening up to me, and it was such a rare occurrence that I didn't dare interrupt him with my own words. I held the *I'm sorry* between my teeth and let him continue.

"She would have been twenty-two. She probably would have had a boyfriend or a fiancé. She always said she wanted to be a lawyer, the kind that are assigned to foster kids, so maybe she would be graduating this year with her bachelor's. Maybe she'd be applying to law school. Or maybe she'd have a couple of years left before that. I have no fucking idea because I haven't amounted to a damn thing in my life. I have no concept of school or goals or what it takes to make something of a person."

I wanted to pipe up then, to tell him he wasn't worthless, but he shook his head to stop me.

"And I was a complete dick to you today because I don't know how to handle her being gone," he said, his eyes finally finding mine. His voice didn't break, but I saw how cracked he was beneath the baritone. "And I'm sorry. Because you didn't deserve it. You don't deserve any of the shit I give you."

I stood then, wrapping my arms around him and planting small kisses on the exposed skin of his arm. He stiffened at first, not returning my embrace, but then finally, his arms went slack and his forehead fell down to rest on top of mine.

And that's when I realized.

"If it's her birthday, that means…"

He nodded against my shoulder bone. "It's my birthday, too."

A pang shot through my chest and I held him tighter.

"Every year on this day, I'm reminded that I'm still here and she's not. I can't even think of celebrating another year of my life when I can't be sure when hers stopped. Or *if* it stopped." He lifted his head, eyes on mine. "And the worst part is that I may never know which it is."

"I know," I whispered, pulling him in closer, just barely touching my forehead to his. "I'm here, Rhodes. I'm right here."

He breathed in once.

Let the air out.

And then he kissed me.

He leaned back, sitting on the table and pulling me to straddle him. My legs fell on either side of him, my feet resting on the bench seats, my core pressed firmly against him. Rhodes gripped my hips and I fisted my hands in his shirt, returning the urgency, letting him feel the need. He bucked his hips to meet mine and the friction evoked a guttural moan from my lips.

I tried with every kiss to erase the crease in his brow, but I never succeeded. Rhodes kissed me and touched me and brought me to the edge of desire with all of our clothes still intact on a frail, beaten down picnic table, all the while with a pained expression on his face. He touched me as if it hurt. He kissed me as if it were the last time.

And somewhere inside my heart, I felt the demise, too.

# CHAPTER

# 14

Dale apologized to me as I cooked an egg white omelet the next morning. His dark eyes were framed by even darker circles and his black hair fell greasily onto his face. He looked like shit, and in a way, I hoped he felt like it, too.

He wanted to make up for the night before, even though it was really Mom he should be apologizing to, so he asked if he could take me shopping. He'd noticed my clothes were fitting loosely with all the weight I'd lost, and he wanted me to have something perfect to wear to Willow's party on Saturday. Though I wanted to be mad at him, Mom seemed to already have forgiven him, and I loved him enough to want to be able to do the same.

Plus, I really did want to look good for Willow's party. It would be the first time Mason and everyone else would see me since the fair, and I was anxious to see their reactions. Nervous, but curious, still. It wasn't that I wanted Mason back anymore, because I didn't, but I still wanted him to see that I was doing it, I was changing my lifestyle — for me, not for him.

Realizing her party was so near, I invited Willow to tag along with us. I missed my best friend, and soon, she'd be far enough away that I wouldn't be able to cure missing her with just a phone call and a trip to the mall. I wanted to take advantage of it as much as I could.

"I can't believe you waited until now to tell me all of this!" Willow whisper-yelled at me in the dressing room of a chic little dress boutique. I'd just filled her in on the Rhodes situation that had developed quickly in her absence, and she was pretty much losing her mind. "I mean honestly," she added, pulling her small breasts to rest higher in the bright pink dress she was trying on. "This is insane. You. And *Rhodes*. Do you hear how weird that sounds?" She paused. "Does he even have a first name? I only know him as Rhodes."

I giggled. "Actually, I don't know. I only know him as Rhodes, too." I made a mental note to ask him about that later. "And trust me, it may seem that way, but it's not as strange as you're making it out to be. We kind of… fit. We balance each other."

"So are you dating him now?" She quirked a brow.

"No, not exactly."

"What exactly does *not exactly* mean?"

"It means I don't know what we are. We're having fun, I guess."

Willow groaned, whipping around and motioning for me to undo her zipper. "Don't, Nat. Don't let him play that game with you. If y'all don't title it or give it some sort of definition, one of you is going to end up hurt." She turned to face me once the zipper hit her lower back, shimmying out of the soft fabric. "My bet is on you."

"Yeah, I get it," I said, sighing. "Stop mothering me now and let me tell you about the mind-blowing orgasms." I blushed at my own words and Willow's mouth popped open.

Braiding her long dark hair to the side as we exited the dressing room, she gushed. "Spare no details, woman. I want them all."

When Dale wasn't around, we talked about Rhodes, which was more therapeutic than I thought. I hadn't told anyone about him, and telling Willow what I'd been experiencing with him made it all feel real. She also made me talk about Mason, which solidified that I really didn't have a desire to be back with him again. Still, she and I both wondered what it would be like for me the next time I saw him face-to-face, which would be at her party that weekend.

We found my outfit for the party almost three hours into our shopping trip. Surprisingly, Dale was patient with us the entire day, and he only pumped me full of encouraging praises each time I tried on something new. With every passing minute, I forgave him more, and I realized I wasn't in any position to judge him when I had my own issues to deal with.

After we dropped Willow off at her place, Dale turned down the radio in the Vette. It was a hot day and the top was down, but the air was dry, and I knew that would fade the deeper we got into summer. Eventually, the air would be so sticky it'd be hard to breathe.

"I know I apologized this morning, but I wanted to say I'm sorry again. It can't be easy seeing your mother cry and I hate that I'm the reason behind her tears." I listened to him intently, my hands folded in my lap, but his eyes remained on the road. "I battle with a lot of inner addictions, Natalie, but I'm not a fiend. I have myself under control, and I'm working on handling the small parts of myself I may not have completely mastered yet. I think we all have demons, don't you?"

He turned to me then, and his dark eyes were so sad, so torn, I knew what happened the night before was wearing down on him. I smiled, grabbing his hand with my own. "It's all good, Dale. I know you love my mom, and she loves you. I'm sure you two will work out whatever is happening between you."

Dale squeezed my hand once and I pulled away, looking out my window. I thought maybe Dale would say more, but he just reached to turn up the volume again. Before he did, I thanked him — for the day out of the house, for the new clothes, and for his honesty. He smiled, swallowed, and gave a curt nod.

There were still so many questions in my head — for Rhodes, for my parents, for life in general — but at the same time, I felt like I was finally finding some sort of footing. My body was changing, and it seemed it was morphing my mind, my goals, my expectations, and so much more right along with it. I didn't know where the summer would end, but in that moment, I didn't care. With the sun on my skin and the wind in my hair, I felt alive — adventurous, free, and maybe confident, too — even if just a little.

I missed my training session with Rhodes the day of the shopping trip, so I went for a long run instead. Running was becoming a sort of release for me. I would click on the voice recorder on my watch from time to time to talk through some of my struggles or just jot down random things I wanted to remember later, and I was getting better at remembering to turn it off at the end — though I wasn't sure I wouldn't drain another battery or two.

Rhodes cancelled our session on Tuesday, and his texts were few and far between. By the end of Wednesday, my day off, they had pretty much diminished altogether. Suddenly, the happiness I felt earlier in the week had faded right along with them. When I parked the Rover in front of the club on Thursday, I had to give myself a pep talk to walk inside.

I wanted to believe it would all be okay, but I knew better.

My first clue should have been the dark storm clouds rolling in. I didn't think much of them, though — just pulled my light jacket tighter around me as I hustled inside. Three strikingly gorgeous women walking out of the training room caused me to slow my steps. They were all laughing, and the pack leader — a tall brunette with long legs and a nose job — clearly had the amusing story responsible for their giggles.

"It's kind of fun pushing his buttons," she said in a voice too nasally for my taste. "I mean *honestly*, he must know that his… *services*… are all he's good for."

I kept my eyes down, adjusting my bag on my shoulder, but I slowed down even more to catch the next part of the conversation.

"I will say, for Poxton Beach trash, he definitely has more than a few talents hidden beneath that scowl of his." They all giggled at that and my fist tightened around the strap I was holding fast to. I knocked into the woman a little harder than necessary as I passed her and she stumbled a bit.

"Excuse you," she scoffed before returning to her posse. I kept walking, and she kept being a bitch. "It's kind of a shame. He'll never be more than a good lay, but I guess there are worse things to be."

Those were the last words I heard before I stepped into the training room the women had just left. I didn't have to look hard to find Rhodes. He was sprinting on the treadmill, its unsteady tracks rocking each time his feet made contact. He stared straight ahead, his mouth pursed, his face hard, and my heart squeezed.

I had no idea what Mrs. Nose Job said to him, but if his strained jade eyes were really windows to his soul, I could see how badly they'd bruised him. He already felt like he was nothing, and these women knew exactly what to say to him to keep those thoughts in place.

"Hey," I said timidly, dropping my bag to the ground in front of his machine. He continued running, keeping his eyes trained on the window ahead of him, but he slowed his pace. "Ready to train?"

It's as if those words snapped him out of his daze. "Yep." The word popped off his lips and he dropped down hard next to me, motioning to where he'd just been. "Hop up. We're starting with cardio."

I tried not to analyze it, but Rhodes remained quiet throughout the entire training session. I wanted him to apologize again, to say I didn't deserve his silent treatment, to say it wasn't my fault — but he didn't. After two hours and one of the most grueling sessions we'd had yet, I attempted to break through.

"Are you busy Saturday night?"

"Probably."

I stuttered at his bluntness, but tried to swallow the embarrassment. "Oh. Well, it's Willow's going away party. I was sort of hoping you would come with me."

"No."

"No?" I asked, but Rhodes just grabbed his water bottle and took off in the opposite direction. I followed. "Why not?"

"Because I might have plans."

"Might? You won't make plans with me, your..." I trailed off. *What was I to him?* "You won't make plans with me because you *might* have plans?"

"Damnit, Natalie." Rhodes huffed, looking around at who might be listening. We were the only ones in the training room, so I dared him to try to make that excuse. "I'm not going to your friend's party. Or on any dates, for that matter."

I wouldn't exactly have classified Willow's party as a date, but hearing him say that derailed my thoughts. "Why not?"

"Because you're my client."

"That's it?" I asked, my voice breaking. I could feel my heart close on its heels. "We're back to this again?"

He didn't answer, and his silence fueled my anger.

"Really. Huh. Well, I guess you just decided to toss in your *extra services* free of charge then, right? So gracious!" I regretted the words as soon as they left my mouth, but my pride wouldn't let me take them back.

Rhodes stopped mid-stride. He was walking away from me, but my comment had cut that motive short. For a moment, he just stared at me, his eyes hollow, and almost questioning. It was like he couldn't believe I'd said that to him, like he wasn't prepared for that hit — not from me. I thought I saw him wince, his mouth opening slightly before he closed it again.

Then, he smirked — but not in a friendly way. Rhodes smiled in a way that made me want to cower in the furthest corner of the room.

"Yeah, Natalie, I guess so." He shook his head. "You're welcome. I hope I lived up to my reputation."

I sighed. "Rhodes," I started, feeling like a fool, but my apology was cut short. One of the women who'd been with the pack earlier sidled up beside Rhodes. His eyes had intensified to almost a neon green and they remained fixed on me as he threw his arm around her shoulder.

"Ew," the small blonde said, swatting at him playfully. She was the shortest of the group I'd seen earlier, but by far the prettiest. "You're all sweaty." She laughed a little before appraising me, her smile faltering just slightly. "Who's this?"

"This is Natalie. She's a client." He said the words so harshly, as if they were the nails to drive his point home. His eyes were wild. They mirrored my heartrate. "And we just finished up. See you tomorrow?" He asked me the question, but we both knew he didn't expect a response.

"Rhodes," I blurted out, boldly reaching for his arm. He shrugged out from beneath my touch as if it offended him. "It's *me*. Please. Don't do this."

The woman under his arm looked bored, and she pulled out her cell phone to type out a text. I thought I saw Rhodes falter, I thought I saw him soften, but he frowned so quickly that I couldn't be sure if I'd imagined it.

"Do what?" His jaw tensed.

I moved closer, whispering so only he could hear me. "Don't leave with her. Please, Rhodes. This isn't you. You *can't* do this. Not after everything we've done... everything we've become."

His nose flared and his eyes wouldn't meet mine. He waited. For what, I wasn't sure. Clearly, nothing I could say would stop him now. He had given me the final push, throwing me to the cold hard ground, and even though it killed me, I didn't try to get back up again.

I could let him walk away from me, but I couldn't bear to watch this time.

So I turned first.

My feet numbly carried me through the club and to my car. I started the engine, put the gear in drive, and the rest was a blur. My mind raced, thoughts blending together in a colorful disaster as I drove. Rhodes was going home with that woman tonight, and I felt physically ill at that realization. Even worse, I'd pushed him there. I knew he was upset, I knew those women had said something to him, but instead of giving him space or trying carefully to help him when he pulled away, I threw his way of life in his face. I brought up his *services*, making fun of him, letting him think I saw him the same way everyone else did.

Now I felt sick for a completely different reason.

Eventually, I found myself at the park he'd taken me just a few days before. I pulled out my camera and took pictures without studying the frame. As the soft shutter button sounded over and over again, I wondered if Rhodes would have been different had his sister not disappeared. I snapped the swings, their empty seats blowing in the wind of the impending storm, and I imagined a younger Rhodes there. I asked myself if he would have looked peaceful, if he would have smiled, if he would have laughed — all questions I had no answer to.

I sat on the same picnic bench he'd kissed me on just a few nights before. I could still feel his lips on mine, hear his words in my ear as he told me I didn't deserve the shit he gave me. But the strange thing was, I wanted that pain. I wanted to help him when he felt low, push him up to solid ground, carry him when he couldn't carry himself. But he didn't want me.

Even after everything, he would lay with another woman that night, and what killed me most was that I knew he was better than that.

The first echo of thunder rumbled the playground around me and filtered through my core, twisting in to fill the gaps between my guilt and anger. It shook me so hard I dropped my camera, the strap around my neck the only thing saving it from shattering.

If only I'd had a safety strap, too.

# CHAPTER

# 15

Sleep didn't come that night. I was restless, tossing and turning, twisting in the sheets and huffing out in frustration when my mind still wouldn't shut off. When dawn finally broke, I pretended to be asleep long enough for Mom to wake me up to have breakfast with her. She and Dale were leaving in just a few hours for another business trip, and Mom wanted to make me pancakes — even though they weren't on my meal plan and Christina was already there and could have cooked, instead.

I didn't fight her on it.

Once they left, the silence of our large house surrounded me, but I found it strangely comforting. I expected to feel more broken than I did. Was I just numb? Maybe. Or maybe I knew this would happen all along. Had I ever *really* thought I'd be able to keep Rhodes?

My training appointment came and went with me still lying in bed. I didn't bother to call or text Rhodes and let him know I wasn't coming and he didn't reach out to me, either.

I did somehow manage to find enough motivation to call Willow, who then drove over as fast as she could. She greeted me with ice cream, but I asked her to go for a run with me, instead. And though Willow was tiny and fit, I kept up with her pace, and when she wanted to quit, I still had steam left. It was the first time I realized I was stronger.

Maybe in more ways than one.

Willow stayed the night, but left early the next morning to get ready for the party. I still felt strange that morning, but not as numb as the day before. In a way, I was ready. I was ready to celebrate my best friend's accomplishments. I was ready to say goodbye to her, at least for the rest of the summer. And I was ready to face Mason and the rest of Poxton Beach. Because as much as Rhodes had wounded me, he had strengthened me just the same.

I knew eventually, I would have to face him again. I'd have to come to terms with the fact that I couldn't have him, not the way I wanted, and I wasn't sure if there would even be a friendship between us at all again. Maybe he would go back to just being my trainer. Maybe he'd pass me off to someone else. I couldn't be sure, but I decided to try not to dwell on it.

For one night, I was going to just be an eighteen-year-old girl.

I was going to have fun.

Moses drove me to Willow's around nine o'clock. I planned on drinking, *a lot*, and Moses was happy to be my safe ride. He probably didn't realize he'd also be my confidant, too.

"I'm nervous, Mo."

He smiled, glancing at me quickly before facing the road again. "Why is that, Miss Natalie?"

I fidgeted with the black and white pleather fabric of my skirt. It was a sort of snakeskin pattern, high-waisted, and I'd paired it with an equally slimming black, scoop-neck tank top. My newly toned legs and arms were on display, my jewelry was loud and blingy, my hair was falling in soft waves over my shoulders. I was wearing an outfit that demanded attention, and I wasn't sure I was ready to handle it.

"Remember when you picked me up from The Crawl earlier this summer and I was a complete mess? Well, I'm facing the people who made me that way tonight, and I thought I was ready, but every mile you drive makes my stomach hurt worse."

Moses chuckled, but didn't say anything. I didn't expect him to. That was part of Moses' appeal — he listened. So, I kept talking. By the time we pulled up to Willow's house where the party seemed to already be in full swing, I had not only confided my fears about the night, but also all of my worries tied to Rhodes. I didn't know if Moses would judge me, but if he did, he didn't show any indication of it. He put the Rover in park and set his hands lightly in his lap.

"You'll be okay, Miss Natalie. You're not as timid as you think you are. I can see a confident, stronger version of yourself waiting to emerge. You just have to let her out." He winked. "Text me when you're ready?"

I smiled, nodding, and placed my hand on the door handle. Hesitating, I quickly wrapped Moses in a tight hug and thanked him. Even though he hadn't said much, it had been exactly what I needed. In a way, I knew he was right — I did feel a stronger me just below the surface. I only hoped I could finally bring her up for air.

Moses squeezed me in return and gave me a reassuring smile when I pulled back. Blowing out a long breath, I ignored the nerves and opened my door.

No one was outside, but I could hear the music spilling out onto the driveway. Willow loved to celebrate, and I knew she would go all out for her last party in Poxton Beach.

Surprisingly, I didn't fall flat on my face walking up her cobblestone drive to the door. I was wearing high heels — not wedges, not kitten heels — but high, red pumps. They were the only pop of color in my entire outfit other than the red lipstick I'd let Willow convince me to pair with them. When I reached the door, I placed my right hand on the handle and felt the music and laughter vibrating through it. Taking one last deep breath, I relaxed my shoulders, swallowed, and gently pushed it open.

It wasn't like a movie — not everyone stopped what they were doing to turn and look my way. In fact, nothing stopped as I walked in. Cliques were spread throughout the house, and I smiled at a few people I recognized as I wandered around looking for Willow. It was in her large living room that I noticed the effect I had on people apparently came once I had already passed. I heard a quiet whisper ringing out, and when I glanced over my shoulder, several heads snapped in the opposite direction. They were staring at me.

Oh God, I wasn't ready.

"Natalie?" Dustin was the first to approach me. His eyes that reminded me so much of Mason's were almost as wide as his mouth. "Wow. You look—"

"Amazing? Incredible? Sexy as hell?" Willow had popped out from the kitchen and was bellowing toward me, her voice much louder than I preferred, calling even more attention to us. "All of thee above?"

She pulled me in for a tight hug when she reached me and I squeezed her in return, trying to ignore the eyes I had from practically every person in the room. When Willow pulled back, she gave me a reassuring wink and I smiled in return.

"Pretty much all of that," Dustin said, chuckling.

"Thank you," I murmured. I tucked a strand of my curled hair behind my ear and cleared my throat, looking to Willow as if she would have the answer for what I needed to do next in this situation.

"Let's get my best friend a drink."

"Let's."

There were still a lot of eyes on our backs as we retreated to the kitchen, but the noise of the party gradually increased until it was back to normal. I downed the first fruity drink Willow mixed up for me, which just made her laugh and mix a new one along with a straight shot of the rum she'd used to make it. She poured one for herself, too, and we clinked our shot glasses together before throwing them back. My limbs warmed and I smiled.

"Do you feel weird?" Willow asked, sipping from her own bright pink solo cup. Of course she couldn't go with regular red ones at her going away party. Pink wasn't really her favorite color, but she did love all things girly. Plus, the cups matched her outfit — bright pink shorts that showed off her long dark legs paired with a crisp white crop top. She was the brightest thing in the house. In my opinion, she was the brightest thing no matter where she was.

"I should be asking you the same thing."

She shrugged. "I don't feel it yet. I mean, I know I'm leaving on Monday, but I guess I just know I'll be back on weekends sometimes and for holidays. It just feels like a temporary goodbye, nothing serious."

"At least it's an excuse to throw a party, right?"

Willow pointed at me. "Exactly." Giggling, she laced her arm through mine and dragged me out to her back patio area where they'd just lit her fire pit.

The energy Willow exuded was infectious. She was so bubbly and confident, and I soaked it up like a sponge. We were laughing loudly, making jokes, dancing and playing drinking games I'd only ever watched from the sidelines before. Mason and Shay showed up about a half hour after I did, but I barely noticed them. I was too busy letting loose to care if they were there.

They, however, definitely seemed to notice me.

After finally losing a game of flip cup after a three game winning streak, Willow and I stumbled into the kitchen to grab some water. We wanted to last all night, so it was time to rehydrate a little. We were sipping from our cups, still laughing, when Shay and her friend from the fair walked in.

I tensed immediately.

"Interesting outfit choice, Natalie," she mocked. "For a girl of your size, I mean." Her friend, who I remembered to be named Tawnya, placed a hand on her hip and giggled. I was waiting for them to high five themselves for their awesomeness. How was I ever afraid of these two? How did these self-centered bullies ever intimidate me?

"Bitch, I will cut—"

I held up my hand, stopping Willow's sentence. She eyed them manically before turning to me with a more questioning stare. I just smiled and shook my head.

"Oh, are you actually going to try to defend that hideous skirt? This ought to be good." Shay nudged Tawnya, flipping her long brown locks over her shoulder.

I flinched at her insult, fingering the hem of my skirt, but the insecurity only lasted for a moment. The more I watched her lips curl, the stronger my urge to kick her in the face became. Since I wasn't sure I'd still be standing if I tried to balance my weight on one of the heels I was wearing, I chose to use my words carefully instead of my foot.

"You know what, Shay? This is *my* town. These are *my* friends, this is *my* best friend's party, and you're only here because you took the sloppy seconds of *my* ex-boyfriend and thought that made you one of us. Well guess what? It doesn't." I could feel the same quietness that surrounded me when I first entered the party creeping up again. Everyone was watching us. "I'm still trying to figure out where Mason's lapse in judgement came from when he decided it'd be a good idea to date you, but since you have to be here until he wises up and realizes he can do better, maybe you could stop obsessing over how I look and what I wear and worry about your own damn self?"

Shay's mouth popped open and Tawnya's followed. Adrenaline was coursing through my veins at the speed of a freight train. Inside I was shaking, but I didn't let it show.

"Come on, Willow." I laced my arm through hers and strutted toward the back door. "We have a game to win. Oh, and since I know you're watching," I added, throwing one last glance over my shoulder at Shay's white face. "How's my ass look, Shay?"

The kitchen and living room both broke out into a mixture of laughter and *oooh*'s. Willow was cracking up and I bit against my urge to do the same. When we finally made it outside, I let it out.

"Oh my God! I cannot believe that just happened. I fucking love you." Willow wrapped me in a crushing hug before turning to the party that was outside. "My best friend is the sexiest bitch alive!" Everyone laughed and a few of the guys whistled. I only blushed in return.

I didn't see Shay or Mason at all in the next hour. They either left or stayed inside, either option worked for me. It felt good to stand up for myself, even if I did have to stoop to her level to do so, but after the adrenaline crashed, I made my way up to Willow's bedroom to gather myself. I thought I'd escaped alone, but Willow tailed me, closing the door softly behind us and falling down to sit on the bed with me.

"I'm fine, Lo," I said with a sigh. "Go back to the party."

"Listen, as much as I want to believe that, especially with your little show in the kitchen, I know there's something bothering you." She winked when she mentioned my showdown with Shay, but her smile fell quickly. "You're thinking about Rhodes, aren't you?"

I chewed my lip and nodded, just the mention of his name making my stomach drop. The adrenaline rush had practically sobered me, which just let all the thoughts consumed with him crash in all at once.

"I just… I almost wish none of it had ever happened, Lo. I wish I would have stopped prying. If I could have just left him alone, let him train me and then gone home and forgot about him until the next session, maybe none of this would have ever happened. He's either going to treat me like I'm just a client again or he's going to make it where he never has to see me. Either option kills me."

And it did. My stomach may have dropped at the sound of his name, but it twisted and ached at the thought of completely losing him. I was angry with him, I was hurt, I was confused, but I still yearned for him. I had no idea how to handle what was happening.

It was Willow's turn to sigh. She shook her head, grabbing my hand and giving it a gentle squeeze. "The worst part of all of this is that now you know what having more of him is like. That's what changes everything, and that's why you're struggling with wanting it back and wishing it never happened at all." She shrugged, her brown eyes softening. "Ignorance is a blessing as much as it is a curse. You can't crave what you don't know exists."

The truth of her observation hit me harder than anything Rhodes had said to me two nights before. I wasn't sure what it was that I was feeling until Willow laid it out in front of me like a photograph.

A knock at the door startled both of us. It slowly opened, and suddenly my adrenaline was back. Or was it nerves? I couldn't be sure. Mason was standing in the frame, hands in the pockets of his faded jeans, messy brown hair curling at his ears and falling into his eyes slightly.

"Hey," he said timidly, looking to me first and then Willow. "Could I... um... would you mind if I talked to Natalie for a second?"

Willow's face was stone. She'd invited Mason and Shay only after I'd convinced her that she needed to.

She was hell bent on keeping both of them away after she found out what had happened at the fair, but I knew it would kill Mason not to be there for her last night in town. Mason and Willow were almost as close as Mason and I were, and I didn't want Willow to have to choose. Still, as Mason waited for her to respond, I swore I could feel the daggers she was throwing his way piercing my own skin.

"Depends. Are you going to be an ass like Shay tried to be?"

"Willow," Mason said softly, shaking his head. "You know I never would be. That's part of why I'm here." He cleared his throat. "I just wanted to apologize."

Willow sniffed, seemingly debating his sincerity. After glancing at me to check if I was okay with it, she pulled her long hair to the side and lifted herself from the bed. "Fine, but don't make me kick your ass, Mason Carter."

Once Willow pulled the door closed behind her, Mason stepped further into the room and it was just the two of us. The last time we'd been alone in a room together was under much different circumstances, and I tucked my hands under my legs at the discomforting comparison.

After a minute of silence, Mason crookedly smiled, shaking his head. "Natalie, you look incredible."

My cheeks heated and I looked down at my red heels, crossing my ankles. "Thanks, Mase."

"I'm really sorry for what happened with Shay."

"It's fine. I handled it."

At that, Mason laughed. "Yeah. So I heard." Feeling more comfortable, he took the empty seat on the bed next to me. "I can't remember you ever standing up for yourself like that, Natalie."

I shrugged. "Well, I never felt strong enough to do it before now."

Mason's eyes softened, and I could tell it was from pity. Pity for my insecurities or for his own ignorance of them, I wasn't sure. Either way, he was staring at me in a familiar way that made me want to curl up under the covers with him. I didn't want anything more — just the friend who'd left me behind. I couldn't decide if I was angrier with myself for wanting anything at all from him or confused because before Rhodes, I wanted a lot more.

"Why are you even with her, Mason?" I couldn't stop myself from asking. "She isn't right for you. She's awful."

"She's not always like that," he defended, but he still ran his hand through his messy hair and sighed. "I guess I hoped being with me would change her. The first night I met her, she showed me a vulnerable side. She doesn't show it to anyone else. Most of the time, she puts her guard up." His eyes met mine. "Kind of like how she did tonight with you."

"I don't think that's a guard, Mase. I think that's her being a bitch." I blushed at the curse word and Mason laughed.

"Maybe you're right. I don't know, I do care about her but…" I swallowed as his words trailed off because he'd moved closer to me, his jeans touching my bare leg. "I have to admit, something is missing."

I didn't have to guess what he meant by *something* because his Adam's apple bobbed in his throat and his eyes fell to my lips. He was thinking of kissing me, and my heart raced at the thought.

Suddenly, the door to Willow's bedroom flew open.

"Uh, Natalie?" Willow asked, panic evident in her voice. "Did you invite Rhodes?"

Mason and I both jumped up from the bed, each for a different reason.

"He's here?"

She nodded.

I glanced at Mason briefly, his face as shocked as mine, before brushing past Willow and flying down the stairs. Willow was on my tail, yelling how he'd just walked in and poured himself a drink. She'd asked him what he was doing there and he said I'd invited him.

And technically, I had.

I tried to remain calm as my foot hit the bottom stair. It took no time at all to find him. The room had cleared where he was standing, which was at the edge of the fireplace in Willow's living room. He was casually leaned against it, one hand tucked in his pocket and the other lifting a pink solo cup to his lips. It was almost comical, except I couldn't find it in me to smile.

He probably didn't notice, but I knew the volume of the party had decreased. People were staring at him, though they tried not to make it obvious, and whispers were flying everywhere. Seeing him standing there so strong and unaffected made it hard to breathe and when his eyes met mine, I gripped the banister of the stairs to steady myself. I needed to know why he was there and what that meant, but before I could build up the strength to walk across the room, Mason's voice broke through.

"Wait, Natalie," he pleaded, grabbing both of my hands in his own. "I don't know what's going on with you and that guy, but you have to know your options before you make your next move." He swallowed and I internally freaked out. "I've been going crazy trying to figure out what's missing with Shay, and seeing you tonight, I know now what it is. It's you. It's us. It's our friendship and our once in a lifetime love that I stupidly threw away." He squeezed my hands in his and stepped closer. "I want our movie nights and our long drives around town. I want our family cookouts and days at the beach. I want to kiss you whenever I feel like it." Mason inched even closer and I stepped back. "I want you, Natalie. I want you back."

My eyes flicked to Rhodes, and even from the distance I could see his jaw tensed. His hand was gripping the cup he was holding with more force than necessary, the pink plastic warping from the force. I needed to say something, but I had no idea what.

I looked back to Mason, who smiled softly. "Please, say you feel the same." His hands cupped my face and he slowly brought my lips toward his. My breath hitched, everything stopped, and my insides were screaming for me to react but I couldn't.

"Mason, wait."

"I've been waiting all night to say this," he said, his lips dangerously close to me. "I'm not waiting any longer."

He was drunk, I could smell the liquor on his breath, but that wasn't why I didn't want him to kiss me. I *should* have wanted him, that was always the plan, but I just didn't. I tried to find the words to explain, but I couldn't.

Or should I say, I didn't have the chance.

Just before our lips met, Mason's hands ripped from where they were cradling my face as a fist crashed into the side of his. In an instant, he was on the ground, curled into fetal position, crying out in agony. His hands flew up quickly to cover the wound but the blood poured through them. I snapped my eyes up to the force responsible and was met with Rhodes' hard glare. His nose was flared, his eyes wild, and he glanced once at Mason on the floor before turning and rushing toward the door.

"Oh my God!" Willow sprang into action, dropping to the floor where Mason was still crying out. Dustin quickly followed and the rest of the room crowded around us. My eyes found Mason before searching out Rhodes again in the crowd. My heart was racing. My fingers were icy cold.

"Natalie," Mason groaned, reaching out for me. I stared at his hand, but then looked toward the door. When I looked back once more, Mason's eyes were wide. He dropped the hand covering his face and

I winced at the sight of his eye and cheekbone. They were both already swollen, his brow was busted open and blood was leaking down the side of his face. "Don't go. Did you see what he just did? He punched me. He almost hit *you*, Nat. The guy's a monster!"

I swallowed, searching my heart for the right answer. Mason had almost kissed me, and the me who existed just one month ago would have been cherishing that. She would have fallen to the ground with him, held him, told him it would be alright. She would have taken him back. But the new me, the me that existed in this moment, standing in Willow's living room with everyone crowded around, didn't feel any of those desires. I didn't want Mason back.

I wanted Rhodes.

"I'm sorry," I whispered, my eyes moving from Mason to Willow. I was apologizing to both of them, but really I wasn't sorry at all. Willow's brows bent, but only in a way that warned me to be careful. I knew she would support me no matter what.

The rest of the room would do the exact opposite.

Still, I left.

I parted the crowd with Mason calling after me. Pushing through the front door, my eyes searched in the darkness for Rhodes. He was almost to his bike, so I kicked off my heels and ran. I knew he felt me coming. He heard as I called out his name, but he didn't stop — not until I reached out and yanked his arm so he would face me. His eyes were still wild.

"Go back inside, Natalie."

"No."

"Natalie."

"Don't," I warned. "What was that about?"

He shrugged me off, striding more purposefully toward his bike. "Nothing. Go back inside. You heard your little boyfriend. He wants you back."

"I don't care. I want you. I *choose* you."

He laughed. "Wrong decision."

Tears pricked my eyes my chest surged with a familiar ache. "Stop this, Rhodes!" He kept walking with me right on his heels. "One minute you're kissing me, the next you're telling me I'm nothing to you. Now you're here." Desperation sparked through me. "Why won't you just let me in?" I choked.

Rhodes spun around, the veins in his neck on full display.

"Because you can't fucking fix me, Natalie!"

"But you fixed me!"

The pain broke free from my chest and wrapped itself around my entire body, forcing the tears down my cheeks. Rhodes swallowed, his eyes fixed on mine, his face screwed up in a mixture of pain and confusion. He was looking at me as if he had no idea how I could possibly care for him. I stared back wondering how he could be so blind to not see it himself.

"You came here for a reason tonight, Rhodes. Why? Why are you here?"

His jaw ticked. "I came to apologize."

He wasn't walking away anymore, so I took a confident step toward him. "So, apologize then."

"I didn't have... I didn't go home with that woman. From the club."

"I know."

Rhodes blanched. "You know?"

Nodding, I moved forward again, this time invading his space to the point of nearly touching him. "I knew you wouldn't do that to me. I knew you were hurting, and you just wouldn't tell me why. That's what you don't get, Rhodes. You may not want to let me in, but I'm still going to be here, pushing, and prodding, and picking at every single lock until you finally do."

"I don't deserve that, Bug." He swallowed, but my heart thumped hard against my rib cage at the mention of my nickname. "Do you not see me? Do you not see the kind of person I am?"

And I knew in that moment that I should have let him go. Every nerve was at attention, as if I were in the presence of a ghost. Maybe it was the ghosts in his eyes, the ones of his past, or maybe it was the ghost of a future I knew we couldn't have. I should have run. But I reached for him, instead.

"That's just it," I breathed, grabbing his tense arm in my shaking grasp. I slid my index finger to his wrist and pressed hard. "I *do* see you. I see your heart, Rhodes." I swallowed. "I feel it."

Rhodes winced as if my words had permanently scarred him, then his hands were in my hair and he was kissing me. "I tried to stay away from you," he murmured against my lips before claiming them again.

"I know."

"I can't."

I shook in his grasp, his kisses stirring up every emotion I had held inside for so long.

"I know."

His lips were fervent, his body pressed against mine like if he didn't feel me everywhere then I wasn't real at all. Pulling back, Rhodes ran his thumb over my bottom lip, his neon eyes blazing in the darkness as he searched my own. He was looking for an answer to a question maybe I hadn't even heard, and I hoped with every ounce of blood in my heart that he would find it.

"I don't want to be alone tonight," I whispered.

Rhodes lifted his backpack from his bike and pulled out his spare helmet, handing it to me as a response. In a way, that helmet said more than he ever could have with words. He had wanted me to leave with him. He'd planned on it.

"Your house or mine?"

# CHAPTER

# 16

Rhodes was quiet when we pulled into my drive. I had him park his bike around back just in case one of the neighbors decided to be nosey, and then I led him inside.

"Do you want something to drink or anything?" I asked nervously, dropping my heels by the door. My feet were dirty from chasing him, but I embraced it.

"I'm okay."

I nodded, smoothing my skirt with my damp hands. "I can make us some food, if you want."

Rhodes smirked, and his fierce eyes smoldered with it. "I ate earlier."

"Oh. Okay." I chewed my lip and he stepped a little closer.

"Are you nervous, Bug?"

I laughed, and it was a higher pitched noise than I'd ever experienced from my own mouth. I couldn't even try to deny it after that, so I cringed. "Yes. And I don't know why."

That was a lie. I did know why. Rhodes was alone with me in my house and I wanted him to touch me. I wanted all of him. I just didn't know if he would be willing to let me have him.

Rhodes chuckled, reaching out and pulling me into his chest. I wrapped my arms around him and tried to calm my breathing. Slowly, he lifted my chin and pressed his lips to mine.

He kissed me slow at first, but I pulled at his shirt, demanding more intensity. Groaning, Rhodes delivered, snaking his tongue into my mouth and gently tugging on my curls. I opened my mouth with a moan and he kissed down my neck, sucking at my collarbone before moving to pull my ear lobe into his mouth. "Take me to your room."

My mouth collided with his again as we stumbled up the stairs, stripping off clothing as we went. Rhodes' hands were hard on my hips as he slammed my back against the railing, breaking our kiss just long enough to make quick work of his shirt. His lips found mine again in a frenzy and he lifted me, my ankles hooking behind his waist as he took me a few more stairs. My back hit the wall next and I dropped my legs so he could pull his jeans to the floor as I unclasped my bra. We were all hands and breaths and lips, clothes landing on each step. By the time we fell into my sheets, I was completely nude and Rhodes wore nothing but his boxer briefs. Straddling him, I pushed off his chest and ran my fingers over his abdomen.

"This is the first time I've really seen you without a shirt on." His abs were just as tight and defined as

I'd imagined, and my fingertips lightly traced each crevice. Chills raced from where I touched him to cover his entire body and I smiled.

"I'm nothing special."

I frowned when I realized there were faint scars that ran across his lower stomach. When I touched them, Rhodes grabbed my wrists firmly and flipped us over, thrusting between my hips and kissing me hard.

"I want you tonight, Rhodes. Please," I pleaded, kissing the bare skin of his shoulder. I could feel his hard on through the cotton fabric of his briefs. When I moaned against his skin and bit his shoulder lightly, he hardened more.

"Jesus Christ," he whispered, burying his face in my neck. "I don't know how to do this. You're not like the women I've had before. I want to take you slowly, gently, but I don't know how."

My breath quickened at his honesty. "So take me how you want to. Hard, fast, rough..." I pulled my hands from his grasp and raked my nails down his back. "I don't want you easy."

Rhodes groaned from deep within his chest at the contact, but shook his head, lifting it to look down at me. "That's just it, though. I disconnect when I have sex, Bug. I've never... it's never meant anything to me before." He swallowed, his thumb tracing the edge of my jaw. "It means something tonight. And I want to feel every single moment with you."

He kissed me again, slower this time, his lips sticking to mine each time he pulled back. When his index finger found the inside of my wrist and he pressed there gently, I sighed contently, mirroring his grip and feeling his heart, too. Mine wasn't the only one racing.

I slipped my fingers beneath the band of his briefs and tugged them down halfway before Rhodes took control. He kicked them off, pressing himself at my entrance as he balanced on shaky arms. My breath hitched. Every nerve was at full alert. He was so close, and I'd never wanted anything more than to close the distance between us.

Quickly, Rhodes tore open the condom package he'd retrieved from his jeans when we were on the stairs. Pullling away slightly, he slid the condom over his length. He was bigger than I'd realized, even after having him strained against his shorts so many nights before, and my breath was too much to exhale only through my nose anymore. My mouth parted when he positioned himself between my thighs again, my chest tight with anticipation.

He felt the weight, too, because he kissed me softer once more before whispering, "Are you sure?"

I nodded, digging my heels into his backside to pull him nearer. His tip grazed my wet opening and we both moaned together. Rhodes sucked my lip into his mouth and then he filled me. All at once. Completely and unapologetically.

He groaned, withdrawing before rocking into me once more. It stung a little, and I held on tighter.

"Are you okay?"

I nodded again, words completely lost at that point. I felt him holding back just like I had every night before then. He entered me slowly, carefully, but each thrust hit deeper, and when he picked up the pace, I couldn't control my moans anymore. They echoed through my room and down the hall, and it was like hearing them obliterated his self-control. Rhodes fisted his hands in my hair and yanked my head back, sucking my left nipple into his mouth and flexing into me harder, hitting a space inside me I'd never known existed.

Rhodes slid into me over and over until I fit his length more comfortably, then he rolled me over onto my hands and knees. Grasping the back of my neck, he pressed my face into the hot comforter and splayed his hand on my upper back before slamming into me from behind. I cried out, but not from pain. Rhodes inside me gave me nothing but pure, unimaginable pleasure.

"Yes," I breathed, but I was still so unsure of my own voice when I was in bed with him. Rhodes gripped my hips firmly and pounded into me again. "Yes," I cried louder. He filled every inch of me in this position. I could feel my orgasm mounting, and I prayed for the release.

But Rhodes waited.

He pulled me to straddle him once more, only this time he remained sitting up. Every part of our bodies were pressed together. My legs were wrapped around his waist, his mouth was hard on mine, and he rocked into me with such calculated pressure I whimpered at the sensation.

"I love the way you feel," he growled, moving his hands from my waist to grip the top of my shoulders.

It was as if he was doing a pull up, but instead, he was pulling me down onto him, burying himself deeper. "Tight. Wet." He flexed his hips. "Fucking incredible."

His words lit me on fire — from the deepest part of my core to the hairs standing on edge at his touch. I felt like I was drowning in a wildfire, burning and gasping for a clean breath of air. Yet still, I wanted to inhale his smoke, I wanted him to consume me completely. It was the most terrifying and arousing contradiction.

"Harder," I whispered, and then my cheeks immediately flushed. Rhodes smiled, biting his lower lip and letting his teeth rake the tender flesh.

He stood, my legs still wrapped around his waist, then he dropped me down to the bed and grabbed my ankles, lifting them to rest on his shoulders. I was completely exposed as Rhodes delivered on my request, and each time he pounded into me, my breasts bounce with the force. I should have been embarrassed, but he gazed down at me with such desire that I only felt sexy.

And I'd never felt that way before.

"Oh," I moaned, gripping the sheets and the edge of the bed. "Yes, Rhodes. *Yes.*"

He slid his hand around my thigh and applied just the faintest bit of pressure to my clit, but it was all it took to send me spiraling. The combination of him inside me and the friction from his touch crashed into my senses from every side, swallowing the world around me until I was in a sensational frenzy. I felt everything. I felt nothing. I was numb. I was *burning*.

He came with me, and watching his face as I

brought him to ecstasy only fueled my release more. I felt powerful, desired, and beautiful.

For once, I actually felt what he had been saying for so long.

Rhodes groaned and pulled me down onto the floor. He was still inside me, both of us pulsing. He kissed me long and soft, his fingers brushing through my hair. We stayed tangled together on the floor, breathing each other in, lightly touching and kissing. But before long, Rhodes was hard again, and I was aching for more.

We didn't speak another word that night.

Rhodes took his time exploring my body until well after the sun had peeked through the white curtains in my window. We stopped only because there were no other condoms, and Rhodes refused to take the chance without me being on birth control. How he was able to think straight in that moment, I'd never know.

I was completely sated when Rhodes finally wrapped me in his arms, cradling my body with his own. His breaths evened out before mine, but soon they lulled me to sleep, too. And for the first time since I'd met him, I didn't wish for a dream of Rhodes. In that moment, reality was better.

I woke later that evening. The sunlight was still shining through my window, basking the room in an orange glow. Quietly, I carefully peeled myself out of bed and grabbed my camera. After finding the right setting, I snapped one simple photo of Rhodes sleeping. I knew the photograph wouldn't ever compare to the actual view, but I had to try to capture it somehow.

After Rhodes had pointed out that I didn't have a mirror in my room, I'd asked Dale to buy me one. It was a free-standing full-length mirror with a light blue, wooden frame. Hesitantly, I moved to stand in front of it.

My curls were still intact, though they were messy and wilder from the night. My cheeks were rosy, my lips dark and plump, eyes wide. Slowly, I positioned my camera at my chest and tilted the lens upward to focus on my face in the mirror. Then, for the first time ever, I took a photo of myself.

*Click.*

It was such a simple noise — *too* simple for what I felt in that moment. It was soft and almost nonexistent, which was the exact opposite of what I felt.

Rhodes' hands touched my elbows first and I jumped, but then leaned back against him as he traced my skin down to my hands. He grabbed the camera, and I dropped my grip, letting him take control. I turned to face him just as he looked through the viewfinder and it clicked again. I smiled.

"What are you doing?" I asked, my voice raspy.

He smiled, too. "Finding something beautiful in the chaos."

Rhodes photographed me from every angle imaginable. He focused on my lips, my hands, my eyes. Sometimes he captured everything, sometimes he zeroed in. I let him shoot until he decided he'd had enough, then I turned the camera in his hands and leaned in close, tucking my head into his chest and snapping a picture of the two of us, careful to crop it to just our faces. It was our first picture, and we both looked calm, sated — happy.

Rhodes kissed my cheek as he dropped my camera back on the nightstand and I wrapped my arms around his neck.

"What's your first name?"

He kissed me back, his hands resting on my waist. "Rhodes"

"Your name is Rhodes Rhodes?" I smirked, nudging him.

Rhodes' jaw flexed and he swallowed. It never occurred to me that maybe he hadn't told anyone before. Why would anyone want to hide their name?

"It's William."

I smiled. "William." He shivered when the syllables left my lips. "I like that name."

# CHAPTER
# 17

Rhodes and I did eventually make it to the gym that Sunday for my weigh-in, after staying in bed all afternoon and evening. I was officially down thirty pounds, and I'd lost another two inches off my hips and three off my waist since my last measurement three weeks ago. It was a huge milestone, and we celebrated, though Rhodes warned me that it would be more difficult to lose from that point on.

It was surreal to me. In six weeks, I'd lost more weight than I thought I was even capable of. More than that, I'd gained muscle and strength — in more ways than one. At the beginning of the summer, I'd felt like I was floating. I was trying to find a purpose, a drive, a passion, but I kept coming up short. The more my body changed, the more I let myself see the beauty in my life and my choices. Maybe I wasn't on the traditional path that society had lined up for me. Did that really mean I wouldn't find my own way?

After our session, I drove straight to Willow's to spend her last night in town together, though it was extremely difficult to say goodbye to Rhodes. I knew he had made the decision to not fight whatever we had anymore, but still, something inside me knew what we had was fleeting. When we were apart, he had the chance to think — and when he had time to think, he thought about all the reasons we couldn't be together. I had a constant ache in my chest that told me not to hold on too tight, but it only made me squeeze my fists harder.

Willow was completely packed and ready to go when I showed up, so I took a quick shower and we fell onto her couch to watch a string of movies we'd seen a thousand times before. We hadn't even made it through the credits of *10 Things I Hate About You* when Willow turned to me, popping a sour gummy worm in her mouth.

"Okay, now that we have background noise, I need to know every detail of your night after you left last night."

I chuckled. "I already told you. Rhodes and I talked, then we went back to my place."

"And?" She dragged the word out, spinning the worm in her hand. I laughed.

"And," I exaggerated. "None of your business."

"Boo!" Willow tossed her half-eaten worm at me, the sugar crystals flying all over my sweatpants. "You're the worst. You can't bone the bad boy of Poxton High and not tell your best friend how big his wang is."

"His *wang*, Lo? Really?"

"Yes, really!"

I laughed, retrieving the airborne worm and biting off its tail. "Fine. Let's just say I'm still sore... and not from the squats today."

"SHUT UP."

"Okay, stop." I blushed, sitting up straighter. "That's all you get. Did people freak out when I left?"

I could tell Willow wanted to ask more, but she conceded. "Oh, of course."

"I'm sure they're still talking," I groaned.

"Whatever. People are always going to talk, might as well give them something to yap about. And believe me, you and Rhodes are *definitely* gossip-worthy."

"I just feel like we're already so complicated, the last thing we need is everyone else in our business. But I know that's how it'll be." I could feel how fragile our relationship was, and I wondered if Rhodes felt the same. He was always more confident than I was, but I wasn't sure if that applied to us or just my training. "And what if they're right? I mean, what do you think? Did I make a mistake choosing Rhodes? Am I just too naïve to see the signs of something that's going to end up crushing me? I mean, look at him." I gestured toward the door and then back to my own body. "And look at me."

Willow popped up from the couch and skipped over to a large shopping bag leaning against the fireplace. Falling back down into the cushions, she shoved it toward me. "Forget what they think. Or what they say. You walked out that door because you knew in your heart it was the right thing to do, right?"

I nodded. "I've never been surer of anything in my entire life."

She shook her head, her dark eyes sincere, a small smile reaching her lips. "We only have so much time to *be*, Natalie. So be wild, be crazy, be spontaneous, and be passionate. Never be sorry. And when someone tells you you'll regret your choice later, be confident in the fact that you won't."

I pulled a smooth, red scrap of fabric from the bag. It was the top to a swim suit. Which meant there was a bottom. Which meant it was two pieces, not one.

Willow smiled wider, pointing at the string dangling from my fingers. "And this weekend, when you're celebrating the Fourth of July with Rhodes, be sexy as fuck."

I choked out a laugh. "I can't wear this. It's a two-piece."

"And you're a fox. I mean it," she said, lowering her head to meet my gaze. "Just promise me you'll try it on. Please?"

I nodded. "Okay."

Even though the thought terrified me, maybe it was time to start finding comfort in my new skin. Willow's words played over and over in my head, growing in volume each time. I didn't know if what I had with Rhodes would last. I could end up in a blissful heaven or I could fall to the floor and break into a million tiny pieces. Either way, I wasn't going to waste any of the moments I did have with him.

Pulling Willow in for a long hug, I let my eyes brim with tears knowing she was leaving in just twelve short hours. "Thank you. I don't know what I'll do without you here."

"Don't sweat it," she said, squeezing me in return. "And something tells me Rhodes and his wang will keep you busy."

"Don't say wang ever again."

"No promises."

The first days of July flew by in a heated frenzy. Rhodes trained me harder during the days and loved me longer through the nights. If I thought the heat I felt from him was dangerous before, I was practically jumping into a volcano at this point. But I craved the burn.

Standing in front of my full-length mirror in nothing but a tiny swim suit on the Fourth of July, I felt particularly sweaty. Rubbing my palms against the tops of my thighs, I turned to the left, inspecting my exposed skin. The cherry red top and bright white bottoms blazed against my tan, though my stomach was a few shades lighter. I was far from being able to walk without jiggling, but at the same time, my curves were more defined than before. My waist was smaller, the skin around my hips more taut — I felt like maybe I could pull it off.

Blowing out a long breath, I threw on my navy blue cover up and beach hat before I could talk myself out of it. Just as I was about to walk out the door to meet Rhodes, my phone pinged.

"Hey guys!" I said when the video of Mom and Dale came into focus. They were spending the holiday in the Hamptons with Dale's friends from New York.

"Oh sweetie!" Mom squealed, her hands flying to her mouth. "You look so great!"

"Mom, you just saw me last week."

"It feels like longer."

Dale laughed. "She's right though, Natalie. How did the weigh-in go?"

I filled them in on Willow's party and my milestone weigh-in. I left out everything about Rhodes other than our training sessions, of course. I knew they'd find out eventually, but I still wasn't sure how Mom would take me choosing Rhodes over Mason. That was definitely an in-person conversation.

Dale high-fived me through the screen for standing up to Shay and Mom swatted at him, but she seemed to be proud, too. Dale went into detail about their planned day out on the yacht, too, which made me miss them more than I realized. In a way, I wished they were home, even if I was enjoying the time alone with Rhodes.

Mom nodded along with Dale as he talked, her blonde hair blowing slightly in the breeze from the porch where they were standing. She was smiling, though she looked more tired than usual. I noted the dark skin above her cheeks and the tensed edges of her eyes. I wondered if Dale was still working on his addiction, but I didn't chance asking. After blowing them each a kiss, I ended the call and sprinted out the door to the Rover.

I was still nervous each time I knew I was about to see Rhodes. When he bounded out of his apartment, his backpack slung over his shoulder and a wide smile on his lips, I faltered, nearly revving the engine. He swung open the door and tossed his bag in the back before grabbing my face between his hands and kissing me like he hadn't spent the night before in my sheets.

"Nice hat," he said, flicking it with his finger as he pulled back and fastened his seatbelt. He was dressed in black and gray, simple swim trunks and a white shirt that I knew would eventually be pulled off to reveal his god-like abdomen. Realizing I would be showing my own midriff soon, I swallowed.

"You're in a good mood."

"Should I not be?" He quirked a brow just above the rim of his dark aviators, smile still glued to his face. "I have the day off, we're heading to the beach." Rhodes leaned over the console, sliding his rough hand up the inside of my thigh. "And I get to spend all day with you."

"You better scowl or something," I joked. "People might actually think you like me."

He smirked, moving my hand to his lips for a swift kiss before leaning back in his seat. "People might actually be right, then."

The drive to the beach was slow, traffic picking up even though we'd left Rhodes' apartment just after nine. Poxton Beach was always packed on the Fourth of July. With a mixture of tourists and regulars, it was nearly impossible to find parking or a spot on the beach after eleven.

We didn't really have to worry about that, though. I parked us in Dale's reserved spot right by one of the boardwalks leading to the beach and led Rhodes to our cabana in front of the Poxton Inn. There were two chaise lounge chairs, a small couch, a hammock, a coffee table and a small bar complete with mini fridge inside and we were just thirty feet from the water.

Rhodes shook his head, dropping his bag on the couch as I pulled a cold water bottle from the fridge. "So this is how the other half lives. Here I thought we'd have to slum it with towels on the beach like the common folk."

"Having a dad who owns the town has some perks."

"That's the understatement of the year." Rhodes watched me tip the water bottle to my lips before quickly stripping off his shirt. "Want to get in the water?"

My heartrate accelerated. It was a damn good thing I wasn't wearing my watch, because I knew it'd be an embarrassing number on that little screen. "Uh, yeah. Sure."

I screwed the lid back on my water slower than necessary and tucked it back into the fridge. Rhodes just watched me, an amused look on his face.

"You wearing your dress in?"

I swallowed, but didn't respond. Gripping the hem of each side, I slowly peeled off my cover up, dropping it into the lounge chair and pulling my long blonde hair forward to shield whatever skin it could. I wanted to squeeze my eyes shut and somehow teleport to the ocean, but I knew I wouldn't be so lucky. Glancing up at him through my lashes, I bit my lip and attempted to lift my head higher.

"Jesus Christ, Bug," Rhodes groaned, shaking his head. He crossed the space between us and reached out, his hands just barely grazing my bare hips. I shivered.

"You like the suit?"

"I'm not looking at the suit," he murmured, trailing his fingers across my sensitive skin before finding my eyes with his own. "Your confidence is the sexiest thing you have on right now."

I blushed. "I'm not sure I remembered that accessory, now that you mention it."

"I disagree. The girl who walked into my gym almost two months ago would never have worn this. And she damn sure wouldn't have worn it in front of me. You look incredible, Natalie, and you know it. And that's okay. It's okay to feel good about yourself."

I smiled, chewing the inside of my cheek. It was one of those moments where Rhodes was completely uninhibited. Suddenly, I wanted to blow off the entire beach day and pull him back to my place and under my sheets. Whatever he saw in me, it was starting to wear off on me, too. I wanted to soak him in.

"Come on," he said, grabbing my hand. His green eyes danced in the bright morning light. "Let's show you off."

I'd never seen Rhodes more free-spirited than that day on the beach.

We played in the water, splashing and laughing and occasionally diving for seashells. When we needed a break from the sun, we'd retreat to our cabana to lounge in the shade, but Rhodes' hand never left mine. We built a sad looking sandcastle and even joined in a game of volleyball with some of our classmates, though we were more of a distraction than anything else. The busier the beach got, the more eyes I felt glued to my back.

"People are staring at us," I said as Rhodes balanced me on a boogie board we'd rented. There were plenty of women from the club eying us, but I felt a particular glare coming from the group I'd spent all my past Independence Days with. Mason included.

"Let them stare."

I smirked, assessing him through the wet strands of my hair. "What's gotten into you?"

He shrugged, his smile falling. "Last night, you fell asleep in my arms, and I just kept thinking about how I don't deserve you." I went to interrupt him, but he continued. "But then I realized I've had a lot of shitty years in my life, maybe too many. But I'm not a bad person, at least, maybe not as bad as I've always believed." He pulled off his shades and squinted against the sun to meet my eyes. "You're the one who made me realize that, Bug. You make me feel like maybe I deserve more. Like maybe my dreams matter. Do you realize how much that means to me?" He shook his head, his jaw tight. Sliding his sunglasses back into place, he pushed me out further into the waves. "I'm never letting that go."

I smiled. "Would it be weird if I called you William?"

"Yes."

"Why?"

"It's not my name."

I frowned, struggling to find my balance on the board. "Well, technically, it is."

"It just doesn't fit me."

"What do you mean?"

Rhodes sighed, shaking his head but still smiling. "Always with the questions. I'll tell you, but I don't want to talk about it right now. Not today. Deal?"

My curiosity was piqued even more, but I'd learned not to push Rhodes. "Deal."

Even with reapplying sunscreen every hour, my skin was tight and a slight shade of pink by the time the sun started sinking in the west. I pulled my hair into a messy bun and threw on Rhodes' long sleeve shirt over my suit, loving the scent of him surrounding me. We grabbed our beach towels and strolled down closer to the water, finding the perfect spot for the fireworks show.

I watched Rhodes with fascination as he spread out both of our towels and then sat down easily, patting the spot next to him. He was so different, so happy — and I reveled in the fact that I had a part in making him that way. I was just about to lower myself next to him when Mason's voice pulled me out of the trance I'd been in all day.

"Hey Natalie," he said timidly, his eyes flicking from mine to Rhodes and back again. I flinched at the sight of his bruised face. "Can I talk to you for a minute?"

I hesitated, glancing to Rhodes quickly before meeting Mason's stare again. "Um, sure."

Rhodes' jaw ticked as I walked a few feet away with Mason, but I made sure I kept within a safe distance. This wasn't a pissing contest. I'd chosen Rhodes, and I wanted him to know I was solid in that choice.

"How are you?" Mason asked, tucking his hands in the pockets of his swim trunks. His messy brown hair was wind-blown and still damp from the ocean.

"I'm good, Mase. What did you want to talk about?"

He sighed, looking off into the water before pulling his attention back to me. The sun was fading quicker, casting shadows on the beach. "What are you doing with him? He's not good for you."

"Mason."

"I'm serious. Do you not remember his reputation from high school? All the times he was in juvie? Or how about his current reputation down at the club?" I swallowed, which seemed to fuel Mason's fire. "Yeah, I take it from that expression that you do know of his *activities*. So then what the hell are you doing? Do you think he's going to change for you, Natalie? He's dangerous. This whole thing is going to blow up in your face."

"What happens between us is none of your concern, Mason. You gave up the privilege to get a say in what I do and don't do with my life." I said the words with conviction, but I was shaking beneath Rhodes' sweater.

"I know that, okay?" He ran his hands back through his hair, glancing once more at where Rhodes was seated behind me. "Just please, be careful. And think about what you're doing. I just don't want to see you hurt."

"I'll be fine."

He nodded. "I hope you're right. Enjoy the show." With one last hard look at Rhodes, Mason walked back to where our group of friends was gathered on the beach. I noted Shay wasn't in attendance.

"Sorry about that," I said, falling down onto the towel next to Rhodes. He pulled my back against his chest, wrapping his arms around me. He was tense for a moment, but then I felt him sigh and relax against me. His lips moved to my neck timidly, kissing me as if he were just as afraid he'd hurt me as Mason was.

Rhodes was quiet after that as we watched the first fireworks being lit off the boats in the distance. The big show hadn't yet started, so I pushed my luck to get deeper into his thoughts.

"There's that scowl I've been looking for all day."

Rhodes smirked, holding me tighter. "I was just thinking. About Lana."

I stiffened, but snuggled into him more. "What about her?"

He was silent a moment, but I waited, letting him take his time. "I just wonder if she sees any of this anymore. I want to believe she does, that she's still out there somewhere, living. But I know I'm stupid for thinking that way." He swallowed. "Sometimes it's just easier than facing the truth that if she is alive, she's not safe enough to call me and let me know."

"Do you feel like she is?"

Rhodes cleared his throat. "Sometimes. Every now and then, I feel her — like her presence. It's almost as if she's watching over me."

"Maybe she is."

He smiled, pulling me in closer. "Maybe."

The first loud crack of the pier fireworks show sounded and the beach cheered. Leaning up from Rhodes' grasp, I retrieved my camera from my beach bag and flicked through the settings. Just as I lifted it to focus on a red and white burst firework, Rhodes grabbed my hands.

"Why do you always do that?"

"Do what?"

"Try to photograph every moment. Trust me," he said, lowering my hands back into my lap and pulling the camera from my grasp. He dropped it on the towel next to us and pulled me back into him. "Sometimes, it's better with your own eyes."

And it was. Every loud boom echoed off the water and reverberated through my chest as the fireworks lit up the beach. I tried to keep my eyes on the sky, but I was drawn to Rhodes each time his face was illuminated. His strong jaw, his barely-there scruff, his beachy hair. Even though his eyes took on whatever color the fireworks decided, I could still see the bright green shining through.

"What are you afraid of, Natalie?" He asked, his voice just above a whisper as he repeated the question I'd asked the first time he set foot in my room. It felt heavier this time. Everything with Rhodes felt heavier.

"Loving you."

He frowned, two perfectly symmetrical lines forming in his brow. Chewing my lip, I looked back to the sky, afraid that maybe I'd said too much. *Did I love him already?* I loved being with him. I loved the way he made me feel. To me, that was dangerously close. And it was the truth — there was nothing I was more afraid of than waking up one morning to find my heart belonged to the one man I knew could break it.

One single firework broke the sound barrier before the finale began. As lights and booms chased each other over the water, Rhodes tilted my chin toward him, catching my eyes with his own. Then, he closed the distance and pressed his lips to mine. It was a slow kiss, passionate and calculating. Maybe he was telling me it was okay to be scared, or that he felt the same fear, too.

Or maybe, he was telling me to leap.

# CHAPTER

# 18

"Natalie," Rhodes warned, leaning his broad chest against my hamstring to apply pressure again. I felt the stretch deep in my muscles and I moaned louder. Rhodes instantly dropped my leg, letting it fall to the floor as he sat back on his heels.

"What?" I feigned innocence. "It feels so *good*, Rhodes. I can't help it."

He shook his head. "You're going to get me fired."

"How? You're just stretching me out. I'm your client."

"Yeah, but if stretching leads to you moaning which in turn leads to me fucking you against the wall in the sauna, I think that might go against club policy."

My mouth grew dry at the image he'd painted and I chewed my lip. Lifting my left wrist, I thumbed through the options of my watch until I found the voice recorder. "Note to self: Ask Dale to install a sauna in the pool house."

"You have a pool house?"

"Yep. Come over tonight and I'll give you the tour."

Rhodes chuckled, standing and making his way toward the back office. "Can't, Bug."

"Why not?" I asked, scrambling to my feet to follow him. It wasn't easy, and I internally groaned. Rhodes had been pushing me hard all week. I was getting stronger, and he was testing my limits — though I couldn't really complain. Every time he showed me how to lower into a new squat position or illustrated a glute exercise, I took advantage, touching him longer than necessary or leaning my body into his. We were garnering glares from nearly every woman in the gym, but I didn't care.

I was branding him, just like he'd branded me.

"I have to be somewhere."

I swallowed, staring down at my sneakers as Rhodes filed through paperwork on his desk. His t-shirt was ripped at the sleeves and the sides drooped down low, giving me full visual access of his ripped abdomen. The muscles flexed with each small movement as he shuffled random client files into place.

I hadn't thought about the possibility that he might still be offering his after hour services. I clutched my stomach. "Are you… do you have to meet another client?"

Rhodes' eyes met mine, his brows knitted together in confusion. "What?" When realization hit, he dropped the papers in his hand and crossed the room to me in two full strides. "Oh fuck, Natalie, no. I'm done with that. It's me and you now, okay? I'm only touching you. And you're the only one touching me." He weaved his hands into my still damp hair and forced me to meet his gaze. "I swear."

Sighing, I nodded. "I'm sorry."

"Don't be. You had every right to assume." Clearing his throat, he stepped back, filtering through the papers once more. "That's actually part of why I can't hang out this evening, though. I have a job interview."

"A job interview?"

He nodded. "It's at this new bar they just opened down at The Crawl. Nothing big, but it'll be enough to cover what training can't."

"Oh God." My hands flew to my face. "You have to get a second job. Because of me."

Rhodes chuckled, tossing a paperclip in my direction. It bounced off my forearm and landed next to my sneaker. "Stop, Bug. This is a good thing. I don't want to do what I've been doing to earn a living." I peeked at him through my fingers and his nose flared slightly. "I'm worth more than what they think I am."

My heart squeezed and a smile met my lips. Was it possible Rhodes was finally seeing what I'd always seen in him? Still, I knew the extra money he made wasn't just spent on worthless material things. I frowned. "What about the private investigator for your sister?"

He moved to me again, taking me in his arms. "I'm giving him his last payment tonight. It's time for me to start letting go, and this is step one."

"Wait." I pushed my hands into his chest. "I can help. I'll pay for him to keep looking. This is my fault, and I know you still believe she's out there." His jaw tensed. "Please, let me help. How much do you pay him?"

"Stop." Rhodes pinched the bridge of his nose, but still kept the other arm secured at my waist. "You're not paying for him. After this week, his services are done. And that's it. And we don't talk about it again. Okay?"

I wasn't happy about that decision, but I nodded. I knew there was no point arguing with Rhodes, but a part of me still ached thinking I was possibly responsible for him giving up on the search for his sister.

Forcing a smile, Rhodes pulled me in for a quick kiss.

"It's okay," he promised against my lips. "I think I'm ready. I think I need to start letting go."

Fisting my hands in his wet t-shirt, I pulled him closer. "I can help."

His throat constricted and he slid his hand into mine, pressing his index finger hard into my wrist. "You already have."

Willow called to catch up the next day while I was enjoying my day off from training. She was so excited about her program and everyone she was meeting at Appalachian State. If I didn't have Rhodes, I would have been jealous. Since I did, I was able to be completely happy for her. We only talked for twenty minutes before she had to run, but it was nice hearing her voice. Especially when she squealed after hearing I'd worn the swimsuit she bought me.

It was a lazy Wednesday, which I actually cherished. I spent the day watching more episodes of *Lost* and even took a nap, which I couldn't remember doing all summer. I had a big night planned with Rhodes, and I wanted to be awake and energized.

When I woke around five, I had a missed text from Mason.

**— I'm worried about you.**
**Did you think about what I said? —**

I rolled my eyes, stifling a yawn as I padded across the cool hardwood floor to the stairs. Funny, Mason seemed more invested in my wellbeing now than he ever had the two years we'd dated. For once, I was beginning not to care what Mason thought of me. Or anyone else, for that matter.

I took my time getting dressed, applying my makeup with careful precision. It paid off when Rhodes slid into my passenger seat with a whistle at just past eight.

"You look gorgeous," he said, planting a sweet kiss on my lips as I threw the Rover into drive. "So, are you going to tell me where you're taking me yet?"

"That would ruin the surprise, silly."

He grumbled. "I'm too impatient for surprises."

"Clearly." I laughed, but the sound caught in my throat when his hand reached across the console and ran up the inside of my thigh. I was wearing a short white dress with a modest top and A-line hem. The more his fingers inched north, the more I squirmed.

"Rhodes," I warned.

"What? Am I distracting you?"

I hesitated longer than normal when the red light turned green, which was all the answer Rhodes needed. He chuckled from a place deep in his chest.

"I fucking *love* the way I affect you," he whispered, trailing his hand higher. I gripped the wheel.

"Rhodes, seriously." I bit my lip, nervous to tell him exactly why he needed to stop, but when his fingers crawled even higher, the words flew from my mouth. "I'm not wearing any panties!"

I had whisper-yelled, just barely audible over the sound of the radio, but I might as well have announced it through a microphone at a stadium. Rhodes stopped, his hand just inches from my center, and a devilish grin curled on his lips.

"Well I'm *definitely* not stopping now."

The air conditioning was on full blast, but suddenly it felt too hot to breathe.

"Move your seat back as far as you can to still be able to drive."

My shaking hand found the control on the door and my seat slowly slid back a few more inches.

"Put both hands on the steering wheel," he demanded next. "And keep them there."

I gripped the wheel at two and ten, my knuckles whitening with the force. Rhodes kissed up my neck and sucked my earlobe into his mouth, his hand riding higher and higher up my thigh.

"Tilt your hips forward," he whispered, and when

I did, he filled me with two fingers. I gasped, my eyes fluttering closed. "And don't crash."

My eyes snapped open again.

With his fingers still dancing inside me, Rhodes kissed and sucked the sensitive skin of my neck, making it practically impossible to keep my focus on the road. The sun hadn't even completely set yet, but the Range Rover had illegally dark tinted windows, which almost eliminated my concern that passing cars would get a peek of the show. For once, I was thankful for Dale's obsession with his cars.

"It's a good thing you're not wearing panties," Rhodes breathed, withdrawing his fingers slowly before thrusting them inside once more. "Because they would definitely be soaked now."

I moaned, biting my lower lip with enough pressure to draw blood. Rhodes' eyes caught the motion and he snaked in to replace my teeth with his own. I was trying so desperately to pay attention to the road, but his mouth was everywhere and his fingers were relentlessly pushing me closer to the release I was anxious to find.

My hands shook on the wheel. My breaths were labored. Adrenaline pumped through my veins as if I'd stolen the car we were driving. My core was tight, my legs tense, and I could feel myself on the brink of desire.

Rhodes maneuvered his left arm from where it had been holding him up on the console and he gripped the bottom of the steering wheel. "Hit the cruise control."

I did as he said before snapping my hands right

back into position. I was squirming in his hand, moans ripping from my throat.

"You're not going to come unless you let go."

Glancing at him through heavy eyelids, I blanched when I realized what he meant.

"I can't," I started, but his thumb found my clit and I moaned instead of finishing my sentence.

"Trust me. I've got the wheel. Let go, Natalie."

I hesitated, but slowly, my hands fell down the sides of the wheel. One gripped the door while the other rested on top of where his was between my thighs. Pushing him into me with more force, I ground my hips against his palm under mine, finding the perfect friction to send me spiraling. My eyes closed, my lips parted, and I fell. It was a release unlike any I'd had before — quick, electric, forbidden.

Incredible.

When I opened my eyes again, I jerked my hands back into place on the wheel, realizing Rhodes was only steering with his left hand. He held it steady, but my sated mind was still afraid of losing control.

Rhodes only smirked, slowly removing his fingers before lifting them to his lips. My breath caught as he slid them inside his mouth, sucking my desire off his skin. I was still panting, my mind racing with what we'd just done.

Leaning back in his seat, Rhodes fastened his seatbelt and didn't say another word.

Ten minutes later, we pulled into the parking lot of LaRue's, a small beach-front restaurant known for its high-end dining experience. Dale and Mom liked to eat there at least once a month, and usually while there was a special event or show. I was hoping to give Rhodes a more hands-on introduction.

"We can't eat here," Rhodes said, shaking his head as I put the Rover in park. He was staring up at the restaurant logo with wide eyes. I straightened out the slightly wrinkled fabric of my dress, heart still racing.

"We're not just eating here."

Rhodes cocked his head, questioning.

"We're *cooking* here."

Before he could ask questions, I hopped out of the car and made my way toward the entrance. I tried to hide the smile on my face as he jogged to catch up to me just as the tall glass and mahogany door gently swung open.

"Good evening, Miss Poxton," the gentleman holding the door greeted. He was tall, with skin as dark as Willow's and bright hazel eyes. "Always a pleasure to see you."

"And you, Marcus."

"This must be Mr. Rhodes." Marcus extended his hand and Rhodes stared at it for a short moment before giving it a firm shake. "Our Executive Chef is ready for you in the kitchen. This way, please."

Marcus escorted us through the pleasantly crowded restaurant to the back kitchen. I watched Rhodes' eyes as we passed each intricate section of the dining area. LaRue's was famous for its various dining environments, from the cozy palace corner donned with rich reds and browns to the bright whites and blues of the outside beach-themed experience. Rhodes had so many firsts of mine, it was nice to finally get to experience a first of his.

When Marcus led us through the swinging double doors, an entirely new atmosphere engulfed us. There were chefs running everywhere, flames burning high, orders being shouted. In a normal universe, I might have been alarmed, but in the current one with Rhodes' wide eyes and curious smile, I was nothing but excited.

"Ah! Miss Poxton!" Chef Karsak wiped his forehead with an off-white towel, tucking it in his back pocket just in time to reach out his hands for mine. He kissed them with a wide, toothy grin and I returned the smile. "It's such an honor to have you in my house. Come, come," he gestured to the stove he was just working. "Thank you, Marcus. I'll take it from here."

"This is incredible," Rhodes murmured, taking in the chaos of the kitchen. Chef Karsak smiled, folding his arms across his chest.

"Isn't it? Never gets old. I take it you must be Mr. Rhodes?" Again, Rhodes hesitated just a short moment before shaking his hand. Chef Karsak shouted out a few expletives at a chef across the kitchen before returning his eyes to Rhodes, still smiling. "I'm Joseph Karsak, the Executive Chef here at LaRue's. Miss Poxton said over our phone call that you are quite the cook yourself. That right?"

For the first time, Rhodes almost looked embarrassed. He cleared his throat and slightly nodded.

"Brilliant. Let's get started, Mr. Rhodes." Chef Karsak clapped his hands together. He was slightly shorter than Rhodes, but it was easy to see Rhodes looked up to him, anyway. The two of them went to work, mixing and searing and tossing and baking. I helped out a little here and there, but for the most part, I just watched. It was fascinating seeing Rhodes in his element. He understood everything Chef Karsak said, while I, on the other hand, was just as confused as when I ordered from the menu. None of the cooking techniques or dish names made sense to me, but they were like a second language to Rhodes.

I had only asked for an hour of Chef Karsak's time, but the pair was getting along so well that we ended up staying until the last dish was prepared. It was comical at times, watching them work together, because they were such opposites. Chef Karsak had ashy blonde hair and dark chocolate eyes, a stark contrast to Rhodes' dark hair and bright eyes. He shouted and cursed and was just generally a larger-than-life character, but Rhodes was quiet, focused, meticulous. Rhodes was tall and built, the kitchen tools almost looking too small for him since I was used to seeing him surrounded by weights, whereas Chef Karsak was shorter but lanky and almost perfectly matched to his kitchen. And where Chef Karsak seemed to do everything with neat precision, Rhodes had more of a sporadic style, though it was still controlled. The fire in his eyes was just as hot as that on the stoves and I knew he would eventually find a way to make this his life. He had to.

When midnight rolled around, the rest of the chefs in the kitchen were still cleaning and prepping ingredients for the next day as Chef Karsak pulled Rhodes in for a manly hug and hard clap on the back.

"You know, I think I might have learned a thing or two from you tonight," he said through a grin.

"This has been incredible." Rhodes' eyes found mine. "I don't think I can thank you enough."

"It was my pleasure." Chef Karsak kissed my cheeks and Rhodes and I made our way outside, but he stopped us one last time. "Listen, you go get your culinary arts degree, hone in on your skill and tighten up your methods, and you have a spot on my team." Rhodes' jaw dropped slightly, but Chef Karsak just smiled, handing him a business card. "Don't waste any time. You need to be in the kitchen, Mr. Rhodes. It's your home, and you've been away too long as it is." He nodded to me once more. "Take care, Miss Poxton."

"Thank you again, Chef."

With one last wink, Chef Karsak disappeared behind the swinging doors, instructions flying from his mouth immediately. I led Rhodes out the back door of the restaurant and down to the beach, kicking off my sandals when we reached the sand. He still hadn't said anything, so I slid my hand into his.

"You're quiet. Should I be scared?"

Rhodes shook his head, a peaceful look on his face as he stared out at the moonlit waves. He wasn't smiling, but he wasn't scowling, either. He just looked content. Pensive.

"Did you at least have fun?"

Rhodes stopped then, his hand still firmly grasping mine. My breath caught at the way the soft blue lighting of the night reflected in his eyes. "Are you kidding? Natalie, this is one of the best nights of my life, right behind the night you chose me outside of Willow's house." My heart jumped. "I still can't wrap my head around what just happened."

"You were amazing to watch in there."

The left corner of his lips pulled into the faintest smile. "No one has ever called me *Mr. Rhodes.*" He shook his head, wetting his lips. "No one has ever shaken my hand like that. Like I mattered. Like I meant something."

I frowned. "You do matter, Rhodes."

His eyes gleamed. "I'm starting to believe you."

Tentatively, his hands found my hips. He pulled me closer, pressing his forehead to mine, and I threaded my arms around his neck, kissing him softly.

"Can we stay for a while?"

Pulling him down into the sand with me, I answered without words. We were close to the water's edge, the waves gently rolling in just over the tops of my toes. Rhodes slipped off his shoes and joined me, and we sat in comfortable silence, our minds replaying the evening.

I felt alive with Rhodes next to me in this state. He had changed so much since the beginning of the summer. I wanted to say it was like I was peeling back his layers, but the truth was, Rhodes didn't work in that simple of a manner. I couldn't just break down one wall and step easily through to the next. He was a constantly altering maze, a Rubik's cube of complexity I wasn't sure I would ever fully understand.

But I knew with absolution that Rhodes was like the wet sand I tried so desperately to grasp that night. I could feel him, he was real, and he was slowly letting me mold him into how I'd seen him in my mind all along. But eventually, the moon would fade, the tide would recede, and the sand would dry beneath the heat of the sun, slipping effortlessly through my fingers.

Still, I held on tight, anyway.

# CHAPTER

# 19

That Friday at training, I felt like I was back with the Rhodes I met day one. He was quiet, broody, and he was on my ass like he had something to prove. I was already dripping in sweat and we were only forty-five minutes into our session.

"Is everything okay?" I asked finally, starting on my third set of lunges.

"Fine."

I rolled my eyes. "Seriously? We're back to this?"

"Back to what?" Rhodes sniffed, gently pushing down on my shoulders to force me lower. My legs shook and I gritted my teeth.

"Rhodes."

He sighed, giving me the sign that I could stand and I exhaled with loud relief, shaking out my legs. "I'm sorry. I'm fine. I just had a late night."

I couldn't ignore the way my stomach dropped at his insinuation of a late night that I wasn't a part of. "But we're okay?"

His brows bent over his intense emerald pools, but he nodded.

I knew better than to push him, but still, his reflex moods bothered me. He wasn't like a roller coaster, he was like a car crash — one that I felt like I'd have to live over and over again forever. I wanted him to stay the way he was at the beach on the Fourth of July, the way he was just two nights ago outside of LaRue's. But those bright times were fleeting.

I somehow managed to make it through the rest of the session without vomiting, but just barely. When I was mid-cooldown on the treadmill, my phone pinged in my gym bag.

"Want me to get that for you?" Rhodes asked, wiping down his machine.

"Yeah, it might be Dale."

Rhodes fished my phone out and the screen lit up again just as he handed it to me.

With Mason's name.

His jaw ticked, his eyes taking on a dark forest green hue. Tossing his white towel over his shoulder, Rhodes made his way back to the office without another word. I groaned.

"Wait, Rhodes," I called out, ending my session and jogging after him.

"Are you still fucking around with him?" Rhodes asked as soon as I shut the office door behind us. My mouth popped open.

"Is that a serious question?"

"Why wouldn't it be? Your body is changing more every day, he's clearly noticing, and the whole reason you ever walked into this gym was because of him. Makes perfect sense to me."

"Rhodes, I don't want Mason. I chose *you*, remember?"

"Yeah. Why is that exactly, Natalie?"

Without warning, my fingers began to tremor, mirroring my unsteady heartbeat. Rhodes was looking at me like I'd betrayed him, and I had no idea why.

I shook my head, confused. "What do you mean? I told you all this already, Rhodes. Isn't it obvious?"

"Well, I thought so, but I don't know anymore."

"Don't do this," I pleaded, reaching out for him. He jerked his arm back. "Please. Talk to me."

"What are you hiding from me, Natalie?!" Rhodes pounded his fists on the desk and I jumped. His voice boomed with anger, but his eyes gleamed with fear. It was the strangest combination.

I just stood there, dumbstruck, like his question was in a foreign language. What did he mean? I was nothing but open and honest with Rhodes.

"Fuck!" he shouted, flipping a stack of papers. They fluttered to the ground and Rhodes ran his hands roughly over his head. He held them there for a moment before slowly reaching into his pocket and retrieving a small, folded piece of paper. He handed it to me without looking at it.

Hesitantly, I took it from his grasp, unfolding it as if it were tied to an explosive. When I read the words written in neat script in the middle of the fold, my heart stopped.

Stay away from Natalie Poxton.

I read those five words slowly, then all at once, then one-by-one, until they didn't make sense anymore. Not that they had to begin with. My brows knitted together and I lifted my eyes to Rhodes, dropped them back to the note, and lifted them again. His expression was unreadable.

"What is this?"

"I found it taped to my bike windshield when I left the gym last night."

"I," I whispered, my voice hoarse. "I don't understand."

Rhodes exhaled through his nose, tucking his bottom lip between his teeth. "If there's something you're not telling me—"

"There's not!" I cut him off, reaching for him again. He jerked away and my eyes blurred, lips trembling.

"Rhodes, please, you have to believe me. I don't know what this means."

He was quiet a moment, his jaw tense, his arms crossed. The sweat had dried on my skin and I was suddenly freezing. Rhodes wouldn't look at me, but I could tell he was battling with what the note meant, too.

Then it hit me.

"God." My hand found my forehead and I closed my eyes tight. "It's Mason. It has to be." When I opened my eyes to find Rhodes, he was already shaking his head. "No, listen to me. He told me you were bad for me when he pulled me to the side on the Fourth of July. He texted me a few days later asking if I'd thought about what he said. And he just texted me again asking me to call him."

"Natalie," Rhodes argued, saying my name like a warning, but I didn't give him the chance to finish the thought.

"He's jealous. And he's an immature little boy. He's playing a stupid game. Please, you have to believe me."

"I can't."

I shook my head, my mouth still open, my hands extended toward him. I was so cold. Everything was so cold. "Why not?"

Rhodes cracked his neck, bending over slightly and splaying his hands on the desk. The muscles in his arms tensed, and he stared at the wooden surface between his thumbs. When he glanced up at me from beneath his still furrowed brow, I waited for his answer.

I never could have imagined the words that left his mouth next.

"Because it's my sister's handwriting."

# CHAPTER

# 20

I convinced Rhodes to let me take the note home with me.

There was something about it, something familiar, but I didn't know what. He was hesitant at first, but given that I was its main subject, he agreed to let me study it for a while.

The house felt emptier than usual that night. I was lying on the floor in the living room, staring up at the chandelier above our coffee table, replaying the scene at the gym. Rhodes let me take the note, and though I wanted him to believe me, I knew a part of him was still wary. How could he not be? The note had a clear warning, one that I couldn't begin to understand, and it was written in his sister's handwriting.

Rhodes held me after dropping the bomb about his sister, but I still felt a hesitance even with his arms around me. He was trying to figure it all out, and even though he might not have wanted to believe that I could hurt him, his basic instinct told him otherwise. I couldn't blame him.

My only suspect was Mason, but did he know about Rhodes' sister? I guess everyone in the town did the year that it happened. Still, I couldn't see him being that cruel to try to pull over an illusion that she wrote it. With him crossed off the list, I didn't have any other ideas as to who could have written the note.

Unless it was his sister.

That possibility shook me to my core.

If that were the case, that meant Lana was alive. Furthermore, it meant that she was alive and that she hated me, or at least wanted her brother to stay away from me.

But why?

Groaning, I grabbed a pillow from the couch and covered my face with it before tossing it to the side again. My head was spinning with no chance of finding steady ground anytime soon. Everything I thought I knew about Rhodes was back in limbo, in a place where I couldn't be sure of anything.

Yanking my phone off the charger, I thumbed through the contacts. I debated calling Willow, but it was Friday night and she was supposed to be at her first college party. Part of me ached to be there with her, part of me was selfish enough to wish she was home with me, instead. Mom and Dale were still up north and wouldn't be back for a few more days. I could have called them, but they didn't know about my relationship with Rhodes, so they couldn't help, either.

Sighing, I dropped my phone back to the floor and continued staring up at the ceiling. A loud knock at the front door woke me from my daydream a few minutes later and I reluctantly climbed to my feet. Padding over to the foyer, I peeked through the peephole, and I didn't know how to feel when I saw him standing there.

Slowly, I unlocked the door and propped it open with my hip. "Hi."

Rhodes' brows pulled inward. "I'm so, so sorry, Bug."

I opened my mouth to speak, but simply closed it again. I wasn't expecting an apology.

"I can't believe I treated you like that today. I can't stop thinking about it. I have no idea what this note means, but I do know that staying away from you isn't going to make anything in my life better. You're the only light I have, Natalie."

My stomach felt light and heavy at the same time. I expected Rhodes to call me tomorrow and tell me I had a new trainer. I thought he was gone. I thought I'd lost him. But we'd grown in the short time we'd known each other. Him standing on my front porch was living proof of that.

My voice cracked along with my strength. "I don't know what the note means. I swear I don't."

"I know," he said quickly, reaching out and pulling me into him. I tucked my nose into the crook of his neck, squeezing my eyes tight. "I don't want to think about it right now."

I pulled back. "I don't know how *not* to think about it."

Rhodes grabbed my hand in his and led me back into the house. Stretching out on the couch, he dragged me down with him and wrapped his arms around my middle. My back was flush against his chest and he softly kissed the skin on my neck.

"I want to take you somewhere tomorrow."

I sighed, my chest tight. I was emotionally spent from the day, yet his hands on my waist and his words on my skin were all I needed to feel whole again.

"Anywhere," I answered, sliding my hand into his. I pressed my index and middle fingers together into the center of his wrist, exhaling through the ache in my chest when I felt his steady heartbeat. "I'll go anywhere with you."

Rhodes woke me early the next morning. He insisted on me letting him pack my bag for whatever we were doing, and I guess a normal girl would have objected. I was pretty low maintenance, though, and was more excited about the fact that he was surprising me. I couldn't remember a time Mason had ever thought to surprise me with anything. I didn't mean to always compare them, but being that Mason was the only example of a relationship that I had to go off of, it happened frequently.

Rhodes outshined him in every category.

We were on the road by six, Rhodes behind the wheel of the Rover. He had one hand fixed at the top of the steering wheel and the other firmly on my thigh. It was so cliché, Willow would have hated it, but it made me smile for the first time in twenty-four hours.

We didn't talk much as Rhodes drove. I stared out the window, sipping on the tropical smoothie I'd picked up at the gas station before we left Poxton Beach. I didn't know where we were going, but I was relieved we were getting out of town, even if it were just for a while.

A little less than three hours later, we pulled into a small gravel parking lot in front of an open-faced, wooden gazebo type building. Rhodes jumped out and shook hands with a large bearded man who asked him a few questions before throwing me a wink and jogging off.

"Come on," Rhodes said, opening my door. I stepped out and helped him load up the few bags and cooler he'd packed. We made our way to a small shuttle, tucking our items around our feet as the same bearded man climbed into the driver's seat.

"Alright, y'all. You ready to spend some time on Edisto River?"

I smiled. "We're canoeing?"

"We are."

"All day?"

This time, Rhodes smirked. "Something like that."

I lifted a brow in question, but he just kissed my hand still locked in his.

The drive was short, but our driver, Clint, chatted animatedly about the river the entire time. It was one of the longest free-flowing blackwater rivers in North America and ran all the way down to its end in Edisto Beach, where it met the Atlantic. We were still in the same state, just a few hours from Poxton Beach, but it was as if we were in an entirely different country. It was so quiet, nothing but wildlife and the gentle rustling of the wind through the leaves.

Clint helped us unload the canoe when we arrived at the drop spot, lowering it steadily into the water. Rhodes secured our bags inside the canoe before attaching the small cooler to the back. It floated easily, and I marveled at bad boy Rhodes showing off his boy scout skills.

"Ready?" he asked, still steadying the canoe with his hands. He was glancing up at me through his slightly-longer-than-usual hair with a boyish grin.

I nodded, his excitement infectious. Rhodes and Clint both helped me inside the canoe, which really wasn't necessary, but I accepted the extra help. Lord knows I was far from graceful.

"We'll see you two tomorrow. Have fun!" Clint shook hands with Rhodes quickly before jogging back to the shuttle.

"Tomorrow?"

Rhodes grinned, climbing in to sit on the small bench behind mine in the canoe. We each had an oar, and Rhodes used his to kick us off the riverbank. "Relax. We're not paddling all that time."

"Then where are we going?"

"You'll see."

The Edisto River was smooth and easy to maneuver, its dark waters reflecting the bright blue sky and tall green trees surrounding it. We passed a few other canoes and kayaks and the occasional paddle board along the way, but for the most part, we had the river to ourselves. Each mile housed something new to see, from turtles to tree swings, and Rhodes surprised me by pulling my camera from one of the bags he packed so I could capture the moments. I tried focusing on what he'd said before, about not striving for so much control in my shots. I played with settings, filters, zoom and lighting, not letting my need to find the perfect shot drive my direction.

It was freeing.

We stopped at a shallow section for lunch, jumping out of the canoe and into the cool water after we ate. Rhodes had packed simple sandwiches for lunch, but I could see other ingredients in the cooler that were more suited to be cooked, which only made my curiosity grow.

Once we were back in the canoe, Rhodes took over paddling completely, letting me face him and relax a little. He was absolutely gorgeous to watch. The muscles in his chest and arms flexed with each row, and he had a permanent smile glued to his face. His fierce green eyes were set ablaze among the backdrop of the dark water and cypress trees.

"Can I ask you something?"

"Uh oh," Rhodes answered, smirking.

"Why don't you let anyone call you by your first name?"

He sighed, dropping the oars back into the water before leaning back and smoothly propelling us forward. For a long moment, he was quiet, and I almost told him he didn't have to tell me, though I desperately wanted to know. But after searching for the right words, he finally spoke.

"Do you know what the name William means?"

I shook my head.

"Resolute protector." Rhodes squinted against the sun fighting its way through the trees. "I believed in it when I was younger. One of my early foster moms, the only one I can recall who wasn't a drugged out loser, told me it meant I was born to protect those around me, so that's what I did. I stood up for those who couldn't defend themselves, whether that was a kid in school being bullied or one of my foster moms being smacked down by their piece of shit husbands." I flinched at that image, wondering how much Rhodes had to see in his formative years. I didn't have to wonder anymore where the scars on his abdomen came from.

"That's part of why I was seen as such a delinquent when I was in high school. Yeah, I got in a lot of fights and got caught in a lot of bad situations, but I was always in those situations because I was helping someone else. It was the one thing I clung on to. I wanted to be worth something to someone. I protected kids, teachers, friends, strangers, foster siblings, pets." He swallowed, his Adam 's apple bobbing beneath his stubble-covered neck. "And above all else, I protected Lana."

He didn't have to say another word for me to understand why he didn't let anyone call him William. He was her protector, but he wasn't able to save her. He didn't feel like he deserved the title anymore.

"I don't know, after she disappeared, I just felt this ultimate failure seep into my bones. It was like the only claim to worth I had was stolen. Or rather, I had let it go. There were signs leading up to her disappearance. Bruises, scratches. And she was always sad. Tired." He shook his head. "I asked a few times, but she said she was fine. I knew in my gut it was something more. A stalker, a crazy boyfriend — something. But she always tried to shelter me. And I let her. I didn't do shit about it. I just let it all go." His jaw was tense as he rowed. "So, I gave up protecting. I gave up trying to find value in myself. I gave up pretty much everything."

I chewed on his words, aching to reach out to him, but I wasn't sure if he'd let me hold him or not. It killed me to know he somehow felt responsible for Lana. It wasn't the kind of guilt that was easy to let go of.

"Can I ask you something else?"

Rhodes seemed to be still stuck in his own thoughts, but he nodded.

"Yesterday, you were the same Rhodes I met at the beginning of the summer. You pushed me away." He frowned, but didn't argue. "But then you showed up at my door last night. And now we're here. It seemed like you were so sure I'd betrayed you." Tucking my hands between the wood and the backs of my thighs, I glanced at him through my lashes. "What made you change your mind?"

He stopped rowing, letting the soft current of the river take over. His eyes were fixed on mine. "I just realized that I've lived a life without love, without caring for someone else or letting them care for me. And I don't want that to be the only kind of life I have." He shrugged. "I made up my mind that night you gave yourself to me that I was never going to walk away from you or the possibility to feel like I have a purpose again. I'm not letting one note change that."

My heart leapt at the word love leaving his lips. He wasn't saying that he loved me, but he wasn't saying he couldn't. To me, that was just as exhilarating.

We stopped again when we found a large rope swing, taking turns riding it out above the water before dropping in with a splash. I was in another two-piece bathing suit, one I'd purchased myself, and Rhodes took a photo of me in it mid-swing. He motioned me over once I resurfaced to show it to me and I smiled. I looked so free, so happy, so confident.

While Rhodes looked over the map he'd taken from Clint, I pulled on my white cover up and rested on a large log extended out over the water near the swing. I laid on my back, watching the clouds float the opposite way of the current, the sun glittering behind them. There was a soft, cool breeze over the water and it flowed through my hair as I rolled over onto my stomach.

I was face-to-face with my reflection in the dark river as I hung off the log, one arm hanging down toward the water. I studied the girl looking back at me — her long, dark blonde hair, slightly lighter at the ends from the summer sun. Her eyes were wide, cheeks high, smile genuine. She was far from the broken girl I'd seen in the mirror the first night Rhodes touched me.

That summer changed me — not just on the outside, but the inside, too. I didn't look at life as a burden or a puzzle I didn't fit into anymore. Instead, it was a beautiful challenge, one I didn't have to face alone. The girl gazing up at me from the river might have been thirty pounds lighter than the girl who entered that summer, but she was also thirty times stronger. She was smarter, more experienced — and she had no limits.

Extending my pointer finger, the tip just barely touched the surface of the water, sparking a ripple that distorted my face first before taking the rest of my body with it. It was then that I realized my life was my own. I could do anything, be anyone, if I only had the courage.

When Rhodes called my name, motioning back to the canoe, boyish grin locked on his face, I nodded and leaned up on the log. But before I jumped into the water, I glanced back down at River Natalie one more time, appreciating her for how far she'd come and knowing that there was still so much more to come for her, too.

I'd been so focused on losing weight, on getting to a certain point where I thought I'd find happiness. It turned out that joy wasn't made by the destination, but rather discovered in the journey.

I looked forward to the next mile in mine.

# CHAPTER
# 21

About an hour later, we came upon a large treehouse extending about twenty feet above the water. There was a fire pit just below it and a hammock hanging between two trees sticking up through the water of the river.

"Wow," I breathed. "How neat is this?"

"Glad you like our home for the evening."

I spun around. "Are you serious?"

Rhodes smiled, steering the canoe toward the house. Once we reached the bank, he hopped out and steadied it as I did the same before pulling it up onto shore. We each grabbed a bag and Rhodes lifted the cooler.

"We're staying here?"

"We are. It's all ours tonight."

I couldn't help the giddy feeling coming over me. I was never much of a camping kind of girl, but I always wanted a treehouse. Dale never built me one, he said it would be an eyesore on our perfect yard.

This house was the farthest thing from an eyesore.

We climbed up the wooden steps to the entrance, revealing an outdoor dining area complete with a rocking chair and tiki torches. Just inside was a small but clean and cozy futon, a make-shift kitchen with gas grill and cooking utensils and plenty of oil candles. It was just like any treehouse I'd ever dreamed of, except adult-size. All I needed was a *No Boys Allowed* sign. Sneaking a peek at the sliver of skin between the hem of Rhodes' shirt and his swim trunks as he reached up to tuck our cooler onto a shelf in the kitchen, I swallowed.

Never mind about that sign.

"Are you hungry yet?"

"Not really. Can we explore?"

Rhodes smiled. "Absolutely."

We spent the rest of the afternoon hiking, swinging off rope swings into the river, and lounging in the hammock out front. We talked about a little of everything, including how Rhodes had been looking into culinary schools. It was as if we were finding our confidence together — me in my body, Rhodes in his ability to be better than his past. It's amazing how just having someone believe in you can suddenly make something that seemed so impossible to achieve feel like it's only a matter of *when*, not if.

After dinner, Rhodes and I sat around the fire pit listening to the nature all around us. We made s'mores, which shocked me since I'd never seen Rhodes eat anything outside of his strict meal plan, and I played around with my camera, catching different shots of Rhodes through the flames of the fire.

"Why do you love photography?"

I smiled, snapping another photo of him. The orange glow from the fire played against the shadows of the night on his face. "I told you once before. You don't remember?"

"You told me you're nerdy about it and it's your passion. But you never told me *why*."

I frowned, realizing I didn't really know the answer. "I guess I just love the power of being able to temporarily freeze a moment in time, even if it's not as good as the real thing. I like being able to pick up a photo, close my eyes, and feel that place and time again." I flipped through a few settings on my camera and took another shot. "We have thousands of memories and our brain is like a never-ending filing cabinet. But sometimes you forget about something until someone reminds you to pull that file. That's what photos do for me. They take me back."

"And what about the future?"

I dropped my camera into my lap, adjusting my position on the small tree stump. "I don't know. I've always wanted to shoot photos for the future, photos that would drive me and make others who weren't in my memories feel something powerful. But, I guess, to be honest, I'm just kind of lacking inspiration."

It hurt to admit, because I'd always thought photography was the one thing in my life I had complete control over, but the truth was that I knew I had so much work to do to really hone my skills. It was part of the reason I wanted to go to an art school, not a state university.

Rhodes seemed lost in thought across the fire. After a moment, he slowly rose and pulled me to my feet, too. Sliding his hands into my hair, he pressed his lips to mine, claiming my mouth with his own. It was a possessive kiss. It was needy, yet patient and sure. He broke it long enough to whisper against my lips.

"So let me inspire you."

Suddenly, the fire's heat seemed so futile.

In one fluid movement, Rhodes lifted me and I wrapped my legs around his waist, locking my ankles. His mouth never left mine as he climbed the stairs. He laid me down softly onto the futon and stood, grabbing his shirt at the back of his neck and pulling it up and over his head. In the candlelight, the ridges of his abdomen were highlighted even more than usual. I bit my lip in anticipation of having him pressed against me.

Moving to the edge of the futon, I slid my hands over his muscles, and each one tensed with the touch. I pressed my lips to his skin, kissing him over and over. His hands found my hair, and the urge to take control hit me.

"I want to try something," I whispered, untying his board shorts. I tugged them down over his hips and they fell to the floor. Rhodes was so hard, so ready. He kicked the shorts to the side and stared down at me as I took him in my hand. Groaning, he flexed into my grasp as I moved my hand up and down his length in a slow and steady rhythm. Hesitantly, I bent forward and just barely touched his tip with my lips.

Rhodes growled, grabbing my chin between his forefinger and thumb and tilting my face to meet his. "Natalie," he breathed. I wasn't sure if it was a warning or a plea.

"I want to try," I repeated, swallowing. "But I need you to show me how." I'd never gone down on Mason, mostly because I'd never had any desire to see him come apart at my touch. With Rhodes, it was all I craved. I wanted to make him feel the way he made me feel — powerful, wanted, sexy.

He cursed, looking up to the ceiling like God would help him maintain composure. I took it as permission, sliding my tongue flat against his length before taking him in my mouth. He groaned, rolling his hips in time with my mouth, careful to not push too deep.

Grabbing my hand in his own, he showed me how to stroke him where my mouth wouldn't meet. He coached me through swirling my tongue and when I pulled him in too deep and gagged, he moaned. Apparently, gagging was a good thing.

Who knew?

I did it again, pulling him in a little deeper and letting my natural reflexes take over. This time, he cursed and pulled back.

"You're trying to kill me."

"On the contrary. I'm trying to make you come."

Rhodes smirked at my forwardness and I blushed. He bent to my lips, covering them with his own and slowly laying me back on the thin mattress. Effortlessly, he stripped my clothes off, piece by piece, littering the treehouse with them as he did. When he slid between my legs, pressing his hard on against my inner thigh, my breath caught and I held on tight to his biceps. He reached blindly for his wallet, but I grabbed his hand with my own.

"I just want you."

Rhodes furrowed his brows, unsure. I'd been on birth control for two weeks and I wanted nothing more than to feel him, *only* him, inside me. I physically ached for that uncensored connection.

"Please," I thrusted my hips up to meet his, the tip of him sliding to my wet opening. He inhaled stiffly, pressing his forehead to mine.

"You're so light, Natalie." He shook his head, but gripped me tighter. "I'm afraid I'll ruin you with my darkness."

I kissed him hard, tugging on his bottom lip with my teeth as I struggled for a way to make him understand.

Pressing my hands firmly against his chest, I slipped from beneath him and crossed the room. I blew out the candle on the small coffee table before moving to the next in the small kitchen. One by one, I extinguished the flames before making my way back to him.

He pulled me to straddle his lap and I locked my fingers behind his neck. I could barely see him, only the soft natural light from the stars and moon sneaking in through the open windows lit the house. Still, I could feel every inch of him pressed against me, I could hear his heart hammering in his chest, I could smell the scent of his body wash mixed with his desire.

"Sometimes, the darkness is where you find yourself." Carefully, I slid down onto his length, feeling every naked inch of him for the first time as I took control. "Let me find myself in you."

Rhodes groaned, his jaw falling slack as he tilted his eyes to the sky.

He rolled his hips into me and I gasped at the fullness. We blindly felt for each other, kissing and touching to find where we wanted to be. His breaths were in my ear, his tongue was on my skin. He was everywhere. I was nowhere. He completely surrounded me.

Just like the darkness.

It was in the moonlit shadows of that night that I found myself. Rhodes wanted to inspire me, but the truth was that it was the possibility of what we could be together that inspired me most. For one night, even if that was all there could be, I lived inside a passion I never knew existed with a man I never saw coming.

Rhodes was an unanticipated thunderstorm.

And I danced in his rain.

# CHAPTER

# 22

"So let me get this straight," Willow said, tucking her long, caramel-colored legs underneath her. They were dark against the soft yellow of her new dorm room comforter. "Rhodes is actually his last name, but you can't tell me what his first name is because it's personal?"

I nodded, smiling at the screen of my laptop where Willow was framed in a video chat window. It was Wednesday, my day off from training, so we made sure to schedule time to catch up. She had already shown me her room and told me every detail about her first college party, and now we had moved on to Rhodes, which was always her favorite topic of conversation.

"And the same Rhodes who made Nathan Arnold piss himself during weightlifting practice from simply yelling at him to move benches took you on a canoe trip down Edisto River to a beautiful tree house tucked into the trees, where you let him teach you how to suck his wang?"

I blushed, covering my face with my pillow. "Lo!"

"Well, am I on track so far?"

Rolling my eyes, I waved my hand at her to continue, cocking a brow in amusement.

"So you had this super romantic weekend together, which is already weird because it's Rhodes, but on top of it all, you did so with both of you knowing in the back of your mind that he found a note on his bike that said to stay away from you and he thinks it's written in his dead sister's handwriting?"

"Willow," I warned, shaking my head. "Have a little respect."

"Okay, his *assumed*-to-be-dead sister."

"That's not any better."

"But am I right?"

I sighed, tucking my pillow closer to my chest and resting my chin on the edge. "Pretty much."

Willow clicked her tongue. "Jeepers, chica. I think your summer is more interesting than my entire life." I chuckled, not moving my head from its resting place on the pillow. She watched me through the screen for a moment. "You really like him, don't you?"

I nodded.

"It scares the shit out of you." She said it as a statement, not a question. I simply nodded again.

"It's just, when I first met Rhodes, he was so closed off to me. To the world. And now that he's letting me in, it's like he's pulling me down fast into an ocean of feelings I've never felt before."

"And you think you'll drown?"

I swallowed. "I know I will. I'm the ship, he's the water. It never ends well for me when there's a storm."

Willow blinked. "Are you turning into me? That totally sounds like some shit I would say."

"Someone in Poxton Beach has to take your place. Might as well be me."

"Please," she said, waving her hand at the screen and checking the polish on her nails. "No one can think of bullshit clichés like I can. But valiant effort, Nat."

She winked and we both laughed. Willow took it as an opportunity to change the subject, which I was grateful for.

"So Mom and Dale come home tonight?"

"Yeah, they should be here in a couple of hours."

"You going to tell them about you and Rhodes?"

I frowned. "I don't know yet."

Willow shook her head. "You couldn't just fall for a banker's son? Or wait until college and find a lawyer-to-be? Something boring and predictable that would save you this emotional tug of war and make your parents happy?"

"I've been doing boring my entire life," I said, shrugging. "I'll take whatever heartache is coming to feel this alive for a while longer."

Willow smirked, braiding her long hair to the side. "My best friend is growing up."

"I'll have wrinkles soon."

"Or gray hair."

"Probably both."

"Don't worry," Willow assured me. "I've read anti-aging blog posts. I know just the cream and hair dye to fix all of that. As long as your vag doesn't dry up, we should be good."

I laughed. "I miss you."

"Miss you more."

After hearing horror stories about Willow's roommate and refusing to tell her anything about my experience going down on Rhodes, we reluctantly ended our video chat just as I heard the front door opening downstairs. Christina had already gone home for the evening, so I knew it was Mom and Dale.

Tossing my hair up into a messy bun, I skipped downstairs, excited to hear about their trip up north. As soon as my feet hit the bottom stair and I saw my mom's mascara-streaked face, my stomach fell.

"Mom?"

She choked on a sob, her hand flying up to cover her lips.

"Oh my God, what's wrong? What happened?" I flew from the stairs and pulled her into a hug. She folded into me easily, leaving all of her weight for me to hold. I felt the tears run from her eyes and soak through my t-shirt, but I only held her tighter.

When another car door slammed outside, Mom's head snapped up. Wiping at her face, she urged me toward the stairs. "Go upstairs, honey. I'll come to your room in a little bit."

"No, I'm not going anywhere. Is he high?"

She smiled, but another tear fell from the apple of her cheek onto the hardwood floor. "It's okay, sweetie.

I just want to get him to bed and then I'll come up. I promise."

"I can help you," I said, making a move toward the door.

"No!" The tone of her voice surprised me and I halted. "Damnit, Natalie, do as you're told and go to your room!" My mouth popped open and Mom bit her lip, closing her eyes tight. "I'm sorry. Please, honey, just give me a few minutes."

The door swung open behind her and Dale stumbled through the frame. His dark hair was slick with sweat, his eyes rimmed in red. When they found mine, I gulped.

I'd always seen Dale as nurturing, kind of like the father I'd never had. He was caring and calm, patient and understanding. He was a businessman, firm but compassionate. But that night, all I saw when I looked into his eyes was a menacing calm that scared me more than I would admit to myself.

"Natalie, please," my mom begged. I looked to her once more, feeling my heart ache at the sight of her tears, before I did as she asked. I didn't chance another look at Dale before jogging up the stairs and into my room. Shutting the door behind me, I reached for my phone and quickly typed out a text to Rhodes. He was working the first night shift at his new job, serving as one of the cooks in the small diner right across the street from the high school. It wasn't everything he wanted, but it was a start. And right now, it was a major inconvenience to me. I hated how selfish I felt, but I needed him. When ten minutes went by without him responding, I knew I wouldn't hear from him until his shift ended.

Fighting back my own tears, I collapsed into the covers of my bed and wrapped them around me. I stared at my closed door, listening to the shuffling and muffled voices of Mom and Dale down the hall. I had no idea what was happening. Was it Dale's addiction? What exactly was he addicted to? Had he hit Mom? *Would* he hit Mom?

It seemed like an eternity had passed by when Mom finally slipped through my door, holding her finger to her lips to ask me to stay quiet. I simply held up the covers so she could crawl into bed with me. When she did, I wrapped my arms around her and told her I loved her.

And she cried.

I wanted to ask her what happened. I wanted her to stop acting like I wasn't old enough to handle whatever was happening. But, in that moment, I knew all she needed was for me to be there, so I didn't ask anything at all. I hugged her and let her know she wasn't alone. That was what she needed.

Mom fell asleep after a while, and I tried to rest, but failed. Around one, Mom kissed me on the forehead and slipped out of bed. I pretended to be asleep, but I listened to her feet pad down the hallway to her and Dale's room. Once she was inside, I reached for my phone and sighed with relief when I saw the text from Rhodes.

## - Come over. -

I pulled on a pair of yoga pants and a PBHS hoodie before quietly sneaking out. Although I probably didn't need to be quiet at all — Dale was clearly wasted and I knew Mom had left my room to go take a sleeping pill. She'd been self-medicating almost every night that summer and didn't think I had noticed.

Rhodes was standing outside when I pulled into his apartment. He yanked the driver door open and I leapt into his arms, burying my face into his neck. He held me tight, gently took the keys from my hand, locked the Rover, and carried me inside.

He helped me to the couch and brought me a glass of water, but I set it to the side without taking a drink. Rhodes opened his arm for me and I snuggled into his chest.

"Want to talk about it?"

I shook my head, kissing the hot skin of his neck. He had already changed into navy blue basketball shorts and a plain white t-shirt and his hair was damp from a shower, but he still smelled faintly of grease.

"You sure?"

"I don't really know what's going on, to be honest. Dale has a problem, Mom is treating me like I'm too young to understand, and I just don't want to be home right now."

He nodded. "I know that feeling. Are you hungry?"

"Not really."

"Tired?"

"Definitely not."

Rhodes frowned. "Tell me how to help you, Bug." He lifted my chin with his knuckle, his viridescent eyes flicking back and forth between my chocolate irises. My eyes fell to his lips, and without hesitating, he answered the request I didn't have to speak aloud.

He winced as his lips met mine, as if my mouth had burned his, and maybe it had. I felt the heat every time Rhodes touched me, and at this point, I wasn't ruling out that maybe I had the power to do the same to him.

No matter how many times Rhodes kissed me, my heart still hammered in my chest every time his tongue snaked in to meet mine. He sensed it, gently laying me down on the couch. He moved between my thighs, his rough hand hiking one up and hitching it around his waist. I gasped at the feel of him pressed against me and he smirked against my lips.

"How do you do that?" I breathed.

He sucked my lower lip between his teeth and released it with a pop. "Do what?"

"Make me forget all the pain?"

Rhodes stilled, his thumb softly grazing the exposed skin between my pants and hoodie. His eyes searched mine before he pulled me up just enough to strip my sweater over my head. Dropping it to the floor, he ran the pad of his thumb across my lower lip where his teeth had just marked me for his own.

"I don't know, but I don't ever want to stop." His mouth found the sensitive skin of my neck, my collarbone, the swell of my breast. He used both hands to push my tank top up so he could kiss down my navel. When his teeth grazed my hip bone, I bucked, and he took it as permission to slide my pants down to my knees. Leaning back on his heels, he slowly grabbed the fabric bunched over my left leg and pulled it off, his eyes locked on mine the entire time. He did the same to what was left hanging from my right leg before dropping them to the ground next to my hoodie.

Rhodes pulled me to sit up straight. My feet were on the floor for only a moment before he fell to the ground and hiked both of my knees up on his shoulders. I gasped at the sight of his neon eyes piercing the darkness as he gazed up at me.

"Give me all your pain, Natalie," he whispered, his skin hot against my center. Chills raced from the contact in all directions, blanketing me completely. "Let me take it as my own."

He dropped his mouth to my clit, surrounding it with wet, hot ecstasy. I moaned, gripping the edge of the couch and fighting the urge to grind my hips into him. He was sucking, licking, kissing, driving me wild.

Rhodes slipped a finger inside me and my hands found his hair, holding on tight for the orgasm I felt building with each flick of his tongue.

"Don't hold back," he growled, sliding another finger inside. It glided in effortlessly and I bucked my hips. "Take control."

Using my hands in his hair, I guided his mouth, tugging his hair when he found the sweet spot. When he sucked my clit hard between his teeth, I cried out, grinding my pelvis into him. He gripped my behind in his large hand and pulled me even closer, nipping and sucking me closer and closer to the edge.

"I'm so close," I panted, my hands flying to the couch again. I kept trying to grip the sharp pleasure I felt floating in space between us. I was right there, but I couldn't quite grasp it.

He was so hot against my sensitive skin, anytime he pulled back the sharp contrast of the cool air of his apartment sent a jolt through me. When I felt myself nearing the edge again, I squeezed my eyes tight, moving my hips in time with his tongue and fingers.

Rhodes' free hand found my nipple and he rolled it between his fingers, adding a new jolt of pleasure. Gripping his hair again, I wriggled my hips and he slid his fingers in deeper, feeding my need. Then, he looked up at me, dragging his tongue up my slit before sucking my clit hard as he thrust even deeper.

That's all it took.

I tumbled over the cliff, falling forever into nothing. Blackness invaded my vision and heat spread from his mouth to every end of my body. I felt the blood rush all the way down to my toes.

As I came down from my high, Rhodes crawled up my body and kissed me every inch of the way until he reached my mouth. I tasted myself on his lips. I felt my soul in his eyes.

He hadn't just taken my pain. He'd taken all of me.

And I only wanted all of him in return.

# CHAPTER

# 23

Reluctantly, I slipped out of Rhodes' bed and drove home just before dawn. Though I barely slept that night, I stayed in bed until just after noon, dragging myself downstairs with just enough time to eat something light and digest before my training session. I was exhausted, but ready to work. Now that I knew my body had the capability to change, I wanted to push harder — see how far I could go. Still, my hip flexors were deliciously sore from my night with Rhodes and I wasn't exactly looking forward to multiplying that tenfold.

When I rounded the corner into the kitchen, Mom was leaning back against the counter, sipping from a large white mug that read *But First, Coffee*. From the looks of it, she hadn't been up long, either.

"Morning," she said cheerily, smiling over the steam. The dark circles beneath her eyes were a subtle reminder of the night before.

"Hey, Mom. How are you feeling?"

"Oh I'm great, sweetie. Everything is fine."

I frowned. "Mom. Stop lying to me."

She took another sip, staring blankly across the kitchen and out the sliding glass door to our pool area. Sighing, I stepped in front of her and grabbed her wrists in my hands.

"Momma, if Dale hurt you, or if you're unhappy with him, we can leave. Just say the word."

She laughed, though her face twisted in a way that I thought she might cry again. "I'm not lying, sweetie. Everything *is* fine. Dale and I are just like any other couple. We have our issues. But at the end of the day, we love each other. In fact," she added, taking a last sip of her coffee before pouring the rest down the drain. "He was gone early this morning. How much do you want to bet he bounds through that door with flowers any second now?"

"Do flowers fix what happened last night?"

She shrugged. "They're a start."

My stomach knotted. I knew there was more that she wasn't telling me, but I couldn't force it out of her. Mom and I had never talked about her and Dale's relationship. I knew that they started dating shortly after my father took off and Dale had whisked Mom away in a whirlwind romance. All my life, I'd watched Dale love her like I wanted a man to love me one day. Now, I felt like I had been standing in a thick blanket of fog that was suddenly being fought off by the sun.

"So," Mom said, clearing her throat and tidying a stack of paper on the counter. "I heard Mason asked you out at Willow's party."

I scoffed. "First of all, how in the world are you hearing stories from a high school party? And secondly, no, he didn't." I shifted. "He may have said something along the lines of wanting me back, but he did not ask me on a date."

"Natalie," my mom said, crossing her arms over her chest. She was still dressed in her pajamas. That's how I knew she'd had a rough night. Jillian Poxton did not lounge around in pajama pants and a t-shirt. She must have stolen them from my dresser. "That is essentially the same thing. And why are you telling me this story like you didn't take him up on his offer?"

I shrugged, pouring myself a glass of water. "Because I didn't."

Mom's mouth popped open.

"I don't want to be with Mason anymore," I explained, sipping from the glass. "I didn't see it when it happened, but I think him breaking up with me was one of the best things that could have happened."

"I don't understand." Mom shook her head, her blonde locks falling from the loose ponytail she'd tied. "Mason is from a good family, Natalie. He could make you happy. And you'd be comfortable."

"I don't want to be just comfortable, Mom. I want a love that makes me everything *but* comfortable. If it doesn't drive me mad, if it doesn't break my heart at the thought of losing it, if it doesn't push me to new places and force me to grow — what kind of love is it, really?"

Mom appraised me for a moment, chewing the inside of her cheek. "You talk about it like you might have already found it."

I dropped my gaze to my water, tracing the lid of the glass with my pointer finger.

She sighed. "Honey, as a woman, sometimes you have to make sacrifices. Sometimes you have to make *choices* about what you need in life and how to get it."

"Did you have to make sacrifices with Dale?" I lifted my eyes to hers again.

She swallowed. "Yes. And with your father, too. But every choice I made was to better my life. And yours." She cleared her throat, fingering the sweatpants she was wearing as if she just realized she was in them. "They weren't always the easiest choices, but women don't exactly have it easy when it comes to the battle of life versus love."

Shrugging, I finished the last of my water and dropped the glass in the sink. "I don't think the two have to be on opposite sides of the war line."

Mom eyed me again, opening her mouth to say more before quickly closing it and standing up straighter. "I suppose it's something you'll have to learn on your own, sweetie." She snapped her fingers. "Oh! That reminds me. I need to start a grocery list for Christina. You have any requests?"

I chuckled, watching Mom snap right back into business mode. "Life, love, and battle reminded you of groceries?"

She stuck her tongue out and I giggled again, but when my eyes focused on the notepad she was writing on, the laugh caught in my throat.

"Oh my God," I whispered.

"You okay, sweetie?" Mom had stopped writing, but my eyes were still glued to the page.

Snapping out of my haze, I grabbed the keys to the Rover and jogged toward the door, grabbing my gym bag off the couch as I passed.

"Sweetie?"

"Fine, Mom!" I yelled over my shoulder as I blew through the front door. "Just late for training. See you later!"

Slamming the door behind me a little harder than I meant, I sprinted for the car and threw it in drive, tearing out of the driveway. My foot was hard on the gas pedal all the way to the gym and I parked across two parking spots before leaving my bag behind and running straight back to the training room.

Rhodes was spotting one of his clients as she benched just the bar. I was tempted to roll my eyes at the way she was drooling as she gazed up at him, but I had more important emotions rolling through me.

"I know where the note came from," I blurted out. Rhodes' brows turned in and he eyed me curiously. I wasn't sure if it was because I was an hour early to training or what I had just said or both.

"What?"

"Just," I stopped his question with my hand, motioning to the woman on the bench. "Wrap this up and come back to the office."

"I'm in the middle of a session, Natalie," he warned. Even though he had his new job at the restaurant, he still needed his training job and I knew that. But this couldn't wait.

I gave him a pointed look to emphasize the urgency and he blew out a breath through his nose, motioning with a nod of his head for me to go back to the office. I heard him tell his client to take a water break and hit cardio. She whined, literally whined, and I ground my teeth. Before I acted on my annoyance, I closed the glass office door behind me and paced around the desk.

Rhodes opened the door moments later and I started rambling before he had the chance to close it again. "It's from the marina. The note. It's Dale's stationery. I knew I had seen this mark before." I unfolded the note and smoothed it out on the desk, pointing to the small orange markings where the tear line was. The note was torn at the bottom edge, like someone had tried to tear off the logo, but even with just the top of it there — I recognized it.

"I don't understand." Rhodes shook his head, brows furrowed.

"This is the top of Dale's stationery logo. But see how it's an ugly orange color?" Rhodes nodded. "It's supposed to be red. Sometimes, the notepads like the one this paper came from get printed incorrectly. It drives my mom absolutely insane because she's a perfectionist. But, she hates being wasteful, too. She won't let Dale use them for anything customer-facing, so she takes all the misprints down to the Poxton Beach Dry Boat Storage Marina. They're always writing notes and putting them on the boats so the employees know where to put them and what customer and such. Since it's just them that see it, Mom figures it's a way to get use out of the stationery without hurting Dale's 'brand' or whatever."

Rhodes lifted a brow. "Your mom is strange."

"Rhodes, did you hear what I said?" I asked, ignoring his attempt at humor. "The note came from the marina. It was in your sister's handwriting." I swallowed. "We may be able to find some answers. We may be able to find *her*."

Rhodes frowned, leaning back against the edge of the desk. He raked his hands over his stubble before crossing his arms hard across his chest. "How?"

"I know where Dale keeps his keys," I whispered. "*All* of his keys." Rhodes' eyes widened at my implication. "Are you up for a little recon mission?"

# CHAPTER

# 24

"I don't even understand the concept of this place," Rhodes whispered as I unlocked the large gate guarding the boat barn. I used to find it funny when Mom called it that, but that's exactly what it was really — a big metal barn full of boats.

"It's just a different way to store your boat. It's actually better for a lot of the ones around here. Keeps them from sitting in salt water and stuff."

Rhodes didn't comment further as we slipped through the gate. I locked it again behind us and we made our way toward the large building.

The night air was warm and wet against my skin and the small tendrils of hair hanging from my bun onto my neck were already soaked. Rhodes didn't seem nervous or tense as we approached the entrance to the building.

I was both.

We gazed up at the columns and rows of boats once we walked inside the barn. I clicked on the flashlight I'd taken from Dale's garage to illuminate them better and scanned the length of the barn. They were stacked ten high and hundreds across, all facing us stern side.

"What are we even looking for?"

"I don't know, Rhodes. Anything that might connect that note and your sister." His brows were furrowed, his jaw set. "Why do I get the feeling that you don't want to be here?"

He sighed. "Sorry. I'm just not sure how to feel about all of this." It was then that I noticed the worry hidden behind his strong eyes. I knew what he was feeling. He didn't want to get his hopes up only to be let down. Or maybe he was afraid of what he'd find. Either way, it was apparent that he may not have been nervous or tense, but he was clearly uncomfortable.

"Try not to think too much about it. If we find something, great. If not, then we move forward and figure something else out. Okay?"

Rhodes took a moment to process before gently nodding. "Okay."

Grabbing his hand, I pointed the flashlight forward and we dove deeper into the barn.

We walked slowly down the main hall, shining the light between each row of boats and up through the various columns. Neither of us spoke, and neither of us found anything to speak of. The longer we were there, the more I worried if I'd made a stupid decision. What exactly *did* I expect to find?

"Hey wait a second," Rhodes whispered, his eyes trained on the row of boats to our right. "What is that?"

I pointed the flashlight to follow his gaze,

illuminating something shiny and small near the back wall. Rhodes glanced back at me questioningly before taking a step toward it.

My heart hammered in my ears as we inched between the boats. When Rhodes and I rounded the front of the boat, he bent slowly, retrieving the object on the ground.

"What is it?" I asked, voice just above a whisper. Rhodes was staring at whatever was in his hands so intently I wondered if he even heard me.

"Oh my God."

"What?" I leaned up to look closer. "What is it?"

He shook his head, forehead wrinkled between his eyebrows. "It's hers." He held the object out to me — a bracelet. It dangled over his pointer finger as his eyes found mine. "It's Lana's. She wore this every day." He swallowed. "It was a gift from me when we turned sixteen."

My heart stopped.

It was a small, dainty bracelet — a thin chain with one solo pearl charm. Their birthstone. Carefully, I reached out to touch the cool silver and rolled the pearl between my fingers, bringing away a film of dust with them. "It doesn't seem like it's been worn in a while."

"What the hell?" He shook his head and I was at a loss for words, too. Nothing was making sense. "Do you think it's the person who took her? Did it happen here?"

"Maybe," I said, my stomach knotting at the thought. The soft click of the shutter sounded as I pulled out my camera and took a photo of the bracelet still hanging from his fingers. Every hair on my body was standing at attention, my fight or flight instincts kicking in. I hadn't been scared before, but I was now. "It wouldn't be weird for it to be left alone back here. These are the vacationer boats. The employees are lucky if they get sent down here more than once a year to pull one of these boats out."

"And you're positive that the note had to have come from here?"

I glanced around, trying to find one of the stationery pages stuck in the window of one of the boats around us. Scanning the windshields, I finally found a sheet four rows down. Peeling it from its careful placement, I held it up for Rhodes to inspect.

"See the bottom logo?" I asked. He nodded, and I pulled the note he'd found on his bike from my pocket. When I held them up next to each other, there was no refuting it. There was just a tiny little piece of the logo on the bottom of the note from Rhodes' sister, but it was there. I snapped another photo.

Rhodes pinched the bridge of his nose. I knew his head was spinning, too. "What the fuck is going on?"

"My thoughts exactly," a rough voice responded. Rhodes and I turned quickly and were met with a blinding white light. Instinctively, Rhodes threw himself between the offender and myself, serving as a human shield.

The light dropped, and my stomach fell right along with it when I realized who was holding it.

A cop.

"Shit," Rhodes muttered.

The cop was young, maybe in his thirties, with caramel skin and a dark buzz cut. His eyes were shaded, but soft, as if he didn't like busting us any more than we liked getting busted. My eyes adjusted to the light difference and I noticed his name badge read *MARTINO*.

"Do you two realize you're trespassing right now?"

"I'm sorry sir," I tried, maneuvering my way around Rhodes. "It's my fault. I just wanted to—"

"And do you realize that because you climbed over that fence to get into a clearly marked no-trespassing property, you could face a first-degree trespassing charge?" He shook his head, almost like he was our parent, before calling out some sort of code into his radio along with our location. "Couldn't even be smart about it. Flashlights? Really? I saw them from the road."

"And do *you* realize you're being a class A fuck boy right now?"

"Rhodes!" I warned, shocked at his disrespect. I was trying to talk us out of the situation, Rhodes was ready to make it worse.

"Wait," Officer Martino interrupted. "Rhodes? As in William Rhodes?"

Rhodes didn't answer. His jaw ticked and he kept his hard eyes trained on the cop, who was now looking at Rhodes in a completely different way. It was as if he recognized him, or as if he was seeing a ghost of his past rise right out of the ground. I knew Rhodes was in and out of juvie when we were younger, but had that reputation really stuck for this long?

"Copy. Calling the property owner now," a woman's voice called over the radio fastened to the officer's hip, breaking the awkward silence stretching between us. It was my turn to add another twist to the night.

"Here," I offered, reaching into my pocket for my phone. The officer pulled his gun, pointing it straight at my chest.

"Whoa whoa whoa!" Rhodes stepped in front of me again, scowling at the cop. "Are you fucking crazy?"

"Keep your hands where I can see them!"

I panicked, dropping my phone completely and letting it shatter on the ground as I lifted my arms above my head. "I'm sorry," I said with shaky voice. I sounded weak, and in that moment, maybe I was. I'd never been in trouble with law enforcement. I didn't know how to act. I didn't understand why this man looked at me like a criminal. "I was just going to call him for you."

"What are you talking about?"

Shifting on my feet, I glanced at Rhodes before answering. "I'm Natalie Poxton." My eyes found the officer's just in time to see recognition set in. "The property owner is my dad."

I'd never stared at my feet for so long.

My eyes were tracing the stitches on my Keds, following the lining of the laces through each hoop and back. I could hear Mom tapping her finger on the edge of the kitchen counter and even though I hadn't looked yet, I could feel Dale's eyes on the point of contact where Rhodes' hand held mine. None of us had said a word since Officer Martino left, and I definitely didn't want to be the first to break that silence.

Disappointing Mom and Dale wasn't something I was used to. Before now, my only offenses had been minor party incidents that they usually scolded me for before breaking out into laughter. It was child's play. Something all teenagers in Poxton Beach went through.

This, however, was not.

"Mr. and Mrs. Poxton," Rhodes started, his deep baritone sounding so foreign beneath the blanket of silence we'd been under. "I just want to apologize for our actions tonight. Natalie had nothing to do with what happened. It was my idea."

I snapped my attention to Rhodes, mouth open and ready to correct him, but he gave me a stern look that made me shut it, instead.

"Well that much is obvious," Dale retorted. "But you're notorious for bad ideas, aren't you, Rhodes?"

"Dale!" Rhodes squeezed my hand tighter, but I refused to let Dale talk to him that way.

"Don't raise your voice at us, young lady," Mom warned. I couldn't remember the last time she'd called me *young lady*.

"Mom, it wasn't his fault. It was my idea to break into the boat barn tonight."

"Honey," she said the pet name with a hint of sympathy, as if I didn't know what I was saying.

"It's true! It was my idea. And I'm sorry. But look, nothing was taken, we didn't break anything. We were just…" My voice trailed off when I realized I couldn't exactly tell them what we were doing.

"You were just *what*, Natalie?" Dale probed. His brows were set in a firm straight line over his hard eyes.

"I can't tell you." I murmured the words, just barely audible over the hum of the refrigerator.

"Why?" Mom asked. She was heated, angrier than I'd ever seen her. I glanced to Rhodes, but that only fueled her fire. "It's clear that whatever you were doing, it was something you didn't want us finding out. And that won't fly in this household."

"I'm sorry. It won't happen—"

"Again?" Dale asked, laughing a little. "Oh, you bet your ass it won't. I don't know who you've become hanging out with this delinquent," he added, gesturing to Rhodes. "But stealing my keys and trespassing on a property you know you shouldn't be on is absolutely unacceptable."

"Stop talking about him like he's not standing right next to me!"

"Bug, it's fine," Rhodes soothed, rubbing the pad of his thumb along my hand. "I'm just going to wait outside."

"Oh no you are not, young man," Mom said. She was shaking slightly, her face red and blotchy. "You are never to see my daughter again. Ever. Do you hear me?"

"Mom!" I choked on her name, my heart jumping to attention at her implication. It didn't slowly accelerate. It jumped. It galloped. I felt it threatening to break through the confines of my rib cage.

"Do not argue with me, Natalie! Now I have had enough of this nonsense. Rhodes was your trainer and that was all he was ever meant to be. Clearly he has seduced you, that much is obvious, but that all ends tonight. I will not stand for this any longer."

"Are you serious?" I cried incredulously. I dropped Rhodes' hand, stepping toward her. "Do you *hear* yourself? Do you hear the way you're talking about a human being who's standing right here in your kitchen?"

"This isn't up for discussion."

"You don't get to decide what I do with my life!"

"As long as you live under this roof, we do. Now stop disrespecting your mother and walk him out," Dale demanded. He wouldn't even say Rhodes' name.

"Then I'll move out!"

"And go where?" Mom asked incredulously. "You're not enrolled in college, you don't have a job, and you won't have a cent to your name if you disobey us."

"I'm not staying away from him." I shook my head, my eyes blurring with tears that quickly bubbled and fell over my cheeks. Faintly, I heard our front door close, and I whipped around to find Rhodes gone. "Rhodes?"

"Just let him go, sweetie." Mom reached out to touch my hand but I jerked back. I plead with my eyes for her to stop, for her to wake up and realize what she was doing, but she remained unmoved.

"You're awful," I whispered, my eyes bouncing between the two of them. "Just because you have your own fucked up shit going on doesn't mean you have to drag me down with you."

"Natalie!" Dale chastised, but I turned on my heel and sprinted out the door without another word.

I expected Rhodes to be gone, but he was still standing in the driveway, hands in his pockets, facing the road. The moon was barely a sliver that night, and the darkness only made me feel more helpless as I walked slowly toward him. My steps were soft, the night was quiet — such a contrast from the war raging inside me.

Sliding my hands through the space between his arms and his middle, I wrapped myself around him, pressing my forehead into the hard muscles of his back. He was shivering, just slightly, just barely enough to notice.

"I'm so sorry."

He cleared his throat, lifting one arm to pull me into his side. "Don't be."

"I can't believe them. If they think I'm going to listen to them, they've seriously lost their minds."

"They're right, Natalie."

I lifted my head from his chest and glanced up at his stoic expression. "What? Rhodes, no, they're not. They don't know anything about you."

"And you do?" he challenged, dropping his hold on me. I was suddenly so cold.

"Yes," I whispered, though the way he was looking at me made me feel like I shouldn't be so sure. His emerald eyes were wild, mouth pressed into a thin line, jaw set.

"I'm not right for you, Natalie. I don't fit into this life. Into *your* life."

"Stop, Rhodes. You know they aren't me."

"But this *is* your life, Natalie," he said again. "This is how it's supposed to be for you. It's what you deserve. Great parents, a nice house, a rich husband with the means to take care of you." He licked his lower lip, his brows knitting together. "You deserve a good life, one without the pain I've already brought you and that I know I'll bring continually, over and over again. I'm trouble. I'm fucked up. I have baggage. I have weight."

"You're none of those things!" I argued. "You're strong. And passionate. And you've pushed me to be someone I never knew I could be this summer."

"And that's just it," he said. "That's all I am for you, Natalie. Yes, I do think I changed you this summer, just the way you changed me. And that's where it ends. I'm not your prince, Bug. I'm not the one you marry and live a long happy life with, the one you have kids with, the one you sit in a rocking chair next to when you're old." He shook his head but I shook mine harder. I could feel it. He was pulling back, retreating into the same shell I'd found him in just two months before. "I. Don't. Fit. I'm a stage for you. A chapter. And this is the last page."

"Please, Rhodes," I begged, but he pushed past me to the side of the house where he'd parked his bike. I followed. "You don't mean this. You said you promised yourself you were done walking away from me. You know this isn't it. This isn't over." I was on his tail every step, but he kept pace until he reached his bike. He climbed on, not saying another word. "Damnit, Rhodes, look at me!"

It was then I noticed how hard his breaths were coming. His chest rose and fell in an unsteady rhythm, the tremble still evident in his hands. He gripped his helmet, but paused, turning to face me. His Adam's apple bobbed in his throat as he waited for my move. I knew he didn't *want* to leave me, but for some reason he felt he needed to.

If he was going to walk away, I wasn't going to let him do it without knowing the truth.

"I chose you. Remember?"

"I didn't ask you to choose me."

"You didn't ask me to love you, either."

He scowled, but I saw him crack beneath it. "You don't love me, Natalie."

"Don't tell me what I feel," I cried. My voice was shaky, breaking with every word. "I wish I didn't love you, but I do." Rhodes' eyes softened, but his lips were still pressed together. I could see it. He was trying not to feel, and I was determined to make him. "It hit me all at once, like a thought or a memory of something I've known all along. I don't have a choice, Rhodes. I love you because there is no other option for me."

I knew he wouldn't say it back, and I didn't expect him to. I only wanted him to stay. Because in my heart,

I already knew he loved me. He loved me with such intensity that I should have been terrified. Instead, I was fascinated. And desperate for more.

My heart wasn't ready to let him go.

Rhodes swallowed, and his eyes fell to my lips. For a moment, I thought he might reach for me. His hand twitched where it held the straps of his helmet, and I willed him to follow through with the instinct.

But he didn't.

There were no physical walls to be seen, but I still watched as they slammed down around him. I watched his eyes gloss over. I watched the scowl form over his softened features, hardening them again, maybe even more so than before.

Slipping the helmet over his head, he buckled the straps and gripped the handlebars, turning to face the road. "I told you that night that you were making the wrong decision," he said, his voice low. He hesitated for just a moment before revving the engine to life. "You should have listened to me."

I squeezed my eyes shut and let two tears fall parallel down my cheeks. I kept them shut and listened to him drive away. Even when the last sound of the engine had faded and I was alone again in the still night air, I refused to open my eyes. I wouldn't watch him leave. I wouldn't face the fact that he was gone. I wouldn't admit that he left, not after what I'd told him.

All that time, I had felt the break coming. I had seen the warning signs. We both had. I guess in a way, we knew it was only a matter of time before the fragile shell of our relationship cracked beneath the weight of reality. I was content to live in that dream with him until it all came crashing down and the rubble killed us both, but he had left without me. Now, I was alone, clinging to the *what ifs* that he refused to hear. The crack was spreading faster and faster, and I watched helplessly as it creaked across the only foundation I had ever built.

I still stayed, waiting to be crushed, praying to be saved.

And the only comfort I found was that regardless of the outcome, it would all be over soon.

# CHAPTER

# 25

There's something so strangely satisfying about heartbreak. It's almost like if you can feel that much for anything, maybe life is worth it. There was a constant ache in my chest after Rhodes left. It wasn't dull, yet it wasn't quite sharp — but it was always present. Thoughts of him filled me with hope just as much as they crushed me. I told myself I should forget him, but I listened to songs with words that made me think of him, instead. It was a repetitive, modern form of torture that I somehow found solace in.

I didn't even try to reach out to him over the weekend. I weighed in by myself on my mom's scale at the house. I was down another four pounds, which was more than I had lost in a while. I guess when you run for hours every day and get sick at even the thought of food, that tends to happen. It wasn't a healthy diet, but I didn't know how else to handle my new reality.

But it was Monday, and to me, that felt like a new beginning of sorts.

Crawling out of bed, I talked myself through getting dressed, taking the time to make myself look somewhat presentable. Willow made me promise to call her after her morning class. She had taken it upon herself to check on me, like I might disappear off the face of the earth if she didn't.

If only it were that easy.

"Wait, are you wearing makeup?" Willow asked as soon as the video chat connected.

"I think I'm going to go see him."

Her face fell. "Um, what?"

"Hear me out," I offered, holding up my hands. "Our normal training session starts in an hour. I figured I'll just show up. If he's there, then maybe we can talk. And if he's not, well... then I'll take it as my cue to leave it alone."

"Don't you think him peeling out of your driveway should have been your cue to leave it alone?"

"He didn't peel out, Willow."

"He might as well have!" Willow's face softened a bit when she saw the sadness I knew perfectly well was outshining my makeup. She sighed. "Look, I can't tell you what to do. I know he means a lot to you. And he's made a huge impact on your life. But look at how much you're already hurting," she said. "What if he's there with a client? I don't want my best friend to break, Nat. I still need you around."

"I don't know. I just feel like I can't *not* fight for him."

"You told him you loved him," she gently reminded me, though I felt a knife twist between my ribs anyway.

"Well, I can try something else."

"Like what?"

"I don't know!" I screamed the words, breathing harder. I was losing control with every passing moment. "I have no idea what I'll say or do if he's there today, Lo, but I can't just sit here. I'm going insane."

"Come to Boone," she urged. "You can stay with me in my dorm for a while. We'll go out to some parties, you can sit in class with me. You'll see. Life is a lot bigger than Poxton Beach."

My stomach lurched, because just two months ago I was telling myself those same words. Now, it seemed nothing was bigger than Rhodes. He was all I could breathe. I didn't want to imagine a life outside of Poxton Beach unless he was in it, too.

"Just promise me you'll think about it, okay?"

I nodded. "Okay."

"And if you go today, just prepare for the worst."

"I think I've already experienced that."

She shrugged. "Still. You can never be too careful with your heart."

I half-laughed. "Sounds like something you should sew on a pillow."

"I just might."

A soft knock at my bedroom door startled me, and when my mom peeked through, I swallowed. "I'll text you later tonight, Lo."

She nodded, eying where my mom stood in the doorway before blowing me a kiss and ending the chat.

"What?" I asked, not even bothering to look at my mom. It was a new experience for me, being disrespectful to her, but she'd taught me my entire life to never give respect to someone who hadn't earned it.

She was the last person who deserved my respect in that moment.

"You can't honestly still be angry with me."

I didn't respond. I was already dressed for the gym, but I packed extra clothes in my gym bag anyway. Anything to keep from looking at her.

"I'm doing this because I love you, sweetie. Trust me. I know it doesn't seem like it right now, but one day you're going to look back at this and thank me. It feels like Rhodes is everything to you right now, but it's just because you're so young, Natalie. You'll understand when you're older that this was just a phase."

"Oh cut the shit, Mom," I spat at her, finally bringing my eyes to hers.

She pursed her lips. "Do not take that tone with me. I'm your mother, and I know what's best for you."

"Oh, is that so?" I scoffed. "Do you really think anything about Poxton Beach has been good for me? You think just because you married a rich man and I had new clothes and plenty of money to go out, that I should have been completely happy?"

"I love Dale," she said, her voice shaky. She was starting to turn red again just like she had in the kitchen a few nights before. "Don't you dare insinuate otherwise. And the fact that you're ungrateful for all he's given us just shows me how immature you still are."

"I'm not ungrateful. Yes, I know we're fortunate. But money and status aren't important to me. They never have been. All I've wanted my entire life was to feel loved without having to change. For so long, I thought maybe I had it all, maybe I was just strange because I wasn't happy even though my life was perfect. But the truth is, I've been stuck in this false sense of security and belonging my entire life." I shook my head, the realization hitting me as the words spilled from my lips. "Willow was my only true friend in this town and now she's gone."

"You have a lot of friends."

"No, that's just it. I don't. And it's okay that you didn't see that before because neither did I. It took Rhodes loving me for exactly who I am and not who I could be or *should* be for me to realize it."

"He doesn't love you, honey," she said with a sigh. "Mason loved you. And he's a good boy who will someday turn into a good man. I know you don't see it right now, and it kills me that we're fighting, but trust me. You'll understand one day. If you just listen to me, your life will be better."

Zipping up my bag with force, I slung it over my shoulder. "I'm done with this conversation. Going to the gym. Be back later."

"You are not to see him, young lady," she demanded to my back as I walked away.

"Try to stop me."

My hands were trembling as I pulled the Rover into the club parking lot. Killing the engine, I gripped the wheel tighter and didn't move. Why was I even here? Rhodes had walked away from me. Did I have anything more to say that would make him change his mind?

Sighing, I slowly slid out of the car and walked shakily toward the entrance. The closer I got to the gym, the heavier I breathed, but that all changed when I walked through the door. I saw him immediately, almost as if no one else was in the room at all. He must have sensed me, because his blazing eyes lifted to mine and he scowled. I wasn't breathing heavy anymore. I wasn't breathing at all.

There was a woman with him, but it wasn't a client — it was the same woman who had walked me into the gym that first day over two months ago. He was signing paperwork and when he finished, they shook hands, and she watched with sad eyes as he walked toward me.

Except he didn't stop.

Rhodes brushed right past me, his body wash leaving an all-too-familiar scent in his wake. For a moment I was stunned, but I quickly shook my daze and jogged after him.

"Rhodes, wait," I pleaded just as we exited the club. It was one of those dreadful summer days where the heat suffocates you, working in constant measure with the steady beating of the sun. It was already so hard to breathe, the humidity wasn't helping make it any easier.

He didn't stop. Slinging his backpack over his shoulders, Rhodes strode purposefully toward his bike. I felt the tears starting to sting the corners of my eyes, but I refused to cry. That's not what I had come for.

"Listen. I know things are complicated between us. I know the two of us together doesn't make sense, not to anyone else, anyway." I was trying to say anything, everything to make him change his mind. I'd never babbled so much in my life. "But you're all that makes sense to me anymore." He was still walking. I watched as the muscles moved beneath the soft fabric of his navy blue shirt. "My parents are idiots. I don't care what they think. I don't care what anyone in this town thinks." He climbed onto his bike, but paused, his helmet in his hands. One lone bead of sweat gathered on his neck before slowly trickling down. "And I know you don't either."

I waited, and for a moment he just sat there, staring at where his hands held fast to the straps of his helmet. Finally, he lifted his eyes to mine. They were soft, almost apologetic. It made me fear him more than when they were beneath his furrowed brow.

"I'm leaving Poxton Beach." The words left his lips as if they were easy to say, though his eyes told me otherwise. "Friday."

I tried to swallow, but not even dry air would go down. I sort of hiccupped, trying to control the emotions

I knew were scrolling across my face but failing miserably. "You're what?" I shook my head. "No. No, oh my God. Is it Dale? Did he get you fired?" Rhodes didn't answer, but I watched his throat constrict with the same emotion taking over my body and I knew the answer without him saying another word.

"It doesn't matter. I don't belong in this town and I don't want to be here anymore. There's nothing here for me, and I've known that for years now. I was stalling. I was holding onto something impossible."

"What about me?"

He chewed the inside of his cheek, his jaw tense, his eyes looking almost past me rather than at me.

My stomach lurched and I wrapped both of my arms tightly around it. "Oh God," I whispered. I felt sick. I felt numb. And more than anything, I felt helpless. "Rhodes," I breathed his name, a shiver breaking through me. "Please. Don't go. Don't leave." I stepped closer, my hand shaking as I untucked it and reached out for Rhodes. He flinched, but didn't pull away as I slid my index finger down his forearm to press hard on the inside of his wrist. "I feel your heart. It beats the same as mine. And I know you love me, too."

His nostrils flared, his brows pulled in, and the slightest tremble quaked through his bottom lip. The sight of him almost breaking was all it took to completely shatter the fragile piece of myself I was trying to hold on to. When he shrugged me off, a sob choked through me, and suddenly the desperation I felt was too much. I lunged at him, shoving him hard enough to knock him

342

off balance. He caught the weight of his bike, shutting his eyes but letting me hit him again and again.

"Fine! Leave!" I screamed so loud my throat hurt, my voice like a line of razor blades in my esophagus as my tiny fists pounded against his chest. "This is what you do, right? This is how it goes? I've memorized every inch of your back from all the times you've walked away from me this summer!"

Rhodes was chewing the corner of his lip, a fresh tear falling in the same line down his cheek. He was hurting, too. *Why was he doing this?*

I hit him once more before my hands flew to cover my mouth and I sobbed. Straightening, I sniffed, shaking my head. "You don't get to be the one who walks away this time." He still wouldn't look at me. I was tired of trying to make him.

I took one last longing look at him, my body remembering everything he'd made me feel that summer all at once, and then I turned. I thought he'd spark his bike to life and leave me in the dust again, but he didn't. He watched me go.

One final penance.

I had always felt like there was this invisible string between Rhodes and me, fastened to his heart and my own. He had pulled me toward him all summer, reeling me in, and as I climbed into the Rover and sped away, I felt the string snap, knocking me backward with the force. I choked, covering my mouth with the hand not glued to the wheel, muffling my cries.

He was leaving me, *really* leaving me, and there was nothing I could do about it. In less than a week, he'd be free of Poxton Beach — of me. But I would never be free of him.

I was getting a crash course in love and loss and I knew in my heart I wouldn't be able to survive the wreckage without Rhodes to help me find the rest of my missing pieces. But he wasn't giving me that choice.

I either had to pull myself together on my own or stay broken.

I hated both options.

# CHAPTER

# 26

It was interesting to compare my break-up with Mason to the one I was having with Rhodes. Even though we hadn't technically been in an official relationship, I felt more for him in two months than I had ever felt with Mason in the two years we'd dated.

Still, it's like my mind wouldn't let me pout the way I did with Mason. I could almost hear Rhodes in my head, yelling at me not to wallow, screaming for me to be strong and pick myself up. Move forward. Forget. Leave it behind.

I didn't try reaching out to Rhodes again. Instead, I threw all of my focus into myself. For two days, I just thought. I would run to think, take an ice bath to think, sit outside by our pool to think, call Willow to think out loud, dream with what little sleep I was getting. I was asking myself all the tough questions I had let myself ignore all summer. What did I want to do next? Where did I want to go? What mattered to me?

In a way, I was avoiding making any moves because Rhodes was here — in Poxton Beach — and so, that's where I wanted to be. And before I met him, before he was the anchor, I just hadn't thought about what I truly wanted aside from the fact that I *didn't* want to go to Appalachian State and be like everyone else in my class.

So, after swallowing back all the fear and self-doubt, I put in my application to the Savannah College of Art and Design. I didn't tell Mom or Dale, not that I was talking to them at all anyway, but I did tell Willow, who screamed over video chat for a solid sixty seconds. She was half-screaming because she was excited for me and half-screaming because I wasn't going to be anywhere near her if I got in. All I could think while we talked was that I really wanted to tell Rhodes. I wanted to see the wide grin spread across his face and watch as his eyes sparkled with pride. I wanted him to pull me in for a long kiss. I wanted him to be there.

But he just wasn't.

Still, I felt him all around me. A part of me wondered if maybe I would always have that sensation. It was strangely comforting just as much as it was terribly agonizing.

My mom always told me that before I could love anyone else, I'd have to learn to love myself. But I didn't believe that anymore. I was beginning to realize it takes a special heart — one stronger than our own — loving us for us to realize that maybe there's something there worth loving, after all. Maybe it was about finding love in the one person who loved you before you had the chance to love yourself.

For me, that someone was William Rhodes.

And I was forever changed by his love, regardless of the fact that I wouldn't get to keep it.

I couldn't sit still the night before Rhodes was supposed to leave town.

I had woken up that morning with a sickening weight in my stomach. Looking back, it's like I could feel what was coming — almost as if I knew that day, July twenty-third, was going to be the last day I would ever be the person I was. Something was brewing, but I didn't know what.

In my desperate attempt to keep myself busy and not thinking about Rhodes and the fact that he was leaving in less than twenty-four hours, I had decided to watch the last three episodes of *Lost*. But when the final episode ended, I simply clicked off the television and stared at the dark screen, thinking back to the beginning of the summer.

Dale was right. I shouldn't have watched it.

Feeling even more lost than before, I strapped on my running sneakers and watch. Mom popped her head into my room just as I was piling my hair into a messy bun on top of my head.

"Going for a run?"

I nodded, pulling my hair tight and checking my watch battery.

"I'm not feeling very well, so I think I'm just going to go to bed." She waited for me to acknowledge her words. Maybe she wanted me to wish her better. Maybe she just wanted me to understand her "wise" view of the world. I didn't do either.

She sighed.

"I love you, baby girl. I know you hate me right now, and I wish I could tell you how much that breaks my heart." Her eyes welled with tears and I felt that familiar sting and tingle in my nose. Mom and I had always been close, and we'd never fought like this before. Still, I couldn't find it in myself to forgive her without an apology, first. "Just know I'm always here for you. No matter what. And I really do care about your best interest."

At that last line, I rolled my eyes. "Okay. Well I'm just going to run a couple of miles. I'll be back soon."

One single tear dropped straight from her high cheek bone to my floor and she hastily wiped at the trail it left behind. "Goodnight, sweetie."

I ducked out of my room right behind her. She went left toward the master bedroom and I went right, jogging quickly down the stairs and out into the warm evening air. The sun was beginning to set, streaking the sky with bright, fiery oranges and pinks. Thumbing through my phone for the right playlist, I strapped it to my arm and tapped a few settings on my watch. Then, I ran.

Each step struck every nerve in my body. I felt myself tearing at the seams and being reborn all at once. I was in such an unfamiliar place mentally, the only way I knew how to get out of my head was to get into my body.

So, I focused on each foot hitting the pavement. I tried counting the steps as my watch counted the calories, but when I clicked over to voice mode, every word that left my lips was about Rhodes. Some of what I spoke into my watch made sense, some of it was just a string of broken sentences about memories and feelings I would never understand nor forget. I ran and ran until my chest ached and sweat leaked into my eyes to replace the salt lost in the tears I'd shed. It wasn't that I was sad, but it wasn't that I was okay, either. I was stuck in a confusing limbo, a sort of healing purgatory.

When I couldn't run anymore, I walked. When I could barely walk, I hobbled. Blisters were forming on my heels and my legs burned fiercely, but I kept going. I spilled my thoughts to the watch and my sweat to the road. Finally, at just past eleven, I limped up the drive, into the house, and up the stairs to my room. Sprawling out on the floor, I stared up at the ceiling, but my eyes quickly lost focus.

I don't know how much time passed. Maybe it was an hour, maybe it was only a minute, but sometime in the future my daze was broken by the soft buzzing of my cell phone on the carpet. I blindly felt for it, answering it without looking at the screen and holding it to my ear.

"I'm fine, Willow."

"Bug?"

The sound of his voice jerked me upright. "Rhodes?"

Silence.

"I can't not see you tonight," he finally said. I could hear the pain in his words. It was like he'd been fighting them for so long that finally letting them slip into the atmosphere killed him a little. "I'm still leaving in the morning, and I can't promise you anything more than tonight. I know I treated you like shit because I somehow always manage to fuck up the best things in my life." He exhaled, slowly breathing life back into me. "I don't deserve for you to come over. But I'm asking you anyway."

I bit my bottom lip with enough force to draw blood. Relief washed over me at the same time the delicious ache from running echoed through my muscles. He wanted to see me. Nothing more, nothing less, but it was just enough to reaffirm the hope I'd been clinging to. "Give me fifteen."

"Bug?"

"Yeah?"

There was a pause, and I felt my heartrate accelerate.

"Hurry."

I debated not showering, but one look in the mirror changed my mind. I could barely stand as the hot water washed over me. My body was caught in a mixture of the anticipation to see Rhodes and the extreme fatigue from my run. Adrenaline could only push me so far before the aches would take over. Still, I hurried through the shower and dressed in shorts and a tank top, throwing my still-wet hair up into a bun. Foregoing makeup, I looked at myself one last time before quietly sneaking out of my room.

Tiptoeing down the stairs, I willed my heart to calm itself so I could make it the rest of the way out of the house without being detected. Mom had ripped into me after I ran out to see Rhodes at the club earlier that week. I didn't want to take the chance of her catching me now and keeping me from him.

My hand reached for the handle on our front door just as a deep voice rang through the darkness.

"Going somewhere?"

I jumped, turning quickly and scanning the black foyer until I spotted Dale. He was kicked back in the recliner next to the couch, hands folded in his lap, amused smirk on his face. I could barely make him out, but the soft light from the kitchen illuminated him just enough for me to realize he wasn't sober.

*Great.*

"Jesus, Dale," I said, blowing out a breath. "You scared me."

He didn't respond.

"Um, I'm just going out for a run. I know it's late, but I can't sleep."

"A run, huh?"

I swallowed, realizing I probably wasn't too convincing at the moment. Thankfully, I had forgotten to take off my watch. Holding up my wrist, I smiled. "Yep. Got my watch set and my shoes are out in the Rover. Just going to throw them on and get started. I won't go too far."

He laughed, but it wasn't the laugh I was so familiar with. It seemed sinister, and suddenly the hairs on my arms were at attention. "You honestly expect me to believe that, don't you?" He shook his head, folding the recliner down with a pop. He was sitting up straight now, his eyes hard on me even through the dim light. "Your hair is still wet from the shower I just heard you taking upstairs. You went for a run earlier, and I know that because your mom told me just before she took her sleeping pills. I can see why you thought you'd be able to sneak out easily, what with those things knocking her out and all, but unfortunately for you, I'm still here. And I see right through your little charade. You're sneaking out to see him, and I can tell you right now, that's not going to happen."

My throat was tight, my hands cold. "Dale, please," I begged. I hated the shakiness of my voice. I wanted to demand respect, I wanted to storm out, but I knew Dale. He wanted to feel like everything was his decision. My only chance of seeing Rhodes was to make him think this was. "You got what you wanted. Rhodes is leaving. I'm never going to see him again. Just… please, give me tonight." Hoping to play into the father-daughter relationship, I even tried a joke. "I watched the last episode of *Lost* today. Have some pity." I laughed, and a smile creaked over his lips, but it fell too quickly for my taste.

Standing, Dale made his way into the foyer, crossing his arms over his chest. He scanned me from head to toe with glazed eyes, that same smug smirk reappearing as he did. I could tell he was on something, but I didn't know what. "He really did do a number on you, didn't he?"

I gulped, stepping back but running straight into the front door. "Dale… you're not thinking straight. I think you should go up to bed. Sleep it off."

He stepped closer, and I could clearly smell it — he'd been drinking. Whiskey. But the way he was acting, there was no way he was just drunk. Something else was intoxicating him.

"It's just amazing. You were always pretty, but he made you…" His voice trailed off and he shook his head, reaching out a hand to thumb my chin. I jerked away from his touch. "Let's just say I can see why he was so quick to claim you as his own."

"Dale. Stop. You're being creepy." I tried to sound firm, pushing my fist into his chest to put space between us. He only stepped closer, wrapping his fingers around my wrist. For some reason, that simple move violated me more than his words. I only wanted Rhodes' fingers on my wrist.

"You really want to go see him tonight, don't you?"

I nodded, swallowing a sandpaper-covered cotton ball as he leaned even closer. He was squeezing my wrist with enough force to make my nerves jump to life. Something was wrong. And I realized at that very moment, I was scared of my step-dad.

"Well, I can let you go and not tell your mother," he said, and though those words should have brought me relief, they only made me shake in his grip. His next sentence proved my fear to be warranted. "But you'll have to do something for me."

He grinned wider, licking his bottom lip as his eyes fell to mine. Bile rose in my throat and I couldn't hide the horror that quickly appeared on my face. "Oh my God, Dale." I tried to shove him away, but he only grabbed my other wrist, and now he had both of them in a tight grip. My heart pounded in my ears. He was serious. *Oh God*, he was serious.

A mixture of fear and disgust rolled through me and I jerked my arms with as much force as I could, but it barely fazed him. My muscles were exhausted, and Dale was stronger. It didn't take me long to realize the sickening implication behind those two facts.

"Dale, please, let me go," I cried, tugging my arms again. He shoved me back hard against the door, knocking the wind from my chest. Wide-eyed and shaking, I flexed my knee forward and connected with his groin. Dale coughed and bent forward, but kept his grip on my wrists. I squirmed against his grasp, trying to wriggle free as he strained to catch his breath again. But I was trapped. And when he lifted his head again, his dark eyes were venomous. He released one of my wrists long enough to rear back and slap my face.

The force hurled me to the ground and I hit the hardwood floor with a smack. Groaning, I grabbed my head between my hands, trying to stop my vision from spinning. Pain echoed through my skull as I tried to focus on the legs of our coffee table across the room. I blinked over and over, but the room kept sliding quickly from the left to the right in my vision. I squeezed my eyes tight, willing my head to settle, praying the dizziness would pass.

Dale dropped down on top of me, pinning my wrists above my head. My chest was tight, my breaths labored. I felt the panic setting in and I couldn't think straight. Shaking my head wildly, I thrashed against his grip, my eyes wide, vision still blurred.

"Dale! Stop! Please!" I screamed for Mom, but that only made him laugh. He knew as well as I did that she was passed out and not even my screaming was going to wake her. When a sickening snarl curled on his lip, I realized this was how he liked it. He wanted me to fight. He wanted me to struggle.

I swallowed back the acid rising in my throat, squeezing my eyes tight again. *This isn't happening. This isn't happening.*

"God, you smell so good," Dale whispered, inhaling a deep breath against my neck. I squeezed my eyes tighter as hot tears leaked out of each one. I focused on them as they seared a trail from my cheeks to my ears. When I felt Dale fidgeting with the spandex band of his sweatpants, my eyes snapped open.

I bucked against him, thrashing, kicking, screaming, crying. A rush of adrenaline had sparked to life and I tried so hard to help it catch fire. I tried to head butt him, to knee him again, but every attempt was futile. My muscles wouldn't cooperate, and Dale wouldn't budge.

"Dale," I groaned, tears streaming, throat aching. "God, please. Please stop. Please. *Please.*" I said the word over and over, praying to his humanity or God or whoever would listen first.

"Shhh," he whispered, touching his finger to my lips as his other hand still held my wrists firmly in place. I shook my head against the touch. "Just relax."

I choked on a sob, writhing beneath him. My heart was pounding in my ears. It was beating so fast. Too fast. I was going to pass out. I was sure of it.

My eyes fluttered open, the beat growing louder and louder in my ears. Dale was still saying something, but I couldn't make it out anymore. Everything was muted, vision still like a dream, or rather a nightmare. I simply stared up at the chandelier, watching it shimmer and glitter like the horrific scene just beneath it weren't real. Like I wasn't real. Like I didn't exist.

Everything was in slow motion. Time was morphing. *Inhale. Exhale.* Dale's hand slid up my inner thigh and two more tears slid down to join the puddles forming in my ears. A cry left my lips, but I didn't hear it. I didn't hear anything. I didn't smell or feel or taste. I only saw through blurred, distorted vision. The chandelier. The chandelier was all that existed.

Something broke the edges of my vision, but still, no sound came. There was commotion, muffled voices and screams pierced through the barrier. I blinked. Dale was off me. I blinked again. Still the chandelier. I blinked once more.

Rhodes.

All of my senses came rushing back at once.

I gasped, bolting upright as the breath hit my lungs. Eyes wide, I clawed at Rhodes as he lifted me into him. He wrapped his arms around me. He was kissing my hair. He was saying something. *What was he saying?* Nothing made sense. *My head.* I reached up, fingering a tender spot on the back of my skull. My hand was wet. Blood.

Dale was on the ground. A woman stood over him. She had a gun. *Who was she?*

Dale's laugh was the first sound to truly register. It broke through the fog, and it was as if I were hearing for the first time.

"You," he seethed. "Well, well. Look who's risen from the dead!" His mouth was bleeding, staining his teeth as he smiled up at us. The woman still had the gun trained on him. All I could see was the back of her head. She had short brown hair and a dove tattoo on the back of her neck.

"You would love me to be dead, wouldn't you?" Her voice was sweet, but firm. Her hands shook just slightly as she adjusted her grip on the gun.

Dale laughed again. "You going to shoot me, sweetheart? Go ahead. I'd just love to see your pretty little ass thrown in jail."

"Lana, don't," Rhodes warned as the woman's finger wavered on the trigger. I gasped.

"Lana?"

Her eyes flicked to mine, but all I saw was Rhodes. She looked just like him. Same green eyes, same strong jaw, same bent brow. Eying Rhodes' arms around me for just a moment, she snapped her attention back to Dale.

"As much as I'd love to be the one to kill you, I'd rather see you rot in prison."

Dale laughed harder and Rhodes lurched forward. Lana held out one arm to stop him. I knew more than anyone that he could have easily plowed through her, but he didn't.

"I don't know what you don't get about this situation, sweetheart. I'm Dale *Poxton*. This is *Poxton* Beach. I own this fucking town."

"I've been gathering witnesses. I have fourteen girls willing to testify against you."

"And I've got three highly-respected doctors who will diagnose every single one of them with some form of mental instability," he argued, not even fazed in the slightest. He lifted himself from the ground, still sitting but leaning back against the wall. "It's my word against yours. And theirs. Sexual assault is one of the hardest crimes to prove, baby, and let me assure you, I am the only one who comes out a winner in the end."

I watched as Lana's face crumbled. Rhodes lurched forward again.

"You mother fucking son of a bitch!" Lana didn't stop him this time and I watched as his fist connected with Dale's jaw. His face flew to the left with a loud crack, blood spurting from his mouth and painting the wall behind him.

"It's okay," Lana tried to soothe Rhodes, but she didn't seem sure herself. "Phil will know what to do. We have the witnesses. We can do this."

"Who the fuck is Phil?" Dale asked.

"Not every cop on your squad is crooked," Rhodes spat at him. His eyes connected with mine and recognition hit. *Officer Martino.*

Dale shook his head, thumbing the fresh wound on his lower lip and chuckling at the blood. "Again. No evidence." He shook his head, still smiling. "I knew you were still out there. One by one, girls I had an eye on for so long started disappearing. Moving away. None of them went to the cops but I knew something was going on. And I just had a feeling it was you." His eyes were so dark, so venomous. "You drove me to drink pretty hard this summer, little girl. But let me just remind you, you've got one cop and fifteen mentally unstable girls against a man whose family has owned this town since it was founded. Who do you think comes out on top, baby cakes?"

I cringed at his pet name for Lana. She fired off something else, but I didn't hear it, because an idea of my own set my heart racing again. Thumbing through the settings on my watch, I ended the voice recording and used my finger to slide the playback option. When I hit play, the yelling in the room ceased.

*"It's just amazing. You were always pretty, but he made you…"* A rustling noise. *"Let's just say I can see why he was so quick to claim you as his own."*

I shivered at the replay and slid the playback further. Rhodes' eyes were wild as recognition hit. He heard what Dale had said to me and he layed into him again, his fist rearing back before connecting again and again, but I screamed at him to stop.

"Just wait!" I hit play again. Dale was now bleeding from one eye, too.

*"I've been gathering witnesses. I have fourteen girls willing to testify against you."*

*"And I've got three highly-respected doctors who will diagnose every single one of them with some form of mental*

*instability. It's my word against yours. And theirs. Sexual assault is one of the hardest crimes to prove, baby, and let me assure you, I am the only one who comes out a winner in the end."*

Dale's voice was soft, but I could still make it out. My nose flared as I held the watch higher. "Let's see you try to refute that in court."

Lana's eyes glossed over, a smile spreading on her face. Red and blue lights broke through the dark foyer and sirens surrounded us. I watched the lights play off the horrified look on Dale's face as cops burst through our front door that had already been broken down.

"Oh my God!" My mom's voice rang from the stairs. She flew down them, hugging her nightgown tightly to her body, her bright blonde hair in disarray. "What the hell is going on?!"

"Dale Poxton, you're under arrest for the sexual assault of Lana Rhodes," an officer said as he forced cuffs on Dale's wrists. Dale laughed at him, but the cop was clearly not amused as he continued reading his Miranda Rights. Lana eyed him with disbelief just as Officer Martino slid up beside her. She jumped into his arms, hugging him tight.

"I don't understand," she breathed, pulling back to face him.

"What, you think I'm the only good cop in the Poxton Beach Police Department?" He smiled crookedly at her and she gazed up at him like he was her hero. I realized that for all I knew, he might have been.

"What are you doing? Let him go!" My mom chased after the cops as they hauled Dale out of the house, still reading his rights along the way. We all followed them outside, though Rhodes had to support me as we walked. I was shaking so violently I couldn't stand on my own.

The scene in the yard was so surreal. I should have been focused on Rhodes' arms around me or Lana's face as she smiled through the tears of happiness in her eyes. I should have ran to my mom to explain what happened, except I didn't really know myself. I wish I remembered what it felt like to be safe again in that moment, but I don't.

I remember the lights.

I remember I wanted to photograph them, the way the red and blue splashed across his cold, emotionless face. But I knew even if my feet could move from the place where they had cemented themselves to the ground and I could run for my camera, I wouldn't be able to capture that moment. There was no shutter speed, no lens, no lighting technique that could properly encapsulate everything I felt as I stared into his eyes. I had trusted him, I had loved him, and even though my body had changed that summer, he'd made sure to help me hold on to who I was inside regardless of how the exterior altered.

But then everything changed.

He stole my innocence. He scarred my heart. He took everything I thought I knew about my life and fast-pitched it out the window, shattering the glass that held my world together in the process.

I remember the lights.

The passionate, desperate, hot strikes of red. The harsh, cruel, icy bolts of blue.

They symbolized everything I endured that summer.

And everything I would never face again.

I squeezed my eyes shut as if it were the lights that had attacked me and not Dale. Rhodes pulled me closer and I buried my face into his chest.

"I trusted him," I choked out.

"I know you did, Bug." He ran his rough hands through my hair, trying but failing to soothe me.

"It hurts," I groaned, clutching at my heart through the thin fabric of my tank top. My chest burned, like acid was slowly leaking between my ribs. Fresh tears fell in lines down my cheeks in the same course as those before them. "It physically hurts. *So bad*. Why does it hurt?"

Rhodes sighed, holding me tighter. He held me as close to him as he could, shielding me from Dale, from the lights, from the pain. "It's weight," he said, kissing my hair. And that's when I felt it — all of it — all at once. "This is your weight."

# CHAPTER

# 27

It took hours to file the police reports and get medically cleared. I had a pretty nasty gash on my head from hitting the floor when Dale smacked me, but other than that, I was just "shaken up," at least that's what the paramedic said. It seemed too simple to describe how I felt in that moment, but I was just thankful Rhodes got there when he did. I couldn't imagine what would have happened if he hadn't shown up.

I didn't know what time it was when our yard finally cleared of all the cop cars. Our neighbors were still lingering in their lawns or behind their windows, phones glued to their ears, no doubt spreading gossip through the town about Dale Poxton being tossed in the back of a police car. When the last car other than Officer Martino's pulled away, it was just him, Rhodes, Lana, Mom and I left. We all stared at each other, no one moving, no one really knowing what to do next.

"I think we should talk," Lana finally said, clearing her throat. "Can we?" She motioned toward the house and I nodded, leading us all inside.

Mom was in a zombie sort of state, her hair wild and her eyes heavy, but she brewed up a pot of coffee for all of us as we gathered around the kitchen island. Rhodes took the bar stool next to mine and pulled me close, resting his hand on my leg. He hadn't stopped touching me since Dale was hauled off. I was thankful. It seemed his touch was the only thing keeping me from losing myself.

"I don't even know where to start," Lana tried, looking to Officer Martino for help. He smiled encouragingly and rubbed her lower back.

"Why did you leave?" Rhodes asked. His lips were pressed together, his jaw tense, but his eyes were bright green and soft. I was so confused, so lost, but I couldn't even imagine what was going through his head. His sister, who he assumed was dead just a few hours before, was now standing in my kitchen with us.

Lana sighed, twisting her short brown hair around her fingers before letting it spring back into shape. "I can't start there. It goes back further than that."

"So start from the beginning."

Lana took a moment, a pondering look on her face. It was as if she were racking her brain for the right words to say, or maybe she was pulling a memory from an ocean so deep she thought she'd never have to see it again. I sipped my coffee and eyed my mom as we waited. I wondered how she was feeling, and even though we were on weird terms, I found myself wanting to hug her.

"When I turned eighteen, I started interning at the Poxton Beach Law Firm. I wanted to go to law school, but it was going to take me a few years of waitressing to get enough cash saved up to even think of applying. I thought interning would be the best way to stay relevant in that down time, and lucky for me, a spot had just opened up." She said *lucky* sarcastically, and I knew if she could go back now, she wouldn't have applied at all.

"I knew Dale was on the board, obviously, being that he owns the firm, but I didn't realize that he was a lawyer and that he worked on certain cases. So, I was surprised and excited, to say the least, when I was assigned to the case he was working on at the time." I noticed Mom sniffle at the mention of Dale, but she just continued stirring her coffee.

"I remember when you started there," Rhodes said. "You would go to school all day, then intern, and sometimes serve after." He shook his head. "I was so impressed."

"It was important to me. And Dale made me feel like I was special, like I was one-of-a-kind. At first, it was normal — nothing alarming. He coached me, he was a good instructor. A lot of the interns got stuck pushing paperwork, but he always asked me questions and made me think. He trusted me. And I trusted him." She swallowed. "One night, he asked me to stay late with him to wrap up paperwork on a case. I felt honored, he hadn't even asked any of the partners to stay. But that was the night that changed my life."

"Oh God," Mom whispered, her trembling fingertips touching her lips.

Lana's face was pale and I could see her arms shaking a bit. Officer Martino squeezed her hip to let her know he was there. "When he was finished with me, he threatened me. He said if I told anyone, I would be fired from my internship and blackballed from every college within a five-state distance. He said if I worked with him, he could make all my dreams come true, but I had to be willing to give him something in return."

I shuddered at the similarity between those words and the ones he'd said to me earlier.

"So, naturally, because I'm a Rhodes, I told him to go fuck himself. Told him I would report him to the cops, even though he said I'd never win." I tried to force a smile, because that did sound like a Rhodes thing to do, but I wasn't sure if one actually appeared. "That only fueled his anger. So he went after what he knew was the most important thing in the world to me, the only way he knew he could get me to keep my mouth shut." Her eyes found Rhodes' and her nose flared. "He said he'd kill you."

Rhodes shook his head. "Why didn't you just fucking tell me? I would have killed *him*, Lana."

"That's just it," she said. "Either he would have killed you, or you would have killed him and ended up in prison for the rest of your life. Both scenarios meant me losing you forever."

Rhodes bit his tongue, but his grip tightened on my leg.

"I was your twin sister, William. And everyone else who was supposed to care for you in your life had failed. I couldn't be the next one." She paused for a moment. "So, I did what I had to do. I just needed time to make a plan, but in the meantime, I played his game."

Officer Martino and Rhodes both ground their teeth at that.

"But every time he assaulted me, it got worse and worse. He started leaving bruises, marks that were calling attention from you."

"I thought you had an asshole boyfriend," Rhodes said. "I was trying to find out who it was so I could pummel the little fuck."

"And you were asking me questions. Too many questions. I knew it was only a matter of time before you found out and went after Dale. I couldn't take that chance. I refused to lose you to some monster." She swallowed. "So I left."

I felt Rhodes arms go slack next to me, and I found his hand, squeezing it with my own. I was still shaking, still broken from the night, but I tried to be his strength.

"So you've been hiding out ever since?" I asked.

She laughed a little. "I wish it were that easy. The first night I was gone, I stayed in a hotel under a fake name. Paid with cash. But when I went out to get food, I came back to a trashed room, all my belongings gone or ripped to shreds. It was Dale. He wasn't going to let me leave.

"I didn't know where to go, but I knew I couldn't stay there, so I just started walking. I packed the blanket off the hotel bed and a pillow and I just walked. That's when I found the boat yard."

"So that's why we found your bracelet there," I breathed.

Lana nodded. "It must have snagged on one of the boat lifts when I left. I stayed there for two weeks. I was trying to lay low, figure out my next move, but I was scared. Dale's crooked ass cops had already raided two nearby hotels and I felt them getting closer. I barely ate, I was dehydrated, I was scarred and depressed and terrified."

"And that's when I found her," Officer Martino said, pulling her a little closer. She smiled up into his dark eyes and he brushed her hair behind her ear.

"That's when he found me."

"Where did you go?" Mom asked. I had almost forgotten she was in the room.

"Phil took me to his place. He lives alone about twenty miles out of town, never has friends over since his place is so far and everyone else lives close to the station. It was easy enough to hide me, though we had a few close calls.

"He fed me, got me back to health, and I confided in him. He knew about Dale and though I had a hunch, he confirmed that I wasn't the first girl this had happened to."

A small cry escaped Mom's lips.

I turned to her again, a sick realization settling in. "Did you know about this?" I asked, my face twisted in disgust. "Is this his addiction, Mom?"

"I knew he was addicted to sex," she said with a cough. "He cheated on me, that much I knew. But I never knew… I didn't realize it was with… that he… that they didn't… Oh God." She shook her head, covering her mouth with both hands as she squeezed her eyes tight.

"It's okay," Lana soothed her. "Trust me, Dale was good at covering his tracks. His cop and doctor friends were practically the only ones who knew. And he paid them very, very well to keep it that way."

"I just… I feel responsible. I'm his wife, I should have known."

"It's not your fault. You're not him, Mrs. Poxton." Mom squeezed her eyes tighter and shook her head at her own last name. It was no longer a name of privilege. It was tainted, disgraced.

"So you just stayed holed up in his house for three years?" Rhodes asked, snapping us back to the story.

"Phil and his partner were sick of Dale's shit, but anyone who stood up to him was quickly fired and left without any other possible job prospects. Dale wasn't afraid to exude his power. So, they kept the peace at work, did what they had to do to fly under the radar, but secretly, they helped me find other girls who had been through what I had. We started with old police reports, tracked down the girls, found other girls through them — it was a chain of discovery. A painful one, but one that we slowly unraveled until we had a solid case."

"We didn't want to even try to go after him with anything less than ten credible victims," Officer Martino explained. "And we were stuck at seven for two years."

"Until about a month ago, when seven other girls showed up at Phil's house saying they heard it was a safe haven. They had all been living by Dale's rules, but word slowly spread about what we were doing." She looked to Mom. "I think that's why Dale started acting crazy. He was losing it, he knew we were up to something, he just didn't know what."

Mom squeezed her eyes tight and I thought back through the summer of hell she'd endured. Suddenly, it all made sense. Maybe she didn't tell me what was going on with Dale because she truly didn't know herself.

Lana shrugged. "Once they came to us, we knew we had enough, and that's when we started planning our move."

"Why didn't you call me? Leave a note? Let me know you were alive?"

Lana swallowed, her eyes glossing over. "I wanted to, William. I hated leaving you behind, watching you suffer, watching you worry. But Dale was watching you, too. The private detective you were paying was one of his crooked cops. He was keeping tabs on you, making you believe I was being looked for when I wasn't. He was exerting control over the situation by stunting you and at the same time warning me. It's as if he was letting me know how easy it would be for him to end you." She shook her head. "Dale was acting crazy the more girls disappeared. I listened to girl after girl tell me the horror stories about their families or boyfriends killed in 'freak accidents.' I didn't want you to be next."

"He killed people?" Mom and I asked at the same time. The horror on her face matched what I felt deep in my gut, but I wasn't sure if I was showing any emotion.

Lana swallowed, her brows bending in sympathy for our ignorance. "He didn't, no… but he had them taken care of… by others."

Mom sobbed and I covered my mouth with my hand, my stomach sinking even lower as chills broke out on my arms.

"But she still looked after you, and made sure I did, too," Officer Martino said, bringing our attention back to the story. "I know it feels like she abandoned you, but I had to fight her every night to get her to stay away. You're the only thing that matters to her, William. She wanted you safe."

"But I'm supposed to be the one who protects her," he said, his voice shaky. I gripped his hand tighter.

"This was something I had to do on my own, William. It was messy, and involving you would have only made the situation worse."

"But you did leave him a note," I pointed out. Shifting uncomfortably on my bar stool, I dropped my head. "The one about me."

Officer Martino's face hardened and Lana cringed. "I'm so sorry, Natalie. You weren't the only one I hurt with that note. I seriously put myself and our entire investigation at risk, but I couldn't help it." She sighed. "I always checked in on William, and when I found out he was your trainer, I was already wary. But one night, you left his house late, and I watched him run out after you had already peeled away. He was standing there with his hands on his head and this look on his face... I knew right then that he was falling for you, and all these red flags flew up in my head. You were Dale's daughter. Dale wanted to kill William. I felt like I had to warn him."

"Even though I made her swear to me that she wouldn't," Officer Marino muttered through clenched teeth.

"He did. And I begged him to let me reach out to you but he refused. We were so close, we just needed a little more time. But I couldn't take it. I snuck out of his house and went back to the boat yard with a bottle of whiskey I stole from under his sink." She eyed where my mom's hands were gripped around her coffee mug. "I don't know. I was just so unstable, so afraid of what would happen. For a while, I just sat there, wondering if everything I did up until that point was right. I was drinking, I was emotional, and by the end of the night I decided I couldn't just sit back anymore. So I wrote that note. I thought I tore the bottom off completely, I figured there was no way he would figure out where it came from."

"When I found you two trespassing, I discovered she didn't keep her promise to me," Officer Martino added. "I had already radioed in the call when I realized who you two were. By that time, it was too late — they'd already called Dale."

My head was spinning. Pinching the bridge of my nose, I tried to make sense of everything. "I still don't understand tonight. How did you know he would... that Dale would..." I couldn't even finish my sentence.

"We didn't," Rhodes said, rubbing my hand still clasped in his. "Right after I ended the call with you, Lana showed up at my door." He paused, his face as white as if he were still seeing Lana as a ghost. "She was trying to tell me this same story, about Dale, about why she left, about finally being able to be back now that she had a case. She wanted me to come away with her to finish what she'd started. She was ready. She was talking so fast but I didn't really grasp anything because all I knew was that you were late. You should have been at my place by then. I don't know..." his voice trailed off. "I can't explain it. I just felt it. I knew something was wrong. Then I tried calling you and your phone went straight to voicemail."

It was then that I realized I had left my phone upstairs after my shower.

"We took my bike, got here as fast as we could and I heard you screaming from the driveway." His jaw ticked and he clenched the fist not holding mine. "I didn't know what to expect when I broke through that door."

My mom cried, and I just stared at the still broken door he was referring to. It was all too much. I couldn't wrap my mind around the information dump we'd just experienced.

All the pain Rhodes had experienced in the past three and a half years was because of my step-dad. The same step-dad who I'd grown up loving, trusting, idolizing. I wanted to be like him. The thought now made me sick and I lurched forward off my barstool, reaching the sink just in time to lose what little food and coffee I had left in my system. Rhodes rushed to my side, pulling my hair back and rubbing my back.

"I know this is a lot," Officer Martino said softly. "I think we all need a night to just process everything. Mrs. Poxton, you should get some rest."

"I'm not feeling very well, either," Lana said, leaning her weight on his shoulder.

"Come on, let me take you home."

"Wait." Rhodes made sure I was okay as I turned to face the room again. He offered me a cup of water and I took it gratefully as he crossed the room to his sister. For a moment, they stared at one another, and the rest of us stared at how similar they looked. Rhodes pulled her into him, crushing her with a hug so fierce, so strong, built from more than three years of loss and given with a sigh of relief. She squeezed her eyes tight, tears sliding through the creases of her skin as she buried her face into his shoulder.

"I love you, William. I'm so sorry I left you. I'm so sorry about everything."

"Don't," he stopped her. "You're alive. You're here. That's all I care about."

They held each other a while longer before Rhodes finally pulled back, letting Officer Martino escort Lana outside. We promised to all meet up for a late lunch the next day to talk more. There was a lot to do now that Dale was in jail and witnesses were gathered, and we all knew they wouldn't hold him long. He would likely post bail in the morning. We wouldn't be truly free of him until after the trial.

Rhodes and I packed up bags for my mom and myself, grabbing everything we thought we'd need. We had no way of knowing if or when Dale would return, but we did know it wouldn't be safe for any of us to stay in the house. Mom was a complete mess. She had stopped talking, and Rhodes had to carry her out to the Rover. We drove in silence to his house, Rhodes following behind us on his bike.

When we got to Rhodes' apartment, he waited in the kitchen as I laid Mom down in his bed. She was shaking slightly, so I pulled the covers up to her chin.

"I'm so sorry, baby," she whispered, fresh tears brimming her eyes before falling to the sheets. "I didn't know. I thought our issues were between us — a cheating husband, a faithful wife. I never knew… I never would have imagined…"

"I know, Mom. It's not your fault."

She squeezed her eyes tight, fighting back a sob. "But it is. I brought you up in the same household as a monster. I put you in danger. He almost… he could have… Oh God, baby, I'm so sorry!" She reached out for me and I hugged her fiercely, shaking my head against her.

"You didn't know, Mom. It's not your fault. I'm okay. We're okay."

She cried, and I held her, trying to be the support she needed while still battling with the night on my own. After a while, her cries softened and she closed her eyes, resting back against Rhodes' pillows. I brought her a glass of water and set it on the bedside table before quietly shutting the bedroom door behind me and rejoining Rhodes in the kitchen.

We looked at each other for what felt like the first time that night.

"Can we go somewhere?"

Rhodes didn't answer, only grabbed the keys to his bike.

I called Christina, telling her what I could about what happened and asking her to go to Rhodes' place to keep an eye on mom. I hoped she would sleep, but just in case, I didn't want her to be alone.

The sun was on the horizon as we drove toward the beach. Rhodes parked his bike in one of Dale's reserved spots and held my hand as we made our way to the water. I fell down into the sand right at the water's edge and Rhodes slowly maneuvered himself down to sit next to me.

"I would give every last penny in my savings account to know what you're thinking right now," he whispered over the waves. His eyes were on me, mine were on the soft yellows and blues of the sunrise over the ocean.

"My step-dad is the reason you've spent the last three years of your life in absolute hell," I said. "I'm tied to the biggest pain in your life. I can't believe I never saw him for what he was. I can't believe I trusted him. I loved him. I thought he loved me." My voice broke a little, but I cleared my throat. I refused to shed any more tears over Dale Poxton.

"Bug, *he* was the reason for what happened to Lana. To me. Not you."

"Are you okay?" I asked, turning to face him. I didn't want to talk about Dale anymore.

"Honestly? No," he answered. His bright green eyes were tinged a sort of aqua with the blue of the sky playing in them. "But I think I will be. I'm more worried about you at the moment."

"Me?"

He nodded.

"I'm fine. *Shaken up* was my diagnosis," I joked. Rhodes didn't return my smile.

"What happened to you tonight was serious, Natalie."

"It didn't happen. You saved me."

He swallowed. "Even still. I wasn't there to stop him from hitting you, or saying what I can only imagine were words you'll never forget."

An ache squeezed around my heart and I clutched at the fabric of my tank top. Rhodes pulled me into him, kissing my hair.

"I think I'll be okay, too." I finally whispered into his chest.

"Maybe we both will be."

I sniffed. "Are you really leaving?"

Rhodes sighed, tilting my chin up to look into my eyes. "Not without you."

He captured my lips with his own, promises dancing between us in the morning light. I tangled my fingers in his hair and he held me tighter, deepening our kiss. Neither of us had any idea where we went from that moment, but finally, and without any doubt, we knew we'd never face whatever it was without the other.

"I love you," he whispered against my lips. "I don't want you to think I'm just saying it now because of what happened tonight. I've felt it for weeks, maybe longer. I should have said it when you did, or hell, before then. You said it hit you all at once, but I felt every single inch of the fall. I tried so hard to fight it, to not let myself be selfish enough to love you knowing who I am and what I'm capable of."

"Stop," I breathed, kissing him again. "I know. You never had to say it."

He frowned, his eyes on mine. "Well now I'm never going to stop."

I smiled against his mouth as he kissed me again, harder this time, with promise and purpose, greed and carefulness. His brows knitted together, and I wondered if he'd ever be able to kiss me without feeling like he didn't deserve to.

"I love you too, William," I said softly. He pulled back, his eyes questioning the name. He opened his mouth to argue, but after a pause, simply closed it once more. Because he knew then what I had known all along.

He was *my* resolute protector now.

Sliding his hand into mine, he pressed two fingers firmly against my inner wrist. I felt my heartbeat pound beneath his touch and I moved my own fingers to mirror his. My heart was racing, but his was slow and steady. Soon, they evened out, beating as one together. William pressed his forehead to mine and I inhaled the first breath of my new life.

That summer had changed me in more ways than I could even understand. I had challenged myself and found strength I didn't know I had. I'd taken risks, risks that lead to a passion and love unlike anything I'd experienced before. And yes, I had lost an innocence that up until that point had played a huge role in who I was.

But in the end, I'd emerged on the other side of summer ready to shed my leaves along with the fall trees. The truth was William had brought a sleeping giant to life. I felt a new me — a better me — waiting just below the surface for her chance to shine in the spring. I didn't shield my eyes as the morning light grew brighter and brighter on the beach around us. I simply held on tighter to the one person whose darkness offered the perfect balance.

The sun was rising.

And we were rising with it.

# THE END

# EPILOGUE

*TWO YEARS LATER*

I smoothed my hands down the thin black fabric of my dress, turning to inspect myself in the mirror once more. My new, shorter, brighter blonde hair was slightly curled and it framed my face at the chin. There were no lumps showing beneath the tight dress, still I stretched it and smoothed it over and over again.

"You look perfect." William's deep voice echoed through our bedroom as he slid up behind me, wrapping his arms around my middle.

"I think it's too small."

A smirk curved on his lips. "Just because it's a single digit doesn't mean it's too small, Bug." He kissed my temple and I turned in his arms, running my hands up his biceps currently covered by a blazer.

"I don't think I'll ever get used to a size eight. I guess I have you to thank for that."

"Don't thank me," he said, kissing my nose. "Thank the squats."

I giggled.

"Ready?"

Licking my lower lip, I slid my hands down his chest and hooked them into the band of his dress pants. He inhaled a stiff breath and I felt him grow hard through the fabric. "Are you *sure* we have to leave the house?"

He groaned, running his hands back through my hair and tugging it gently, forcing my face up to his. He pressed his lips against mine and bit the lower lip I'd just licked to tease him. "Go ahead. Tease me all you want tonight, Bug. Just remember that later when I pay you back."

His words sent a jolt straight between my legs and my thighs tensed. William didn't break the kiss, though — he deepened it, running his rough hands down the open back of my dress to firmly palm my ass. I moaned into his mouth and he finally pulled away, leaving me panting for more.

"Looking forward to it," I said, breathless. I went to steal another kiss, but Zipper ran between our legs, tail wagging furiously, knocking both of us back a step.

"What do you say, Zip? You going to be good while we're gone?"

Our rough-around-the-edges pit bull sat down quickly, planting his front feet and looking up at us with wide eyes and tongue flopped out. I rubbed the white spot on his head before leaning down to kiss his nose, to which he responded with a sneeze and another sprint through the house.

We rescued Zipper last Christmas and he'd been a part of our little dysfunctional family ever since. He was hyper, got into trouble more days than not, and I'd lost count of how many pairs of shoes had fallen victim to his chewing habit. Still, he reminded me a lot of Rhodes when we first met — people were scared of him, he seemed dangerous, but inside he was kind and caring and brave. One more week in the shelter and he would have been put down. Some say we saved him, but I think it might be the other way around. Where therapy failed over the last few months, Zipper succeeded.

He ran through the house full speed, using the front door as a backboard before bounding back toward us.

William chuckled, watching Zipper run another lap before smacking my ass playfully as he motioned toward the door. If it weren't such an important dinner, I likely would have continued my teasing until he gave up and let me stay home with him. As it was, we were expected to meet with his sister and my mom — neither of who we saw much anymore.

The drive to the restaurant was short, but I stared out the window the entire time. Even though we'd lived in Savannah for over a year, I still marveled at how beautiful the town was. There was so much history, but more than that — life. Every square of the city buzzed with beauty and excitement.

Still, any time I was quiet, the noise in my head would creep in. I'd come a long way in the two years since everything happened, but I wasn't sure I'd ever truly move on and forget. Therapy had helped, in the beginning at least, but I realized after a while that the only person I wanted to talk to about everything was William. He knew me better than I even knew myself. And so we leaned on each other, in the good times and the bad, and our foundation that had once been cracked and breaking was rebuilt slowly and steadily. It was stronger than ever now.

William's hand gently squeezing my knee brought my attention back inside the car. He knew when I drifted, but just feeling his skin on mine would bring me back to the moment — back to him. "I have some exciting news."

I arched a brow. "Yeah?"

He nodded, the cutest smirk quirking at the corner of his lips. "I applied for a summer job a while back. I didn't want to say anything to you because I figured with all the competition at school, I probably wouldn't get it. But... well... I did."

I smiled, wrinkling my nose. "And... what are you doing?"

William chewed his lip. "You know how Bradley Schumaker from Food Network is the guest chef at that little Italian restaurant downtown?"

"Oh my God... are you?"

He nodded again, this time a huge smile lighting up his face. It was the kind that still had the power to knock the breath from my chest. "I'm going to be one of his cooks."

"William!" I wrapped my hand around the one he had on my knee and squeezed. "That's amazing!"

I shook my head, overwhelmed with pride. The man I'd met that summer two years ago had absolutely zero confidence in his cooking. The man beside me now was almost finished with his culinary degree and was going to be cooking all summer with one of the hottest chefs in the industry.

He shrugged. "Just trying to keep up with my all-star girlfriend."

"I hardly think working at the art museum qualifies as all-star. Or compares to what you'll be doing in any way."

"They're asking you to curate and you're still in school, Bug. And your photos are the first to sell any time you let them display them. Stop selling yourself short."

I blushed. "Confidence is still a work in progress for me."

"I know. That's why I'm always here to remind you." He threw me a wink just as we pulled into the quaint seafood restaurant where Mom had asked us to meet her and Lana. William parked our small Camry and ran around to open my door, extending one hand to help me out. It wasn't the Rover or a Corvette, but it was ours — we had both worked hard for it. And for that reason alone, I was proud every time I rode inside it.

I couldn't help but stare at William as we walked toward the front door. His chestnut hair was carefully styled, his suit crisp, and the slight stubble on his chin made it look like he didn't even try too hard to look that way. His bright green eyes were happy — the happiest I'd ever seen them. He hardly ever scowled anymore, the expression so rare that I almost forgot what it looked like at all. Nowadays, he always wore the most comfortable smile.

It completed his outfit.

Before we'd even reached the table, Mom was up and out of her seat, wrapping me in a crushing hug. I embraced her, laughing a little when she pulled back swiping at the wetness on her cheeks.

"Oh heavens, I've missed you so much, sweetie."

"I've missed you, too, Mom." She looked good — incredible, actually. Her long blonde hair was tied up into an elegant updo and her eyes were free from the dark circles they'd worn for so long after the incident with Dale. She seemed to be happy. I hoped she truly was.

"No but really, she's missed you. I think I know your whole life now. She talks about you every night," Lana said with a smile, wrapping me in a light hug. "Good to see you, Natalie. You look amazing."

"Thank you, so do you." We shared a smile before taking our seats at the table. A waiter placed our napkins in our laps and left us with menus after we placed our drink order.

"So, how was today's tour stop?" I asked, eying Lana as she texted away on her phone. A smile was plastered on her face and I didn't need more than one guess as to who she was texting. She and Officer Martino had been shy about their relationship at first, unsure of it just like Rhodes and I in the beginning. But there was no denying it now.

"So good," Mom answered. "I feel like we're really making a difference in some of these young ladies' lives. It's like while we're speaking, I look out at them, and I can tell which ones have gone through something. I can't explain it, but you can see it in their eyes. They're listening — they want to know their options."

"It's terrifying, in a way," Lana added, tucking her phone back in her clutch.

Mom nodded. "It is. But that's what reminds me why we do this." They shared a knowing smile and William found my hand under the table, giving it a soft squeeze.

After the trial, Lana and Mom became really close. It was interesting, since they were on two very opposite sides of what happened with Dale, but they really seemed to help each other cope. They decided to write a book together and, mostly because of the popularity of Dale's case nation-wide, it sold tremendously. Now, they were booked through December with tour stops all over the country speaking to high schools, colleges, women's groups and more. They were signing and selling books and telling their story, giving other women hope and strength to fight through their own situations. It was actually quite incredible.

"How have you two been? How's school?"

William told them about his new summer job and I filled them in on the latest projects at the museum. It was finals week at school and I was going to take the summer off to focus on curating and honing in on my own skills. I was looking forward to the months off, especially since it meant more time with William.

"Is Willow still coming to visit you this summer?"

I grinned. "Yeah, she flies in next week. She's supposedly bringing her flavor of the semester with her, so this should be interesting." Willow was the only friend I still kept in contact with from Poxton Beach. Mason had checked on me after everything happened, but once he left for college and I left for Savannah, we lost contact completely. In a way, I preferred it like that. Poxton Beach was in my past — just where I wanted it.

Mom and William laughed as the waiter refilled our glasses. Lifting hers high in the air, Mom cleared her throat. "A toast," she said. We all lifted our glasses to join hers in unison. "To survival. And healing. And family."

"Cheers," we all sang together. I clinked my glass with Lana's and Mom's first before ending with William's. He held my gaze for a moment, and his eyes spoke more words than any toast could. The love I felt from those two jade irises astounded me sometimes.

As we sipped from our glasses, I couldn't help but think about all the amazing things that had come from such a horrific experience. Dale was finally paying for the pain he'd caused so many women to suffer, William had his sister back in his life, my mom had finally found something she was passionate about, and I was following a dream I'd had no confidence in before.

Maybe everything really does happen for a reason.

I thought about that more as we drove home, the radio playing softly as William ran his thumb along the bare skin on my knee. We were both quiet, reflective, and I realized that in a way, I kind of had Mason to thank for bringing me to him. If he hadn't been my first boyfriend, my first heartbreak, I may have never found the courage or the motivation to take that first step into the Poxton Beach Country Club. And I surely never would have known what waited for me behind its doors.

Or rather, who.

Zipper jumped on me as soon as William unlocked the door to our apartment. His large paws connected with my shoulders and I braced myself against the wall in the foyer, kicking off my heels as he licked at my face. This was our routine, and it always made me smile.

"Hey, Zip. Missed you too, bud."

He dropped back down to the floor and sat, patiently waiting as William shrugged off his suit jacket and slung it over one of our dining room chairs before grabbing Zipper's leash.

"I'm going to walk him real quick and I'll be back," he said, leaning in to kiss my cheek. He lingered there for just a moment, kissing up to my ear before whispering, "Don't get too undressed before I get back."

I shivered, biting my lip as he pulled back with a wink and led Zipper out the door.

Tossing my clutch on the kitchen table, I grabbed my heels off the floor and slowly walked back to our bedroom, stomach full and eyes heavy from the night. I trailed my fingers along the wall of photos that lined the hallway, each frame filled with a memory of William and I. The first photo we'd ever taken together was there, the one we'd snapped that evening after he took me for the first time. It sat in the middle, surrounded by new memories, everything from our lazy Sunday picnics in the park and sweaty after-gym selfies to dressed-up nights at the gallery and adventures with Zipper.

A smile tugged at my lips as I dropped my heels into the bottom of our closet and unfastened my earrings. I didn't even get the second one out before I heard the front door open and close, followed by a stampede of paws as Zipper ran wild once again. I tossed his bone onto his bed near the foot of ours and he flopped down happily, gnawing away with his tail still wagging.

"Let me help with that," William murmured, sliding up behind me before moving the hair off my neck. His hand found the zipper at the back of my dress and he slowly guided it down, planting small kisses on my neck as he trailed it lower. I slipped out of the fabric, letting it hit the floor before turning and hooking my arms around his neck.

William's eyes raked over me slowly and he shook his head. "You're so beautiful."

I smiled. "Thank you."

I didn't have to fight hard to believe him anymore.

I half-expected him to take me right then and there, but he let me go long enough for each of us to dress in our pajamas before we crawled between our sheets. Only William's bedside lamp illuminated the room as he propped himself on one elbow, eyes pensive.

"What are you thinking about over there?" I asked, quirking a brow. He ran his free hand through my hair with a lazy grin before swallowing hard.

"I got you something."

He rolled, opening the small drawer on his bedside table before shutting it again softly. When he turned back to me, he held a box I recognized — the one my watch had come in when he gave it to me two years ago at the club.

"You know my watch still works, right?" I asked with a smile, propping myself up against the pillows. "I just ran the battery down. Again."

William held the box out anyway and I took it, eying him curiously as I opened it. When I looked down again, it wasn't a watch at all.

"Oh my God," I breathed, eyes snapping to William. "What is this?"

It was a stupid question because I knew what it was. It was a ring — a beautiful ring, slender and gold with an eternity symbol that linked two tiny hearts together. My eyes flicked between it and William over and over.

"It's a promise," he finally said, reaching out to grab the box from my shaking hands. He removed the ring, setting the box to the side before his eyes found mine again. "That I'm here. That I'll always *be* here, through your dark times and your light, shouldering whatever weight you can't carry on your own. It's a promise that I'll always help you feel beautiful when you don't on your own, that I'll hold you when you need to cry and spin you in my arms when you need to celebrate." We both laughed a little, tears brimming my eyes at the memory of him doing just that in the middle of the gym the day I hit my goal weight. "And one day, when we're ready, I'll replace it with a ring that promises forever, even though you don't need it — not really. Because the truth is that you've had me since the day we met, and you already have my forever… if you want it."

He held the ring out, eyes on mine, waiting. But I didn't hesitate. I extended my hand, fingers spread wide, and he slipped it over the knuckle of the ring finger on my right hand with a sigh.

"Do you even have to ask?" I slid my hand into his, index finger pressing against the small tattooed circle on the inside of his wrist. He did the same, finding the matching circle on my wrist as I whispered what we both knew all along. "I want all of you, William."

He answered me with a kiss, his hands finding my hair as he rolled over, my thighs framing his strong middle as he pressed me into the sheets. Sometimes he still kissed me like it hurt him, like he was afraid he'd hurt *me*, and this was one of those times. But eventually, the crease between his brows faded, each new touch and kiss erasing it slowly. He kissed me until I felt beautiful and I kissed him until he felt worthy, and we never cared how long it took to get us there.

I've always hated weight.

Before I met William, I hated the weight that crowded my body, making me feel inadequate in every aspect of my life. Then, when I first started training with him, he pushed me harder than anyone ever had. Whenever I thought I was finally rising to meet his standards, he would add more weight to my set, making me work harder, forcing me to find the motivation to push through.

And maybe that's the thing about weight — though it hurts when we feel its added pressure on our lives, it only makes us stronger in the end. Looking at William now, I couldn't imagine him without the weight that had shaped him. His past made him into the man I loved — no matter how scarred. He was the man who fixed me, who changed me, and who helped me carry my own weight when it grew too heavy to handle on my own.

I was beginning to realize that weight really wasn't a bad thing, after all.

# ACKNOWLEDGEMENTS

This is always the hardest part, because the truth is there are too many people in my life to thank for getting me to where I am today in my writing journey. I'd love nothing more than to just gather all of you around a fire with a cooler full of beer and tell you how much I love you, but for now, a few sentences will have to do.

Ryan — AKA Hubs — AKA hot bearded man who keeps me going when it feels impossible to do. Thank you for being my William, my never-ending stream of support, the trainer in my ear telling me I can do it. Thanks for the late night dinners and foiled weekend plans when writing deadlines snuck up on me. This book is the most difficult book I've written thus far, and I couldn't have done it without you. I love you.

This book would have been dead and buried in an RIP file on my hard drive if it weren't for Staci Brillhart, who has become one of my very best friends in the short year we've known each other. You will forever be the Hype Man to my Polly Pocket, and I can never truly thank you enough for helping me elevate this book to the next level. #JuiceBoxHero

Becca Hensley Mysoor, you helped me build Weightless up from a little tiny outline. You saved the ending, but more than that you saved me from my crippling self-doubt. Thank you for your love and your friendship — both which are invaluable and cherished more than you know.

To my lifelong best friend Sasha Whittington, thank you once again for reading my work in every stage along the way and helping me make it better. I've written you into every acknowledgement I've had and I know you'll be in every single one until the day I stop writing because you're not just my best friend, but my biggest fan, too. Now, prepare yourself — we've got a big job ahead of us with this next one. ;) #ALLTW

A big shout out goes out to the Circle of Trust — Erin Spencer, Cassie Graham, Ashlei Davison and Jess Vogel for beta reading, helping me choose teasers, saving me on the late nights when I felt like quitting and always knowing how to make me laugh. I love you all so much it hurts and I can't imagine doing this without you.

Momma, thank you for letting me stay up past my bedtime to read Harry Potter and for not judging me when I majored in Creative Writing. You will forever be my biggest inspiration and the wind beneath my wings.

Brittainy C. Cherry, thank you for breathing confidence back into me with every message you sent as you read Weightless. Thank you for believing in me, for sharing my work, for loving my words and for being literally the best human being I know. Period. My life wouldn't be as bright without you.

A HUGE, special shout out goes to Angie Doyle McKeon for being the best damn Bumble Bee to ever buzz around in the land of lifeless flowers. You bring life and color to everything and everyone you touch and I appreciate your support and love more than you know.

To the rest of the beta readers — Kellee, Sahar, Novo, Monique, Trish (Queen Mintness), Maegan, and Tina, thank you for petting my hair and helping me whip this thing into submission. You're the best ride or die team and I'm so thankful for each and every one of you.

Kash Monay and Elaine Hudson York — thanks for editing and formatting Weightless to perfection. Now it's pretty inside and out, and it's all thanks to you two.

Two the two groups who keep me going — Tribe and Kandiland (https://www.facebook.com/profile.php?id=1408360979440689) — thank you for the daily posts and messages, the support, the love, the giggles, the whiskey, and everything in-between. I'm convinced that I'm the luckiest writer because I have y'all, and I hope the day never comes where I learn what it is to do this without you in my corner.

To you — the reader — for loving my characters and stories as much as I do and for reading all the way through the acknowledgments (Like seriously, who are you?! You rock.). Thanks for choosing indie. I hope I didn't let you down.

Lastly, as always, I have to thank God. Without His blessings and love, I wouldn't be able to chase my dreams the way I do. I only pray he gives me the strength and the courage to never stop.

# MORE FROM
# KANDI STEINER

A Love Letter to Whiskey

Weightless

Black Number Four

The Palm South University Serial

PSU Season 1

PSU Season 2

(Season 3 coming August 2017!)

The Chaser Series

Tag Chaser

Song Chaser

Straight, No Chaser

Tag Catcher

# ABOUT THE
# AUTHOR

Kandi Steiner is a bestselling author and whiskey connoisseur living in Tampa, FL. Best known for writing "emotional rollercoaster" stories, she loves bringing flawed characters to life and writing about real, raw romance — in all its forms. No two Kandi Steiner books are the same, and if you're a lover of angsty, emotional, and inspirational reads, she's your gal.

An alumna of the University of Central Florida, Kandi graduated with a double major in Creative Writing and Advertising/PR with a minor in Women's Studies. She started writing back in the 4th grade after reading the first Harry Potter installment. In 6th grade, she wrote and edited her own newspaper and distributed to her classmates. Eventually, the principal caught on and the newspaper was quickly halted, though Kandi tried fighting for her "freedom of press." She took particular interest in writing romance after college, as she has always been a die hard hopeless romantic, and likes to highlight all the challenges of love as well as the triumphs.

When Kandi isn't writing, you can find her reading books of all kinds, talking with her extremely vocal cat, and spending time with her friends and family. She enjoys live music, traveling, anything heavy in carbs, beach days, movie marathons, craft beer and sweet wine — not necessarily in that order.

CONNECT WITH KANDI:
NEWSLETTER: bit.ly/NewsletterKS
FACEBOOK: facebook.com/kandisteiner
FACEBOOK READER GROUP (Kandiland): facebook.com/groups/
kandischasers
INSTAGRAM: Instagram.com/kandisteiner
TWITTER: twitter.com/kandisteiner
PINTEREST: pinterest.com/kandicoffman
WEBSITE: www.kandisteiner.com

Kandi Steiner may be coming to a city near you! Check out her "events" tab to see all the signings she's attending in the near future www.kandisteiner.com/events

Made in the USA
Middletown, DE
17 September 2022

10657191R00225